PENGUIN BOOKS

The Bomb Girl Brides

Daisy Styles grew up in Lancashire surrounded by a family and community of strong women. She loved to listen to their stories of life in the cotton mill, in the home, at the pub, on the dance floor, in the local church, or just what happened to them on the bus going into town. It was from these women, particularly her vibrant mother and Irish grandmother, that Daisy learnt the art of storytelling.

The Bomb Girl Brides

DAISY STYLES

PENGUIN BOOKS

PENGUIN BOOKS

UK | USA | Canada | Ireland | Australia
India | New Zealand | South Africa

Penguin Books is part of the Penguin Random House group of companies
whose addresses can be found at global.penguinrandomhouse.com.

First published 2018

001

Set in 12.5/14.75 pt Garamond MT Std
Typeset by Jouve (UK), Milton Keynes
Printed and bound in Great Britain by Clays Ltd, Elcograf S.p.A.

A CIP catalogue record for this book is available from the British Library

ISBN: 978–1–405–93617–0

www.greenpenguin.co.uk

For my youngest daughter, Isabella, who when she was a little girl liked nothing more than sitting on church benches watching weddings with her mum!
Love you x

1. London, January 1944

Julia Thorpe hurled an armful of clothes into her suitcase; as skirts, blouses and cardigans fell in a heap on top of her precious books, she began to cry. She wouldn't need Shakespeare, Jane Austen and T. S. Eliot where she was going!

Falling on to her bed, Julia abandoned herself to tears, which just made her feel even guiltier. What if all the millions of conscripted women across the nation reacted in the same self-indulgent manner as she had? There'd be no bombs or planes built and who would work the land to provide food for a nation that was on the edge of starvation? Buses and Red Cross ambulances would stand empty without their female drivers; the country would literally grind to a halt.

Julia knew that signing on as a Bomb Girl was unquestionably her duty, but she'd been so close to her dream of going to Oxford. In her mind she'd walked the streets of the old city on her way to early-morning lectures; she'd pictured her garret room overlooking a leafy quad; and she'd imagined herself on autumn days cycling around the town with a long scarf wrapped around her college gown.

'Damn! Damn! Damn!' Julia seethed as she pummelled her lilac satin eiderdown.

Her sobs were too loud for her to hear a tap at the door, so she was startled when her older brother, Hugo, walked in, calmly puffing on his pipe.

'Cheer up, sis, it's not that bad,' he said with a cheery smile.

'Go away!' she mumbled as she wiped away her tell-tale tears on the eiderdown.

Ignoring her red, scowling face, Hugo settled himself on the pretty padded chair beside her dressing table.

'Can't you see I'm busy packing?' Julia said, as she struggled to her feet and straightened her golden-blonde bobbed hair.

Hugo hid a smile at the sight of the flimsy silk under-wear and nylons she'd flung into her case.

'You'll need something more substantial than that lot to keep you warm up North,' he joked.

'What do you suggest? Clogs and shawl?' she asked crossly.

'Warm jumpers, trousers and skirts – and stout boots,' he suggested with a knowing wink.

'I'm not going on a walking tour of the bloody Alps,' she snapped, as she turned her back on him to resume her packing.

'Okay, okay,' Hugo said, as he rose to his feet. 'I'll leave you to your bad mood.'

'It's all right for *you*,' Julia grumbled. 'Just because you're a man you get away with everything!'

Hugo burst out laughing. 'Don't be so damned silly!'

'Daddy would have let you go to Oxford,' she said sulkily.

'He would not!' Hugo exclaimed. 'He wouldn't have let either of us shirk our duty and you know it.'

Their eyes locked: Julia knew exactly what her brother was talking about. Hugo had lost his left hand when he'd been attacked by a German Messerschmitt as he was heading home across the Channel after a night raid. He'd insisted he could fly with one hand, but, for all his bravado, he'd been discharged from military service and now worked for the Ministry of Information in London. It was a worthy enough job, but Hugo never got over leaving his beloved RAF.

'So why didn't he stop me taking the wretched entrance exam in the first place?' Julia continued. 'Did he hope I'd fail and that would be the end of my academic ambitions?'

'We're in the middle of a war, sis. I actually doubt the old man gave your Oxbridge exam much thought,' Hugo said in his father's defence.

'That sums it up perfectly!' Julia cried miserably. 'Daddy's life belongs to the army and Mummy's to the Red Cross – duty's really all that counts in this house.'

Hugo's expression darkened as he listened to his younger sister. 'Stop right there, Jay!' he commanded. 'Damn it, of course father's life belongs to the British Army: he's deploying troops all over Europe. You can hardly blame him for not keeping up with what's going on at home.'

Feeling embarrassed, Julia flushed at his words.

'And as for Ma, she's a bloody hero,' Hugo continued. 'Driving around the city during enemy air attacks, risking her life to dig out the dead and the wounded from blazing ruins.'

Julia's head drooped. Swallowing back tears, she managed to murmur, 'I'm sorry. I know I'm behaving badly. It just seems so cruel to get a place at Oxford and then have it snatched away because of this damn, blasted war.'

Hugo's heart ached to see his sister so wretched. Pulling her into his arms, he held her close to his chest and kissed the top of her head. 'Darling girl, when this filthy war is over you can follow your dreams, but for now you must do your duty, just like millions of other men and women up and down the country.'

Julia lifted her beautiful green eyes flecked with little golden flashes to gaze into Hugo's sombre face. 'I know. I'll buckle down once I get there,' she promised feebly.

'That's my girl,' he said, as he gave her a kiss on each cheek. 'Now finish your packing and I'll drive you to the station.'

After he'd left the room and closed the door behind him, Julia stared at her suitcase. Damn it! She'd take the books, even if she didn't read a single one – the sight of their familiar covers would make her feel better. And she'd take her typewriter too; she'd started to write her first novel when she thought she was going to Oxford, and there was no reason why she shouldn't continue with it just because her circumstances had changed. She packed all the sensible clothes Hugo had suggested – plus, seeing as she was going to Lancashire, a raincoat as well!

'You shouldn't be wasting your precious petrol ration

coupons on me,' Julia said, as they bounced along the rutted streets littered with shattered concrete, brick-work and broken glass. Areas that had once been leafy and green were now blocked by trees that had been uprooted by bomb blasts. Julia stared at a tenement block that looked as though it had been sliced in half with a knife: upstairs, beds and wardrobes seemed to be balancing precariously, as if any minute they would tumble and fall into the street far below.

'God!' groaned Hugo, as he expertly steered his ministry car around a gaping man-hole. 'There'll be nothing left of London before long.'

Julia gazed sadly at the wretched sights all around them. 'Do you think the war will end soon?' she asked.

'Ah, if only, sis,' Hugo sighed. 'I fear Herr Hitler will never capitulate — even though the war is turning in our favour, megalomaniacs like him never give in. The best we can hope for is that his generals will shoot him themselves!'

'Miracles happen,' Julia said with a sigh.

The Manchester train was packed to bursting point with soldiers, sailors and young men in RAF uniforms, all on the move up and down the country. But they were happy enough to give up their seats for a stunning slender girl with a winning smile.

'Here, love, take mine,' a cheerful sergeant said, as he rose from his window seat.

'That's very kind of you,' Julia responded gratefully. 'If you're sure you don't mind?'

'Nah,' the cheery sergeant replied. 'Me and the lads' – he indicated with a nod his men in the compartment and the outside corridor who seemed barely more than boys – 'we'll be hopping out at Watford Junction.'

Julia gratefully accepted his seat and sat down just in time to wave to her brother standing on the platform. Smiling at his sister, who looked small and vulnerable in a carriage packed with uniformed men, Hugo gave her a cheery grin as the huge locomotive belched a cloud of sooty black smoke, then started to shunt slowly out of Euston Station. Standing on the empty platform littered with discarded cigarette packets, spent matches and trampled newspapers, Hugo wondered how his clever but often too outspoken sister would fare in the bomb-building factory in Lancashire.

2. New Digs

Flushed, hot and excited, Maggie and Nora staggered into the cowshed, a modernized farm building that the Phoenix Munitions Factory had requisitioned to accommodate some of their residential female workers. Bearing bulging shopping bags and heavy suitcases, they were red in the face and gasping for breath.

'I've packed everything but the kitchen sink!' Nora giggled as she collapsed on the sofa, which Rosa, already a resident of the cowshed, quickly vacated.

Keen to share her home with her best friends, she gave both girls a quick kiss. '*Benvenuto*, welcome!'

'I'm too tired to understand Italian, our kid, just put kettle on for a brew,' Maggie said affectionately to Rosa, who, though Italian, now spoke English with a heavy Lancashire accent and understood all the idioms her workmates used, though she still kept to Italian endearments for the ones she loved best.

'*Certo, cara*,' Rosa replied, as she quickly put the little black kettle on top of the wood-burning stove that kept the cowshed warm and cosy all through the cold winter months. 'Promise me you two won't squabble when you're sharing a bedroom together,' she teased.

'I'm so happy to be here I'd agree to anything,' Nora admitted with her sweet, gap-toothed smile. 'I'll never get over mi dad allowing me to leave home and come up here to live on't moors with mi best friends,' she said with a rush of pure joy. 'I feel right proper grown up now,' she announced, as she handed round a packet of Woodbines.

Maggie eagerly accepted a cigarette, but Rosa preferred to roll one of her own strong-tasting cheroots.

'Mi mother couldn't get me out of house quick enough,' Maggie confessed. 'I know I've been driving her and mi dad round the bend and back again since me and Les got engaged.'

'You can say that again!' Nora exclaimed. 'It's wedding this and wedding that with you these days.'

'So?' an aggrieved Maggie cried. 'A girl only gets married once in her life.'

'If she's lucky,' Rosa said sceptically. Seeing a hurt expression flash across her friend's happy, glowing face, Rosa quickly adjusted her comment. 'Though I am quite sure in the case of you and Les, your marriage will last a lifetime, *carissima*.'

When the little kettle whistled on the stove, Rosa brewed the tea, which she then poured into mugs. 'A letter arrived from Gladys today,' she told her friends excitedly. 'It's to all of us,' she added, as she drew the envelope out of her cardigan pocket.

'Oh, read it out,' Nora implored. 'I miss her so much.'

'Me too,' Maggie said. 'But, you know, we should be grateful for small mercies: if it weren't for Gladys going to London, we'd never be living here in the cowshed.'

All three girls smiled a little sadly as they recalled

darling Gladys with her long, dark-mahogany brown hair and brilliant deep-blue eyes dancing round the cowshed in her new nurse's uniform. She'd had to re-train as a nurse when her skin reacted violently to the cordite she handled daily. She'd struggled at first, but it turned out Gladys loved her new job, was born for it, in fact. She'd done so well she'd been offered a job working alongside her handsome boyfriend, Dr Reggie Lloyd, at St Thomas' Hospital in London. But taking up that position had left an empty space not just in the cow-shed, where she'd lived happily for almost two years, but in her friends' hearts too.

Rosa unfolded the letter and started to read:

Dearest Mags, Nora, and Rosa,

I'm snatching a few moments to write to you as I've not had time to draw my breath since I arrived in London. Reggie was waiting for me at Euston Station and when I stepped off the train he presented me with a bouquet. (I dread to think how much he paid on the black market for red roses in winter!)

'Ah, lucky Glad. I wish I could see my Les,' Maggie said in a low yearning voice.

I'm back on the post-op ward, which I requested and which I love. It's not a pretty sight, nursing men with terrible wounds who need life-saving surgery, but I admire their strength and humour and their determination to return to the front just as soon as they can.

'Only to be shot at again, poor sods,' Nora murmured sadly.

They're heroes in my opinion and I'm proud to be able to ease their pain when they're recovering from surgery; some don't make it, which always upsets me, especially when they're no more than boys and call out for their mothers on their death beds. Anyway, on a more cheerful note, it's lovely that I'm so close to Reggie – even if I only see him for five minutes a day, it's more than I would ever see him if I were still at the Phoenix. How is everybody? Are you all well? Rosa told me that you two girls would be moving in with her – I'm glad she'll have company. Don't give the poor girl earache with your nattering every night! I miss you all so much. Write when you've got five minutes to spare and give my love to everybody.

Yours ever, Gladys xxx

As Rosa folded the letter and returned it to the envelope, there was a thoughtful silence.

'Do you think she'll ever come back here?' Nora asked.

Rosa slowly shook her head. 'I don't think so, not if she wants to do specialist nursing and be with her beloved Reggie,' she replied.

'Nothing ever stays the same,' Nora murmured mournfully. 'There's always somebody coming or going.'

'That's wartime for you,' Maggie groaned. 'Nobody's in one place for long.'

'We're sure to have somebody new in here with us

soon,' Rosa added as she topped up everybody's mug of tea.

'That will make a full house,' Nora commented.

'What difference does it make?' Maggie said mournfully. 'Whoever comes next won't hold a candle to our lovely Glad.'

A few hours later, after the girls had shared a frugal supper of baked beans and slices of cold spam, there was a knock at the door. It was Nora, wearing an old woolly dressing gown, who got up to answer it. Swinging open the door, she squinted in the dark, and was just about able to make out the tall, slender figure of a woman silhouetted against the night sky.

'I think this might be my new lodgings?' the woman declared in a clear, ringing voice, as she handed Nora a sheet of official-looking typewritten paper.

'Oh . . . yes, come in, please,' Nora warmly responded. 'We were told to expect somebody soon but we didn't think it would be right away,' she added, as she bustled the newcomer into the warm room.

After her long walk up the dark cobbled lane to the cowshed, with a fox-fur stole thrown carelessly around her neck and a soft brown felt trilby hat set at a jaunty angle on her blonde bob, Julia blinked as she entered the room; the other three girls blinked for altogether another reason. Who was this willowy, elegant woman dressed like a model in expensive tweed trousers and smart brown tie-up brogues?

'Pleased to meet you,' she said, as she extended a

slim pale hand to the three women in their nightwear. 'I'm Julia Thorpe.'

Overawed, the three girls just about managed to make their own introductions, before Nora, thinking the tight-lipped girl might loosen up with tea inside her, moved forwards.

'Fancy a cuppa?'

'I'm awfully tired,' Julia said apologetically. 'I've been travelling all day and I'm longing for my bed. Would you mind very much showing me to my room?'

'Yes, of course.' Though taken aback by Julia's formal tone, Rosa nevertheless responded politely as she led her towards the vacant bedroom.

Rosa was quick to notice that Julia's face appeared to fall as she took in the stark metal bed and cheap flimsy wardrobe. She wondered what kind of surroundings Julia had come from, given her stylish clothes. No doubt she had her own lovely room with a luxurious double bed, and a deep closet full of glamorous ball gowns, the likes of which most of the girls at the Phoenix would never even have seen, let alone owned.

'And here's the toilet and bathroom,' Nora chipped in, anxious to help. 'We've got running hot water,' she added proudly. 'Fancy that! No more soaking in a tin bath in front of the fire, eh?' she said with genuine pleasure.

Seeing Julia's bleak expression, Maggie gave a warm smile. 'Would you like us to help you make up your bed?'

Tears pricked the back of Julia's eyes as she gazed at the

sheets and blankets piled up in military fashion at the end of the bed. Gritting her teeth, she recalled her father's stern words. 'Make us proud, do your duty and do it well, my darling.'

Before her resolve broke and she made a complete fool of herself, Julia turned abruptly to Nora, Maggie and Rosa who were all hovering uncertainly in the doorway.

'No, thank you. Goodnight,' she said in a tight clipped voice, before quickly shutting the door on their startled faces.

Creeping back into the living room, the girls sat around the crackling wood-burner, where they whispered to one another.

'Oh, my God!' said Maggie in a barely suppressed voice. 'She's so *posh*!'

'Shhh!' Rosa hissed. 'She might hear you.'

'One thing's for sure,' said Nora. 'Miss Julia Thorpe in yon back bedroom is never, ever going to fit in at the Phoenix!'

3. The Shop Floor

Rosa, Nora and Maggie were keen to relate the latest domestic events to their old friend Kit, who worked in the filling shed, whilst the three of them worked on the cordite line. On long, twelve-hour shifts they filled bomb cases to a specified level with cordite, then inserted an empty tube for the detonator, which would be loaded further down the line. The Canary Girls, as the girls on the cordite line were nicknamed because of the yellow chemical staining on their skin, made sure they tucked their hair tightly under their turbans (which were part of the mandatory factory uniform); if they didn't, any escaping hair would be bleached bright yellow by the dangerous explosive. Older, more experienced Canary Girls said the unsightly stains could be removed with milk, but, as far as Rosa, Maggie and Nora were concerned, it never completely worked.

A former resident of the cowshed, Kit had moved out after she'd married; she now lived with her husband, Ian, and her young son Billy, and another baby was on the way. Their home was a big old farmhouse on the Pennine Moors, which meant she regularly needed an update on the latest developments in her former home.

'You'll never believe it!' Nora cried, as Kit settled down at the canteen table beside her friends.

Seeing Nora's flushed face, Kit responded with an indulgent smile. 'Go on, I can see you're dying to tell me.'

'We've got a new girl in the cowshed!' Nora announced.

'A POSH new girl,' Maggie added, as she handed round cigarettes, which Kit, previously a heavy smoker, just couldn't take these days and therefore politely turned down. 'She's rich too, from the look of her smart clothes,' Maggie said a little enviously.

'Is she nice?' Kit asked.

'She seems pleasant enough,' Rosa said diplomatically. 'It's early days for the poor girl.'

'She went straight to bed almost as soon as she arrived,' Nora said in a disappointed voice.

'She's definitely not from these parts,' Maggie informed Kit. 'You can tell by her accent that she's a Southerner.'

'All lah-di-dah!' Nora giggled. 'She won't understand a word us Lancashire lasses have to say.'

Rosa burst out laughing. 'Hell fire!' she exclaimed in a deep Lancashire accent. 'I didn't understand anything when I first arrived at the Phoenix.'

Nora immediately made an excuse for Rosa, whom she unconditionally adored. 'You're different,' she said with a smile. 'You're Italian!'

'It doesn't matter where anybody's from,' Rosa

pointed out. 'You Bomb Girls are a tight-knit community; it takes time to get to know you.'

'Are you saying we're stand-offish?' Nora asked in astonishment.

'No, not at all, you're welcoming – but behind the welcome you can, occasionally,' Rosa added cautiously, 'be harsh to judge.'

Feeling guilty, big-hearted Nora turned to Maggie. 'We didn't say owt to upset Julia, did we?'

Maggie shook her long thick auburn curls that she'd just released from the restraints of her white turban. 'How could we have?' she demanded. 'She went straight to bed.'

'Where is she now?' Kit asked curiously, as she looked around the canteen packed with women smoking cigarettes and drinking large mugs of hot tea.

'She's being debriefed by Malc,' Maggie said, as she rolled her eyes in amusement.

'I don't know how she'll ever fit in,' Nora said bleakly, repeating her words from the previous night. 'Not here at work or in the cowshed with us either.'

'Just give her time,' Rosa urged.

Kit smiled as she recalled her emotions when she first entered the cowshed. 'I thought it was the most wonderful place on God's earth,' she confessed.

'Me too, I love it,' Maggie agreed.

'But if you've been brought up posh, unlike us, it might come as a bit of a shock,' Nora pointed out.

Maggie lit up a Woodbine, and, after slowly blowing out a plume of smoke, she murmured thoughtfully,

'God only knows what Malc will make of Miss High and Mighty!'

Malc, in fact, had taken to the new girl, who – although not from the same class as most of the other women in the factory – seemed bright and willing, and very curious about the bomb-making process.

'What happens to the bombs once they leave here?' Julia asked.

'Well, that information is top secret,' Malc replied. 'But I don't think I'm giving away any state secrets by saying they're taken where they're most needed on the front line. You'll see them being shipped out of the Phoenix just about every day.'

After Malc had carefully explained the dangerous sparking potential of jewellery, hairpins and slides on the factory floor, Julia assiduously checked there was nothing metal about her person before changing into the Bomb Girls' uniform in the ladies' toilets: white overalls, a white turban and heavy-soled rubber boots. Once Julia was kitted up, Malc led her to the filling shed, where he introduced her to Kit, who was back on her shift after the break.

'This is where you'll be working, and this is Kit: she'll show you the ropes,' Malc said confidently, then left the two women to get to know each other.

Though they were both wearing identical white overalls, Kit could immediately see that Julia had style. Even though weighed down by ugly rubber boots (which, like the jewellery ban, reduced the danger of sparking on the factory floor), Julia walked with an easy confidence, and she carried herself with a barely perceivable elegance. Sitting beside Kit, Julia listened intently to her teacher's instructions on how to fill fuses.

'Our job is to blend this mucky grey gunpowder,' Kit started as she rolled around the explosive with her fingertips. 'Once it's smooth, we pack it into one of these metal cases,' she said. 'When the case is full, tap it gently, then stack it on to the tray.' Kit carefully deposited the fuse on to a wooden tray on her workbench. 'We work with twenty-five fuses per tray, and these are regularly collected by Malc, who replaces the full trays with empty ones.'

Always curious, Julia asked, 'What happens to the fuse cases once they leave us?'

'Further down the production line the loaded fuses will be attached to a variety of bombs and explosives,' Kit explained. 'Now, come on,' she said with a grin. 'Your turn.'

Kit smiled sympathetically as Julia handled the fine gunpowder that trickled from her fumbling fingers. 'Don't worry if it's awkward to start with,' she said reassuringly. 'It's close work and back-breaking too, especially if you're pregnant,' she said with a shy smile.

Julia glanced at Kit's uniform, which masked her pregnancy.

'I'm four months gone; my baby's due in June,' Kit said with a happy smile.

'Is it wise for a pregnant woman to be working in these conditions?' Julia asked abruptly.

'I'm sure it isn't. This stuff' – Kit nodded towards the tray of dark-grey gunpowder – 'sometimes makes me retch,' she confessed. 'But there's a war on and we're conscripted women, so who am I to pick a fight with Mr Churchill?' Kit said, as she turned her attention to expertly filling the fuse cases, which poor, inexperienced Julia continued to struggle with. It was a relief when the factory hooter sounded and they could both get up and stretch their aching backs.

'Time for a cuppa,' Kit announced. 'I don't know about you, but I'm starving.'

They walked side by side to the bathroom, where they scrupulously cleaned the gunpowder off their hands in the sinks that lined one side of the long bare room, then made their way to the canteen, passing a crowd of bustling girls and chattering women, several of whom called out to Kit.

'Hiya, Kitty!'

'How's that bonny little Billy of yours?'

After warmly responding to her colleagues, Kit turned to Julia and said earnestly, 'The Phoenix women are good women. They might take some getting used to but, believe me, they've got hearts of gold – you've just got to dig a bit to find them.'

Thinking that she had no intention of digging around for people's hearts, least of all their affections, Julia smiled bleakly and followed Kit into the canteen, where they picked up mugs of tea and chip butties from the counter.

'This way,' Kit called to the new girl, who looked all set to go and sit at a table on her own. 'We usually sit together at break time,' Kit explained as she led Julia (who would love to have sat on her own and read the morning papers) to the table where Rosa, Maggie and Nora were waiting for them. As they approached, Julia bowed her head at the curious, staring women all around her and obediently followed Kit, who drew out a metal chair for her.

'How did Julia get on in the filling shed?' Maggie asked curiously.

'Very well,' Kit replied. 'She's a quick learner.'

Julia wriggled uncomfortably; she wished they'd all stop talking about her like she wasn't there.

'We're all on the cordite line,' Rosa explained to Julia. 'On the other side of the factory.'

'I don't know which is worse, cordite staining your skin and hair bright yellow or working with mucky black gunpowder,' Nora said with a grimace. 'Neither does owt for your complexion.'

'I'm sure I'll get used to it,' Julia said, as she smothered a yawn; she was only three hours into her twelve-hour shift and she was already longing for her bed.

'Were you working in munitions before you came here?' Maggie inquired.

With her mug of tea halfway to her lips, Julia paused; how much should she say? Even though she'd only recently arrived, she could already see that she was an oddball;

she certainly didn't want to flag up anything that might set her even further apart from the Bomb Girls.

'No, I, er, I worked in a library,' she answered.

Nora in her guileless innocent way turned wide-eyed with wonder. 'You worked in a proper library, with all them books?' she gasped.

Julia smiled tightly as she nodded. 'Yes, I like books; in fact, I read a lot.'

Nora shook her head. 'I'm a rotten reader,' she confessed without any shame. 'I can't concentrate and the words seem to dance before mi eyes till I get a belting headache. I suppose I'm just a numb bugger, that's what mi mam always used to say to me,' she said with a cheerful laugh.

'Nora, you must stop putting yourself down,' Rosa protested. 'You taught me more about working on the cordite line than any of the bosses.'

Nora blushed at her words of praise. 'That's nowt,' she answered dismissively. 'Building bombs is what we do at the Phoenix.'

Not to be outdone, Nora – who was inordinately proud of her darling Rosa – said with a ring in her voice, 'Rosa's Italian! She's been on a gondola – and she's been to university too, studying summat . . .' Her voice trailed away as she turned to Maggie for advice. 'What were it she were studying in them foreign parts?' she whispered.

'Painting,' Maggie said, as she burst out laughing. 'And we're not talking about redecorating the back bedroom – she's a proper artist,' Maggie boasted.

Rosa blushed at her friends' sweet but rather embarrassing disclosure. 'I studied art in my home town of Padua, before the war,' she modestly explained to Julia, who was struggling with her bulky chip butty, which kept slipping sideways out of her fingers.

'Oh, how interesting,' she replied unenthusiastically, as she gave up the battle and dropped the greasy sandwich on to her plate.

Nora, who could have eaten chip butties till they came out of her ears, gaped in disbelief at the discarded food. 'Are you not eating that?' she gasped in disbelief.

Julia's stomach turned as she gazed at the congealed chips on the dense white bread. 'No, I'm not hungry.'

'Can I have it?' Nora asked.

'Eeh, she's got no shame that one!' teased Maggie. 'She'd eat owt!'

'I hate to see good food go to waste,' Nora remonstrated.

Feeling like she was behaving like a spoilt brat, Julia couldn't get rid of the offending chip butty quickly enough. 'Have it,' she said dismissively. 'Please take it!'

Rosa exchanged a disapproving look with Kit. Why did Julia have to be so brusque? It would do her no good if she wanted to make friends in the Phoenix; but Rosa had a strong feeling that Julia really wasn't interested in making friends; she sensed that the new girl merely tolerated the munitions factory and everybody in it as part of her war effort.

As Nora chomped contentedly on Julia's rejected

food, Maggie had a novel thought that amused her immensely, 'What with Kit from Ireland, Rosa from Italy and now Julia from London, it looks like me and you, Nora, are the only locals.'

Quickly swallowing the last of the sandwich, Nora reached across the table for her Woodbines. 'Local yokels!' she joked.

As the girls around the table giggled at Nora's silly joke, Maggie threw her a mock haughty glance.

'You won't call me a yokel on my wedding day!' she promised. Hamming it up and putting on a posh voice, Maggie continued, 'In fact – with a bit of luck – you won't recognize me in my bridal gown and veil!'

'OOOOH!' came a collective teasing cry from her friends.

Julia, longing for the work hooter to go off so she could escape the endless round of banter, stared gloomily at the dirty Formica table-top and said nothing.

Julia's first day at the Phoenix was long and hard. The cold from the floors, constantly kept damp to reduce the risk of sparking, seeped up her legs until they were numb, and the bitter north wind whistling in through the permanently open factory doors made her shiver until her teeth chattered.

'Remember to wear a woolly under your overall tomorrow,' Kit advised at the end of an interminably long day. 'It can only get colder.'

As Kit hurried away to pick up her little son from the

Phoenix's nursery, Julia, tired to the bone, staggered up the dark lane, slipping and sliding on the unfamiliar wet cobbles. The cowshed was warm and welcoming, with the wood-burner crackling, but tea was no more than sardines on toast and a few leftover baked beans. Julia volunteered to wash up, and then – too tired to talk – she bade goodnight to her housemates.

'I'm sorry to be unsociable,' she said apologetically. 'I'm just done in.'

'Don't worry, you'll get used to it,' Nora said with a kindly smile. 'After my first shift I could have slept on a clothes line!'

Shivering in her cold bedroom, Julia quickly changed into one of her pretty embroidered nightdresses.

'God!' she thought to herself. 'What I need in this bloody ice-box is a thick winceyette nightie and a pair of bed-socks.'

Grabbing a book, she gritted her teeth as she opened the covers and jumped into bed. Even though she'd put a stone hot-water bottle between the sheets earlier, they still felt damp – how she longed for an India-rubber one that she could clutch to her chest instead of the primitive heavy bottle that barely gave off any heat. And the heavy blanket that lay like a brick on top of her and smelt vaguely of mould Julia was sure had served time in the Crimean War. Shivering with cold and feeling utterly miserable, Julia fought back tears as she tried not to remember the warmth and comfort of her cosy bed at home, with its pretty eiderdown and plump feather pillows. There'd always be a glass of hot milk on the bedside, left by their devoted housekeeper, who'd spoilt Julia rotten since she was a child, and, if she was lucky, a few homemade shortbread biscuits. Forcing herself to focus on the here and now, she began to read her favourite Shakespeare play, *A Midsummer Night's Dream*, but got no further than the second page before the book slipped from her fingers and she fell into a deep sleep of complete exhaustion.

4. Settling In

As freezing January slipped into wet February and a cloying grey mist covered the moors, Julia slowly became accustomed to her work. She was soon so quick and deft at packing fuse cases that Malc, who wasn't given to flowery compliments, congratulated her.

'Eeh, you're a regular little fire-cracker,' he chuckled, as he removed the filled tray from her bench and replaced it with an empty one. 'You'll break the world record for shell-filling if you carry on at this rate.'

Julia liked Malc enormously, but she hadn't the heart to tell him that his cheerful banter was wasted on her. Because of his broad Lancashire accent and use of local quirky idioms, she could understand only half of what he actually said.

'Anyway,' Julia told herself wearily, 'I'm not at the Phoenix to make friends; this is my duty, and duty comes first in my family.'

Malc wasn't oblivious to the strains the new girl was under; he'd gathered from Kit she was pleasant enough but rather withdrawn. As far as Nora and Maggie were concerned, Julia was 'too posh', but Malc gleaned more from observant Rosa, who knew all about heartache brought on by homesickness.

'She's a hard worker and a loner, and she doesn't

volunteer much information about her personal life, but I quite understand that,' Rosa said, as she recalled how shy and withdrawn she had been when she first arrived at the Phoenix from Germany. 'As I told the girls, these things take time.'

'Nevertheless, I think I should have a little word,' Malc insisted.

'Be subtle,' Rosa warned. 'Julia's a very private person.'

'Trust me, I'll be so subtle she won't even notice I'm there!' Malc joked. 'Haven't you heard I have a winning way with the ladies?'

Rosa wagged her finger at him, 'I'll report you to Edna for flirting,' she teased.

'Bloody 'ell!' Malc chuckled. 'Don't do that – she'll be after me with her rolling pin.'

One morning, as Malc was passing Julia's bench, he caught sight of her wiping a dirty stained hand across her tired face.

'Are you bearing up, kiddo?' he asked cheerily.

'I'm fine, thank you,' Julia answered politely.

'Not missing your family down South?' he inquired.

Julia shook her head. 'I hardly saw my family even when I lived with them – we were always so busy, dashing about at the oddest hours. Occasionally we'd bump into each other on the way in or out,' she said with a distracted smile.

After Malc wandered off, pushing his trolley stacked with fuse cases, Kit, who'd grown up with a brother and a sister in a squat, peat-thatched cottage where privacy had always been impossible, turned to her new workmate. 'Is that right?' she asked incredulously. 'That you didn't see so much of your family even when you were all living together under the same roof?'

Julia gazed into Kit's deep, dark eyes; she was so tempted to open up to her new workmate, who was honest, genuine and kind; it would have been a relief to be able to tell somebody just how much she missed London and the comforts of home, and her family too, but, scared that she'd come across as a spoilt brat, Julia said with a shrug and a dismissive laugh, 'It wasn't that we weren't fond of each other – we just lived very independent lives and worked odd hours too.'

How could she possibly tell Kit that her father was a major in the British Army and spent all his days massing troops for battle? Or that her brother did something mysterious in the Ministry of Information that he wouldn't even talk to her about? Kit, who was no fool, paused in her work when she saw an awkward expression hover over Julia's face.

'I know what it's like to be an outsider here,' she murmured softly. 'I was one miself for quite some time. I had a secret, you see, that I didn't dare share with anybody; it took time until I knew who I could trust, if you get my meaning?'

Feeling like Kit was reading her mind, Julia blushed. 'Thank you,' she said. 'I'll remember that.'

'Never be afraid – I'll always understand,' Kit concluded, and with a sweet smile she returned to her monotonous work that was only lightened by the dreamy voice of Vera Lynn singing 'The White Cliffs of Dover' followed by 'We'll Meet Again' on the factory loudspeaker.

A few hours later, standing in a queue at the canteen counter, Julia smiled to herself as she realized with surprise that she was salivating at the sight of the meat-and-potato pie and mushy peas – a meal she would have turned up her nose at a mere month ago. Maybe eventually she would get used to chip butties after all, she thought ruefully.

During the afternoon, in between bursts of song from Joe Loss, Glenn Miller and the Andrews Sisters, Kit startled Julia by returning to the subject of her family. With no hidden agenda, Kit deftly filled one fuse case after another as she chatted.

'So what is it you and your family do in London that keeps you all so busy?'

Choosing her words carefully, Julia said, 'My father's in the army and my mother's a volunteer driver with the Red Cross.'

Kit, who'd read a great deal about the work of the Red Cross during the Blitz, looked impressed. 'Are you after telling me your ma drives an ambulance around the city as bombs are raining down?' she cried.

Feeling rather ashamed that she'd always taken her mother's war work so much for granted, Julia nodded. 'Yes, she's been an ambulance driver since the start of the war.'

Kit quickly crossed herself. 'She's a braver woman than me, that's for sure,' she announced.

'I suppose she is brave,' Julia admitted. 'I've never thought about it that way before.'

'Glory be to God and all the saints!' shocked Kit cried. 'Your ma could have copped it every day she drove an ambulance, and it never crossed your mind she could be hit by a German bomb!'

Now feeling positively guilty, Julia recalled how she and her mother, both clutching their obligatory gas masks, would breeze past each other most days, barely exchanging more than a polite greeting.

'Everything all right, darling?' her mother would always call out.

'Everything's fine, Mummy,' Julia would quickly reply over her shoulder as she dashed off to meet a friend or go to the library.

When Julia compared the strong bonds the Phoenix women had with their friends and families, she realized that, though she loved her parents very much, her relationship with both of them was distant. She briefly wondered if going away to school had forged a more independent relationship with her mother, and indeed her father too.

Kit interrupted her line of thought. 'Have you any brothers or sisters?'

'An older brother, Hugo,' Julia replied. 'He used to fly fighter planes in the RAF.'

Kit raised her eyebrows. 'That's what I call taking your life into your own hands.'

'He took a hit after a successful raid over Berlin – he lost a hand,' Julia added, managing to damp down as she always did any emotion when she spoke about the tragic accident. 'Thank God he survived.'

Kit held a hand to her mouth. 'Poor soul! Did he have to leave the RAF?'

'Oh, yes,' Julia said with a sad smile. 'Although he insisted until he was blue in the face that he could fly perfectly well with his right hand he was finally discharged.'

Completely fascinated by Julia's family, who seemed like altogether another race compared with her own, Kit couldn't stop asking questions.

'So what does your brother do now?'

'Oh, something in the Ministry of Information,' Julia said vaguely.

'Jesus, Mary and Joseph!' well-meaning Kit thought to herself. 'It's like getting blood out of a stone talking to this one.'

Julia's mind flew back to her last meal with Hugo, just before she left for Lancashire. Hugo had taken her to a Hungarian restaurant, almost hidden by banks of sand bags, in the West End. They'd had a rich goulash with spicy dumplings and thick wedges of seeded brown bread. Over pudding, sweet pancakes laced with cognac, Julia had interrogated Hugo about his new posting.

'You're so secretive these days,' she'd teased. 'I'm really beginning to think you're a spy.'

'Trust you, Jay,' Hugo had mocked. 'Always the over-imaginative one.'

'Well, don't leave it to my imagination,' she'd insisted. 'Tell me the truth!'

Hugo glanced around the crowded popular restaurant.

'Don't be ridiculous, sis,' he'd whispered. 'You're the daughter of a major, you know damn well we're all sworn to secrecy, so stop pushing for a story.'

'I don't believe you're shuffling papers all day.' she scoffed.

Seeing his sister's mutinous expression, Hugo knew she wouldn't be happy until he threw her a bone.

Dropping his voice, Hugo muttered, 'My department is responsible for radar mapping – now, does that satisfy your overactive imagination?'

Disappointed, she'd retorted, 'Sounds boring – you were made for finer things.'

Hugo held up the stump of his left hand. 'Something got in the way – now buck up or I won't take you out to dinner again.'

Kit roused Julia from her reverie. 'Your family all seem to be doing their bit for the war effort,' she said. 'And so are you! Coming up here and joining us Bomb Girls takes guts.'

Fingering the gunpowder, which she could now deftly trickle into the shell case, Julia shrugged. 'It's not exactly like we've got any choice, is it?' she said candidly. 'You go where you're sent.'

Taken aback by Julia's throw-away response, Kit said passionately, 'I never cease to thank God for sending me here to the Phoenix: it's the first real home I've ever had and the people here are like a family – they took me in and made me feel welcome,' she said, stifling a grateful sob. 'I've never known anything like it in my life,' she admitted.

Julia marvelled at Kit's statement; she couldn't ever imagine feeling like that about the windswept Phoenix high on the Pennine Moors, or about any of the workers, who were as alien to her as Martians on a distant planet.

5. Maggie's Grand Plans

As Julia became familiar with her work and the rotation of her twelve-hour shifts, she grew less exhausted; instead of falling asleep straight after tea or even during her dinner-break, she was able to take in some of the conversations going on around her. One such conversation was Maggie's favourite subject: her forthcoming marriage.

'I can't afford to have my wedding invitations printed,' she said during their tea-break one dark February afternoon. 'So I thought I'd get them typed out.'

Nora burst out laughing, 'Bomb Girls don't have typewriters!' she scoffed.

'Mebbe Mr Featherstone's secretary would let you borrow hers?' Kit joked.

Everybody knew that Mr Featherstone's granite-faced secretary, Marjorie, guarded her boss and his belongings like a Rottweiler guards a bone.

'She'd sooner part with her right arm than let anybody near her bloody typewriter,' Nora said realistically.

'Back to the drawing board,' said Maggie with a long sigh.

'You could try sending your invitations by mi dad's carrier pigeon!' Nora joked. 'He's got loads of the bally birds in the pigeon loft in our backyard.'

Maggie shot Nora a furious look that curtailed any further dark humour at her expense.

'Why don't you just write them?' Rosa asked. 'Surely it would be simpler?'

'Because I'm trying to be different,' Maggie answered with her typical honesty.

As a moody silence fell, Julia said in an embarrassed rush, 'I've got a typewriter.'

The girls around the table gazed at Julia in disbelief; not because she'd got a typewriter, but because she was actually joining in their conversation. The minute the words were out of her mouth Julia regretted them.

'Stupid!' she seethed to herself. 'Now you'll have to explain why you've actually got a bloody typewriter in a munitions factory!'

Adopting a careless manner, Julia said with a shrug, 'I don't know why I brought the wretched thing.' She certainly wasn't going to admit that she'd stupidly thought that during her stay in Lancashire she'd have plenty of time on her hands to knock out a few novels! 'I thought I might use it to write letters home.'

No longer despondent, Maggie looked excitedly at Julia. 'So could I have a go at typing out my wedding invitations?' she asked incredulously.

'I suppose so, if you'd like to?' Julia answered lamely.

Ignoring her rather less than enthusiastic response, Maggie grinned. 'I'd love to – can we start tonight?'

Julia's polite smile hid her unkind thoughts; now she'd have to spend all night drinking strong tea and inhaling other people's tobacco smoke whilst she typed out wedding invitations for Maggie. 'Bloody fool!' she crossly chided herself. 'Next time keep your big mouth shut.'

After tea Julia dutifully produced her typewriter from the bottom of her wardrobe, where she'd kept it since her arrival.

'Here we are,' she said, as she carried it into the sitting room, where Maggie, Nora and Rosa were gathered around the wood-burning stove, smoking cigarettes and drinking strong tea, just as Julia had glumly anticipated.

'I've got some typewriting paper to practise on,' she told the girls, who nudged up so that Julia could sit beside Maggie on the battered, old mock leatherette sofa. 'Where shall we start?' Julia asked, as she deftly wound paper into the typewriter.

Maggie, usually so forthright, suddenly seemed nervous and uncertain. 'What do people usually write?'

In a hurry to get the tiresome task over with, Julia said briskly as she started to type, 'Usually it would go something like . . .' – Julia read out the words as she quickly typed them – 'Mr and Mrs Yates request the pleasure of your company at the wedding of their youngest daughter, Margaret.'

Maggie interrupted her: 'Margaret Mary Sybil is my full name,' she said.

'What's your fiancé's surname?' Julia continued.

'Leslie Gordon Johnson – and he lives in Leeds,' Maggie told her.

Julia dutifully typed in the groom's details, then looked up to ask, 'Have you set a date?'

'Yes, eighth of May, my birthday – *if* Les gets leave,' Maggie told her.

'That's a bit hit-and-miss!' Nora giggled. 'Don't put any *ifs* on the invite – nobody'll come if they think the groom's gone missing!'

Seeing Maggie looking cross, Rosa gave Nora a gentle nudge in the ribs. 'Stop interrupting, *cara*,' she said softly.

Unperturbed, Nora added a defiant, 'You can't get wed if your fella's not there!'

After many interruptions Julia finally finished the first draft, which she removed from the typewriter.

'Take a look,' she said, as she handed the sheet of paper to Maggie.

'Oh, it does look smart,' the bride-to-be enthused.

'If you pasted the invitations on to pieces of card, I could decorate them with little painted flowers and lovebirds,' Rosa generously suggested.

Maggie's eyes glowed with pleasure. 'Thank you,' she exclaimed as she flung her arms around Rosa. 'My wedding is going to be *so* stylish!'

Feeling relieved that Maggie hadn't hugged her too, Julia got to her feet. 'I'll leave the typewriter for you to play around with,' she said, as she smothered a yawn. 'If you'll excuse me, I think I might go to bed and read.'

'Oh, rightio,' said Maggie, sounding just the tiniest bit disappointed that the fun was over. 'Thanks for your help.'

'Pleasure,' said Julia. 'Night,' she added as she left the room.

The minute they heard Julia's bedroom door click shut, Nora whispered naughtily, 'Goodnight, Ice Queen!'

'Shhh!' hissed shocked Rosa. 'She was very kind lending Maggie her typewriter.'

'I'm not saying she wasn't,' Nora continued in a whisper. 'It's just that every time you think she might drop her guard, she takes herself off as if she can't stand the sight of us.'

'I'm quite sure it's not like that, *cara*,' Rosa said diplomatically, as she rolled a cheroot.

'I'm quite sure it is!' naughty Nora muttered mutinously.

Before Nora could make another comment, Maggie whispered, 'It is disappointing, though, you must admit, Rosa. Not only was Julia kind and helpful for once, but she really got into the swing of things – then *ping*! It's like a light goes out and she's had enough.'

'People react differently to different situations; you have to accept that,' Rosa said smoothly. 'I like Julia,' she added staunchly.

'I'd like her a lot more if she'd just come down from her bloody high pedestal,' Nora concluded crossly.

Maggie's ambitious plans for a stylish wedding certainly didn't end with the invitations. She announced the next day, when they were joined by Kit in the canteen, that she wouldn't settle for anything less than a white silk wedding dress, a long veil and a bouquet of red roses.

'Darling!' Kit exclaimed. 'You've got to be joking.'

'I am not!' Maggie answered defiantly. 'You had what you wanted, Kit,' she hotly pointed out.

Kit nodded as she recalled how lavish her wedding had been, thanks to Ian's family's generosity and her husband's determination that she would be dressed like a princess on their wedding day.

'I'd willingly lend you my entire outfit, but unfortunately I'm six inches smaller than you.'

Seeing Maggie's sweet sky-blue eyes cloud over, Rosa quickly changed the subject. 'Have you chosen your bridesmaids yet?'

The word 'bridesmaids' brought a smile back to Maggie's lovely face. 'Nora,' she announced with a grin. 'And I've asked Kit if Billy can be my page boy.'

Modest, undemanding Nora, who expected nothing much of life, gaped at Maggie in astonishment. '*Me!* Why me?'

'Because you're my very best friend,' Maggie replied fondly.

Overcome with emotion, Nora's eyes brimmed with tears. 'I hope I don't show you up,' she muttered humbly. 'I've got two left feet and a big gob!' she reminded Maggie, who was still fretting over her wedding plans.

'I've no idea what any of us are going to wear,' she cried impatiently.

'You've got plenty of time,' Kit soothed. 'Something will turn up, for sure.'

Julia, with her head bent over the daily paper, coolly considered Maggie's wedding plans, which in her opinion were wildly overambitious. In her circle, wedding invitations were sent out at least six months before the ceremony, and the church and wedding reception were booked even before the mailing. Clearly Bomb Girls went about arranging their nuptials in a very different manner from what she was accustomed to.

'One of her friends should have the guts to tell her she's daydreaming,' Julia thought crossly, but she wisely kept her thoughts to herself.

Maggie gave a long, melodramatic moan, 'If things don't improve soon, I'll finish up walking down the aisle in mi bra and knickers!'

The very next evening, after they'd finished another sparse supper, this time faggots and mashed potatoes, Maggie dashed off to pick up her post from the Phoenix, and less than ten minutes later she came dancing back into the cowshed waving a letter.

'A letter from Les!' After running full pelt up the lane from the Phoenix to the cowshed, Maggie paused to draw breath. 'Thank God – he's been granted leave to get married on the eighth of May!'

'That's wonderful, *cara*,' Rosa cried.

Maggie's eyes glowed with happiness. 'Now we can do the invitations properly, Julia,' she exclaimed, startling Julia, who was miles away.

'Rightio, if you say so,' Julia answered civilly.

Nora raised sardonic eyebrows at Julia's response, but Maggie was way too excited even to notice.

'I'll go to see the vicar first thing in the morning

before I clock on for work – and I'll book the Black Bull whilst I'm in town, for the reception,' she added breathlessly. 'Though what we'll eat God only knows!'

Now that the wedding date was fixed, Maggie's brain was in a whirl as she thought of even more things that she had to do. 'I must let Les's parents know, and Gladys and Reg too: they'll have to travel all the way up from London ...' Suddenly she caught sight of Nora and her voice faded away. 'Nora, love, is something wrong?' she said, as she hurried to the window where Nora was standing staring out at the dark, wet moors.

Nora turned to her friend, a single tear falling miserably down her pale face.

'What is it, sweetheart, what's happened?' Maggie murmured, as weeping Nora fell into her open arms.

'That's just it, nothing's happened, nothing *ever* happens to me!' As the tears increased, Nora managed to blurt out what was bothering her. 'I'll – never-ever-get-married!' she said through heart-wrenching sobs. 'Nobody will ever want to marry *me*!'

As Maggie gently stroked Nora's frizzy red hair, Rosa joined her in comforting poor Nora.

'*Cara*, dearest, you have so much love to give,' she murmured. 'One day, I'm sure, the right boy will come along and win your heart.'

Nora sadly shook her head. 'There's nobody out there who would want somebody like me.'

Feeling completely inadequate, Julia watched Maggie and Rosa settle Nora on the sofa; it was impossible for her to respond to the charged emotional scene as the other girls had. But, she thought suddenly, I could do something useful. Turning on her heel, she walked quickly into her bedroom; when she emerged she was carrying the fashion magazines she'd brought from London.

'You might like to look through these,' she said, as she handed Nora the magazines. 'They might give you some ideas for your bridesmaid's dress.'

Stunned by Julia's spontaneous act of kindness, Nora gazed in disbelief, first at the elegant fashion models on the front of *Vogue*, then at Julia.

'Thank you,' she murmured.

After Julia had retired early as usual, Maggie and Nora flicked through the magazines.

'Oh, they're *gorgeous*,' Maggie sighed, as she stared in wonder at the wonderful bridal gowns, beautiful bouquets and pretty accessories.

Nora was less impressed by the tall, willow-slim *Vogue* models. 'I could no more wear summat like that than fly to the moon,' she giggled self-consciously.

Maggie gave a dreamy sigh. 'I'd give my back teeth to look like a princess on my wedding day.'

Rosa gave an inward groan. She knew Julia must have meant well, but by giving Maggie the magazines she'd set the poor girl's standards even higher. 'Damn!' she thought to herself. 'Things can only get worse.'

6. Roger Carrington

Rosa's pretty, heart-shaped face suffused with blushes as Nora bawled across the post room. 'Eh, Rosa! There's a letter in your pigeon-hole – it might be from that fella of yours down South!'

Rosa cringed; much as she loved sweet guileless Nora, there were times when she wished she'd stop being so loud and indiscreet about Rosa's personal life.

'Thanks,' Rosa said quickly, as she shoved the letter into her pocket.

Nora, incredulous that Rosa hadn't ripped open the envelope straight away, spluttered, 'Well, aren't you going to read it?'

Fortunately, Maggie, who was right beside Nora, gave her friend a dig in the ribs. 'Put a sock in it, our kid; love letters are better read in private.'

Now it was poor Nora's turn to blush. 'How would I know?' she muttered grumpily. 'Nobody's ever sent me a love letter.'

After reading Roger's effusive letter (in the privacy of one of the cubicles in the ladies' toilets in order to avoid any awkward questions), Rosa was both excited and nervous. She'd met Roger the previous autumn, when they'd both exhibited their paintings in an art gallery in Salford. Roger, who'd driven all the way up

43

from Norfolk, had been delighted to make her acquaintance, and Rosa fondly remembered his laughter and easy-going manner. When he'd said goodbye and kissed her modestly on the cheek (his sandy moustache tickling her nose!), he'd asked if they could keep in touch. He, she thought with a twinge of guilt, had put more effort into their correspondence than she had.

As she read the letter Rosa could almost hear his soft, cultivated voice.

Dearest Rosa,

I think of you so much and wonder how you are in the bomb factory on the wild Pennine Moors. I miss you terribly and wonder why you haven't written recently. Are they working you munitions girls to death?

His passionate attachment to his RAF squadron and his love of flying came through loud and clear in his letter.

There's nothing like the thrill of take off, taxiing down the runway, the propellers whirling, the engine kicking in, then that breath-taking moment when you take to the skies. Once over enemy territory and Jerry's on your radar, the only thought in your head is survival.

Rosa's stomach gave a sickening turn; she'd seen enough killing at close quarters to last her a lifetime and could cheerfully have forgone Roger's gung-ho descriptions of gunning down the enemy.

The drive back to base in the dawn light is the sweetest
moment – it's the time when I always think of you. I imagine
you standing on the edge of the runway, with your glorious long
dark hair blowing around your face, your eyes wide as you look
out for me with a smile on your lovely face. Please don't mock:
a man must be allowed to dream in wartime and you're the girl
I always dream of, Rosa. Would you ever think of coming to
see me? I've hardly any leave due till March, and the thought
of not seeing you for such an enormous length of time makes
me feel unhinged! I know it's a lot to ask but it would make
me so, so happy.

Yours, in hope of seeing you soon,
All my love, Roger

When Rosa had finished the letter, she sought out
Kit: the eldest of the group of friends, a married woman
and a mother whom she trusted implicitly.

'Roger wants me to visit him at his base near King's
Lynn,' she told Kit anxiously.

'Glory be to God!' Kit exclaimed. 'That's way over
on the other side of England.'

'I know,' Rosa laughed. 'I'm owed some leave, but I
suspect I'll spend one day getting there and another
getting back, and if I'm lucky a day with Roger.'

Seeing Rosa's doubtful expression, Kit gently asked,
'What's troubling you, lovie?'

Rosa paused to consider before she answered. 'Well,
I hardly know the man for a start,' she laughed.

'Do you like him?'

'Yes, I do like him,' Rosa replied.

'Do you want to go?'

Rosa nodded. 'It might be a bit strange, but, yes, it would be nice to see him again.'

'Well, then, I'd throw caution to the wind – nothing ventured, nothing gained,' Kit exclaimed. 'Book your ticket and tell the RAF to roll out the red carpet!'

As Rosa packed a small suitcase for her brief trip South, Nora became very anxious. 'Are you sure you'll be able to find your way back to us safely?' she fretted.

'You mean because I'm Italian and might get arrested as an enemy spy?' Rosa asked, her merry eyes twinkling.

Anxious Nora nodded. 'I wouldn't want owt awful to happen to you,' she blurted out.

Rosa patiently laid aside the black crêpe skirt she was packing in order to reassure Nora, who worried if any of her best friends travelled further than Manchester. '*Cara*, there is nothing to worry about.'

Determined to cheer up Nora, Rosa said with a teasing smile, 'Do you think if I talk like you Bomb Girls people down South will understand me?'

Nora gave her a quizzical look. 'Go on, then,' she challenged. 'Just you try.'

Rosa took a deep breath, then launched off. 'I were sayin' to our Nora t'other day, if thou dusn't shape up we'll get nowt done soon,' she said in a thick Lancashire accent. 'Well, was that convincing?' she asked with a laugh.

Nora grinned with relief. 'Thou'll pass alreet,' she

46

said with an approving nod. 'Talking like that you sound like one of us,' she finished with a loving smile.

'Of course I'm one of you, silly,' Rosa said, as she gave sweet Nora a hug. 'I'm a Lancashire Bomb Girl and right proud of it too!'

When Rosa set off on her long journey across England a few days later, she was at times overwhelmed by the sheer mass of troops on the move. At every station hundreds of uniformed soldiers, sailors and RAF servicemen poured out of compartments reeking of cigarette smoke and sweat. Then, in what seemed like no time at all, even more servicemen poured on to the steam train, until it was almost impossible to walk down the corridor to use the lavatories.

The bustling crowds started to dwindle when they left the major cities behind, and, as the train chugged through the flat Norfolk landscape, Rosa was able to stand up and lower the window: the blast of fresh air combined with the salty tang of the sea took her breath away. As they approached King's Lynn, the train started to shunt slowly forwards.

'Are you getting off here, sweetheart?' a handsome young sailor with his hat worn at a jaunty angle asked Rosa, as she reached up for her suitcase, lodged in the netted luggage rack.

'Yes,' she gasped as she tugged hard to release the case.

'Let me help,' he said with a confident smile. 'Hope you've got a boyfriend to meet you at the station?' he asked cheekily.

Rosa blushed and nodded. 'Yes, somebody is meeting me.'

'Lucky fella!' the cocky sailor joked.

Rosa descended the steep steps of the train with her heart beating double time – would she recognize Roger? The one and only time she'd seen him he'd been swamped in a huge RAF flying jacket. Would he even be there to pick her up as promised? Just as she was beginning to feel panicky, a voice rang out along the blustery platform: *'Rosa!'*

Rosa smiled at the sight of Roger, tearing up the platform, waving madly at her. He emerged from the crowd, and without a hint of self-consciousness sprinted forwards and lifted her high in the air.

'Hahh!' Rosa cried, as she laughed out loud in surprise.

'Hello again!' Roger responded with a broad smile as he set her down on her feet, then planted kisses on each of her pretty blushing cheeks. 'It's wonderful to see you.'

Relieving Rosa of her suitcase, he threw an arm around her shoulders, then led her along the platform and out of the station.

'Hop in,' he said, when they reached his parked up, battered old Morgan sports car, which Rosa remembered from the first time she'd met him.

'She's still going?' Rosa teased.

'I occasionally have to get out and push the old girl,' Roger admitted. 'Luckily the Norfolk lanes are kinder on her than your Pennine roads – she nearly blew a gasket up there.'

Rosa smiled with relief. Roger was just as she'd remembered him: extrovert, energetic, as carefree and open as a boy; it was exactly these qualities that had warmed her to him in the first place.

Like the gent he was, Roger settled her in the front passenger seat, where he lingered in order to softly stroke a ringlet of mahogany-brown hair from her upturned face. 'You're still the loveliest woman I've ever laid eyes on,' he murmured.

Rosa was relieved when Roger was in the driver's seat. It wasn't that she didn't enjoy his praise and tender looks; she simply needed to catch her breath and get used to being in his presence. Driving through the dark town, Rosa noticed there wasn't a single light in sight; even Roger was driving with the headlights off.

'How can you find your way in the pitch dark?' she puzzled.

'You get used to it,' Roger said, as he confidently swept out of Lynn and wound his way along country lanes that were so narrow Rosa felt as if the hedgerows were brushing against the car's wheels. 'We're on the very edge of the East coast, which is dotted with RAF airfields. A chance light could give away a secret location and Jerry would be on us before you could say, "Herr Hitler",' he chuckled. 'Now, tell me, have you done any more Bomb Girl paintings since we last met?'

'I'm afraid to say I haven't,' Rosa admitted with a shame-faced smile. 'Though I have drawn numerous bunches of flowers for Maggie's wedding invitations!'

Roger made a disapproving clucking sound with his

tongue. 'Very disappointing,' he said in a mock-stern voice.

'Since Christmas I haven't had the time, or the inclination, to draw anything much,' Rosa answered honestly. 'How about you?'

Roger shook his head as he dropped gear to take a sharp double bend. 'No, more's the pity; we've hardly time to draw breath here – orders from the top are to keep bombing Jerry day and night.'

Feeling suddenly queasy, Rosa closed her eyes in the inky darkness. How many thousands and thousands of people imprisoned in German camps, just as she had been, and just as her brother probably still was – the old, the sick and the infirm, babies, children and mothers – would die under the relentless barrage of the RAF's bombing raids over Germany? Would it eventually undermine German morale, as the British government hoped, and bring the wretched war to an end? Or would this new wave of attacks slaughter even more helpless innocents?

'So,' said Roger, breaking through her gloomy thoughts. 'I thought we'd go to the officers' mess for supper, then I'll tuck you up in the visitors' quarters for the night, so you'll be as fresh as a daisy for our day out tomorrow.'

Rosa felt a huge surge of relief; she hadn't realized until that moment that she'd been subconsciously worrying about where she would sleep. Fortunately, gallant Roger had thought of everything.

'Don't set your hopes too high on supper,' Roger

continued, as he ground to a halt and yanked on the handbrake. 'The officers' mess is a bit hit-and-miss on the grub front, but it's always hot and plentiful.'

After their long drive in the dark, Rosa blinked as they entered the canteen, loud with the sound of clattering knives and forks, and the deep murmur of men's voices. A brief silence fell as Roger led Rosa towards the serving hatch.

'We don't see many beautiful women,' Roger whispered in her ear, as his arm protectively encircled her slender waist. 'If I weren't here, they might mob you,' he joked.

Piling their trays with boiled beetroot, sprouts and something that looked like shepherd's pie, Roger guided Rosa to a table, where he introduced her to his friends; they gazed admiringly at her shapely frame and slim legs. Shaking her rather untidy hair off her face, she sat down beside Roger and smiled at the men, who could barely keep their eyes off her.

'Where did old man Carrington find a lovely thing like you?' one of them asked.

'We met at an art exhibition in Salford,' Rosa answered.

'Good God! It would be worth taking up painting to meet you!' another of the men chuckled.

'Leave the poor girl alone,' Roger chided good-naturedly. 'She's been travelling all day,' he added protectively.

'Christ! I wouldn't cross the road to see an ugly sod like you, old chap,' his friend joshed.

Rosa broke through the raucous laughter. 'Roger says the RAF are keeping you all busy.'

And they were off: avidly discussing the advantages of Lancasters over Halifaxes well into the second course of stewed apples and custard. Seeing Rosa's eyelids drooping with fatigue and an excess of information on the size of various planes' bomb bases, Roger steered her away from his friends and settled her at a quiet table, where they were able to drink their tumblers of whisky and soda in private.

'Poor buggers,' he said, as they clinked glasses. 'They couldn't believe their eyes when you walked in and lit up the room.'

'They've probably all got devoted girlfriends at home,' Rosa answered with a knowing smile.

'Not one of them could hold a candle to you, my sweet,' Roger said. 'I'm the luckiest man in the world to have met you,' he whispered, as he leant forward to kiss her on her cheek.

Rosa's heart skipped a beat; she liked the smell of his clean skin and the way the ends of his sandy moustache swept against her warm cheek.

'I've not been able to get you out of my head since the moment I first met you.' Roger stared into her deep, dark eyes, so intensely that embarrassed Rosa started to blush. 'I don't want to rush you, my dearest, but do you think you might have feelings for me?'

Though taken aback at his directness, Rosa paused to consider; she'd never been the kind of woman who gushed on request, so her reply was short and direct.

'I do have feelings for you, Roger – that's exactly why I'm here – but please,' she begged, 'can we take things one step at a time? We hardly know each other,' she finished shyly.

'Of course!' he agreed with a grateful smile. 'But I do want to know *everything* about you, darling Rosa.'

Seeing Rosa give a sharp intake of breath, Roger quickly added, 'In time, of course.'

'Time is a luxury in wartime,' Rosa thought ruefully. 'When there's always the fear that there will be no tomorrow.'

Seeing the yearning in Roger's earnest brown eyes, Rosa took his hand and squeezed it. 'It's good to be here with you,' she whispered.

Whatever else she might have said was lost as he crushed her into his arms and held her tight.

'Oh, Rosa, dearest, *dearest* Rosa.'

7. Holkham Beach

The following morning, after a restless night on a hard metal military bed, Rosa woke up, and for a few seconds she wondered where she was. Peeping round the edges of the blackout blind, she saw a line of Nissen huts close to a runway on which fighter planes were parked, ready for take-off. Rosa, who didn't know one plane from another, smiled to herself: Roger would know the name of every one by heart, she thought fondly. As she took in the scene, she heard a long, lone drone overhead, and looking up she saw planes approaching the base. One by one they dropped height and landed with a sharp bump before taxiing to a stop.

Realizing they must have just come back from a night raid, Rosa watched the pilots, grey with fatigue, emerge from their cockpits; immediately their ground crews rushed forward to greet them and to inspect and prepare the planes for their next take-off. Rosa spotted Roger speaking to one of the pilots, who, clearly upset, shook his head despondently; Rosa was touched by Roger's response to his obvious sadness. Without any inhibition he slung an arm around the pilot's burly shoulders, then clapped him hard on the back. Suddenly realizing that some of the pilots must have been lost in the night raid, Rosa's eyes filled with tears; even so, tomorrow night more airmen would fly out over the North Sea, which had become a graveyard for so many shot down by enemy fire – and the killing would go on.

Seeing the pilots heading indoors to log their report, Rosa frantically tried to gather her wits together; she needed to get washed and dressed before Roger came knocking on her door and the day began in earnest. In a quandary about what to wear, she finally opted for a pair of thick tweed trousers that showed off her slim but curvy hips and a sage-green twinset. The outfit would keep her warm on a cold February day, but it also brought out the lustrous glow in her warm olive skin and large dark eyes.

Hoping they wouldn't have to start the day in the officers' mess with men ogling her over their beans on toast, Rosa was delighted when Roger arrived saying they'd eat breakfast in the car. As they sped along the narrow lanes overflowing with aconites and tiny primroses just starting to poke through the cold earth, Roger handed her a packet of sandwiches and a flask.

'Tea's up,' he announced. 'Be a darling and pour one for me.'

Balancing the plastic cup of hot tea on his knees, Roger drove with one hand whilst he ate a cheese-and-pickle sandwich with the other. Laughing, Rosa bit into her sandwich, which really was delicious, then she poured herself a cup of tea that she sipped as she took in the landscape.

'We're going to have the day all to ourselves,' Roger told her. 'Just me and you and the sea and the sky.'

Though familiar with the beauty of the Mediterranean, Rosa was nevertheless stunned by the loveliness of the beach Roger had chosen for their day out. The smooth white sand swept for miles along the coast, which was fringed by a thick pine wood and rolling dunes.

'It's beautiful,' Rosa murmured as Roger, holding her by the hand, led her on to the beach. *'Bellissimo!'* she exclaimed.

'Holkham,' Roger explained. 'One of the most wonderful places in England as far as I'm concerned,' he added, as they walked hand in hand towards the distant grey sea. 'I often come here and think about you,' he admitted without a hint of embarrassment. 'I worry that you might have forgotten me or that some other chap might have stolen your heart?' He turned abruptly towards Rosa. 'Tell me truthfully, dearest, is there anyone else?'

Rosa blushed. 'Don't be ridiculous!' she cried. 'I work in a munitions factory on top of the moors – how am I going to meet any man who isn't over fifty?'

'Well, that's a relief!' he laughed, as he held her hand tighter, and then, to her astonishment, set off running along the beach, pulling her along with him.

The sound of crashing waves combined with the whistling east wind momentarily took Rosa's breath away, making her feel as giddy and reckless as a child. Grasping Roger's hand, she kept up with his long legs, running as fast as he did, until finally she shook him off and ran even faster.

'Catch me!' she called over the sound of the wind.

Diving into the dark woods, Rosa stopped and looked around. Spotting a stout pine tree, she crept behind it, stifled a giggle and waited. As her breath quietened, she heard Roger's feet cracking on the fallen pinecones as he approached her hiding place; startled by his presence, several young rabbits shot past her when he loudly called her name.

'*Rosa!* Where are you?'

Smiling impishly, Rosa hunkered down closer to the bole of the tree.

'Stop teasing, Rosa, where are you?'

Just as he was about to pass the tree, she sprang out at him like a wild cat.

'Haha!' she yelled.

Flinging her strong arms around his shoulders, she held on to him as he swung her round; then, when she was completely dizzy, he gently lowered her on to the sandy ground soft with pine needles, and she lay spreadeagled, helpless with laughter.

'I gave you a fright!' she giggled.

'You bloody well frightened me to death,' he chuckled. 'Little minx!' he declared, as he threw himself on to the ground beside her. 'Darling little minx,' he murmured and gathered her into his arms, kissing her long and lingeringly on the lips.

This time Rosa had no doubts about responding to the warm lovable man who held her safe in the fold of his arms. In fact, she was surprised by the sudden surge of passion she felt as his lips pressed against hers and his hand wound around tresses of her silky dark hair. As they drew apart, Roger's eyes, gentle with emotion, gazed down at her.

'You pack quite a punch,' he whispered, as he traced the line of her small nose, whose tip he kissed.

'Have you forgotten I'm Italian?' she teased. Assuming a phony Italian accent, she rattled on, 'I am passionate, dramatic, eh, *sono fantastico*!'

Roger stopped her silliness with more kisses, which she returned with fervour. Coming up for air, she buried her face against his strong chest and inhaled the smell of his flesh through his RAF shirt.

'You smell of soap,' she murmured dreamily. 'Sweet, scented soap.'

'Mother sends me a bar of homemade soap every month,' he admitted.

'She must love her little boy,' Rosa remarked without a hint of sarcasm.

'She's worried sick about me,' Roger said in an unusually quiet voice.

'How could she not be?' Rosa asked. 'It's a heavy load to carry, knowing your son flies fighter planes over enemy territory almost every night.' She shivered involuntarily. 'I also worry.'

'Your sweet face brings me winging back home, believe me,' Roger assured her. 'I would do anything just to be with you,' he added in a voice that was tight with emotion.

Feeling empowered by his conviction that she kept him safe, Rosa couldn't help but smile.

'Why does opening my heart to you make you smile?' Roger said, as her smile widened underneath his scrutiny.

'The thought that I could save you,' she replied. 'When I couldn't even save my own beloved brother.' Looking Roger square in the eye, she asked sharply, 'You do remember I have a brother, Gabriel?'

'Of course,' he assured her. 'You told me about him when we met.'

She and Gabriel, her elder brother, had been forced to leave their home and their family only two years ago. On the run, they'd soon been captured and dispatched to a concentration camp in Germany, where Gabriel had bribed the guards by giving them everything he possessed to free his sister. Rosa never even got a chance to say goodbye to her brother, let alone to thank him for his selfless sacrifice; all the time she was making her perilous escape she knew in her heart that by buying her freedom from the Nazis, Gabriel had put himself in an even more vulnerable position. If it was ever leaked that he had bribed the guards, he would be shot on the spot.

After grieving so long for her lost family and brother, Rosa was wary; was she ready to fall in love with a man who took his life in his hands every day of the week?

She struggled free of his embrace in order to sit up and say something that was of the most fundamental importance to her; if they were to have any kind of relationship, she needed to be totally honest with him.

'I can't take any more heartache,' she said. Determined

not to give in to tears, she swallowed hard and added, 'I could not bear to love and lose another.'

Seeing tears brimming over Rosa's eyes, wetting her long black lashes and slipping down her sweet, sad face, Roger sat up too.

'Dearest girl, I would do anything to avoid giving you even more grief, but I cannot lie to you, Rosa,' he responded in complete honesty. 'I can't guarantee that nothing will ever happen to me – my first duty is to my King and Country, and if my life is required I would offer it up, but' – he took a deep ragged breath – 'I will do my very best to stay safe, I promise. I want to have a future with you, Rosa, beyond this bloody war. I want to be with you forever.'

Rosa's thoughts flew back to a poem she'd read in Pendleton Library not very long ago. Grieving her lost loved ones in the Great War, Vera Brittain had written:

> Perhaps some day the sun will shine again,
> And I shall see that still the skies are blue,
> And feel once more I do not live in vain,
> Although bereft of You.

The poem had haunted Rosa, who often murmured it when she thought of Gabriel. But now, here in these pinewoods with the breakers crashing on the beach, it came back to her with a powerful personal resonance. Why was she holding her emotions in so tightly? In the political climate of the moment, why was she hesitating? Why didn't she take life by the throat and squeeze everything that was worthwhile out of it? Look what had happened with her and Gabriel: one minute they were in the concentration camp together, the next they were parted. This man with unruly hair that fell in a fringe over his earnest hazel eyes was laying his heart at her feet, and she – she was prevaricating!

'What's the matter with me?' she demanded of herself. 'Have I forgotten how to love?'

Seeing Rosa's flushed cheeks, Roger misinterpreted her anguished expression; fearing he'd gone too far too quickly, he apologized. 'I'm so awfully sorry,' he blustered. 'I didn't mean it to be this way.'

Rosa smiled gently as she stroked his cheek. 'What way is that?' she whispered.

'So quick and rushed,' he blurted out. 'I wanted to woo you, buy you presents, write you poetry, send you flowers – not swamp you with emotional declarations. Oh, God!' he exclaimed, furious with himself. 'Why do I always make such a damn mess of things?' he said, as he laid his head on her chest and groaned in despair.

Rosa steadily stroked Roger's sandy-brown hair until she felt his breath steady.

'I've never met anybody like you, and I'm so afraid of losing you,' he confessed. 'You're so beautiful and talented and clever – how could you ever fall for a blundering fool like me?'

'Believe me, I'm having a lovely time,' Rosa said with a sudden surge of giddiness. 'I'm just wondering when you might kiss me again.'

Eager as a puppy, Roger's head shot up. 'Really? Would you mind?'

In answer she held her arms open wide to him and, abandoning her fears and inhibitions she locked her lips with his and sank into his passionate embrace.

8. Wrigg Hall

Sitting in her comfy sitting room, which was in fact the back room of her chip shop, Edna Chadderton's green eyes grew as wide as saucers as she read, then reread, an article in the *Manchester Evening News*.

'Malc!' she cried excitedly to her husband. 'Listen to this.' Straightening her glasses, she read out loud from the paper.

'Wrigg Hall, the ancient Jacobean seat of the Leonard family, has been requisitioned by the Red Cross. The need for more hospitals has necessitated the government taking over several stately homes in the area, primarily for nursing the sick and providing specialist care for those returning from hospital stations on the front line. Because of the acute shortage of nurses, the Red Cross are keen to recruit local volunteers – especially those who might have some past experience in physiotherapy and convalescent care. The British Red Cross are in the process of adapting the ancient building for the sick and wounded, who will shortly be arriving at Wrigg Hall.'

'I wouldn't have thought that draughty old mansion would be suitable for sick men,' Malc commented.

'They'll have to do summat about keeping it warm

or the poor lads will freeze to death on arrival,' Edna agreed.

'I wonder what happens to the toffs when the government walk in and claim their ancestral pile?' Malc mused.

'There's only old Lord Leonard in the Hall these days,' Edna told him. 'Mebbe he'll move out when the Red Cross move in.'

Malc gazed fondly at his wife, whom he'd married on Christmas Eve only a couple of months ago. Since then he'd experienced such contentment and companionship with his new wife that he could hardly believe it. He could tell from the look in her eyes as she gazed into the fireplace, banked up with logs collected from the moors now that coal was sparse, that she was 'cogitating', as she would say. Nevertheless he was taken aback by what she had to say when she did speak.

'I might just put myself forward as a volunteer,' she announced.

Malc hid a smile as he shook his head; generous, impulsive Edna never ceased to surprise him.

'And just how are you going to do that, sweetheart?' he inquired. 'You're working every hour God sends as it is.'

Edna ran a flourishing chip shop that provided hot and cheap hearty food for the local mill workers. Though the workforce was depleted, with men having been called up for active service, the cotton mill had stayed open, and Lancashire cotton continued to roll off the looms. Edna's customers arrived with their own tin bowls every dinnertime, which Edna heaped with chips, scallops, butter beans or mushy peas. In the good old days there'd been fresh cod from Fleetwood, but over the past five years of war fresh fish was a rarity. When Edna was lucky enough to be able to buy mince-meat or scrag end of mutton with her ration coupons, she always made delicious meat pies swimming in onions and rich gravy for her grateful customers.

Apart from her thriving chip shop, Edna also had another business: well before she'd met Malc she'd con-verted an old van into a mobile chip shop, which she drove up the hill to the Phoenix factory most evenings. Parked up in the dispatch yard, Edna served out a lot more than chips to the Bomb Girls, who were initially drawn to the van by the tantalizing smell of sizzling hot fat. As time went by, Edna's mobile chip shop became a familiar land-mark, which the workers were attracted to like iron to a magnet. Edna's warmth and humour were special indeed, but the advice she doled out was fair and sensible, and she could always be trusted to keep a secret, For Edna the Phoenix became her second home. Initially she'd gone there for business, but these days she went out of love. Edna admired the Bomb Girls' tough commitment; supporting them in whatever way she could was her bit towards the war effort. So Malc was right that she was already about as busy as it was possible for a person to be.

'I can't see you giving up your lunchtime openings or your night-time visits to the Phoenix,' Malc continued.

'I could put in a couple of afternoons a week at Wrigg Hall,' Edna replied to her husband.

Knowing full well that when Edna had made her

mind up to do something, there was no point in trying to change it, Malc struck a match and lit up a Player's for both of them. 'Fair enough,' he said, as he exhaled a cloud of smoke. 'Give it a go, lovie, and see how you get on.'

Edna wasn't the only one who'd read and responded to the article in the newspaper. Nora also expressed an interest in volunteering, which amazed Edna, who knew just how squeamish the young girl was.

'You'd better toughen up, my sweetheart,' Edna said with a gentle smile. 'You can't have a touch of the vapours every time you see a drop of blood.'

'I'm just hoping I'll get used to it – I really do want to help them poor buggers coming back from the front,' Nora said with tears in her big blue eyes.

Edna looked at Nora's earnest face: she could see the poor kid meant well, and it would be a shame for her if she fell at the first hurdle.

'Mebbe you should volunteer to do the tea trolley to start with,' she said kindly. 'Just till you get used to the lie of the land, like.'

Nora looked distinctly relieved at Edna's suggestion. 'Yes,' she answered eagerly. 'Tea I can easily do.'

Maggie said she couldn't take on anything extra at the moment.

'I know it sounds selfish,' she said with an embarrassed smile. 'But I want to concentrate on our wedding; I just want everything to be –'

'Don't say it,' Edna laughed.

'*Perfect!*' Maggie's friends around the van shouted in unison.

Maggie blushed at their teasing. 'I know you think I'm mad – mebbe I am, I don't care!' she retaliated. 'When I think of marrying my lovely Les, my knees turn to water,' she confessed. 'I want our wedding day to be a day we'll remember till the end of our lives,' she said romantically.

'So we'll take it that love's young dream is off the volunteers' list till after the wedding?' Edna said cheerfully. 'What about Julia or Rosa? Do you think they'll be interested?'

'We'll ask Rosa when she gets back from Norfolk,' Nora said. 'That's if she ever finds her way safely home,' she added with a fretful sigh.

Using the naughty nickname they'd given the new girl, Maggie quipped, 'I can as much see the Ice Queen ministering to the sick as Mr Featherstone giving us a week's holiday!'

When Rosa returned home late at night, they could all see a startling physical difference in her. Her already natural beauty was magnified by the happiness in her dark eyes; her skin glowed and a smile permanently lingered around the edges of her luscious pink pouty lips. Kit, who saw Rosa the morning after her tediously long journey home, was struck by the change in her. When the girls assembled as usual around their favourite corner table in the packed canteen, all eyes turned to radiant Rosa.

'You didn't say much when you got in last night,' Nora said accusingly.

'Heavens!' Rosa laughed. 'After twelve hours on a packed train that seemed to stop every five minutes, I was just about fainting by the time I walked into the cowshed.'

'We could see that,' said Maggie, as she eyeballed Nora for being abrupt. 'That's why we left you alone.'

'But you do look different!' unstoppable Nora blurted out.

Julia stirred her strong dark tea, the local brew that she was trying to familiarize herself with, and idly wondered when Rosa's friends would stop being so damn nosy.

Kit, the more mature member of the group, turned to Rosa with a warm smile. 'Did it go well?'

Rosa's smile said it all. 'Everything went wonderfully!'

On the point of exploding with curiosity, Nora cried, 'So tell us all about it?'

Feeling distinctly uncomfortable at the silly young girls' constant questioning of Rosa, Julia scraped back her chair. 'I'm going to get more tea,' she announced. 'Would anybody else like some?'

Kit, Nora and Maggie, totally focused on Rosa, quickly shook their heads. 'No thanks,' they said in unison.

'Roger and I had only one day together,' Rosa started. 'We spent the whole of it on a beautiful beach, walking by the sea, or in the woods close to the sea; we sat in the sand dunes and ate a picnic and we talked and talked and talked,' she said in a dreamy voice.

'Did he kiss you?' cheeky Nora couldn't stop herself from asking.

Rosa's eyes shone with love as she recalled Roger's

kisses, which had grown stronger and more passionate as the day progressed. 'Oh, yes!' she replied with a giggle.

'It must have been awful leaving him,' Maggie commiserated. 'Just one day and it was all over.'

'But what a day, a perfect day!' Rosa exclaimed happily.

When Kit and Rosa were briefly alone in the ladies' toilets, Rosa volunteered more information.

'I wasn't at all sure that you'd go,' Kit admitted.

'I don't deny I was nervous, especially when he took me into the officers' mess,' Rosa chuckled. 'You'd think some of those men had never seen a woman before.'

'They've probably never seen a woman as stunning as you, with your lovely Mediterranean looks,' Kit said generously.

'It was only the next day when we went walking on the beach that I began to feel relaxed,' Rosa confessed. 'Roger's so funny and lovable and open and honest. I felt so easy with him.'

'I'm delighted for you,' said Kit. 'I hope you get to see him again soon.'

'Oh, so do I . . . so do I,' Rosa said on a long dreamy sigh.

9. Flora's Visit

Rosa's return coincided with Edna's daughter's visit to Pendleton. Flora had only recently been reunited with her mother, who as a teenager had been forced to give up her baby for adoption. For many years she had kept her daughter's existence to herself, until one day in a burst of passion she'd shared her secret with Kit. It was Kit's solicitor husband, Ian, who against all the odds had helped track Flora down.

To add to Edna's joy, Flora had two little girls, Marilyn and Katherine, who'd been bridesmaids at her recent wedding to Malc on Christmas Eve.

Flora's visits with her little girls were golden days in Edna's calendar; occasionally she had to nip herself just to make sure she wasn't dreaming. She adored her new family and they adored their new 'Mum' and 'Nan'.

Edna had plans for Flora's imminent visit; she'd saved her ration coupons so that she could make jam tarts with her grandchildren and she'd managed (thanks to Malc's dubious connections with the local black market) to get a precious pair of nylons, a treat for Flora; plus she was planning to take them all to see *The Wizard of Oz* at the local picture house.

But this time when Flora arrived with her daughters, Malc noticed a change in the tall slender young woman who had her mother's auburn curls and startling green eyes. She looked tired and had dark circles under her eyes; and though she chatted and laughed as she always had, Malc was aware of a difference in her. Normally sensitive, Edna would usually notice such things, but with her thoughts on baking with Marilyn and Katherine, and singing the songs in *The Wizard of Oz*, Edna was in a happy world of her own that Malc had no intention of spoiling.

Malc pushed his anxiety aside as he peeled and chopped potatoes for the next dinner-time opening along with Marilyn and Katherine in the shed in the backyard. The little girls loved watching Malc pull the metal lever of the chip chopper and seeing slender slices of potatoes pour into a bucket underneath the hand-operated machine.

'Daddy was home from the war last week,' little Katherine, the younger of the sisters, chirped up.

Malc quickly tried to hide his surprise; he'd gathered from Edna that Flora hadn't seen her husband in a long time, so why hadn't she mentioned to her mother that he was home on leave?

'That must have been nice,' he said, as he continued chopping potatoes.

Glancing up, he saw the girls look at each other before shaking their heads.

'It wasn't nice,' Katherine blurted out.

'And why's that, then?' Malc asked as casually as he could manage.

Marilyn, a bright, sensitive seven-year-old, replied, 'He was grumpy.'

'We thought he was grumpy 'cos he was fed up with killing Germans,' Katherine added.

'Mummy told us he was just tired,' Marilyn added.

Careful not to interrupt their innocent childish chatter, Malc didn't say a word.

'But then he kept shouting at Mummy till she cried,' Katherine said sadly.

'We were frightened,' Marilyn confessed.

Wanting to put their fears at rest, Malc said, 'I'm sure they had a good chat when you two were fast asleep. Now then,' he said cheerfully as he stood up, 'let's get these spuds into a bucket of cold water for Nana to cook later.'

After the children had run off, Malc sat for some time thoughtfully smoking a cigarette; there could be only one explanation as to why Flora hadn't mentioned her husband's leave to her mother and that was because she didn't want to talk about it, which in itself was worrying. Especially given what the girls had said. Edna had never met her son-in-law – he'd been fighting with the Lancashire Regiment since the war started – but Malc hadn't heard a bad word said about him. Stubbing out his Pall Mall, Malc determined he'd have a private word with Flora before she and the girls returned to her family home in Penrith.

Malc's chance came the next day when they were all out walking on the snowy moors with Edna ahead, singing 'Follow the Yellow Brick Road' at the top of her voice.

'More, Nana!' cried the giggling little girls, skipping along beside her.

'You two will have me hoarse!' Edna laughed, as she started up again with the catchy chorus. 'Follow the Yellow Brick Road!'

Flora smiled fondly at the sight of her mother and her daughters running along the snowy path together.

'They love her so much,' she sighed.

'And she worships them,' Malc said fondly. Seeing the unexpected tears in Flora's eyes, he gently caught her by the arm. 'Marilyn and Katherine were telling me about their dad coming home on leave, sweetheart.'

Flora's face clouded. 'I asked them not to mention it,' she said quickly.

'You know what kids are like – nothing's a secret long,' Malc retorted with a smile; then, coming straight to the point, he added, 'Can I ask why you didn't want them to mention it?' When his question was met with silence, he probed further. 'The little girls told me that your husband was grumpy.'

'Is that what they said?' Flora asked sharply.

'Aye, and that he made you cry,' Malc added boldly.

Flora swiped away the tears welling in her eyes. 'He came back in a bad mood, that's all,' she said, trying to sound dismissive.

Malc was increasingly aware that he was stepping on eggshells, but he couldn't end the conversation until he knew more. 'Poor little buggers said they were frightened of him,' he told Flora. 'And they were frightened for you too.'

Unable to staunch the tears that began to course down her tired face, Flora murmured miserably, 'John never used to be like this – he never drank nor swore – but now . . .' Her voice broke into a sob. 'When he's home on leave, which isn't very often, thank God, he drinks all the time and shouts and swears in front of his little girls.'

'And does he ever turn on you, lovie?' Malc gently inquired.

Flora slowly nodded. 'Just the once.'

Malc took a deep breath to steady his rising temper. 'They say army life changes some men,' he said diplomatically.

'These days I dread him coming home,' Flora whispered. 'Please don't tell Mum,' she added urgently. 'The last thing I want is her upset too. I'm sure it'll get better.'

Malc nodded. 'I won't mention it, though I can't vouch for your two little chatterboxes not spilling the beans,' he said with a smile.

Anxious that her mother shouldn't see her upset, Flora quickly wiped away her tears. 'We'll be leaving tomorrow, so hopefully Mum won't find out.'

Before she hurried off to catch up with her girls, Malc detained her a moment longer. 'Flora,' he said softly. 'Promise you'll tell me if things should, er . . .' He paused awkwardly. 'Take a turn for the worse. Edna would never forgive me if she knew you'd shared your secret with me and I'd never tried to help you, so promise, please?' he pleaded.

Looking uncomfortable, Flora nodded. 'I promise, but I'm sure it's not necessary, Malc,' she prevaricated.

'Nevertheless, if you need help, contact me – any time, day or night,' Malc insisted.

Flora gave Malc a quick peck on the cheek. 'Thank you,' she whispered, then ran off to join her daughters, who were now throwing snowballs at Edna.

The next day, when Edna waved her family off at Clitheroe Station, she had no idea what dark secret lay behind her daughter's cheerful smile.

'Bye, Nana,' the girls cried, as they waved goodbye.

'Come back soon!' Edna called out, and the steam train pulled out of the station. 'Love you!'

After the train had sped away, Edna took a clean hankie from her handbag. 'I'm a soft old bugger,' she said, wiping her eyes. 'I hate saying goodbye to them.'

Putting a comforting arm around his wife's shoulder, Malc led her down the empty platform. 'Don't fret yourself, lovie: they'll be back soon,' he assured her.

10. Volunteers

Edna read more news about the local volunteers' call-up in the evening paper and made sure that everybody she saw that night, when she drove her mobile chip shop to the Phoenix dispatch yard, knew all about it too.

'Anybody who's interested in helping out at Wrigg Hall has to report there this Thursday,' she said, as she shovelled chips into paper bags, then handed them out to her hungry customers.

'Have the wounded arrived?' one of the girls asked, as she doused her hot chips in salt and vinegar.

'Not yet, according to the paper,' Edna replied. 'The Red Cross are busy preparing the Hall for their arrival, which is why they want to know how many volunteers might be available to help them out.'

Some of the workers said, rather shamefacedly, that they simply couldn't take on anything else.

'I'm dead on mi feet at the end of mi shifts,' one woman said bluntly. 'I'd be neither use nor ornament to anybody at Wrigg Hall if I couldn't keep mi eyes open.'

Rosa told Edna in confidence that she might consider volunteering later on. 'To be honest, I can't even think straight at the moment,' she confessed with a guilty blush.

'Did your visit to Norfolk addle your brains that much?' Edna teased.

Rosa nodded. 'I don't know whether I'm on my head or my heels,' she giggled.

Pregnant Kit, with a toddler at home, had no choice but to decline, and Julia never even mentioned volunteering.

'Typical!' sniffed Nora, who was getting increasingly niggled by the snooty, remote newcomer.

'Leave her be,' Edna chided. 'Malc said she's a good worker, just keeps herself to herself.'

'That's putting it mildly,' Nora grumbled. 'It doesn't cost owt to smile occasionally.'

When the day came, Nora and Edna took the bus to the Wrigg Hall stop, then walked along a cobbled lane, until reaching what had originally been a grand Tudor mansion. The front was decorated traditionally – black timber frames and white stucco – while a large red-brick extension had been tagged on at the back at a later date.

When the volunteers arrived at the top of the drive-way, Red Cross vans were being unloaded by drivers aided by VADs, an acronym that Edna had to explain to a muddled Nora.

'VAD stands for Voluntary Aid Detachment.'

'Are they properly trained staff?' Nora asked.

'Oh, aye, from the British Red Cross and St John Ambulance too – they do valuable work at home and abroad,' Edna replied.

'So who'll be training us?' Nora puzzled.

'Well, I'm hoping the VADs will – but if they're short of staff they might chuck us in at the deep end and see how we survive,' Edna joked.

'Don't say that, Edna!' Nora fretted. 'We need to be told what to do when there are lives at risk.'

Changing the subject, Edna nodded towards a growing line of girls and women converging on the Hall. 'Looks like a fair number have showed up – come on, let's follow the crowd.'

The volunteers were directed into what would once have been a grand entranceway, with elegant staircases sweeping off both sides. The beautiful old tiled floor was covered in mud and grass stains, which grew worse as burly delivery men manoeuvred metal hospital beds around the growing crowd in the packed hallway.

'Welcome, ladies!' an imperious voice called over the clattering din.

The volunteers turned to see a formidable middle-aged woman wearing a nurse's uniform, which was almost covered by a large white starched apron with an enormous red cross emblazoned on the front of the bodice. She wore black stockings and sturdy black shoes, and on top of her iron-grey hair, which was caught up in a tight bun, was a crisp white cap. 'Follow me, please.'

Leading the wide-eyed volunteers into what must have been the library but was now completely bereft of books, the lady in charge wasted no time introducing herself. 'I'm Matron,' she announced. 'On behalf of the staff here at Wrigg Hall I'd like to welcome you and say how extremely grateful we are to you all for taking the trouble to come here today. Now, if I may, I will explain to you the kind of voluntary help we're urgently in need of.'

She briskly unfurled a homemade chart which she stuck on to a free-standing blackboard – then, tapping the chart with a long stick, Matron continued.

'An operating theatre has recently been established in the cellars; it will be staffed by trained surgeons and a nursing team experienced in pre-operative and post-op care. Patients will be nursed at ground level, here in the library and in most of the other rooms on this floor. We are expecting patients with wide-ranging needs.' Turning to the chart, she swiftly ran down the list written in large, bold capitals. 'We shall be treating patients suffering from shell shock, burns, gas poisoning, malnutrition, exhaustion and gangrene. There will be amputees in need of convalescent care and physiotherapy; patients traumatized by shell shock and loss of memory will require counselling and psychiatric help; and there will be others who will need feeding up and restoring to health before they're well enough to be sent back to the front line.'

There was a general murmur of sympathy from the assembled women. 'Poor sods, just as soon as they can stand on their own two feet they're sent back to fighting the Hun!' one older woman said over-loudly.

'I'm afraid that's an inevitable aspect of war,' Matron said curtly.

Edna was the first to speak up, asking the question

on everybody's lips. 'Where do we fit in if we're not qualified?'

Matron gave a brief smile and turned a page on her chart. 'We need cleaners, drivers, cooks, tea ladies, librarians, typists, chemists, stretcher-bearers, stewards, postal workers and women who will sit alongside a dying man and pray with him,' she said. 'Our aim is to send our patients away from here hale and hearty; however, the deaf, the blind, the mentally ill and the crippled who need long-term specialist care may be transferred to more appropriate convalescent homes.' Turning from the blackboard, she pointed to some forms that had been left on tables around the room. 'Please fill in the forms with your name and contact details and whatever skills you might have to offer – and, please, don't say you have no skills: the very fact that you're here means you have something to give. If you have a St John's certificate please make that clear on your form.'

As the volunteers made to move off, Matron called over the growing chatter, 'Finally, I'd like to thank you all again for coming here today.'

Nora and Edna took some time in filling out their forms. 'I'd be happiest hiding behind the tea trolley,' Nora whispered nervously to Edna.

'Then write that down,' Edna advised.

'What have you put?' Nora asked, as she peered at the form Edna was busily filling in.

'I'm best at being with folks,' Edna replied. 'Reading them the paper, chatting and making them laugh – as long as I don't make them split their stitches,' she chuckled, completing her form and dropping it into a box by the front door.

Just as they were about to leave, Edna and Nora spotted Julia talking to the Matron.

'She never mentioned she was coming here!' Nora gasped incredulously.

'The more the merrier,' Edna answered cheerily.

'You'd think she'd have told us,' indignant Nora grumbled.

'Shhh! She's coming over,' Edna hissed as Julia approached them. 'Have you joined up?' she asked with a smile.

Julia nodded. 'Matron noticed on my form that I'd got a St John's certificate so she's put me straight to work on the wards.'

Nora rolled her eyes as if to say, 'Well, she would, wouldn't she?'

'What have you signed up for?' Julia inquired.

'Washing up!' Nora said bluntly.

'General dogsbody,' Edna replied.

Julia checked the time on her slender gold wrist-watch. 'I'd better be off,' she said hurriedly. 'Back to the grindstone.'

A scowling Nora watched her go.

'Pack it in, our lass,' Edna scolded. 'At least the kid's volunteering.'

'Oh, yeah,' sneered Nora. 'And wouldn't she get the poshest job too? Nursing whilst we're skivvying!'

'Oi!' Edna snapped. 'You volunteered for what you

thought you could do best – would you swap with Julia if you could?'

Nora's sky-blue eyes clouded. 'No, I'm not qualified to nurse and I'd be no good at it either.'

'There you go,' Edna said equably. 'Each to his own.'

The scowl on Nora's face grew when she saw Julia striding down the drive ahead of them. 'She didn't even wait to catch the bus home with us,' she snorted. 'Miserable cow!'

11. In Kit's Safekeeping

Shortly after her return to work, Rosa found a letter in her pigeon-hole at the Phoenix. It was less than a week since her emotional farewell from Roger, and she was delighted that a letter had reached her so soon.

My dearest, darling, sweetest Rosa,

For a grown man well into his twenties, I'm ashamed to say I felt like sobbing as your train pulled out of King's Lynn, taking you with it. I was so bereft I've no idea how I got back to the base, but reality kicked in later when we got the command to go and it was action stations for my squadron. I won't elaborate (I know it upsets you) — let's just say we lost some good men in a successful mission. Dawn was breaking as we touched down on the runway, and a blazing pink sun rose over the horizon, bringing light to a new day, and my thoughts immediately flew to you. God, how I would love to return home to you! To walk into your arms, rest my head against your soft breasts and run my hands along the curve of your back and feel the hollow at the base of your spine.

Rosa's face grew hot at his passionate words; did he really discover that much about her body as they lay curled up in the sand dunes?

Coming home safe made me think how fortunate I was to be not only alive but to have you, my sweetest girl, who I cannot bear even to think of losing. Darling Rosa, I want you to consider what I have to say without me breathing down your neck! It is, quite simply this – will you marry me?

Rosa gasped, in shock and delight. 'Marry you!' she squeaked.

I'm not a rich man but my family have land which we farm in the south of England, a place called Wiltshire. When the war is over, I would like to continue with the RAF, which has become my second home and my second love, after you of course! If we married, we could live both in Wiltshire and in London. We could share an artists' studio! I already have one: an old barn on the farm that I stripped out to make a studio; the light is perfect for painting. I have never been more certain about anything in my entire life; I love you and want to marry you, Rosa.

Moved beyond words by the sincerity of Roger's letter, tears appeared in Rosa's deep, dark-brown eyes.

IF you accept a great lumbering loudmouth like me as your future husband, then I have a task for you. You talked to me a lot about Kit, a young woman you work with and like greatly; I remember her name well because you mentioned her so often.

Rosa's brow crinkled as she tried to remember what she had actually told Roger about Kit – whatever it was could only have been good, as she had only good things to say about Kit.

I've taken the liberty of sending a small package, care of the Phoenix factory, to Kit. If you choose to marry me, ask her for the parcel; if you decide against it, then please ask Kit to return the parcel to me (I'll refund any costs) and I will try to mend my broken heart! I'll say no more for now – my destiny lies with you, dearest Rosa.

Roger

With trembling hands Rosa folded the letter, then checked the factory clock. She was on her break and had a bit of time till the hooter went off; she'd been briefly moved from the cordite line to stand in for a sick woman in the filling shed, so she'd have a chance to question Kit, but right now Rosa wanted time to herself. Not wanting to stay indoors, she hurried out of the factory and struck out for the moors that ran alongside the Phoenix. Feeling the wind lift her hair, she quickened her pace and quickly gained height, all the time turning over Roger's proposal in her mind.

'I've only met him TWICE!' she said out loud.

But they were no different from millions of couples who fell head over heels in love at first sight; the war pressurized all relationships – how could it be otherwise when you didn't know from one day to the next if your loved one would die fighting on the front line, or manning a minesweeper in enemy territory, or flying out on nightly bombing raids? Wisdom didn't enter into the argument when the major concern for most couples in love was: would your beloved return safely to your arms or would you never see him again?

'To hell with caution,' she'd heard Maggie say more than once. 'Seize life by the throat and live for the moment!'

When Rosa thought of Roger her insides melted with love; he was honest, kind, funny, impetuous, loyal, devoted, faithful – the list could go on forever as far as she was concerned. As she retraced her steps back to the factory, Rosa wondered what her brother, Gabriel, would have said to her. Rosa smiled as she recalled her brother's voice; she knew exactly what he would say. 'Follow your heart, *cara*.'

'And I will!' Rosa announced to a pair of startled magpies that flew by, squawking crossly.

After adjusting her wild hair, which she always struggled to keep inside her white turban, Rosa entered the filling shed, where she took her place beside Kit. Smiling shyly, Rosa plucked up the courage to ask her dear friend if anything had arrived in the post for her.

Kit let out a long sigh of relief. 'Thank God you asked me!' she laughed. 'I thought you were never going to mention it.'

'Sorry, I've only just received his letter explaining about the parcel,' Rosa said. 'I hope you don't mind?'

Kit shook her head. 'Of course not,' she replied. 'It's just been an agony waiting to see if you wanted it. There was a note from Roger inside the package; he asked me not to mention it unless you did first. I've been on tenterhooks ever since.' Unable to keep her curiosity to herself a minute longer, Kit just about exploded as she cried, '*Well?* What did your man say in his letter?'

'I didn't know what to think when I first started reading it,' Rosa confessed. 'When we were together, Roger promised he wouldn't rush me into making any decisions, but he clearly forgot all about that once we parted,' Rosa said as she burst out laughing. 'Caution went right out of the window!' A pretty pink blush spread up her face and into her turban as she added with a radiant smile, 'He wants me to marry him.'

Kit looked up, beaming at her friend. 'That's wonderful news!' she exclaimed. 'I had assumed it was some grand romantic gesture but marriage, that's really serious!' Kit gave her a hug before quickly adding, 'That's if you want to marry him, of course?'

Rosa nodded happily. 'I think I do,' she said nervously. 'So may I have the package?' she added eagerly.

Kit, who was obviously enjoying the drama and the romantic secrecy, giggled. 'You can't open it now; it's in the changing room.'

'Haha!' Rosa groaned in sheer frustration.

'You'll have to wait till we finish our shift,' Kit added.

'It's hours till the hooter goes,' cried an overexcited Rosa.

'Patience is a virtue,' Kit chided with a playful wink. 'Now come on, fill some of these fuses and the hours will fly.'

The hours didn't fly but the long wait was helped by the popular songs supplied by *Music While You Work*, combined with lots of speculation about what could be inside the package. Kit, who'd handled the package, was sure of the contents. 'It's got to be a ring?'

'But what if it's not?' cried Rosa. 'It might be nylons?'

Kit chuckled. 'That would be very disappointing, though I could do with some new ones – Billy used one of mine to tie his rocking horse to the leg of the kitchen table!'

When the hooter finally blew, releasing the weary workers from their long, hard shift, Rosa all but ran to the changing room, where she was joined by a breathless Kit, who took the package from her handbag and handed it to her flushed young friend.

'I suggest you open it in private,' Kit said hurriedly, as dozens of munitions girls came barging in.

Rosa nodded in agreement. 'Good idea,' she said.

After removing her overall, turban and heavy rubber boots, Rosa donned her usual clothes, then ran all the way home to the cowshed. Though it was bitterly cold, there was a distinct smell of spring in the air; Rosa gazed in delight at the pale primroses and wild daffodils dotted under the drystone walls and smiled at the sound of tweeting birds calling to each other across the blustery moors. Once inside the cowshed, she quickly built up the fading fire in the wood-burner, then by the light of the flickering flames she opened the parcel with trembling fingers. The wrapping paper fell away from a small jewellery box covered in faded midnight-blue velvet. Rosa eased open the clasp and gasped at the sight of a large shimmering garnet set in old gold. Moved beyond words, and with tears not far away, she gingerly slipped the ring on to her engagement finger.

'It fits!' she gasped incredulously.

Hardly able to take her eyes off the garnet, which glowed like dark-red wine in the firelight, Rosa slowly read the letter that Roger had enclosed in the package.

It was my grandmother's engagement ring, which I had sized for you. You may remember I bound some sea grass around your finger that wonderful day we lay in the sand dunes? I kept it and asked the local jeweller to adjust the ring to fit your tiny finger.

I love you, and I hope you will say yes!

Roger

Rosa sat in front of the wood-burner for she didn't know how long, gazing at her vintage engagement ring. Her mother had had beautiful jewellery, some very old heirlooms that were now in the hands of the thieving Nazis. This ring, she thought, represented the start of a new life; no hideous memories attached to it. She was eventually startled from her profound reverie by the arrival of Nora and Maggie, who, eager to get inside the warm cowshed and put the kettle on, made a heck of a noise as they pushed open the front door and took their coats off. Julia trailed after them, looking tired as she usually did at the end of her shift. It was Maggie who almost immediately spotted the delicate gold ring on Rosa's wedding finger.

'Oh, my God!' she almost screamed. 'What's that?'

Nora followed Maggie's pointing finger. 'An engagement ring!' she gasped.

Rosa smiled as she announced with a hint of pride in her voice, 'I'll have you know that, as of today, I am engaged to Roger Carrington.'

'That fella down South?' Nora shrieked. 'Bloody 'ell, he's a fast mover!'

Julia stretched out in an armchair on the other side of the room, wincing as Nora and Maggie cross-examined Rosa on her astonishing announcement. Rosa had no answers to most of their questions, but she was happy to tell them everything she knew, especially the bit about Kit keeping the arrival of the package a secret.

'I don't know how she kept so quiet about it,' Maggie exclaimed. 'I'm sure I would have been tempted to open the package and have a peek inside,' she confessed.

'Kit was very discreet,' Rosa informed her friends. 'She was so relieved when I did ask about the package, but then I had to wait all afternoon till the hooter went before she could give it to me,' Rosa recalled with a smile.

After they'd finished their tea, Rosa rushed off to see Edna, who as usual was parked up in the dispatch yard. Edna was truly delighted but characteristically her thoughts immediately turned to Roger, so many hundreds of miles from his new fiancée.

'Have you had a chance to tell him the good news?' she asked after she'd admired Rosa's unusual ring.

'Sadly not,' Rosa replied. 'I'll have to settle for a letter, which I'll write as soon as I get home,' she added.

Edna reached into her pinafore pocket. 'Here, cock,

take this,' she said, as she handed Rosa her back-door key. 'Use my phone to tell your young man just how much you love him!'

Rosa gazed at Edna in astonishment. 'Really?' she cried.

'Really! Now be off with you,' Edna urged. 'You'll have the place to yourself; Malc's having a couple of pints in the Black Bull, so be sharp about it.'

Rosa didn't need telling twice. 'Thank you, thank you,' she cried as she sped down the hill to Pendleton with wings on her feet.

Once inside Edna's cosy back room, Rosa steadied her breath before she dialled Roger's number; as the line connected she began to fret. 'What if he's not at his desk? What if he's on a raid, or in the officers' mess?'

Her wild thoughts were interrupted by a male voice at the end of the phone. 'Hello! Who is it?'

Rosa gulped before blurting out in a single breath, 'May I speak to Squadron Leader Roger Carrington please?'

There was a clunk as the phone was put aside, but she could still hear the male voice bellowing, 'CAR-RINGTON! I say, old boy, gel on the phone for you.'

Seconds later the phone was picked up by Roger, who was clearly breathless from dashing across the room.

'Hello!' he sputtered.

'It's me,' she squeaked nervously.

'ROSA!' he exclaimed. 'Rosa,' he said again, and with such gentleness that she felt her heart tremble with love.

'I'm wearing your ring,' she said simply with a smile

he couldn't see but could definitely hear. Nor could she see the tears of joy that sprang into his eyes. 'You accept?' he gasped.

'I do!' she answered softly.

At which point they both began to weep. 'I just want to hold you and smother you with kisses,' Roger said, as he tried to control his tumultuous emotion.

'That would be difficult with all those miles between us,' she said with a giggle. 'Maybe you could fly up here and parachute straight into my arms,' she suggested with a romantic smile.

'When will I see you again?' he murmured. 'When will I see my ring on your sweet little wedding finger?'

'I don't know,' Rosa responded with a heavy sigh. 'I used all my days off visiting you, remember?'

'As if I could ever forget,' he whispered. 'Oh, God!' he added. 'I can't believe you've agreed to be my wife!'

'How could I ever have resisted your letter of proposal or the ring you ingeniously sent to Kit for safekeeping – that was very clever,' she told him.

'I hope the poor girl didn't think I was being cheeky?' he asked, suddenly anxious.

'No,' Rosa assured him. 'She liked the drama, and she's eager to meet my new fiancé,' she added shyly.

Feeling anxious about running up an enormous telephone bill at Edna's expense, Rosa eventually tore herself away from the phone with promises of eternal love and an imminent meeting. Locking Edna's back door, she retraced her steps to the Phoenix, where she returned the key to Edna, who smiled at the starry-eyed girl.

'Everything all right?' she asked with a cheeky smile.

Rosa dreamily nodded her head. 'Everything is perfect!' she laughed. 'Thank you for letting me use your phone. I left some money on the sideboard to cover the cost,' she quickly added.

Edna gave an unconcerned shrug, then asked a practical question. 'Is there anybody you should notify?' Aware that she was in danger of upsetting Rosa by mentioning her family, Edna briskly added, 'I was wondering about those relations of yours in Manchester; they're your nearest kin, aren't they?'

'Zio, my uncle,' Rosa murmured. 'Yes, you're right, of course I must tell them the news.'

'It might be a good idea to tell them sooner rather than later,' Edna advised. 'If your fiancé's family should announce your marriage in the paper, your relatives up here might get quite a shock.'

Thanking Edna for her advice and her generous loan of the telephone, Rosa set off for home; a new silver moon gilded the cobbled path to the cowshed and a barn owl hooted at her as she hurried past the field where he was hunting. Before she opened the front door, Rosa smiled up at the stars in the night sky and blew a kiss. 'Goodnight, my love,' she whispered to Roger hundreds of miles away. 'Stay safe and come home to me.'

The effects of a long, highly emotional day had left Rosa exhausted. In the bathroom, almost too tired to clean her teeth, she yawned widely as she struggled into her warm nightgown. She was surprised when Julia, wearing a very pretty blue padded dressing gown and clutching a matching wash bag, walked into the bathroom.

'Oh, sorry, I didn't know you were in here,' Julia said in a clipped formal voice. Rosa nodded as she continued to wipe her face on a towel.

'I suppose congratulations are in order?'

'Thank you,' Rosa replied, as she hung up the towel and prepared to leave the room.

'I hope you'll be happy,' Julia added, with a small frown clouding her face. 'But, I'm sorry – I have to say this as nobody else has – I do believe you're being rather hasty. You yourself have said more than once, you barely know the chap.' Having said her piece, Julia (wondering if she'd done the right thing) hid her rather flushed cheeks with a flannel, with which she busily scrubbed her face.

Stung by her sharp words, Rosa paused by the door; she'd always known that Julia was acerbic but she'd never imagined she'd speak so harshly to her on such an intensely personal subject. Feeling rattled, Rosa could do nothing but stare at Julia, who could not even bring herself to look her in the eye after her outburst. It was only in the privacy of her own bedroom with the door firmly closed that Rosa gave vent to her wrath.

'The cheek of the woman!' she seethed. 'All this time I've been defending her to the other girls and now Miss High and Mighty's trying to ruin my happiness – so much for gratitude!' Rosa dived into bed, where she tossed and turned in fury. 'She's gone too far this time – how bloody dare she?'

12. Good News/Bad News

Rosa wrote to her uncle and aunt in Manchester, asking if she might visit them soon. With no days off due, Rosa could only make the journey after an early shift, which meant she was exhausted even before she caught the bus into Manchester. Rosa sleepily watched the sun glance off her engagement ring; mesmerized by its wine-dark colours, she wondered about the first woman who'd worn it, Roger's grandmother. 'How strange,' she mused. 'Years have passed and now it belongs to me, the woman who loves her grandson – time has come round full circle,' she thought.

As the bus rumbled towards Manchester, Rosa suddenly felt butterflies in her tummy; whilst she'd been living in England her aunt and uncle had stood in place of her parents. Should she have asked them for permission to marry Roger before she accepted his proposal?

'It's too late now,' she thought to herself but she was anxious that her impetuous actions might show a lack of respect.

The winter sun that had shone down in Pendleton disappeared as she approached Manchester, where thick black plumes of smoke belched out from dozens of mill chimneys. Looking out over the bleak landscape lined with row upon row of poor terraced houses stretching right up to the mills, Rosa was glad that she'd been sent to work in Pendleton. As the bus rumbled past bombed-out tenement blocks where children in rags scrambled around in the rubble, Rosa realized how lucky she was to live on the edge of the moors, where she was able to breathe in clean, fresh air every day. When she was working inside the factory, she felt cooped up; but through the factory windows she could still see sunbursts of light after a rainstorm, or a flock of geese honking their way home, and on a late shift there were tiny silver stars pricking the night sky – all precious gifts of nature which she would have struggled to find in industrial Manchester.

When she reached her uncle's semi-detached in Fallowfield to the south of the city, Rosa gently touched the mezuzah by the front door, then kissed the hand that had touched it; the next second she jumped when her aunt flung open the front door and caught the slender girl in a warm embrace.

'Child!' she exclaimed in delight, as she took her hand and led her into the sitting room, where her husband was reading the newspaper.

'Welcome, Rosa,' he said, rising to kiss her on both cheeks before beckoning to her to sit close to him. 'How are you?' he inquired.

'I'm well, Zio,' Rosa replied, as she took the black tea and slice of cake her aunt offered her.

'You look tired,' her aunt fretted when she saw the bags under her niece's beautiful dark eyes.

'I am,' Rosa admitted. 'I've just finished a shift, but

I'll be better after a slice of your delicious seed cake, Zia,' she said gratefully.

'You must have something important to tell us,' her uncle said knowingly. 'If you've come all this way to see us straight after work?'

Rosa wiped crumbs from her lips and laid aside her plate. 'I do have some news, Zio,' she confessed. 'I'm engaged!' she blurted out. 'Look,' she added and held out her left hand to show them the ring.

Her aunt and uncle exchanged a look of complete surprise. There were hardly any eligible men around these days – who could their niece have met up on the lonely moors where she worked? Seeing their puzzled expressions, Rosa hastily explained, 'He's called Roger Carrington and he's a pilot in the RAF. I met him in November when we both showed our paintings at the art gallery in Salford.'

With a frown creasing her lined forehead, Zia said, 'Is there a reason why you agreed to marry this man in such a hurry?'

'You needn't worry, Aunt: nothing you would disapprove of has taken place,' Rosa reassured her with a knowing smile. 'I know I love Roger, and that's enough for me.'

'How many times have you seen this man you intend to spend the rest of your life with?' her uncle asked in a deep growly voice.

Hoping her relatives wouldn't tick her off in the same way that Julia had done only a few nights previously, Rosa answered with a tell-tale blush. 'Just twice: once in Salford and recently when I visited his base in Norfolk. But after spending a short amount of time with Roger, I realized how strong my feelings for him are, so when he proposed I accepted.'

An ominous silence fell as Zio lit his pipe and took several long thoughtful puffs on it.

'Is he a good man?' he asked.

'Yes, Zio.'

'Is he a Jew?'

'No.'

A long pause followed, which her aunt broke. 'Would your parents have approved of your choice?' she asked pointedly.

Rosa's voice wobbled as she thought of her mother and father. 'I'm sure they would have liked Roger.'

'Even though you have religious differences?' her uncle remarked.

In the past Rosa would never have considered consenting to a proposal of marriage without having first consulted her parents – but times had changed. Five years of war had skewed everything.

Zia examined the impressive garnet on Rosa's wedding finger. 'He has good taste,' she said with a smile. 'I would like to meet this fiancé of yours.'

Zio was not quite as effusive. 'I would also like to meet him and ask him how he intends to support a wife,' he said huffily.

'I promise you will meet him soon,' Rosa assured her relatives. 'Though as a fighter pilot he gets hardly any time off at all.'

After her aunt refilled their cups with hot tea, Rosa's Zio turned to her with a sombre expression on his face. 'My dear, we have news too.'

Rosa started, nearly spilling her tea. 'Gabriel?' she asked, her voice cracking with a mixture of emotion and hope.

Her uncle nodded but his expression brought terror rather than the joy she'd hoped for to Rosa's heart. 'Tell me, Zio?' she begged.

Zio nodded grimly. 'We know from our sources that your brother escaped from the German prison camp where he was held,' he started.

Relief so sweet and intense flooded through Rosa's body; she felt like a metal band had been removed from her heart and she could breathe freely for the first time in months. 'Thank God,' she murmured fervently; then, suddenly confused, she asked, 'But why do you not look happier?'

'Rosa, this isn't *new* news. We heard it two months ago,' her aunt replied.

'Two months! Why didn't you tell me?' Rosa gasped.

'Because we've been hoping and waiting to hear more before we spoke of it,' Zia said bleakly. 'But no one has heard a word from Gabriel since he got out.'

'As I understand from our sources, the plan was to get Gabriel into a safe house from where he would be aided by our collaborators,' Zio shrugged. 'But he never reached that safe house.'

Rosa's pulse began to race and her cheeks flushed as she imagined her brother trying to fend for himself, all alone in enemy territory.

'So we have no idea where he is?'

'No. Maybe he abandoned his collaborators for fear of putting them in danger – who knows?' her uncle murmured. 'All we know is they lost track of him.'

'Knowing Gabriel, he could have come up with an alternative plan, a better plan, Zio,' Rosa insisted. 'He *could* be safe.'

'Pray God he is safe, child,' Zio agreed earnestly.

'But to go so long without making contact . . .' Rosa murmured.

'It would be dangerous to do so if he was on the run,' Zio pointed out.

Racked with guilt, Rosa considered what she'd been doing in the last two months; she'd been preoccupied, not with Gabriel but with the events of her own life, something she would never have done a year ago. She'd pursued her own happiness whilst Gabriel was in all kinds of danger. Burying her wet, tear-stained face in her trembling hands, she sobbed as she scourged herself with morbid thoughts.

Her uncle reached for the bottle of brandy he kept in the sideboard cupboard. 'Drink this,' he urged, handing her a generous shot. Rosa stubbornly shook her head, but Zio insisted she swallow some of the spirit, which slowly steadied her erratic breathing.

When Rosa finally stopped crying, she realized to her dismay it was getting late. 'I have to go,' she said urgently. 'But if you hear anything, *anything*,' she beseeched her relatives, 'please tell me right away, whether it be good or bad.'

'We can only hope and pray,' Zia soothed as she hugged her niece tight.

'Hope and pray!' Rosa muttered under her breath, as she ran all the way to the bus stop in the pouring rain. 'I intend to do *a lot* more than that!'

None of Rosa's friends failed to notice the change in her over the next few days.

'She must have had bad news when she went to Manchester,' Nora whispered to Maggie, as they brewed tea in the cowshed kitchen.

Seeing the two whispering girls, Julia sharply intervened. 'I think out of respect for Rosa's privacy it might not be a good idea to start questioning her right now.'

Nora and Maggie glared at the interfering new girl. Ignoring their indignant expressions, Julia added briskly, 'I'm sure she'll talk when she's ready.'

After Julia had walked out of the kitchen, both Nora and Maggie pulled rude faces behind her back.

'What does she think we're going to do?' Maggie seethed. 'Get the thumb screws out and force the truth out of Rosa?'

Nora went red in the face before she exploded with fury. 'That woman is one of the rudest people I have EVER met!' she declared.

But Rosa showed no sign of opening up; if anything, she became even more withdrawn. She seemed to have no interest in her wedding plans and barely wore the ring she'd been so proud of. Kit, like the other girls, kept a respectful distance, but, as time went by and Rosa grew increasingly pale and gaunt, Kit's heart ached for her. One afternoon she simply couldn't stand the tension a moment longer, and when the hooter sounded for a tea-break Kit held back and laid an arm around her friend's shoulders.

'Darlin', for the love of God what's happened to you?' she said in her soft lilting Irish voice. 'Have you cold feet about getting married all of a sudden?'

Rosa stared into Kit's solemn trusting eyes and finally her resolve broke. 'It's not that – it's Gabriel, my brother. Two months ago he escaped from the Nazi camp where he was being held,' she blurted out as her tears flowed unchecked. 'Nobody has seen or heard from him since.'

Taking the sobbing girl in her arms, Kit held her close and tenderly stroked the long dark curls that had escaped from Rosa's turban. 'That's awful news, Rosa. No wonder you're so worried. But listen, darlin', I don't know your brother, but if he's at all like you he'll never give up,' she whispered.

Rosa slowly withdrew from Kit's embrace and stared at her. 'You're right,' she said with a tremulous smile. 'As long as he's got breath in his body, my Gabriel will never give up.'

'And neither must you,' Kit urged. 'It's wrong to lose hope when he could be out there, somewhere – pray for him,' she implored. 'We'll all pray for him. If he's alive, he'll hear your prayers, and if he isn't . . . well, he'll need your prayers wherever he's gone.'

Though the hooter had sounded sombre, Rosa automatically resumed stuffing gunpowder into the fuses lined up before her. 'The time for crying's over, now the fighting begins,' she muttered defiantly under her breath. 'I will find my brother – dead or alive I'll find him – even if it kills me.'

13. Dig for Victory

As the weeks went by, Maggie became increasingly frustrated when most of her hoped for wedding plans turned to ashes.

'Nothing's up to scratch!' she moaned as she stood side by side with Rosa and Nora on the cordite line.

The relentless rattle of the rolling shells, combined with a Glenn Miller number blaring out from the factory loudspeaker, didn't stop her friends from picking up on the petulance in Maggie's voice.

'Nothing will ever be up to scratch as long as this war continues,' said Nora realistically.

Maggie threw up her hands as she cried out in loud frustration, 'If anybody else mentions the war, I swear to God I'll throw one of these bloody shell cases at them!'

Malc, who was supervising the cordite line, couldn't help but overhear her angry comment. 'I wouldn't go talking like that,' he said reprovingly.

Maggie blushed. 'Sorry, Malc, it was just a manner of speaking, nothing more than that,' she replied apologetically.

'She's fed up 'cos nowt's going according to plan for her wedding,' Nora yelled over the racket.

Maggie glared at her friend. 'Thanks, Nora!' she

snapped. 'Now everybody on the cordite line knows my problems!'

'Weddings!' Malc exclaimed as he recalled his own recent one to Edna. 'You can make 'em simple or you can make 'em complicated.'

'Maggie's is right complicated!' Nora assured him.

Maggie scowled at her friend, who added, 'It's *true*! You've barely stopped moaning since you got engaged!'

Before a full-blown row erupted, Malc turned to Maggie. 'What's happened now?'

Maggie's shoulders slumped. 'I was hoping to serve a proper roast to my wedding guests, meat, gravy, roast potatoes, veg –'

'Stop!' Malc begged. 'You'll have me drooling down mi shirt front if you go on any longer,' he joked.

'But when I booked the Black Bull for our wedding breakfast, the landlord said that fresh meat is right out of the question,' she continued, before turning to Nora. 'Don't say it! I know there's a war on – but I am allowed to be disappointed!'

'You could do a mock goose with parsnip legs?' a woman down the line suggested.

'Or a Lord Woolton Pie,' another called out.

Maggie rolled her eyes as she chanted off some of the war-time recipes she was desperately hoping to avoid. 'Yes, or devilled fish, scotch broth, beef hash, roast heart, tripe and onions, liver and bacon. I've had 'em all up to here,' she said, pointing to the top of her head. 'I just want to serve something special, something everybody will remember – what's so wrong with that?'

Rosa, who'd been quiet throughout the entire conversation, suddenly spoke up. 'When I was at home in Italy, our neighbours always kept a pig to fatten up for their feast days; being Jews, we didn't of course, but we kept ducks and geese. Oh, I wish we could find a goose for your wedding, *cara*.'

'Find what?' Maggie giggled. 'A flock of geese like the Goose Girl in the fairy-tale?'

The very idea reduced Maggie and Nora to helpless hysterics.

'Ooh!' gasped Nora. 'I can just see you waltzing down the aisle trailed by honking geese!'

'You're missing Rosa's point, yer daft sods,' Malc said good-humouredly. 'You could fatten up a pig for your wedding breakfast!'

'Fatten up a pig?' Maggie gasped.

'Folks have been doing it for years,' Malc retorted. 'Surely you've had a cut of pork from your local pig?' he inquired.

Maggie nodded. 'Yes, we got cuts and they were good too. I used to take the slops down to the allotment where the pig was penned in; he was the neighbourhood pet until mi dad turned up with a butcher's knife and slit his throat . . . poor bugger! But where on earth would I find a pig these days?'

'You could check all the local allotments – you never know your luck – you might find a runt that's not been spoken for,' he added with a wink. 'You've enough time between now and your wedding day to fatten it up.'

Maggie's summer-sky pale-blue eyes opened wider

and wider. 'Do you really think it's possible?' she asked incredulously.

'Course – you just need to keep your eyes and ears open in these parts. It's always been word of mouth: you know, a quick backhander and Bob's your uncle!' said Malc knowingly. 'There's no harm in trying. Eh, and whilst you're at it you could grow your own veg too.'

Maggie smiled as she quoted one of the popular government slogans of the time. 'Dig for Victory!' she cried. 'You know, I'd never thought of that.'

A few days later the girls gathered as usual in the canteen so they could catch up on each other's news. They all knew by now of Rosa's heartache; they'd been told by Kit. Julia, hidden behind the daily paper so she wouldn't get caught up in any of the ongoing conversations, was immensely relieved to hear Kit advising caution to Nora and Maggie.

'Rosa's got a lot on her mind right now, so take it easy, girls.'

'Do you think she'll call off her engagement?' wide-eyed Nora asked.

'No,' Kit replied. 'Though I do think she should talk to her fiancé.'

'Rosa gets a letter from him nearly every day,' nosy Nora said. 'I don't think she writes to him as much.'

'The poor lad must be wondering what's going on,' Kit murmured.

The conversation around the table was interrupted

by Malc, who came rushing up with a wide grin on his face.

'Guess who's just turned up?' he said excitedly.

'Robert Mitchum!', 'Bing Crosby!', 'Gracie Fields!', the girls chorused back.

'Better than all of them put together,' Malc laughed. 'ARTHUR LEADBETTER!'

There was a stunned silence, followed by a torrent of eager questions.

'Is Stevie with him?'

'Is he coming back to the Phoenix?'

'Where is he now?'

'How does he look?'

Malc answered all of the questions quickly. 'Stevie's not here; Arthur left him with someone. He's not coming back – unfortunately. He's here to advise the new fire-safety officer. He looks fine! Any more questions?'

Still obscured by the paper she held aloft, Julia wondered why the new arrival was causing such a commotion; no doubt she'd find out soon enough – whether she liked it or not!

As Malc turned to go, he threw a last comment over his shoulder. 'He's only here today, so make the most of it, ladies.'

The girls around the table fell silent after he'd left; it was impossible to think of Arthur without thinking of his wife and their dear friend, Violet, who'd tragically died in a factory bomb explosion. Poor heart-broken Arthur had moved to Dundee to start a new life with their baby son, Stevie.

Word got round that Arthur would be in the Phoenix bar later that night.

'Coming, Rosa?' Nora asked, as she and Maggie made themselves up for an evening out.

Rosa shook her head; like everybody, she adored Arthur, but she just couldn't bring herself to go to the noisy bar. 'No, I can't face it,' she replied apologetically. 'Perhaps I'll catch him before he leaves tomorrow – but please give him my love,' she quickly added.

Nora and Maggie rushed off, leaving Rosa and Julia washing up.

'Everybody seems to like this Arthur chap,' Julia remarked.

'He's one of the best and nicest men I've ever met,' Rosa answered honestly.

By the time Nora and Maggie returned from the pub, Rosa and Julia were tucked up in bed with their feet pressed up against their heavy stone hot-water bottles. Rosa could hear the excited girls chatting in the bathroom as they prepared for bed.

'I thought he looked really well,' Nora remarked.

'Better than he did when he left here, that's for sure,' Maggie replied.

'He'll be snapped up by some lucky Dundee lass in no time,' Nora commented.

'I don't think so,' Maggie answered thoughtfully. 'It'll take quite a woman to replace Violet – he worshipped the ground she walked on.'

The following morning, after the other girls had left

for work and Rosa, on a later shift, was washing her smalls in the kitchen sink, she heard a knock on the cowshed door. Thinking it was one of the girls who'd forgotten her key, Rosa flung it open, only to come face to face with Arthur himself!

'Arthur!' she cried in delight. 'Come in, everybody's at work but me,' she explained.

'I'm just on my way to the bus stop, but I couldn't leave without saying hello and goodbye to you,' Arthur said fondly.

As Arthur walked towards the wood-burner to warm his hands, Rosa noticed he'd put on a bit of weight, which suited him; he had virtually been a bag of bones when he'd left the Phoenix just after Christmas.

'How's Stevie?' she asked eagerly.

'Very good,' Arthur replied proudly. 'Growing fast, talking, crawling into everything.'

'Does he like his new nursery?'

'Well enough, though it took a few weeks to settle him in,' he admitted.

Rosa recalled the first time she'd laid eyes on Arthur's son; she'd only just arrived at the Phoenix, a shy and awkward newcomer. When she met Stevie, cooing and gurgling and waving his chubby little legs in the air, Rosa had fallen in love with him. She still remembered the huge surge of emotion he had released in her, and she had visited him whenever she could. Their bond was so great that after Violet had died Rosa had looked after Stevie, and during those awful times when he was screaming for his mother, whom he would never see again, it had only been Rosa who could soothe him. When Arthur had announced that he was leaving the Phoenix, Rosa had been devastated; not that she didn't understand Arthur's motives – she would have done exactly the same in his place – but the thought of losing Stevie almost broke her heart. It had taken weeks to recover from the pain of that loss, and seeing Arthur again now brought it back like a tidal wave.

'I hear congratulations are in order,' Arthur said warmly, as Rosa handed him a mug of hot, strong tea. 'Kit told me your good news.'

'Yes!' Rosa replied. 'It was all a bit fast, but I am engaged.'

'He's a very lucky man. I hope you'll both be happy,' Arthur said, sipping his tea. 'Have you had any news of your brother?' he added in all innocence. 'I remember how worried you were about him when we last talked.'

Before Rosa could stop herself, she felt the tears pouring down her cheeks. Realizing he'd gone and put his foot in it, Arthur laid down his mug of tea and gabbling apologies he took her trembling hands in his. 'Rosa, please forgive me. I truly never meant to upset you.'

Seeing the poor weeping girl doubled up with sorrow, Arthur swept her tumbling, long dark hair from off her face and gave her a hug.

'There . . . there . . .' he soothed as he gently rocked her back and forth.

For the first time in weeks Rosa felt safe; she wanted

to stay right there in the moment with her head pressed against Arthur's strong chest, which smelt strongly of industrial soap. But too soon Arthur gently pulled away. 'Feeling better?'

Rosa nodded and smiled weakly. 'I'm sorry,' she started.

He put a finger on her soft pink lips. 'Shhh,' he whispered. 'How many times have I wept in front of you and the girls? Don't be sorry – I'm here for you.' Gazing into her big brown eyes that sparkled with the last of her tears, Arthur ventured, 'Want to tell me what this is about?'

After she'd told him all that she knew of her brother, Arthur lit up two Pall Mall cigarettes.

'I've *got* to find him,' she said desperately.

'How do you plan to do that?'

'I don't know, but I can't stay here and do nothing!' Rosa exclaimed. 'Surely you of all people understand that.'

'Of course I can see you must do something,' he agreed. 'I'm just wondering exactly *what* you realistically can do,' he admitted.

'I could try talking to some of the contacts who helped me out,' she told him. 'It would involve a bit of travelling, going down South, asking a few questions at the ports,' she answered tentatively. 'I've not properly thought it through – all I know is I'll go mad if I don't at least try to find Gabriel.'

Seeing she was deadly serious, Arthur locked his eyes with hers, his as blue as an open sky, hers dark and brooding. 'Be careful what you take on, Rosa,' he warned.

Rosa flung back her delicate shoulders as she returned his anxious gaze, her dark eyes flashing. 'I know what I'm doing. I'm *not* afraid!'

A slow smile grew on Arthur's wide generous mouth. 'My God, lass, I wouldn't want to bump into you on a dark night!' he chuckled.

14. The Girl with the Tea Trolley

Edna, Nora and Julia were all asked to report for duty at Wrigg Hall on 1 March 1944. They took the bus, Edna and Nora up on the top deck so they could smoke, whilst Julia stayed downstairs, where she was able to sit in peace and admire the majestic beauty of the Pennines through the bus window.

Julia was surprised at how homesick she felt; as she herself said, she'd always taken her home and family for granted, but now, stuck in the far North, she really missed the comforts of home and the care and love she'd been surrounded by there. She also desperately missed her elusive brother, Hugo, who wrote irritatingly infrequently. There was nobody she could talk to in her new life; she didn't fit in. She wasn't interested in tittle-tattle or make-up or boyfriends; she just wanted the bloody war to stop so she could go home, having performed her duty for King and Country and put this ghastly episode of her life behind her.

Up on the top deck, Nora chain-smoked one Woodbine after another.

'Calm down, our kid,' Edna advised. 'We're all in this together, you know?' she reminded Nora, who was as white as a sheet.

'I'm terrified!' the trembling girl blurted out.

'You did volunteer!' Edna reminded her.

'I know!' Nora exclaimed. 'And I bloody well wish I hadn't! I wish I'd stayed at home with Maggie, worrying all day long about what frock she's going to wear for her wedding!'

Edna couldn't help but chuckle at Nora's remark.

'That's just not true,' Edna pointed out. 'You were ready for thumping her the other day.'

Nora deeply inhaled the smoke from her fourth Woodbine. 'She's my best friend and I love her, but Christ! There are times when I wish she'd put a sock in it!'

When they arrived, the new volunteers, of which there were many of all ages, were issued with the standard pinafore emblazoned with a red cross on the front of the bodice.

'I feel official now I've got mi pinny!' Edna joked, as she adjusted her greying red curls under her starched white cap.

'Better than the Phoenix kit,' Nora remarked, sneakily admiring her reflection in one of the full-length windows. Seeing how smart she looked, Nora felt a sudden and very unexpected rush of confidence. 'I can do this,' she muttered under her breath.

After checking the lists in the busy entranceway, Julia was whisked away to the post-op ward she'd been assigned to, leaving Edna and Nora wondering where they should go.

'Can I help you?' a smiling VAD Sister asked the two confused women.

'I'm on teas,' Nora told her.

'And I'm on walks and talks – I know that's not a category, I've just made it up,' Edna said with a grin.

'We call it "recreational",' the Sister informed Edna. 'But walks and talks sums it up nicely.'

Nora was directed to the large kitchens at the back of the Hall, whilst the Sister took Edna to a large, airy garden room dotted with easy-chairs and tables on which were laid out newspapers, packs of cards, dominoes, chess boards and writing paper. The VAD Sister, obviously in a hurry, introduced Edna to another volunteer called Ivy, then left the two of them to get to know each other.

Coming straight to the point, Edna asked, 'Where do I start?'

Ivy led her to a large timetable pinned to a cork noticeboard and pointed to the time of day.

'They've just finished their dinner, and the afternoons are free for the patients to do whatever they fancy: listen to the radio, read, play a game of cards or chess, write home, go for a walk.' Ivy dropped her voice as several men on crutches limped into the room. 'You have to play it by ear, lovie: don't push the men if they don't immediately co-operate; most of them need a bit of gentle persuasion,' she added in a whisper.

Edna was shocked at the sight of the men who slowly filled the room: some sat in huddles, smoking around tables; loners took themselves off to sit in a solitary chair and stare out of the window; some blind patients were guided in by VAD nurses, who handed them into

Ivy and Edna's care; others were wheeled in by porters. Edna's strong heart fluttered nervously. She'd expected to breeze into this, smiling and chatting as she always did, but this was serious; these men needed careful, sensitive treatment and she would have to get to know them slowly if they were ever going to trust her.

Meanwhile Nora was pushing a laden tea trolley into the rest room, where she was hailed with smiles and whistles as the thirsty patients welcomed her. Edna, playing snap with several gentlemen who had either an arm in a sling or a leg in a splint, smiled at Nora, who blushed to the roots of her frizzy red hair as she offered tea and thick wedges of Brown Betty, a wartime cake, to the patients, who wolfed it back and promptly asked for more.

'I can't give anybody more than one slice apiece,' Nora explained, repeating the exact words Wrigg Hall's fearsome cook had told her to say to 'any greedy buggers' who wanted more!

'Awww, go on, just a bit, sweetheart, you wouldn't deny a soldier a bit of cake?' a cheeky lad with a patch over one eye teased.

Just as Nora was on the point of relenting, the VAD nurse gave her directions to Ward D6 and, smiling goodbye, Nora rattled down the panelled corridor that led to the north wing.

When she got to the ward and pushed open the door, poor Nora had no idea what she was walking into. Here there was no light-hearted banter, no welcoming wave of the hand, just a disinterested silence broken by an occasional sound, which Nora thought sounded like a yelp or a sob. Men sat sprawled on their beds and across chairs; some muttered incessantly to themselves; others gazed blankly up at the ceiling. Several men were in the grip of uncontrollable trembling, whilst others paced the room as if they were in prison.

'TEA!' Nora, at a complete loss as to how to handle herself, called out feebly.

Seeing the new volunteer dithering nervously, the VAD relieved her of several mugs of tea, which she distributed to the nearest patients, who showed no interest in what they'd been offered. Nora heard one man say quite briskly, 'Give it to young Tommy in the trenches – poor sods down there need it more than us chaps in the dug-outs.'

The VAD, who didn't argue with her patient's suggestion, gave the tea to his neighbour.

'You'll hear some odd comments,' she told Nora. 'Just go along with them, all right?'

Nora gulped and gave a quick nod.

'Wheel the trolley around the ward,' the VAD quickly added. 'You might get some takers.'

Embarrassed by the loud clattering noise her cups and plates were making, Nora almost crept around the beds, calling softly, 'Tea? Cake?' The sound of sobbing distracted her, and, turning, she saw a young lad sat on the edge of his bed rocking back and forth. Nora forgot her fear as her heart contracted with pity. Picking up a mug of tea, she approached the lad, whose face was turned away from her. 'Cuppa?' she said softly. Nora all but dropped the mug when he jumped at the sound of her voice and turned to her. Nora took in a face that must once have been very handsome; but, now whilst one side of the poor boy's face was almost normal, the other side was burnt and disfigured to such an extent that the skin of his cheekbones was rucked up like a lump of pastry.

'AHHH!' he yelled. 'Go away! Don't come near me – don't touch me!'

As his cries got louder, the VAD came hurrying over. 'Nothing to worry about, Peter,' she soothed, as she sat on the bed beside him and took his hand firmly in her own. 'Just a nice lady offering you some tea.'

Nora, who had frozen when the boy started to yell, hovered nervously.

'Thank you,' said the VAD. 'Just leave the tea for now.'

Nora all but flew back to her trolley, which she hurriedly pushed out of the ward and into the corridor. Once she was well clear of anybody, she flopped against the old oak panelling and took deep breaths.

'God in heaven!' she gasped. She'd never seen anything quite so harrowing as those men, and that poor lad with the disfigured face. 'What the hell have they all been through?' she wondered.

By now the urn was distinctly cool and Nora returned to the warm, busy kitchen, where she made fresh tea, and after a few more rounds it was time to go home. Feeling utterly exhausted, Nora changed out of her pinafore and cap in the cloakroom, where she found not Edna but Julia.

'Edna left a few minutes ago to catch the bus,' Julia explained. 'She didn't want to be late for her evening opening in the dispatch yard.'

Nora's heart sank. 'Sod it!' she thought: now she was on her own with Julia.

'There isn't another one for an hour,' Julia added, fastening the laces of her smart leather brogues. 'You can either wait for the next one or walk over the moors with me.'

Nora hesitated – the very last thing she wanted was to be alone with Julia – but the thought of standing at the chilly bus stop didn't hold much appeal either.

Tying on her headscarf and buttoning up her old winter coat, Nora followed Julia out of Wrigg Hall.

Day was fading to a pearly twilight as they walked back over the springy heather and the slowly uncurling bracken that would soon turn the moors from winter-brown to vernal-green. Deep in thought, Nora walked along in an uncharacteristic stony silence, which surprised Julia, who'd become used to her endless babble. Slowing her long, striding steps, she called over her shoulder, 'Everything all right?'

Stopping in her tracks, Nora was abrupt. 'What's battle fatigue?'

Julia tried hard not to betray her incredulity; she found it impossible to believe that anyone could not know that. Surely, after volunteering to work with the war wounded at Wrigg Hall, Nora would know what battle fatigue was? Registering the genuinely puzzled look on the girl's pale face, Julia answered her question to the best of her ability.

'It goes under several names,' she began. 'The Americans call it "war trauma"; it used to be called "shell shock", especially in the Great War.'

'I've heard mi dad talking about shell shock,' Nora replied, as she kept pace with Julia, who'd resumed walking.

'Men, and women too, can become sick in their minds if they're put under too much pressure during battle,' Julia continued. 'When you've been brought up and educated in a culture where you're taught not to kill or hurt your fellow man, then suddenly you're put in a situation where your actions must go against the grain, it ultimately damages you. Exhausted men, worn down by battle, avoid the pain and guilt by shutting down.'

'Shutting down?' Nora queried.

'It's a sort of self-preservation,' Julia explained. 'The human brain shuts down because the soldier just can't take in any more suffering.'

Julia turned to see if Nora had understood what she was saying.

'You mean they go blank?' Nora remarked.

'Exactly,' Julia responded.

They walked on for a while in silence, then Nora angrily burst out, 'They were wrong to send me to that ward without a word of warning. I breezed in with the tea trolley and was met with a stone wall. I thought it might be because of something I'd done,' she added guiltily. 'I went blundering up to a poor lad who'd had half his face blown away, and when he saw me he started yelling and crying. God, it was awful!' she cried, tears forming in her eyes. 'I never took up volunteering to upset poor wounded soldiers – they should never have let me go to D6 with that bloody tea trolley,' she fumed. 'All I did was trouble folks – I'm just no good at it!'

Julia shook her head. 'You're quite wrong!' she declared. 'Normality and routine are what help patients; they give them a structure.' Thinking hard, Julia tried to recall what else she'd read about battle fatigue that would help Nora not to blame herself the next time she volunteered.

'Sometimes you can't see that the person is sick – they look no different from anybody else – but inside they may be suffering from memory loss, lack of sleep, fear of death, isolation, and all sorts of other horrible things. A warm, smiley, friendly face such as yours can only make these poor men feel better,' Julia added reassuringly.

'Some of the fellas on D6 were crying,' Nora pointed out.

Julia tentatively put a hand on Nora's arm. 'Look, if it upsets you this much, you should make it clear when you next sign on at Wrigg Hall that you'd prefer not to be sent to D6 – nobody will mind,' she assured Nora, who vehemently shook her head.

'NO!' she cried. 'I'm NOT giving up. Them poor lads are suffering a lot more than me, and, more to the point, they suffered because of me, and you, and *every-body* who wants to be free!' she said, as she made a wide sweeping movement with her hand. 'I can and *I will* do this,' she added through gritted teeth.

Julia gazed at Nora in admiration; this was a side of the chatterbox girl that she'd never expected to see.

'Mi mam and mi kid sister were blown up by a stray bomb a year ago,' Nora suddenly said. 'Some bloody Hun emptied his bomb bay to lighten his load and get home quicker over open countryside . . . mi mam and mi sister were blown to smithereens.' Nora took a deep, shuddering breath. 'I got through that and I'll get through this,' she muttered, as she defiantly strode past wide-eyed Julia and over the darkening moors.

Nora kept her word: the next time she visited Wrigg Hall she went to the kitchen area, where she picked up the tea trolley and then made straight for Ward D6. 'No point in putting it off,' she said firmly to herself.

Pushing open the door, she entered the ward but not tentatively, as she had before; this time she went with a bright smile and a cheerful 'Good afternoon, gentle-men'. She progressed along the line of beds and made a point of greeting each patient, offering him tea and cake. And even if he didn't respond, Nora would chat to him about all kinds of banal things.

'The daffodils are coming up,' she said happily. 'A sure sign of spring. And the snow's gone from the moors. I was up there only the other day: it were so beautiful, the birds were singing their little hearts out!'

Nora's comforting presence, her soothing Northern

voice, her infectious sense of humour and ordinary everyday conversations about the weather or what she'd been listening to on the radio seemed to comfort some of the patients.

'Who's got a favourite Gracie Fields' number?' she said as she brought her trolley to a stop near a group of men slouched vacantly in chairs. She had got used to receiving no reply, so their silence no longer bothered her; she just chatted on. 'I don't think anything beats "Bless 'Em All",' she announced, as she poured strong dark tea into mugs. 'Remember how it goes?' she asked, setting the mugs on the table. 'Bless 'em all, bless 'em all, the long, the rich and the tall.' Having steeled herself to expecting no response and knowing that self-aggrandizement was not something that belonged on D6, Nora continued softly singing snatches of Gracie's song as she did her round.

It didn't happen overnight but gradually the patients responded to the warm-hearted, gap-toothed, smiling redhead who was constantly wrestling to keep her wild frizzy hair inside her starched white cap. Nora's heart leapt with happiness when she got her first vague look of recognition; and a few visits later, when she thought she saw the faintest smile on a patient's face, followed by a shy nod, Nora knew instinctively that she was going in the right direction. She was overjoyed when the Ward Sister confirmed her feelings.

'The men are beginning to trust you,' she said. 'Well done.'

If she'd been given the George Cross, Nora couldn't

have been happier! This was trust indeed, she thought: men who'd lost touch with themselves tentatively reaching out – the very thought made Nora weep.

'This volunteering's getting you down, lass,' Edna said sharply when she saw Nora's red-rimmed eyes.

'It's not getting me down,' Nora answered firmly. 'It just breaks my heart to think what the men have been through. I want to hold them and make sure they'll never be hurt again.'

Touched by Nora's guileless simplicity, Edna smiled. 'You're doing a grand job, but just remember it's only voluntary work.'

Edna's words of advice were completely lost on Nora when it came to nursing Peter. At least he'd now stopped reacting to her as if she was a live hand grenade every time she approached his bedside with a cup of tea. Nora had taken a pattern out of the Ward Sister's book: Nora had watched her sitting by Peter's side, talking soothingly as she firmly held his trembling hands, and she'd seen Peter's habitual rocking movement slowly cease.

One day, as Nora was sitting beside Peter herself, holding his hand as Sister did, Nora, having run out of pleasantries about the weather, decided she'd tell Peter about her friends at work.

'I live in a cowshed,' she started. 'It's been done up – we're not knee-deep in cow muck!' she laughed. 'There's four of us – me, Nora' – she pointed to herself – 'mi best pal, Maggie, she's the one that's getting married. My God! You'd think no bugger in the world 'ad ever got wed before, ooh, pardon my French!' she said in an apologetic whisper. Peter didn't make any response, but she noticed that his habitual rocking movement was slowing down. 'Then there's Rosa – she's Italian – but she's not herself these days.' Thinking it might be wise to circumnavigate Rosa's sadness, Nora swiftly moved on. 'And finally there's Julia.' Nora let out a long sigh. 'She's a Southerner, from London, too posh to mix with us common factory girls but . . .' She remembered how understanding Julia had been when she'd talked to her about Peter's condition. 'She has her good moments.'

Fifteen minutes later the tea in the urn was stone cold and Nora was still rattling on about life at the Phoenix to Peter, who had by now stopped rocking altogether. Seeing the time on the wall clock, Nora reluctantly said, 'I'd best go, lovie.'

She rose to her feet and made to let go of Peter's warm hand. 'Bye bye for now, Peter,' she said as she looked into his good eye, on the side of his face that had once been beautiful.

But Peter didn't let go of her hand; his mouth twisted and he made little inarticulate noises that eventually formed something that sounded like 'Nora'.

She smothered a gasp – had he really just said her name?

'Nora,' he said again.

Looking into Peter's smashed face, Nora thought her heart would burst. 'That's right, sweetheart, I'm Nora, and you're Peter.'

Pushing the trolley away from Peter's bed, an elated Nora thought, 'Peter knows me!'

The VAD Sister verified Nora's thoughts. 'You've been a great help with Peter this afternoon.'

Nora glowed with happiness. 'I like helping him,' she answered. 'I like helping them all!' she added passionately.

'I can see that, and they can as well. Keep up the good work,' the Sister said. 'See you next week.'

15. Percy

The 'Dig for Victory' discussion had had a far-reaching effect on Maggie: when she wasn't on late shifts, she visited the local allotments until she found what she wanted: a vacant plot conveniently situated between the cowshed and the Phoenix that she immediately snapped up.

'You can have two if you want, love?' the old man in charge suggested. 'They're going for almost nowt since yon government wants us growing our own grub.'

'*Two* allotments?' Maggie asked.

'Aye, this one and t'other 'long side it. Mind you – they'll keep thee busy from dawn till bloody dusk.'

Maggie threw back her shoulders, thereby (quite innocently) emphasizing her large bust, which brought the old boy's eyes out on stalks.

'I'm a big girl,' she said enthusiastically.

'Aye, yer that alreet!' he grinned.

'All I need now is a pig,' Maggie added.

If it were possible that the old man's eyes could widen even further, they did. 'Are you pulling my leg?'

'No, I want to find a pig to fatten up for my wedding breakfast on the eighth of May,' Maggie replied. 'It might be impossible, with all the government rules and regulations I've been reading about, but,' she added robustly, 'nothing ventured, nothing gained!'

'May, yer say,' he muttered, and did a quick calculation on his fingers. 'You won't be wanting a weaner, then?'

'Weaner?'

'A piglet that's just been weaned,' he explained.

'Oooh, no, I wouldn't want to slaughter a baby!' Maggie gasped.

'Are you in a position to feed a pig?' the old man asked sharply. 'Bloody pigs can eat for England!'

Maggie thought of the brimming waste-food bin at the Phoenix; she was quite sure she could come to some arrangement with the amiable kitchen staff. She nodded enthusiastically.

'I'll see if any of the local pig clubs are wanting to offload a runt?' was his only answer, accompanied by a wink that Maggie found completely aggravating.

'Is that a yes or a no?' she asked crossly.

The old man continued with his maddening allusive line: 'I'll have to make inquiries. How can I get in touch with you if I find one?'

'I live in the cowshed, up the lane from the Phoenix factory.'

'That owd shack!' he said with a chuckle.

'It does for us Bomb Girls.'

'Well, I'll know where to find you – by the way, mi name's Percy.'

'Nice to meet you, Percy. I'm Maggie.'

Convinced that the old man was no doubt just

fantasizing about helping her, and that his promises would come to nothing, Maggie forced out a polite smile as she said goodbye. Walking away from him, aware that he was admiring her shapely backside, she thought to herself, 'Pigs'll fly before he comes up with the goods,' then giggled at her apt choice of words.

A few days later, after a long hard shift, Maggie was soaking in a luke-warm bath – it had been Nora's turn to go first – when she heard a knock at the cowshed door.

'It's for you, Mags,' Nora yelled.

'Bugger! Is there nowhere I can have five minutes' peace?' Maggie groaned, as she hauled herself out of the bath.

Wrapped in her dressing gown, she padded to the door, where she was shocked to see Percy waiting for her. Coming straight to the point, he grinned and said, 'Got summat for you, lass. It's out yonder.'

'Can I get dressed first?' Maggie asked quickly.

'Make it sharpish – this business won't wait.'

Intrigued, Maggie dashed back into her bedroom and threw on some clothes without properly drying herself. 'This had better be worth it,' she thought.

When she returned to the front door, Percy was gone. 'What's the old fool playing at?' Maggie grumbled.

'Oy, lass! Over 'ere!' he called from the gable end of the cowshed.

Shoving her feet into some old wellies she kept by

the door, Maggie hurried around the corner of the building, and there she stood as if turned to stone. Snuffling contentedly around the dustbin was a happy pink pig!

'You got one!' she gasped.

'It weren't easy,' Percy said with a bit of a swagger. 'Pig clubs are proper tight – wouldn't part with a fart! If you'll excuse my language,' he added cheerfully, as he tugged the length of rope he'd looped around the pig's neck. 'I were lucky with a Ramsbottom farmer, a mate o' mine on t'other side of the valley, who didn't mind swapping a runt for fifty Woodbines.'

An astonished Maggie, who could barely drag her eyes from the pig, spluttered, 'RUNT?'

'Aye, smallest, scrag-end of the litter,' Percy explained. 'Jesus! You should've seen the rest of 'em!' he chuckled. 'Size of bloody gable ends!' His eyes swept over the pig's flanks. 'She should fatten up nicely for your wedding if you look after her proper.'

Maggie cringed; could the pig understand what he was saying, she wondered guiltily.

'Well, don't just stand there!' Percy chuckled. 'What're you going to do with her?'

'Her!' Maggie cried. 'A girl?'

'A sow,' Percy corrected her. ''Ave you got owt to feed her?' he added, giving another tug on the rope around the sow's neck. 'It might help her settle in; otherwise she might head back home to Ramsbottom.'

Maggie's brain was in a whirl; she was so unprepared for this; if she'd known she was having a pig to stay, she wouldn't have eaten her tea, pork rissoles. 'Oh, no!' she thought. 'I couldn't have fed rissoles to her – it'd be like eating a relative!'

'Take her down to the allotment, will you?' Maggie said to Percy, as she turned back into the cowshed. 'I'll go and see what I can rustle up for her tea.'

'Be sharp about it – it'll be dark soon,' said Percy, as he set off down the lane with the pig trotting happily at his side.

In the sparse kitchen Maggie rummaged through the cupboards but found nothing but half a packet of salt. 'I might get some slops from the Phoenix canteen,' she frantically thought as she ran out of the cowshed, clutching an aluminium bucket. Nora and Rosa (Julia was, as usual, in her bedroom) watched Maggie's antics in wide-eyed amazement.

'She's running around like a blue-arsed fly!' Nora murmured curiously. 'Something must be up.'

Maggie ran all the way to the Phoenix canteen, where she begged for two buckets of food slops in exchange for ten Woodbines. Never dreaming that two buckets of slops would weigh so much, Maggie staggered back up the path to the allotment with oxtail soup slopping from the buckets into her boots. In her absence Percy had settled the pig in a makeshift pig pen improvised from an old shed with a corrugated-tin roof and a length of fencing he'd strung across the shed door that dangled from one rusty hinge.

'There's no straw,' he complained. 'What's the

132

animal going to sleep on, never mind relieve itself on? Thou's not prepared theeself, woman!' Percy chided sharply.

'I didn't know you were going to turn up with a pig so soon,' Maggie remonstrated. 'Or at all! Not that I'm not grateful,' she quickly added.

'When a fella offers you a pig for fifty fags you don't stand about,' Percy snapped.

Maggie carefully set down the two heavy pails in order to rub her aching hands.

'Fella said he couldn't feed more than a couple of pigs. This one would've 'ad its throat slit if it weren't for you making inquiries,' Percy informed her cheerfully.

By now the pig could smell the slops overflowing from the buckets.

'Best feed her before we've got a riot on our hands,' Percy said. 'Stand back or she'll flatten thee!'

Wondering what he was going to do next, Maggie leapt aside as Percy grabbed one of the buckets; holding it firmly in one hand and with a stick in the other, he poked the pig away from the makeshift fence he'd erected and settled the pail on the ground inside the pen.

'Watch her shift that lot,' Percy said gleefully.

And indeed it was a sight for sore eyes. The hungry animal buried her face in the swill and hardly came up for air until she'd reached the bottom of the bucket, finishing with a loud, satisfied belch.

'I'll be off now,' Percy said, straightening his flat cap.

'Noo!' Maggie exclaimed. Totally panicked, she grabbed Percy's arm to prevent him from leaving her. 'I don't know what to do!' she cried.

'Leave her be for now,' Percy advised. 'I'll come up with some straw tomorrow, for bedding, and a hammer and nails to fix that shed, thee will 'ave to find her grub, and muck her out too.' Seeing her wild look, he added, 'You only need a shovel to shift the muck!'

Laughing to himself, Percy set off down the lane, leaving Maggie staring at the pig, who was butting her head against the fencing Percy had erected.

'Oh, God!' she said out loud. 'What've I done?'

When it was nearly dark and Maggie still hadn't come home, Nora set a stub of a candle in an old lantern and set off down the lane to look for her. Stopping in the pitch dark, she swung the feeble lantern from left to right; she could hardly see a thing but she could hear a low grunting sound.

'That can't be Maggie?' Nora murmured.

With hairs standing up on the back of her neck, Nora crept slowly towards the sound, which was coming from the allotments.

'Who's there?' she cried, as she swung the lantern high.

'Me!' Maggie cried back.

'What're you doing out here in the dark?' Nora scolded as she approached, shedding light on to Maggie, who was crouched on the ground.

'Are you all right?' Nora asked.

'I'm fine,' Maggie replied. 'Come closer, then I can introduce you to my new friend.'

Overcome with curiosity, Nora hurried towards Maggie, who grinned in the candlelight. 'Here she is!'

Nora gazed in disbelief at the pig, who grunted ecstatically as Maggie tickled her pink snout. 'A pig!' she spluttered.

Laying the lantern at Maggie's feet, Nora also hunkered down so she could get a better look at the animal. 'I don't believe it!' she gasped, her face breaking into a huge smile. 'Oh, you're gorgeous, aren't you?' she crooned softly as she gazed in delight at the newcomer.

'I'm going to fatten her up for my wedding breakfast,' Maggie announced.

Nora gazed at her friend in horror. 'You can't!' she protested.

'Well, I've not got her for the bloody fun of it,' yawned Maggie, who was suddenly overcome with exhaustion. 'It's going to be hard work, but Percy said he'd give me a hand.'

'Who's Percy?'

'The fella that found the pig,' Maggie explained.

'I'll help too,' Nora instantly volunteered.

'Thanks,' said Maggie, struggling to her feet. 'Come on, let's leave her to settle down.'

'She might run away,' Nora fretted.

'Percy's penned her in for the night; she should be fine,' Maggie explained.

By the light of the wavering candle, the pig looked at them with her little baleful eyes.

'See you in the morning,' Nora whispered fondly.

The pig gave a grunt as they departed. 'Goodnight, sweetheart!' Nora cooed.

'It does no good to get sentimental, Nora,' Maggie warned as the two tired girls made their way home. 'Remember, this is about my wedding breakfast, nothing more, nothing less.'

The following morning it was Maggie who went in search of Nora. It was the beginning of a perfect spring day: skylarks were singing their hearts out as they rose higher and higher in the arching blue sky and blackbirds were calling across the valley. Lovely Maggie, with her thick auburn hair swinging down her back and her blue eyes sparkling with excitement, was more than surprised to find Nora at the allotment, where she was helping Percy lay straw in the pig pen.

'Just in time to muck out!' Percy called, handing Maggie a shovel.

Wrinkling her delicate nose, Maggie gingerly dropped the pig muck into a bucket, then hurriedly set the spade to one side.

'You can use yon muck on your vegetables,' Percy informed her as he lowered the second bucket of slops that Maggie had collected the previous night over the fence. 'Get stuck in, missis,' he said cheerfully to the pig.

Nora watched in delight as the pig gave the same performance as she had the previous night.

'She's starving!' Nora cried.

'Nay, she's not,' Percy told her knowledgeably. 'Pigs'll eat till it comes out of their ears.'

'We want her nice and plump,' Maggie remarked.

'You shouldn't talk like that when she's around,' Nora hissed as she pressed her finger to her lips.

'She's a pig!' Maggie laughed. 'She doesn't know what we're talking about.'

'I think it's insensitive,' Nora added. 'And, by the way, she's called Polly!'

'You're taking this too far, Nora, you'll regret it,' Maggie warned.

But Nora wasn't listening: she was smiling at Polly, whose head, after it had emerged from the swill bucket, was decorated with potato peelings. After Polly had given a series of satisfied grunts, she rolled on her back in the newly strewn hay.

'Look at her!' giggled Nora in delight.

'Drag yourself away, lovie,' Maggie urged. 'We've got five minutes till clocking-on time and you're still wearing your nightie!'

16. Secrets and Lies

At Edna's insistence, Rosa finally got hold of Roger using the phone in the chip shop.

'I'm so sorry I've been a poor correspondent,' she said apologetically.

Clearly agitated, Roger was torn between relief and frustration.

'Rosa! I've been going mad with worry – why didn't you answer my letters, sweetheart?'

'I'm sorry,' she repeated flatly.

'Is something wrong? Are you all right?' he asked anxiously.

'I'm fine,' she replied. 'But I've had bad news about my brother.'

Clearly thinking it was the worst news, that Gabriel was dead, Roger waited for her to continue. After Rosa had related the latest details, Roger exclaimed, 'Darling, I can't tell you how many stories I've heard about pilots being helped to escape by underground workers. With luck your brother may have been helped too.'

'Yes, I know all about that,' Rosa cut in impatiently.

'Sorry,' Roger said contritely. 'You clearly know a lot more about these things than I do.' When Rosa didn't respond, he added softly, 'I can see why you haven't been in the mood for writing to me.'

'I tried. I just couldn't find the words,' she admitted. 'Phoning seemed easier.'

'You poor love.' His voice gave an emotional lurch as he spoke. 'I feel so useless stuck here in Norfolk with not a hope in hell of getting leave – I should be supporting you in your time of trouble.'

Rosa was in fact secretly relieved that Roger wasn't near at hand; she had plans to put into action that were taking up every spare minute of her time. If Roger had been around, he would have got in the way, and no doubt stop her – best that he was kept in the dark, and at a distance too. Cutting through her thoughts, Roger spoke again. 'How can I help?'

'Say some prayers, and forgive me for being such a poor fiancée,' she said in all sincerity.

'There's nothing to forgive, my darling,' Roger said so tenderly that Rosa flushed with guilt. 'Just tell me you love me and still want to be my wife?' he implored.

'Of course I still want to marry you, Roger,' she retorted quickly.

'As long as you mean that, I can put up with anything,' he replied.

Rosa brought their conversation to a close by announcing that Edna had returned, which was a lie, but she had to make an urgent phone call before Edna really did return. Dialling her uncle's number in Manchester, she asked if there was any news. Hearing to her distress that there was none, she made her decision. She'd write to Gladys and tell her she was coming to London; hopefully she could stay with her dearest friend in the first instance and then see if she could get to the ports. 'I might even get a safe passage to France!' Rosa thought wildly.

She didn't know how far she would get, but she knew if she was ever to find out where Gabriel was, she would have to take some risks. She'd sat around too long waiting for something to happen; the time for action had come.

When Edna returned Rosa was on her second cheroot. 'I've left some money for my calls,' she told Edna, who was busy putting the kettle on.

'Thanks, lovie,' Edna said, lighting up her own cigarette. 'I'm on mi tod tonight,' she added. 'Malc's had to drive over to Doncaster to pick up some safety equipment for the new fella.'

'Why hasn't he gone himself?' Rosa asked. 'Arthur always used to pick up his own stuff.'

'He can't drive,' Edna replied with a grimace. 'So Malc's got lumbered with the job, worse luck. Like you say, it wouldn't have happened if Arthur Leadbetter was still safety officer at the Phoenix; nothing slipped past him when it came to organization.'

'I thought he looked well when he was down here,' Rosa remarked. 'He's put on weight and he doesn't have quite such a terrible haunted look any more.'

Edna nodded. 'He's still a handsome man despite his war wounds,' she said, referring to the scars caused by the factory explosion and the damage done to his hands when he was working with explosives in the army. 'It won't be long till he's spoken for again. Mark my words.'

Rosa's stomach lurched; the thought of Stevie having a stepmother upset her more than anything. 'I hope Arthur chooses carefully,' she said with an unexpected burst of passion. 'I'd hate to see that little boy take second place to anyone.'

'I can't see Arthur letting that happen,' Edna assured her. 'He loves his lad more than life itself.'

Little did Edna know that her husband wasn't in Doncaster on work business; he was in fact in Penrith with Flora. He'd received a frantic phone call from her earlier in the day that had put the fear of God in him.

'Malc!' she cried when he picked up the phone in his office.

'Hello, lovie,' he'd started amiably enough.

'Help me!' Flora wailed.

'What is it?' he asked tensely. 'Take a deep breath,' he said, as she started to sob uncontrollably.

Through her tears, Flora tried to stay coherent. 'You said . . . you said you'd help me, Malc.'

'And I will, lovie,' he assured her calmly. 'But first you've got to tell me what's happened.'

'John came home,' she whispered.

Malc was surprised. 'I thought he'd only recently been granted leave?'

'It wasn't leave,' Flora explained miserably. 'The army doctor's recommended that John should be discharged from his duties.'

'On what grounds?' Malc asked, his alarm growing.

'He's sick, mentally sick,' she said through bursts of

fresh tears. 'They say he's incapable of performing his duties because he's drunk all the time. His sergeant-major as good as said he'd be dishonourably discharged if he wasn't classified as sick.'

Malc couldn't believe he was hearing right. 'Where does all the booze come from?'

'He steals it,' Flora muttered in shame. 'I've known John all my life, and he never touched a drop of alcohol until he joined the army. It's not his fault.'

'War does terrible things to the best of men,' Malc agreed softly. 'Maybe home and family are a safer placer for him until he's over the booze.'

By this time Flora was almost hysterical. 'Noo!' she exclaimed as her voice rose higher. 'He's home now and he's not stopped drinking since he walked through the door. We're terrified.'

On the other end of the line, Malc's brow creased in anxiety as he realized quite how serious things were for young Flora and her precious family.

'It's so bad today I've had to leave the girls with a neighbour. I was frightened for their safety – that's why I'm phoning you,' Flora cried.

'Okay. Where is he now?' Malc asked.

'He passed out about an hour ago – with a bit of luck he might sleep till morning.' The tremble in Flora's terrified voice said it all.

'I'll be up there with you as soon as I can,' Malc promised.

'Don't tell Mum,' Flora begged. 'Please don't tell her,' she implored. 'She'll be so worried.'

Malc took a deep breath; he wasn't at all easy with this request. 'She should know, Flora – after all she is your mother. She'll want to help too.'

'But I've only just found her!' Flora protested. 'I don't want to spoil our lovely new happiness – if she knew about John she'd never have a minute's peace.'

Malc knew for sure that Flora was right; Edna would be on the warpath and God help the man that ever laid a hand on her precious daughter.

'He was a really good man when I married him,' Flora added almost apologetically.

Worried that he should be on his way, Malc quickly brought the conversation to a close. 'I'll make an excuse to Edna and leave right away. Don't do anything to provoke him, Flora,' he warned before he put down the phone.

Hours later, Malc was on Flora's street in Penrith. He was careful not to park outside her house in order to avoid drawing attention to a stranger's car in the area. On his drive North (in the blackout pitch dark), Malc had had time to consider his options. What legal rights did he have over Flora's husband? He wasn't even a blood relative. But he couldn't ignore her plea for help, especially after he'd made a solemn promise to protect her.

Getting out of the car, he strode down the street till he was standing outside Flora's house, which was ominously silent. Malc jumped as a voice hissed in the darkness. 'Oi! Over here.'

Malc turned to see a neighbour waving at him from behind a half-open door. Hurrying towards her, he cast a look over his shoulder to make sure that nobody was watching him.

'Quick, come in,' the nervous neighbour whispered urgently, as she all but pulled him indoors, then quickly closed and locked the door behind him. 'The wee bairns are asleep upstairs,' she continued, still whispering as she led him into her front room, which was gloomy with the blackout blinds pulled down.

'Are they all right?' Malc asked.

'As right as they can be with their dad raving drunk from dawn till dusk,' the neighbour replied. 'He used to be a lovely fella, a real family man, but the war's had its way with him and like so many others he's taken to the bottle.'

Keen to find Flora, Malc was anxious not to spend too long chatting to the anxious neighbour. 'Thanks for taking care of the kiddies,' he said gratefully.

'He'll kill her if he carries on like this,' the neighbour insisted. 'He needs to be locked up for his own safety.'

Feeling his heartbeat quicken, Malc moved towards the door. 'I'd best go to her, then – am I right in thinking she's alone with him?'

The neighbour nodded curtly. 'Take care of yourself,' she said, as she watched him leave, then quickly locked the door behind him.

Malc silently made his way round to the back of Flora's house and tapped on the kitchen window, where he saw a light was on. When Flora let him in, he gasped as a shaft of light fell across her bruised face; he could see she'd ineffectually tried to hide her wounds with face powder, but the swelling was livid where she'd clearly been hit around the face.

'Jesus Christ!' he gasped.

'Shhh!' Flora hissed, as she laid a trembling finger to her lips. 'He's woken up.'

'Good,' said Malc, suddenly so angry that he itched to punch the brute who'd hurt his daughter-in-law. 'I want a word with him.'

Flora flattened herself against the kitchen wall as her husband came staggering into the room. Bleary-eyed and hung-over, he looked like he was spoiling for a fight. Adjusting his braces over his grubby, unbuttoned shirt, he glared at Malc, who stood defiantly before him.

'Who the hell are you?'

'Flora's father-in-law,' Malc replied, looking the man straight in the eye and seeing a brief flash of bewilderment there. Curbing his anger, Malc took a deep breath and tried a more subtle approach. 'Look, son, I know you've had a bloody hard time – we can get help for you, proper advice on how to look after yourself. But' – he stressed his words to make sure the message got home – 'But you really have got to stop hurting your wife.'

At that Flora's husband went off as if somebody had lit a blue touch fuse underneath him.

'Get out!' he bawled as he drunkenly swung a fist at Malc, who neatly ducked the blow. 'Get out!' he shouted again and picked up the kitchen table and threw it across the room.

It wasn't difficult to dodge the table, which landed against the window, its glass panes shattering on impact.

Flora's husband then lunged at Malc, who, for all his bulk, was quicker on his feet than his attacker. Pinning John's arms behind his back, he turned to Flora. 'Go!' he commanded. 'Go to the girls!'

White-faced and trembling, Flora fled, leaving the two men wrestling with each other, rolling around the kitchen floor, the shards of glass cutting into their hands and faces. Malc was just wondering if he'd be able to beat off the younger man when to his relief the back door flew open and two burly policemen rushed in, dragging John off Malc, who was by now gasping for breath.

'You need to cool down, young fella mi lad,' one of the policemen started to say, but John smashed a furious fist into his face, causing blood to gush from the policeman's nose.

'That's it!' shouted the other policeman as he attached handcuffs to John's wrists. 'A night behind bars might make you see sense,' he added as the two of them frog-marched John, shouting every kind of obscenity, out of the back door and down the street towards the waiting police van.

Within seconds of their going Flora was back in the house.

'Malc! Malc!' she cried as she rushed to help him.

'I'm all right; don't worry about me,' he spluttered, as he leant against the kitchen sink and tried to get his breath back.

Flora surveyed her ruined kitchen. 'Thank God he's gone,' she said fervently. 'I was so scared when I heard all the shouting that I ran to the phone box and called the police.'

'I'm glad you did,' Malc replied. 'Drunk or not, your husband's a lot younger and stronger than me.'

Flora reached into a kitchen cupboard for her first-aid box. 'Let me clean those cuts for you,' she said.

'Come back with me,' Malc begged as Flora gently washed his wounds with antiseptic. 'We could put the little girls in the car and drive back to Pendleton tonight – you'll be safe there.'

Flora sadly shook her head. 'He'll be like a lamb when he comes round in the morning,' she murmured. 'He'll have no idea what he's done or why he's in custody; he'll be frightened,' she added. 'I can't leave him like that, Malc.'

Malc struggled to suppress his frustration. 'Sweetheart, don't you see, he's lost all control? It won't help him you being here; it just allows it to start all over again.'

'Maybe I'll be able to get him to the doctor's when he's sober,' she pleaded. 'I've got to give him another chance; I can't just walk away.'

'And what about them little lasses?' Malc asked. 'What kind of example are they growing up with?'

Seeing Flora's green eyes, which were so like Edna's,

fill up with tears, Malc felt his heart melt. 'I'm sorry, sweetheart – it upsets me to see you like this,' he said, as he held out his arms to the weeping woman.

When she nestled her head against his warm shoulder, Malc got a faint whiff of perfume; it made him even sadder to think that Flora had tried to make herself attractive for her husband's return. 'Look where that has got her,' he thought bitterly.

'Let me take you home, lovie?' he implored again.

'I've got to see it through,' Flora said in a muffled voice. 'I've got to do the best I can for the man I once loved. I married him for better or for worse.'

As Malc rocked the suffering woman in his arms, he prayed she'd live long enough to keep her promise.

After a cup of tea and several cigarettes, Malc felt there was no more he could do, so he set off for home.

'Now remember, call me if things go wrong again. Promise? And the police too if you need help sooner.'

'I promise,' Flora replied. 'Thank you, Malc,' she said, as she stood on her tiptoes to kiss his ruddy cheek.

'I'd better get a move on,' Malc said, his normal cheerful grin back again. 'If my Edna finds out I've not been where I said I was going to be, she'll have mi guts for garters.'

Driving as fast as he could through the dark, winding lanes, Malc got home just before dawn. Too exhausted to wash himself, and scared of wakening his sleeping wife, Malc slipped into his pyjamas, then eased himself under the blankets, where he lay with his eyes wide open, staring up at the ceiling.

'God Almighty, what a mess,' he thought before sleep claimed him.

Edna waited until she could hear her husband's steady breathing, then she sat up on one elbow to gaze at him. Did he smell of Evening in Paris or was she imagining it? Carefully lowering herself so as not to disturb him, Edna inhaled deeply – and by God! He did smell of perfume! Edna stared blankly at the bedroom wall; she'd never had her husband down as a lady's man but how in God's name was he going to explain his absence and the state he was in when he got back to her?

17. Grow Your Own

When Maggie and Nora weren't working their shifts at the Phoenix, they could often be found on the allotment, where Polly the pig idled away her days, filling out nicely on stale bread and scrapings of potatoes, carrots and swede, which the girls scrounged from other allotments. Though Maggie had been successful at the beginning in getting buckets of food waste from the Phoenix canteen, the cook was obliged to take her on one side and have a word in her ear.

'You see, lovie,' she said kindly, 'our slops are spoken for. I can slip you the odd bucket now and again, but the pig man from over Bury way picks up the canteen's food waste every week, and if he finds he's short, well,' she chuckled. 'He won't be very happy!'

Faced with a shortage of food for Polly, the anxious girls turned to lugubrious Percy for advice.

'Make yer own pig bin,' he told them. 'Just stick it in't street with a notice on't front and folks will find stuff to drop in.'

'But won't it smell?' Maggie asked.

'Course it'll bloody smell, but Polly won't mind,' Percy chuckled.

Nora found an old dustbin and attached a big notice – PIGSWILL – to the front. Percy was right: the bin filled up, not only with their own waste food from the cowshed but with their neighbours' waste as well. Added to which Polly always had something extra special every day from Nora. Her greatest treat so far was a chip butty that Nora had sneaked out of the canteen; given Nora's passion for chip butties, it was a mark of her love that she willingly sacrificed it to Polly. As the pig slurped ecstatically on the cold chips, Nora smiled. 'I'll try and sneak you a chip butty every day, my sweetheart,' she promised Polly, who grunted solemnly before she lay on her back and rolled in the straw.

Spring showers caused the roof of Polly's pen to leak. Percy was, as ever, forthcoming with advice. 'Bung up the 'oles in't roof so yon pig dun't get soaked t'ut skin,' he said. 'If she gets cowd she'll lose weight and, given we've got less than two months to fatten her up for't wedding, we don't want that, do we?' he said, giving a knowing wink in Polly's direction.

Donning navy-blue overalls borrowed from Malc's stores, the two girls plugged up the leaking holes of the corrugated roof and reinforced all four shed walls, which, if Polly were to lean against them for a comforting scratch, would collapse underneath her bulk. Nora took it upon herself to ensure that Polly had a deep straw bed to settle down on every night.

'Bloody life of Riley!' Percy scoffed as they all stood by the pen watching Polly, lying on her back with her little trotters in the air, wriggling contentedly on her comfy bedding. 'Who's added the extra litter?' he asked.

Maggie's eyes swivelled in the direction of Nora. 'You?' she asked.

Nora blushed. 'I thought it might turn frosty overnight,' she confessed. 'Anyway,' she quickly added, 'Percy just said we don't want her dropping weight.'

'Aye,' he agreed. 'But I never said treat her like the Queen of Sheba. You'll regret being so soft, lass,' Percy warned. 'This beast is for the chop.'

Every time anybody mentioned Polly's inevitable end, Nora felt sick. Since she'd met Polly, she'd not been able to eat any rationed food with a shred of pork in it, and she saved any little titbits, an apple or a crust, for when she visited Polly, who always lolloped up to Nora, grunting in happy anticipation. Of course poor Nora didn't dare to voice her disquiet – the pig was destined to be Maggie's wedding breakfast – but she dreaded the morning when Percy would slit Polly's throat.

It seemed that Percy could get hold of anything; he always had a friend who knew a friend (always over Ramsbottom way) that could lay his hands on whatever they required. When he appeared one day pushing an old trolley piled high with trays of seedlings, Polly frisked forward, clearly expecting to eat the lot.

'Nay, not you, missis,' chuckled Percy, as he brought the trolley to a stop before Maggie and Nora. 'These are for the lasses.'

Both girls stared at the trays containing little seedlings no bigger than the length of a metal nail.

'What're they?' Nora asked unashamedly.

Percy did a double-take. 'Hast thou ne'er set eyes on seedlings before?'

The girls shook their heads; though they lived on the edge of the countryside and several of their neighbours kept an allotment, neither of them had ever shown any interest in growing anything – up until now.

'You're looking at carrots, parsnips, peas, beans, kale and cabbage!' Percy exclaimed. 'Veg for your wedding breakfast,' he added as he grinned at Maggie.

'Them weedy things?' Nora said dismissively. 'They'll blow away in the first high wind.'

Maggie, though an inexperienced gardener, was a lot more enthusiastic than her doubtful friend. 'Are you serious, Percy?' she asked in delight.

'Aye, lass, I'm right proper serious – where do you think veg comes from? D'yer think it falls out o't sky?' he teased.

Keen to show she was eager to learn, Maggie asked, 'What do we do with them?'

'We'll keep 'em undercover, let 'em get stronger,' Percy replied. 'Then when the weather's a bit warmer we'll plant 'em out in separate rows, water and weed 'em and hopefully bring 'em on enough for your wedding do, lass.'

Maggie glowed with excitement. 'For the first time since I started planning our wedding, things are working out!' she announced.

'Thank God for that,' naughty Nora muttered under her breath.

'I'm not saying it'll all be plain sailing,' Percy quickly

intervened. 'It's back-breaking work, and the slugs could destroy the entire crop, not to mention the weather up here on't moors, one sharp frost and the whole bloody lot'll be gone.'

Seeing Maggie's lovely face fall, Percy quickly spoke again. 'Don't fret: we'll know if there's a frost coming, and we can cover 'em up, keep 'em warm,' he assured her.

'And what about the snails?' Maggie fretted.

Percy grimaced. 'We can always pour boiling water over 'em and boil the buggers to death!'

'So,' bright-eyed Maggie enthused, 'when do we start?'

'No time like the present,' Percy replied with undisguised glee.

'But I thought you just said they were too small to plant out now?' Maggie protested.

'Aye,' said Percy as he surveyed the overgrown allotment with a disapproving eye. 'But before we even get to that stage we've got to dig this bugger over,' he added, pointing at the riotous weeds that would strangle any delicate seedlings. Grabbing spades from his trolley, he handed one to Maggie and another to Nora. 'Dig for Victory, lasses!' he chuckled. 'As Mr Churchill says!'

'But . . .' grumbled Nora. 'We start our afternoon shift in an hour and we haven't even had our dinner.'

'You go home and brew up whilst we get cracking,' Percy instructed. 'And be sharp about it – many hands make light work.'

When Nora walked into the cowshed, she found Rosa and Julia washing up their lunch utensils. 'We left some spam sandwiches and radishes for you,' Rosa said, when she saw her friend's flushed face.

'Thanks,' said ravenous Nora, grabbing a butty. 'I can't stop,' she quickly added. 'I've left Maggie at the allotment with Winston Churchill!'

'Winston Churchill?' Rosa inquired with a grin.

'Bossy Percy!' Nora laughed, as she boiled a kettle of water and washed out the teapot. 'He's got more energy in his little finger than I have in my whole body. If it weren't for Maggie and her blasted wedding plans, I'd have now't to do with Percy!' she added, as she stomped out of the cowshed bearing mugs of tea and spam butties on a tin tray.

A few days later, as Edna and Nora travelled on the bus to Wrigg Hall, Edna said, 'Now you've got an allotment, you'll have something new to chat to your patients about.'

'Do you think so?' Nora asked uncertainly.

'You've had me in stitches telling me all about Percy and Polly!' Edna assured her.

'I'm glad I brought a smile to your face,' Nora replied. 'You haven't seemed your usual smiling self recently.'

Edna lit up a Woodbine as she said, 'I've had a lot on mi mind, that's all.'

Nora's face registered genuine concern. 'Ooh, lovie, I hope everything's all right?'

Recalling her husband arriving home smelling like

he'd just left a bordello, Edna muttered through a cloud of smoke, 'So do I, Nora, so do I.'

Nora couldn't wait to get to Ward D6 and tell Peter her news, but, to her surprise, she found his bed empty.

'Where's Peter gone?' she asked the Sister.

'He was taken down to theatre this morning,' she replied. 'We have a visiting plastic surgeon from Birmingham,' Sister explained. 'He's been doing a lot of pioneering work on men with disfiguring face wounds.'

Nora's stomach gave a nervous flip. 'What will they do to the poor lad?' she nervously inquired.

'The procedure is of a somewhat experimental nature,' Sister answered truthfully. 'The surgeon will take good skin from Peter's thigh and use it to rebuild his face,' she explained.

Nora thought she was going to be sick; seeing her turn a deathly white, the kind Sister quickly sat her down and gave her a glass of water, which she dutifully sipped.

'I know it sounds ghastly, but I have seen excellent results,' she assured Nora. 'Peter really is in the very best of hands.'

Feeling slightly less dizzy, Nora asked another question. 'What about his bad eye? Can they fix that too?'

'No, Peter's sight is completely gone in his left eye,' Sister replied. 'Sadly there's nothing anybody can do about that.'

'What happened to him?' Nora asked for the first time since she'd started her voluntary work.

'As far as I know, his regiment was caught up in enemy crossfire.'

'He's so young,' Nora murmured sadly.

'Twenty-one,' Sister told her.

'Same age as me,' Nora sighed guiltily. 'And what have I done to help win this terrible war?'

'You're here helping us,' Sister reminded her. 'The men enjoy your visits, Peter especially so.'

Touched by her words, Nora smiled and rose to go.

'I'd better get a move on or I'll miss the bus back to town,' she said. 'Please will you give Peter my best wishes when he comes round.'

'Of course I will,' Sister assured her. 'I'm sure he'll be very grateful.'

18. Suspicions

Kit wafted a letter high in the air as she called out to Maggie and Nora, 'Got a letter off Gladys!'

Anxious for Kit, now heavily pregnant, Maggie pulled out a chair and pushed a mug of tea forwards. 'Sit down, sweetheart – you look big enough to go into labour,' she half joked.

'Thanks, darlin',' sighed Kit as she lowered herself down on to the chair and rearranged her stomach, which was squashed into her tight overall. 'Glory be to God, this child of mine is a regular bruiser!' she said fondly, as she reached for her tea.

'Was Billy hard to carry?' Nora asked curiously.

Kit's lovely face clouded over. 'Well, now, that's another story,' she said sadly. 'I was so busy hiding my pregnancy from mi dah I don't recall anything other than the terror of being found out.'

Maggie put a comforting hand on her friend's shoulder. 'You can enjoy every minute of this little one,' she said softly.

'To be honest, Ian's enjoying it more than me!' Kit laughed. 'He and Billy are so excited; Billy wants a baby brother, but Ian would die for a little girl, big softie that he is.'

Kit's dark eyes lit up with love as she talked of her

husband, whom she simply adored. 'He's keen for me to stop working, and I will when I can't get behind the bench any more,' she told her friends.

'Wonder how Julia will survive without you?' Maggie mused.

'She'll be fine,' Kit said cheerfully.

'But once you've gone she'll have no pals to talk to in the filling shed,' Maggie pointed out.

'They all think she's a snooty Southerner,' Nora added.

Kit, who always found something positive to say about anybody, replied with characteristic optimism, 'Julia's a good woman and a kind one too – she's just quiet and reserved.'

'HUMPH! Try living with her,' Nora snorted.

In an effort to change the subject, Kit tore open the envelope. 'Let's see what our lovely Glad has to say,' she said excitedly.

Dear Kit,

How are you all?

Life here is wonderful! I know it sounds silly, given we struggle with the nightly bombing raids and the wretched air-raid shelters, plus the long hours we work, sometimes up to eighteen hours a day, but I am so very happy! Reg and I see more of each other when we're working than out of work hours – even so we get on better than ever. Sometimes the other nurses tease me for being handsome Dr Lloyd's girlfriend, but I don't care! I'm so proud of Reg and the work he does on the poor boys brought in from the front line. The staff at St Thomas' are such a dedicated team, working their socks off round the clock to support their patients, whose cheerfulness and bravery often bring tears to my eyes.

Gladys's letter went on to talk about London, the weather, rationing, her digs and the latest films she'd been to see. She concluded the letter by saying:

I miss you all so much, I wish I could see you. I bet you would love the West End, even though it's been blasted to bits by the German bombers. Got to go, the damn air-raid siren's going off again. See you at Maggie's wedding – not long now. Write back with your news.

Hugs and kisses,
Glad
xxx

Around the same time Rosa also received a letter from Gladys, an answer to her own recent one begging for her friend's help. When she saw it in her pigeon-hole and recognized the familiar writing, Rosa (unlike Kit) had no intention of sharing her correspondence with anybody. She quickly hid the letter in her overall pocket and read it later when she was alone.

Dearest Rosa,

You make me feel anxious – what's happened to you? Of course you're welcome to come and stay with me; I shall worry

until I see you. If you need to get in touch urgently, you can
phone me on the ward — Southwark 1100.

All my love,
Glad
xxx

Rosa sighed with relief when she finished the letter —
thank God she had Glad to rely on. By being in London
and visiting ports, she hoped and prayed she'd be able
to pick up some useful information — certainly more
than she'd ever pick up by doing nothing and staying
in Pendleton! Much as she loved Maggie and Nora, she
was determined not to speak to them of her plan;
she didn't want them to get into trouble if they were
questioned. The less they knew the better, though she
sensed that Julia, who was too clever by half, might
have sensed something.

Not long ago she'd caught Rosa flicking through the
little black notebook which she'd carried with her all
the way through France when she was on the run from
the Nazis. It contained some of her memories, some
names and some codes, but more importantly it held
several small black-and-white photographs of Gabriel
and a little poem he'd written for her. Rosa had always
kept the notebook a secret; it was the last link she had
with her past and the last photographs that had been
taken of Gabriel just before the war destroyed their
family life. She'd been so locked in her own thoughts,
gazing at the crinkled black-and-white photos and

thinking of her brother, that she didn't hear Julia walk up behind her. A discreet cough had made her jump, and immediately she snatched up her precious belongings and hurried to her bedroom, where she'd hidden her notebook in her underwear drawer. Since then Rosa had become neurotically aware of Julia's penetrating, clever green eyes that always seemed to be watching her.

The day that Rosa chose to run away came down to one essential factor – it had to be a day when all of her housemates were out the longest. After listening in on several conversations, both in the cowshed and at the canteen, Rosa decided that the following Thursday would be the best day to make her escape. Maggie would be at the allotment with Percy before she clocked on at the Phoenix, and Nora and Julia would be at Wrigg Hall before they too started their shifts.

Knowing she only had a few days to prepare for her trip, Rosa realized she couldn't wander down to Clitheroe Station and book a single ticket to London; if anybody saw her there it would arouse instant suspicion. She'd just have to take the bus into Manchester, hoping that nobody would spot her en route; she could then buy a ticket to London at London Road Station. Troop trains were running all over the country; she was confident that even if she had to wait she would eventually find a seat on one of them.

Rosa wrote a brief note to Gladys, saying when she'd be arriving; as she was unsure of the exact time, she told Gladys that she'd sit and wait for her at the hospital. Next she packed a small rucksack with some warm clothes, several changes of underwear, the little money she'd managed to save, her notebook and the photographs of her brother. Now all she had to do was to wait and hope to God that she wouldn't lose her nerve at the last minute.

Down in Pendleton, Edna was getting grumpier by the day. After trying to forget about her husband coming home smelling of Evening in Paris, she became anxious all over again when a letter went missing. She'd been busy preparing the chip shop for opening, but not so busy that she hadn't seen the postman pass by waving a white envelope, which he normally popped through the letter-box. However, later on, when she went to collect the letter, she found nothing on the doormat. When she questioned Malc, he said he knew nothing about it – so where had it gone? Increasingly suspicious, Edna questioned the postman the next day; he assured her he'd dropped the envelope through her letter-box.

'Well, I've not got it,' Edna thought to herself. 'And there's only one other person who lives at this address so he HAS to have it!'

Malc had in fact seen the letter on the doormat; he'd also immediately recognized the writing on the envelope – it was Flora's, and the letter was addressed to him. He'd snatched it up and shoved it in his coat pocket before Edna could see her daughter's handwriting and start asking awkward questions. Several hours later, Malc read the letter in the privacy of his office at the Phoenix.

Dear Malc,

*God only knows if you'll ever get this as John is keeping me
and the girls prisoners in our own home.*

Malc instantly regretted the delay in reading the letter.
'Oh, no!' he groaned. The letter continued:

*WHY do the army keep giving him sick leave? He needs help
but instead of treating him they've sent him back to me. He's
drunk and abusive, Malc – my girls are crying all the time,
which makes John even angrier. This time I can't get them to
the safety of a neighbour's house, as he's locked all the doors
and keeps the keys. I don't know what to do – I'm so frightened.
My only hope is if I can slip this letter under the back door,
my neighbour might pick it up and post it on to you.*

If you get it please help us.

Flora

'God Almighty!' Malc cried, as he rapidly reread the
letter.

He HAD to tell Edna this time; it simply couldn't
go on this way. But then he remembered his vow to
Flora; he was torn between loyalty to his wife and his
promise to her daughter. One thing he knew for sure
was he had to get to Penrith right away; even by his
calculations Flora and the little girls had been imprisoned in their home for at least as long as it had taken
Malc to get the letter: twenty-four hours – or even
more. Without telling a soul, Malc slipped out of the

Phoenix's back entrance, then ran all the way down the hill into town, where he picked up his car in the back street behind Edna's chip shop. Thanks to his links with the local black market, Malc had been able to ensure that the tank was topped up with petrol in case there was another domestic emergency. Without leaving a message Malc set off on his grim journey North.

Edna was surprised when her husband didn't come home for his tea; usually when he was working late she kept his meal hot in the oven until he got home. After she'd driven up to the Phoenix in her little blue van, and before she lit up the range to start cooking, Edna hurried into the factory to see if she could find her husband, who wasn't in his office. After asking a few questions she realized nobody had seen him all afternoon.

'Mebbe there's an emergency in another part of the factory,' Maggie suggested, as she and Edna smoked their cigarettes in the dispatch yard.

'Mebbe,' Edna replied.

She didn't mention the missing letter or Malc's previous absence; she didn't need advice or comfort. She knew the cold truth in her heart – her husband of a few short months was having an affair behind her back.

19. The Truth

Malc drove like the devil, but when he got to Flora's house he found it empty. After banging hard on the front door and getting no reply, he'd run round the back.

'GOD!' he thought as he began to panic. 'I hope I'm not too late?'

Seeing him furiously hammering on the back door, the kind neighbour he recognized from his previous visit called out to him. 'The police have carted the drunken bugger off in a van – again!' she said sourly.

Frantic with fear, Malc called back to her, 'What happened to Flora and the girls?'

'There was enough screaming to wake the dead – half the street must've heard; we were all out here, wondering what to do for the best. The local bobby called in for help – they were all taken to the hospital, Flora on a stretcher and the bairns hysterical with fear. A terrible thing to happen to a family when you can't trust a man with his kids.'

Malc didn't waste a moment longer talking. He jumped into his car and drove straight to the hospital, where he was told quite firmly that Flora couldn't be seen.

'She's in no state for visitors,' the desk clerk told him crisply.

'Can't I at least see her daughters?' he implored. 'I'm their grandad.'

After much persuasion Malc was shown to a side ward, where Katherine and Marilyn were lying side by side in a single bed, clinging on to each other.

'GRANDAD!' they cried when they saw Malc's familiar burly figure in the doorway.

After hugging them tightly, Malc pointed at the empty bed on the other side of the room.

'Why are you two sleeping in the same bed?' he asked.

'We wanted to be together 'cos we were frightened,' Katherine, the youngest, explained.

'Have you come to take us home?' Marilyn asked nervously.

Malc's eyes filled with tears at the state of the poor mites, who, with dark bags under their eyes, looked like they hadn't slept in days.

'I thought we might go to Nana's – what do you think?' he asked brightly.

Obviously relieved they weren't going back to their real home full of terrifying memories, the girls cried in unison, 'Yes! Yes! Yes!'

'I'll have to ask your mummy's permission first,' Malc warned.

Marilyn said in a low anxious voice, 'We mustn't leave Mummy alone with Daddy; he shouts at her and hits her.'

'Mummy's with the nice nurses right now,' Malc gently explained. 'She's asleep, but as soon as she wakes up I'll ask her if I can take you both to Nana Edna in Pendleton, where you can eat chips and fritters all day long!'

Giggling at his silly remark, the girls snuggled closer to him. 'Now,' he said, as he took a pack of cards from his pocket, 'look what I found in my car.' Flicking the cards, he sat on the chair beside their bed. 'Who fancies a game of snap?'

After what seemed like twenty games of snap, the little girls finally fell asleep, and so did Malc, who slumped over on to their bed with his head in his hands. When he awoke it was to a nurse shaking him by the shoulder.

'I'm afraid you can't stay here,' she whispered.

Malc nodded and rubbed his tired eyes as he followed her out of the room. 'I didn't want to leave the girls until they were sound asleep,' he told the young nurse, who gave an understanding smile.

With nowhere to go but his car, Malc settled himself in the back seat, where in between fitful snatches of sleep, he anxiously tried to work out what he'd say to Edna on his return; only the absolute truth would do this time, he decided.

By seven thirty Malc was back in the hospital asking once again to see Flora.

'I have to get my daughter-in-law's permission to take her children to their grandmother in Pendleton, where they'll be safe from their father,' he pleaded to the new desk clerk. 'After what they've been through, they need proper care and protection.'

Eventually, after the staff had stopped serving breakfast, Malc was briefly allowed to see Flora, who was sitting up in bed with her left arm in a splint.

'What happened?' he gasped, as he bent to give her a quick kiss on the forehead.

'I tried to open the front door to get the girls out, but John grabbed my arm.' She winced as she recalled the pain. 'I thought he'd rip it off.'

Malc also winced as he noticed the multiple bruises on her face and arms.

'Have you seen Marilyn and Katherine?' Flora quickly asked.

Malc smiled reassuringly. 'I stayed with them until I got thrown out of here last night; we played snap,' he added with a wink. 'They won of course!'

Flora's wide green eyes, so like Edna's, filled with tears. 'They were so frightened,' she murmured.

'They're all right now, sweetheart, and you will be too,' Malc promised. 'Now, lovie,' he added briskly, 'whether you like it or not, it's time to put your mother in the picture.'

Flora nodded as tears slipped down her thin cheeks. 'You're right,' she agreed. 'Mum needs to know. I can't go on like this any more – if the army won't protect us from my husband, we'll have to protect ourselves.'

Malc nodded at the woman who had repeatedly taken the brunt of her deranged husband's anger. 'With your permission I'll take the girls to Edna – they'll be safe as houses with her, have no fear,' he chuckled. 'She'll kill anybody who as much as looks at 'em!' he joked. 'As soon as you're fit I'll come back for you and take you home too,' he promised.

Flora nervously bit her nails. 'Mum will be cross with me for keeping her in the dark, won't she?'

'She'll be relieved to know what's going on,' Malc assured her. 'She's had her suspicions,' he added. 'She's not daft, is our Edna.'

Malc insisted on Marilyn and Katherine speaking to their mother before they left. Both of them were quiet when he brought them to the ward, where they stared solemnly at their mother lying in bed.

'Why is your arm in a stick, Mummy?' Katherine piped up.

'Because it's a bit sore,' Flora replied. 'Now listen carefully, girls, Grandad's taking you to Nana's.'

'Will you come too, Mummy?' Marilyn begged.

'I'll come as soon as my poorly arm is better,' Flora promised.

'I'm frightened Daddy will hurt you again,' the terrified child blurted out.

'Daddy's being taken care of, and I'm safe here with the nurses and doctors,' Flora gently reassured her.

After a tearful farewell with lots of hugs and kisses, Malc finally got the girls into his car. Even though they needed fresh clothes, he had no intention of taking them back to their home; instead he tucked them up in the back seat and, after covering them with his heavy tweed overcoat, he set off for Pendleton with them in the back happily singing 'There were Ten in the Bed and the Little One Said, Roll Over!'

*

170

Edna hadn't slept a wink all night long. Lying wide-eyed and staring up at the ceiling, she'd listened to the old clock chiming out the hours; by six o'clock she couldn't stand doing nothing for a minute longer. Hurrying downstairs, she put on the kettle for a brew and lit up her first cigarette of the day. But where in God's name was her husband? When and *if* he ever did get home, there'd be no creeping about this time; she'd get the truth out of Malc, even if she had to wring it out of him with her bare hands. It all added up: the perfume incident, the missing letter and now this – her husband gone all night with no explanation. It was as clear as the nose on her face: her husband, less than four months wed to her, was committing adultery.

She would never have put her money on Malc being an adulterer; the one thing she'd always loved about him was his honesty; often blunt to the point of rudeness, he was a man who always spoke the truth and stood by it too. How could he have broken his marriage vows to her so quickly? Didn't he love her any more? Had he fallen for a younger woman with a better figure? The thought of him with somebody else made Edna's insides turn upside down, and unable to stop herself she was suddenly violently sick in the kitchen sink. Feeling weak and dizzy, she reached out to steady herself on the kitchen table.

'Get a grip, woman,' she told herself. 'The bugger will be back, with his tail between his legs, and you've got to face him! No shilly-shallying, it's the truth you want – you deserve nothing less.'

Half an hour later Edna was dressed and in the chip shop, peering out of the window for the first sight of her wayward husband; in her hand she held her rolling pin, which she had no fear of using if it meant she'd get to the truth. She heard Malc's car before she saw it turn into the street, and, ducking down so he wouldn't see she was waiting for his return, Edna dashed to the front door, which she threw open.

'And where the 'ell do you think you've been?' she raged at her husband standing on the doorstep.

Seeing the rolling pin twitching in his wife's hands, Malc quickly said, 'I can explain everything, Edna.'

'You better bloody had!' she raged. 'And it had better be good too. What kind of a fool do you take me for?'

'Edna,' he pleaded. 'If you'll just give me a minute.'

'A minute!' she shrieked. 'I've been up all night waiting for you. You won't put a foot over this doorstep until you tell me about the floozy you're spending so much time with!'

'Edna –' Malc implored.

'First you come to bed stinking of another woman's perfume, then you lie, deliberately lie to me about a letter that was delivered here and you hid, and now you come home after being out all night.' Looking like she was going to explode, Edna added, 'What do you expect? A welcoming party?'

Keeping his eye on the wavering rolling pin, which Malc had no doubt his wife would use on him if he didn't tell her the truth pretty quickly, he yelled over the top of her ranting, 'If you want proof of my innocence, come and look in the car, right now!' Hurrying back to the car, he called over his shoulder, 'Come on, take a look.'

Edna hesitated. 'This had better be good,' she snapped, as she slowly made her way to his parked car.

'There are my other women!' Malc said, as he pointed at Edna's grandchildren sprawled out and fast asleep on the back seat of his car.

Edna gaped in disbelief at the sweetly sleeping children. 'What . . .'

Taking her trembling hands (and at the same time relieving her of the menacing rolling pin!), Malc quickly said, 'It's a long and not a very pretty story, sweetheart, but it's nowt to do with another woman – well, unless you call your Flora a threat.'

Edna was so shocked she could barely speak. 'What's going on?' she spluttered.

Before Malc could begin to tell his wife about his involvement in Flora's domestic affairs, Katherine woke up and held out her arms to Edna, who rushed to embrace her precious granddaughter.

'Mummy said you'd look after us till she gets out of hospital,' Katherine said sleepily.

'Oh, I will, my sweetheart,' Edna cried with tears in her eyes. 'Nana will always look after you.'

Before Malc could even begin to offer an explanation, Edna's granddaughters poured out the terrible story themselves.

'Mummy told us to hide in the wardrobe.'

'Daddy kept shouting.'

'He hurt Mummy, she was crying a lot.'

'She's poorly in hospital.'

'The nurses are making Mummy better.'

After their tearful outpourings, the girls requested something to eat. Once they were sitting by the fire in the kitchen, Edna started making toast and boiling the few precious eggs she'd been given by a neighbour who kept chickens in his backyard. Glancing up from slicing a loaf of bread, she said in a low voice, 'You'd better explain what's been going on up there, Malc.'

After Malc told her in hurried whispers what had happened, Edna looked both hurt and angry.

'And why did nobody bother to tell me?'

'Flora didn't want to upset you; she made me promise not to tell you,' Malc explained.

Clearly offended, Edna snapped, 'But she told *you*!'

'I *hated* keeping it a secret, but Flora was adamant.'

Edna's eyes swam with tears. 'And there was I thinking you'd run off with a floozy,' she murmured.

Malc took her in his strong arms and held her close to his chest. '*My* sweetheart,' he whispered softly. 'You're the only woman in the world I want.' Then, spying Katherine and Marilyn grinning at them over the top of Edna's bent head, he added with a chuckle, 'Well, apart from those two cheeky little monkeys who are waiting for their breakfast!'

It was shortly after Malc returned to Pendleton with Flora's children that the day dawned that Rosa had been both dreading and longing for: the day she would begin her search for Gabriel. Feigning sickness, she groaned as she lifted her head out of the metal pail she'd been retching into.

'It must have been something I ate.'

Looking concerned, Nora and Maggie offered advice.

'Best stay in bed,' Maggie said.

'We'll tell Malc you're ill,' Nora added.

'Sleep it off,' Maggie suggested, as she turned to go.

'Hopefully you'll feel better in a few hours' time,' Nora called over her shoulder.

As the two girls left for work, Julia popped her head around the doorframe. Catching sight of her, Rosa quickly closed her eyes and groaned loudly.

'Strange . . .' astute Julia observed. 'We've all eaten the same food but you're the only one that's got a tummy bug.'

Not trusting herself to speak, Rosa turned her face to the pail by her bed and retched, after which, seething at Julia, she rolled on to her side so she wouldn't have to look at the interfering girl. Seizing the opportunity, Julia quickly peered into the bucket, which, considering all the noise that Rosa had been making, was surprisingly empty.

After she heard the door bang shut behind Julia, Rosa lay tense on her bed, listening out for the tiniest sound; she had to be absolutely sure that she really was on her own. Hardly daring to breathe, she threw off her bedcovers and slipped fully dressed out of bed. She neatly made up the bed, then took her rucksack from its hiding place and quickly checked the contents for the tenth time: warm clothes, several changes of underwear, the little money she'd managed to save and her notebook with the photographs of her brother.

'Ready,' she said in a trembling whisper.

Still fearful of being discovered, she crept into the sitting room, where she pulled on her stout walking boots and warm winter coat; then, with her rucksack slung over her shoulder, Rosa walked out of the cowshed, wondering, as she slammed the door shut behind her, if she would ever see it again.

20. Consequences

Maggie arrived back at the cowshed first. After a day on the allotment with Percy and Polly, her gardening overalls stank of manure and compost. Keen not to bring the smell into the sitting room, Maggie wriggled out of her overalls on the doorstep before stepping inside.

'Hello,' she called softly, just in case Rosa was asleep.

Getting no reply, she crept towards Rosa's bedroom door, which was standing slightly ajar.

'Hello,' she whispered again.

But when she looked inside, Rosa's bed was empty. With only ten minutes to go before she clocked on for her shift, Maggie dashed into the bathroom, where she quickly washed herself. When she came out, rubbing herself dry with a towel, Julia and Nora, just returned from Wrigg Hall, were also back and preparing for work.

'Rosa's not here, so she must be feeling better,' Maggie informed her friends.

'She's probably nipped over to the canteen to grab a chip butty!' Nora joked.

'Come on,' Maggie giggled as she grabbed Nora by the arm. 'If we're quick we can grab one too.'

After the chattering girls had left in a rush, Julia

checked out Rosa's bedroom, where at first nothing looked unusual. Rosa's slippers were under the bed, her dressing gown was hanging on the back of the door, a cardigan lay neatly folded on a chair. But, just as Julia was turning to leave the room, her eyes fell on a scrap of paper on the floor. She picked it up and guessed immediately that the handsome man with the dark brooding eyes and high cheekbones must be Rosa's brother.

'She must have dropped it when she left,' Julia thought. Turning it over and noting some numbers on the back that looked like possible codes, she decided to keep hold of the photograph. 'It could be useful.' She wondered if Rosa had intended to take it with her to the canteen, if that's where she actually was. 'Surely not,' Julia reasoned. Any photographs would be destroyed in no time in the filthy factory environment.

Without a moment's hesitation, Julia, who right from the start had been unconvinced about Rosa's sudden tummy bug, started to rummage through Rosa's chest of drawers and wardrobe to see if she could find anything else that would help her get to the bottom of Rosa's odd behaviour. But, after searching through her things and finding nothing of any relevance, Julia felt a mixture of irritation and frustration. She remembered seeing her once with a notebook that she'd been suspiciously secretive about, but there was no sign of it anywhere.

'Am I just making this up?' she questioned herself. 'For all I know she might be at work!' Tucking the photograph into her pocket, Julia left the room. 'There's only one way to find out,' she thought as she pulled on her coat and hurriedly made her way to the Phoenix.

After clocking on Julia searched the cordite line, the filling shed and the dispatch yard for Rosa. When the hooter sounded for the start of the new shift, a wave of workers surged out of the canteen; Julia, pressed against a wall, scanned every face in the crowd, but Rosa was not amongst them. Determined not to panic, Julia checked the changing room and the ladies' toilet, then breathlessly joined Kit at their bench in the filling shed.

'Have you seen Rosa?' Julia casually asked, as her fingers, normally so deft and nimble, fumbled with the filthy gunpowder. 'I've looked everywhere but she doesn't appear to be in the building.'

Looking concerned, Kit muttered, 'Where on earth could she have got to?'

Oblivious to the jolly voices of Gracie Fields and Arthur Askey on *Music While You Work*, Julia's brain was racing; she instinctively knew that the girl was up to something. Feigning sickness and disappearing without any explanation required a bold plan, which Rosa must have carefully put together. But *what* is she up to, Julia pondered. The only possible idea that had any kind of logic to it was that desperately unhappy Rosa had taken off to search for her brother.

'If that's the case,' Julia puzzled, 'where would she go? Who would she turn to for advice?'

Within a split-second Julia had answered her own question: there was only one place where Rosa could go if she was serious. *'London!'* she thought.

Keeping her face as composed as possible, Julia turned to Kit. 'Am I right in thinking your friend Gladys works at St Thomas' Hospital?'

Kit looked surprised by her question. 'Yes,' she answered.

'What's the name of her boyfriend again?'

'Reggie Lloyd, Dr Reggie Lloyd,' Kit replied with an anxious frown. 'Why do you ask?'

Not wanting to alarm heavily pregnant Kit with her own fears, Julia smiled. 'Just curious,' she said, and, pretending to be humming along to the music, she started to make her own bold plan.

Edna outmatched a lioness protecting her cubs when it came to taking care of Marilyn and Katherine, who trailed after her like nervous chicks following a mother hen. Edna discovered that the best thing she could do to take their mind off their worries was to let them work alongside her in the shop. She warned them not to go near the red-hot chip range, but they could wipe down the dining tables, fill up the salt and vinegar bottles and shape newspaper squares into little bags. Marilyn was clever enough to write out the daily menu on the blackboard. Being busy kept the girls occupied but night-times were bad. Both girls regularly woke up with screaming nightmares.

'No! Daddy, no!'

'Please don't hurt Mummy.'

It just about broke Edna's heart to hear their anguished cries, but she found if she lay in her big double bed between the two of them she could soothe each in turn and eventually they would snuggle down in the safety of her arms and go back to sleep.

'I could kill that bastard father of theirs with mi bare hands,' Edna said to Malc one night after she'd finally settled the girls in bed.

Malc, who'd seen the madness and the sadness too in Flora's husband's crazed eyes, repeated Flora's words. 'She said he was a good man till he joined up; it's the war that's turned him into what he is now – the war and the booze.'

'But to take it out on children, his own flesh and blood!' Edna insisted. 'It's inhuman.' Taking a hankie from her pinafore pocket, she dabbed at the tears streaming down her face. 'I'll never forgive him, *never*!' she raged. 'He could have killed my Flora – but for you and that neighbour of hers she could be lying dead in her grave!' Edna's ample breast gave a great heartbroken heave.

'Come 'ere, you poor love,' Malc murmured, as he gathered his sobbing wife into his strong arms. 'Thank Christ, given what might have happened, they're all safe.'

'You're a brave man,' Edna murmured as she reached up to kiss Malc's face. 'I'm sorry I thought you were off gallivanting!'

Malc suppressed a guffaw of laughter. 'There's only

one woman I want to gallivant with and she's my wife,' he said, as he gently kissed Edna's soft pink lips.

Nora was delighted to see Marilyn and Katherine back in Pendleton and willingly babysat the little girls whenever she got the chance.

'I've got a new friend I'd like you to meet,' she told them one day after Edna had dropped them off at the cowshed.

'Is she pretty?' Katherine asked.

'She's got pink cheeks and pink skin and quite big ears,' Nora said with a secretive smile.

'What colour's her hair?' Marilyn inquired.

'Silver.'

'How old is she?'

'Younger than you two,' Nora replied.

'Does she go to school?'

'She's not very bright; her favourite thing is eating,' Nora giggled.

'Eating *what*?' asked an intrigued Marilyn.

'Anything – she's not fussy,' Nora chuckled.

By the time they'd trudged up the hill to the allotments, Nora was breathless with answering their endless questions; she was also excited.

'This way, come on, follow me,' she called, as she made her way into the muddy allotment.

'UGH!' groaned the girls. 'Does your friend live here?'

'For the time being this is her home,' Nora said. 'Here she is!' she declared, and Polly came trotting up to the fence, grunting expectantly.

'A PIG!' both girls exclaimed at the same time.

'Not just a pig – Polly the pig!' proud Nora said, as she tickled Polly's ears, then produced from her overall pockets some crusts of bread. 'Here, give her these – careful of your fingers, she might nip.'

Polly devoured the crusts, then gazed up at the girls with her baleful little piggy eyes. 'She wants some more,' Katherine laughed.

'She can wait till supper-time,' Nora answered firmly. 'Me and Maggie bring her buckets of slops morning and night.'

The girls groaned again in loud disgust. 'URGH!'

Nora mucked out Polly's soiled bedding, whilst Marilyn and Katherine inspected the sprouting seedlings kept warm in the shed well away from Polly's greedy eyes.

'We'll soon be planting them out,' Nora explained. 'Look! Carrots, parsnips, peas, beans, kale and cabbage,' she said, showing the girls the seed packets with the images of the vegetables on the front.

'Can you grow chips?' Katherine giggled.

'Don't be daft,' Nora laughed. 'You should know better than anybody; your nana's chips come from fresh potatoes.'

Hearing their collective laughter, Polly joined in the fun with a happy grunt.

'I like her,' Marilyn said and stroked Polly's ears just as she'd seen Nora do earlier.

'How long will she stay here?' Katherine inquired.

A shadow passed over Nora's smiling face. 'Till May,' she said.

'Where will she go after May?' Katherine asked.

Nora gulped. 'Heaven.'

The girls looked shocked. 'Will she die?' Marilyn cried.

Nora replied with a sob in her voice, 'She'll be made into sausages and bacon.'

The girls' eyes grew as wide as saucers. 'You could hide Polly somewhere so no one would ever find her,' gentle-hearted Katherine suggested.

Nora's eyes grew round. 'You know, I'd never thought of that,' she admitted.

'She's too nice to be made into sausages,' Marilyn said, as she hung over the fence to scratch Polly's ample rump.

Polly wriggled in delight. 'HONK!' she grunted. 'HONK! HONK!'

Marilyn broke into peals of laughter and pointed at Polly. 'Listen to her, she agrees with me!'

'So she does.' Nora laughed too, then added under her breath, 'And so do I!'

21. London

Rosa's journey to London literally took all day. Sitting in the same window seat for hour after hour, Rosa stared at the bleak landscape the lumbering train passed through. Every town and city seemed to have been blown up from the inside out; spewed debris and rubble linked the endless ruins, which even the slow emerging spring did nothing to enhance. Occasional bunches of forlorn daffodils by the train tracks or a blasted fruit tree miraculously in bud did nothing to lift Rosa's spirits.

How would this blasted landscape ever recover from a brutal war that had raged for over five years and affected every corner of the land? Rosa's thoughts flew to her own beloved country, in the grip of the Nazis. What would be left of her beautiful ancient city, Padua, with its cloistered medieval centre, its majestic duomo and priceless works of art?

'Don't think about it,' she firmly told herself. 'Or what kind of trouble you'll be in for abandoning the factory without leave. Keep focused and concentrate on finding Gabriel.'

She repeated the sentence like a mantra, until the train finally ground to a halt in Euston Station and disgorged hundreds of bone-weary, hungry troops. Rosa, who had never been to the city before, hadn't a clue where she was; bewildered, she asked a policeman outside the station how to get to St Thomas' Hospital.

'Take the Tube to Westminster, then cross over the bridge to the hospital,' he said.

Totally confused, Rosa scanned the area. 'Where is the Tube?'

'Right behind you,' the policeman said with a smile, and he nodded over her shoulder in the direction of the Underground.

Clutching an overhead strap, Rosa was squashed and jostled inside the packed compartment, until she finally emerged into the fresh air, which she gratefully breathed in as she walked over Westminster Bridge. The view of the Thames, with barrage balloons floating over the river, denying airspace to the German bombers, was a comforting surprise, as was the dome of St Paul's, which (she'd read in the newspaper) had so far miraculously survived the continuous London bombing.

When she reached the hospital entrance Rosa wondered how she was going to locate Gladys. And, even more importantly, what her next step would be now she was actually here in London. Seeing a group of nurses in caps and capes hurrying towards the doors, Rosa stepped forwards.

'Can you tell me how I can find Nurse Gladys Johnson? I think she works on the post-op ward.'

'I don't know her,' one of them replied.

'Hold on a minute,' another nurse remarked. 'Isn't she the good-looking brunette who's going out with Dr Lloyd?'

Rosa's ears pricked up at the mention of Reggie's name.

'Dr Lloyd is her boyfriend,' she said quickly.

'C4 and C5 are acute post-op – check those,' the nurse said, before they all went on their way, with their blue capes billowing out behind them.

Following the hospital signs, Rosa eventually found herself in the corridor that connected the two wards. She was too nervous to walk on to the wards and inquire after Gladys, so she sat on a wooden bench and waited. Suddenly overcome with exhaustion after her long and bewildering journey, she felt her body, which had been tensed up like a sprung coil for weeks, go limp. The loud clattering sound of a metal stretcher made Rosa jump to her feet.

'Excuse me,' she said to a nurse who was pushing a patient on the trolley. 'Do you know where I can find Nurse Gladys Johnson?'

'She's on C5,' the nurse replied. 'It's still visiting time – pop down and see if you can find her,' she suggested.

After thanking her, Rosa pushed open the doors of C5 and walked down the tiled corridor, praying that she wouldn't be interrogated by an officious Ward Sister. Before she even reached the main body of the ward, she heard a lilting laugh that she would have recognized anywhere. Turning in the direction of the laughter, Rosa called softly, 'Gladys?'

And to her absolute joy Gladys's head popped around an open doorway.

'ROSA!' she cried.

Overwhelmed with relief, Rosa all but ran into Gladys's arms. 'Oh, I'm so glad to see you!' she cried on the verge of tears.

Seeing her friend's pale, tired face, Gladys asked, 'How long have you been here, lovie?'

'Not long,' Rosa assured her, then smiled as she took in the pleasing picture of tall, slender Gladys in her crisp uniform and starched white cap that was pinned firmly to her neatly pleated mahogany brown hair. 'When do you finish your shift?' she asked.

'Not for an hour,' Gladys replied.

'I'll wait in the corridor for you,' Rosa replied.

Gladys shook her head. 'You must be worn out after your journey. There's a Lyons Café round the corner – go and get yourself something to eat. I'll meet you there as soon as I can get away.'

A quarter of an hour later Rosa was sitting at a corner table, devouring toast and Marmite and pouring out a third cup of strong Lyons tea. A combination of feeling warm for the first time all day and the low buzz of conversation all around made Rosa's eyes droop, and when Reggie and Gladys arrived they found her fast asleep.

'Poor kid, she looks exhausted,' Gladys murmured.

Hearing their voices, Rosa woke up with a start, rubbing her eyes and looking around in confusion.

'Want a top-up?' Gladys asked, as she pointed at Rosa's empty cup.

'Yes, please,' Rosa replied, then, seeing Reggie standing beside Gladys, she smiled and added, 'Good to see you again, Reggie.'

When Gladys returned with more tea and toast, the three of them sat chatting until eventually Rosa could bear the strain no longer.

'I need your help,' she blurted out.

Gladys gently took hold of her friend's trembling hand. 'What's the matter, sweetheart?'

'I ran away from the Phoenix!'

'Why?' Gladys cried.

'I'll tell you if you promise to hear me out,' Rosa requested.

As Rosa's story unfolded, Gladys more than once looked like she was going to interrupt, but a look from Rosa stifled her. However, when Rosa had finished, Gladys burst out, 'You can't rescue your brother single-handed – it's madness!'

'I'm not asking for your opinion about my plan, *cara*,' Rosa said pointedly. 'I'm asking for your help.'

In a calmer voice than his girlfriend's, Reggie asked, 'Seriously, Rosa, what do you think Gladys and I can do to help you?'

'It's not like we know any powerful people in the government or the forces,' Gladys joked.

Rosa shuffled her chair closer. 'I was hoping to visit some ports to get information. I need advice on how I can get out of the country and I thought you might have some ideas.' She quickly added for Reggie's bene-fit, 'I got into this country as a refugee on the run; there must be people who have contacts?'

'I'm sure there are,' Reggie agreed. 'But I honestly wouldn't know where to start!'

Keeping her voice down, Gladys said urgently, 'I understand you want to do something, Rosa, but your plan is far too dangerous! You could get caught and end up back in a concentration camp yourself.' She paused to shake her head in bewilderment. 'Even if you don't get caught, how on earth do you think you would find your brother!'

Rosa slumped. 'I know all that. But you won't change my mind, *cara*,' she said sadly. There was a long pause as the two friends locked eyes. 'If I don't try to look for Gabriel, I'll never forgive myself. If I die searching for him, so be it – better to die trying than live with the guilt of doing nothing.'

Gladys knew Rosa far too well to continue arguing; she could see that her friend was set on a mission. She was going to have to think of another way to put a stop to this mad plan. Reggie, who had been listening quietly, stepped in to help.

'I was on a warship in the Med for almost a year,' he said, smiling fondly at Gladys, whose blue eyes sparkled as he spoke. 'It's where we met,' he added, as he leant across to kiss Gladys lightly on the cheek. 'I've kept in touch with some of the senior officers; I could ask them a few discreet questions. See if they have any ideas about how we can trace your brother?'

'Oh, Reggie!' Rosa said with suppressed excitement in her voice. 'I'd be so grateful.'

Reggie held out his hands to calm her down. 'Please don't get your hopes up. I'm not agreeing to smuggle you into France,' he added hurriedly, glancing at his wristwatch. 'But you never know – it's worth a try. Look, I'm sorry, I've got to get back to work.' Turning to Gladys, he added, 'I suggest you find a bed for Rosa in the nurses' hostel, darling.'

Feeling the pressure of Reggie's hand on her back, Gladys said to Rosa, 'I'll go and pay the bill – won't be a minute.'

Once they were well away from Rosa, Reggie said in a low, urgent voice, 'I don't think for a moment we can help her. I had to say something just to stall her,' he admitted. 'Given the state Rosa's in, I've no doubt she'd run off to Dover and smuggle herself on the first ship bound for France if we didn't!'

'What can I do to stop her?' a frantic Gladys asked.

'Stall her any way you can – tell her you really think my contacts will help. And don't let her know you're alarmed!' Reggie said, as he gave his anxious girlfriend a quick kiss. 'See you in the morning.'

Reggie returned to St Thomas', where he operated on a young soldier with massive injuries to his bowel; after working on him for several hours, Reggie swabbed down in readiness for leaving for the night when the senior nurse on duty called out to him, 'Phone call for you, Dr Lloyd.'

Wiping his hands dry, Reggie picked up the receiver. 'Lloyd speaking.'

'Hello, I'm sorry to bother you so late and at work too,' a clear confident female voice rang out. 'My name is Julia Thorpe, and I live with Rosa Falco.' Julia came straight to the point: 'Rosa has run away. She left without saying a word to anybody this morning. I thought she might have come to see your fiancée, Gladys.'

Not at all sure which way the conversation was going, Reggie cautiously waited. On the other end of the phone Julia took a deep breath. 'I have to be blunt, Dr Lloyd; I'm very worried for Rosa. I believe she may be planning to try to leave the country to look for her brother.'

Reggie decided it was time to respond. 'Yes, you're right. She is with Gladys and that is exactly what she is planning,' he said heavily.

'Oh no! I hoped I was wrong, but Rosa is in the gravest of danger. For her own sake she must be stopped,' Julia urged.

'I've been racking my brains trying to think how best to stop her,' Reggie agreed.

'There's only one sure way,' Julia told him.

'What are you proposing?' he asked.

'Tell her that I've issued her description to all the ports,' Julia answered without a moment's hesitation.

'That won't go down well,' Reggie warned.

'It doesn't matter, Dr Lloyd, I've got nothing to lose,' Julia retorted. 'You and Gladys must insist that she returns to the Phoenix before the police are called in and she gets arrested.'

Reggie was impressed by Julia's cool, calculated planning. 'You've really thought this through,' he said. 'But she's not going to like it.'

'I know, but I have no choice.'

22. A Change of Plan

The following morning Reggie met up with Gladys and Rosa at the entrance to St Thomas'. Gladys immediately noticed her boyfriend's sickly pallor; assuming he'd been working most of the night, she kissed him tenderly on the lips.

'You look exhausted,' she murmured.

But when she saw the stony look in his eyes, Gladys felt alarmed. 'What's the matter, Reggie?' she asked fearfully.

'Let's find somewhere quiet to talk,' he suggested.

When they were settled on one of the long wooden benches in the echoing entrance hall, Reggie didn't beat about the bush. 'Something's come up, Rosa,' he began.

'What?' she cried.

Reggie took a deep breath before he said, 'Your description has been issued to all the major ports. I'm afraid there's very little chance of your leaving the country now.'

Rosa turned so white that Reggie thought she might faint. 'That's impossible!' she protested. 'Nobody knew anything about my plans – apart from you and Gladys.'

Reggie, who was dreading imparting the next piece

of information, briefly hesitated before he added, 'Your housemate, Julia, phoned me. She's the one who contacted the authorities.'

'She did *what*?' Rosa gasped.

Wishing he wasn't the bearer of such acrimonious news, Reggie continued, 'She guessed what you were up to.'

Rosa was so angry she could barely speak. 'How could she possibly know?' she spluttered.

Reggie shrugged. 'Don't ask me,' he remonstrated.

With her fists clenched into tight balls, Rosa leapt to her feet. 'I could kill her!'

Gladys laid a restraining hand on her friend's shaking shoulders. 'Maybe she was thinking of your safety,' she murmured.

'What I choose to do is nothing to do with bloody Julia! How dare she interfere?'

Knowing he was urgently needed in the operating theatre, Reggie said, 'Whatever your feelings about Julia, you must understand, Rosa, that you cannot try to leave the country now this has happened.'

As she opened her mouth to protest, Reggie quickly said, 'The best thing you can do is go back to Pendleton right away.'

On hearing his advice, Rosa burst into floods of tears. 'Julia's ruined everything!' she wailed.

'She might just have saved your life,' Reggie patiently pointed out.

As Rosa wept into her hands, Reggie whispered urgently to Gladys, 'You must take her back; she can't be trusted on her own.'

'How am I going to get time off at such short notice?' Gladys asked in an anxious whisper.

'I'm sure I can fix it as long as you travel back here as soon as you can,' Reggie assured her.

Quickly nodding in agreement with him, Gladys soothingly said to Rosa, 'Sweetheart, you're in no state to be travelling alone. I'll come back to Pendleton with you.'

Rosa glared defiantly through her tears. 'I am *not* going back!'

Gladys softly stroked Rosa's rich mahogany hair. 'You have no choice – you *have* to go back or you'll be in big trouble.'

Heart-broken Rosa laid her head on Gladys's shoulder, where she abandoned herself to grief.

'God help me! I'll never find Gabriel now.'

Rosa hardly spoke a word on the journey back to Pendleton. Gladys knew her too well to trouble her with small talk, so she just sat beside her as the train laboured its way to the North.

When they arrived at the cowshed, it was getting dark. Rosa, who'd been depressed and lethargic all day, suddenly switched gears. Throwing open the cowshed door, she marched in, followed by Gladys, who could see Nora and Maggie standing rooted to the spot as they stared at Rosa in disbelief.

'ROSA!' gasped Maggie. 'Thank God, you're back!'

'We've been worried sick!' Nora cried. 'Where have you been?'

Stony-faced Rosa ignored their welcoming smiles. 'Where is she?' she stormed. 'Where's Julia?'

A bedroom door opened and Julia, tight-lipped, stepped into the sitting room.

'Here.'

All the fury and disappointment of the last twenty-four hours poured out of Rosa in a rush of vicious hatred. Taking a step towards Julia, she shouted, 'How dare you interfere!'

Undaunted, Julia held Rosa's blazing gaze. 'I couldn't stand by and watch once I realized what you were up to.'

'How exactly did you find out?' Rosa demanded. 'Were you snooping through my things like the interfering bitch you really are?'

'I didn't have to snoop,' Julia answered levelly. 'It was perfectly obvious you were desperate to help your brother, and when you disappeared I realized you'd probably run away. I suspected you'd go to Gladys in London, so I phoned Dr Lloyd, who confirmed my suspicions.'

Unable to believe what they were hearing, Nora and Maggie gaped in shock at Rosa. When Nora finally found her voice, she was stung that Rosa hadn't told them anything of her plans.

'Didn't you trust us to keep our mouths shut?' she demanded.

Turning to her emotional friend, Rosa dropped her voice to a normal level as she tried to explain. 'I didn't want to involve anybody, I had to keep it a secret.' She turned back to Julia. 'That is until Miss Big-Mouth here stepped in and played the part of God.'

Bewildered Maggie looked over to Gladys, who was standing by the wood-burning stove.

'What happened, Glad?' she asked in genuine confusion.

'Rosa came to me and Reggie for help.'

'I was trying to get to France,' Rosa blurted out. 'I have contacts there who I hoped would help me to find my brother but' – her blazing eyes swivelled across to Julia, who was standing resolutely still – '*she* threatened to tell the authorities, who would have immediately alerted all the major ports; *she* effectively destroyed all my hopes of finding Gabriel!'

Rosa's anger burned out as she said her brother's name, and she slumped on to the sofa, sobbing. Her friends hovered anxiously over her.

'I'll put the kettle on and make some tea,' mumbled Nora.

'Here, have a cigarette,' Maggie said, holding a packet of Woodbines before Rosa.

Julia waited whilst Rosa smoked down half the cigarette, then said quietly, 'There are safer ways of finding your brother than randomly running off to France.'

Rosa couldn't believe the brass of the woman; did she ever know when to stop? 'And how would you know?' she sneered.

Before Julia could reply, and fearing Rosa really would explode, Gladys intervened. 'It's been a long day, and we're both exhausted. I think we should leave it there,' she said firmly, as she eyed Julia, who briefly nodded, then retired to her room.

'*Judas!*' Rosa hissed after her.

Maggie pulled down the sides of her pretty mouth. 'She's always been a bit of a bloody know-all.'

Gladys sipped her hot tea as she stared thoughtfully into the fire. 'I'm sorry to say this, girls,' she said quietly, 'you might not like Julia Thorpe, but I believe she is a very brave woman.'

After Gladys had left for London early the next morning, Rosa returned to work, telling Malc that her short absence had been due to a chronic stomach bug.

Julia and Rosa saw little of each other in the workplace, where a fair distance separated Julia in the filling shed from Rosa on the cordite line, plus Julia made herself scarce at break times, taking her tea alone whilst she read the papers.

'You really don't need to sit on your own,' a worried Kit said when they were working alone together.

'It's the sensible thing to do,' Julia reasoned. 'I've never been one of the crowd, so nobody will miss me,' she said with a wry smile. 'And Rosa shooting daggers at me wouldn't be relaxing for anyone. I don't mind,' she assured kind-hearted Kit.

Kit rubbed her burgeoning tummy and sighed heavily. 'Rosa will never forgive you for telling on her,' she said. 'In her eyes she thinks she might have got away with it and, more importantly, she might have found Gabriel.'

Julia shook her head. 'There wasn't a hope of that, and you know it!' Fixing her gaze firmly on the gunpowder she was sifting through her stained black fingers, Julia added, 'I have no regrets, Kit; what Rosa was planning was outright madness.'

'I know,' Kit responded sadly. 'But that doesn't stop me feeling sorry for the poor girl. I've never seen her looking quite so lost and forlorn.'

The atmosphere in the cowshed was so tense when Julia and Rosa were in the same space that Julia took to her room, where she typed letters or lay on her bed and read her few books over and over again.

'I hate it!' Nora complained as she, Maggie and Rosa ate their frugal tea in the kitchen. 'The cowshed's always been such a happy place – friends living together, enjoying each other's company – now you can cut the atmosphere with a knife.'

'I have thought of moving out,' Rosa admitted. 'Just to get away from Julia.'

Tears welled up in Nora's big blue eyes. 'NO!' she cried. 'You mustn't do that, Rosa!'

'If anybody should go, it should be blasted Julia,' Maggie fumed. 'She's the one that caused a row in the first place!'

The only place where Nora felt happy in the days that followed the vitriolic row between Julia and Rosa was at Wrigg Hall. The highlight of each visit was seeing Peter, who had responded well to plastic surgery. The left-hand side of his face was still bandaged, but the surgeon, pleased with the young man's quick recovery, was keen to do more restorative work on his damaged face. Lately, though, poor Nora dreaded the journey over the moors to the Hall. Usually she and Edna sat on the top deck of the bus, smoking and chattering, but nobody had seen much of Edna recently. Nora would be on her own with Julia, whom she'd never liked much but whom she now didn't like *at all*.

Rosa's spirits sank day by day. She couldn't see the point of anything, and being in close proximity to Julia nearly drove her mad. Fortunately she overheard Julia asking Malc's permission to take the few days' leave that were owed to her.

'I hope she never comes back!' said Nora, when word got round of Julia's travel plans.

'It'll be such a relief when she's gone,' Maggie said with a grin.

'Hopefully it'll cheer Rosa up,' Nora added.

'Maybe,' Maggie said with a shrug. 'Nothing much does these days.'

Pleased at the thought of Julia's imminent departure, Rosa's spirits were mildly lifted, but the sight of Roger's letters in her pigeon-hole sent them plummeting again. She'd never told her fiancé about her foiled plan to find Gabriel; if the truth were told, she'd barely given him a thought in weeks.

'I should write,' Rosa thought guiltily, as she put Roger's letter in her pocket; and she would . . . but just not right now.

23. Edna and Flora

Edna phoned Penrith Hospital every morning to inquire into her daughter's health. Though she begged to speak to Flora, the Ward Sister refused; until her patient was strong enough to get out of bed, she wouldn't be allowed to use the phone. Then one wonderful day Flora phoned Edna.

'Mum! Oh, Mum!' she sobbed when she heard her mother's voice.

Edna burst into tears and sobbed too.

'Sweetheart!' she exclaimed. 'How are you?'

After several emotional minutes they both calmed down and Flora was able to tell Edna that she was feeling much better and was ready to be discharged.

'We'll come and fetch you,' Edna instantly promised.

When their animated phone call was brought to a close, Edna, breathless with excitement, threw her arms around Malc. 'My little girl's coming home!' she cried.

'I'll go and get Featherstone's permission to pick up Flora, whilst *you*,' he said excitedly, 'you'd best sort out the little lasses.'

Edna popped the girls into her old blue van and roared over the moors, now loud with the call of skylarks in their springtime glory, rising high above the heather trilling their song. Screeching to a halt outside the cowshed, Edna was relieved to find Nora, who was struggling into her muddy wellies.

'Thank God you're home!' Edna called out.

Marilyn and Katherine threw themselves on Nora, who gave them both a hug.

'Can you do me a favour, lovie?' Edna asked. 'Could you have the girls whilst me and Malc do an errand?' Not wanting to alert her granddaughters, she gave Nora a meaningful wink.

'Of course!' kind-hearted Nora retorted. 'I don't start work till later, and Maggie's around too – we'd love to look after these two little monkeys!'

After waving goodbye to Edna, smiling Nora turned to Marilyn and Katherine. 'I know somebody who's waiting for their breakfast,' she said, as she picked up a bucket of pigswill.

'UGH! That's not breakfast!' Katherine giggled. 'It stinks!'

'Polly thinks it's delicious,' Nora laughed. 'Follow me, ladies,' she said and led her helpers to the allotment. Polly greeted them with rapturous grunts before she buried her head in the overflowing bucket!

Edna could barely sit still as they made slow but steady progress to Penrith in Malc's car.

'I can't wait to see her,' she said impatiently.

Remembering the state Flora was in the last time he saw her, Malc felt it was necessary to warn his wife beforehand. 'She might not look like her normal self.'

'She's bound to have her arm in a sling,' Edna said. 'Maybe even a plaster cast.' She gave him a suspicious look. 'Is there something else I should know?'

'She had quite a few bruises about the face,' Malc told her reluctantly.

Edna clenched her fists. 'What happens to men like him?'

'War happens,' Malc said grimly.

'But most fellas don't go knocking their kids and wives about,' Edna pointed out.

Malc gave a wry grin. 'Next time he arrives home, he'll find nobody to knock about,' he said with undisguised satisfaction.

'Do you think he might try to trace them?' Edna fretted.

'He might,' Malc replied. 'Though going by the last time I saw him, when he could barely stand upright, I'd say he was in no state to trace a cat! The army might try and get in touch with Flora on his behalf at some point, but let's worry about that when it happens.'

Edna was glad of Malc's timely warning. It wasn't the sling or the plaster cast that shocked her; it was Flora's pale, bruised, emaciated face that broke her heart. Sitting on her hospital bed, Flora, wearing an oversized hospital nightie, looked like a bag of bones. Mother and daughter clung to each other; then after the nurse had closed the curtains surrounding Flora's bed, Edna helped her weak and rather breathless daughter to dress in the clothes Edna had brought with her from Pendleton.

Anxious that Flora shouldn't know how upset she

really was, Edna tried to sound light-hearted. 'Eeh, lovie,' she said, as she rolled nylons up her daughter's skinny legs and secured them to her suspender belt. 'We'll have to fatten you up when we get you home.'

Flora gave a little chuckle. 'I'm going to the right place for putting on weight – a chip shop! I'll be the size of a house in no time.'

After packing the few things she possessed into a paper bag, Flora said a warm goodbye to the staff who'd taken good care of her; then, supported by Malc and Edna, one on either side of her, she slowly made her way to Malc's car. Once she was settled, Flora shocked them both by making an announcement.

'I need to go home.'

Edna caught her breath as she looked at Malc. 'Is that a good idea, lovie?' she asked nervously.

Flora replied firmly, 'Yes, Mum – I have to.'

The house was cold and damp, the smashed kitchen window was boarded up, and broken furniture lay strewn about the downstairs rooms.

'God in heaven!' Edna said, as she took in the desolation left behind by a violent man who had lost all control.

Flora picked up the pieces of a picture frame. 'This is me and John on our wedding day,' she said and showed it to her mother, who'd never met her husband. 'We were both twenty-one and so happy.' Tears seeped out of the corner of Flora's eyes. 'He was the perfect gent, kind and gentle; he adored our girls.'

Seeing Flora's resolve starting to crumble, Malc said

briskly, 'Let's find a case for your things, sweetheart, and be on our way.'

Edna quickly emulated Malc's manner. 'Best be sharp – the little lasses will be expecting you.'

With the two of them helping her, Flora packed clothes for herself and her daughters; then, with a last look at her ruined home, she locked the front door and, trembling with emotion, she walked down the path, clutching her mother's firm hand.

It didn't take them long to drive back, but when they arrived at the cowshed they found it empty and a note was pinned to the front door. *We're down the lane at the allotment – come and meet us.*

The sound of happy childish laughter led Edna, Flora and Malc to the allotment, where Flora laughed for the first time in weeks at the sight of her daughters sitting on top of a wonky fence.

'MARILYN! KATHERINE!' she cried, as she hurried towards her girls.

'MUMMY! MUMMY!' they exclaimed and jumped off the fence and hugged her.

Though thrilled to see their mother, the little girls were keen to introduce her to Polly.

'Can we have a pig bucket at home, Nana?' Marilyn asked.

Edna tried not to grimace when she caught sight of the potato peelings and cabbage leaves strewn all over Polly's pen. 'We'll see, sweetheart,' she told the girls, who were covered in straw and smelt of pig muck.

'We've had a lovely time,' said Nora, who also smelt a bit whiffy. 'They'll need a bath when they get home,' she added with a grin.

'You can say that again – phew, what a pong!' Malc chuckled.

Maggie, who'd been weeding her vegetables at the other end of the allotment, came up to say hello. 'I never thought growing veg would be such hard work,' she admitted.

'It'll be worth it,' Edna assured her. 'You'll be pleased with yourself when you serve up fresh meat and veg at your wedding breakfast.'

'I'm sure I will,' Maggie agreed.

Flora's eyes strayed from Maggie to Polly. 'OH!' she gasped as the penny dropped.

'Say no more,' Maggie said hastily, as she nodded in the direction of the little girls.

It took quite a bit of persuading to get Marilyn and Katherine away from Polly, but the thought of Nana's chip-and-fritters supper eventually tempted them back home. They immediately found a bucket in the back-yard and stuck on a label: POLLY'S BREAKFAST.

'They'd best not put any good stuff in yon bucket!' Malc joked.

'Only the best for Polly the pig!' Edna laughed.

'Not to worry – in a couple of months' time Polly will be bacon rashers,' Malc added in a dramatic whisper.

'The girls will be heart-broken,' Flora said, as she and Edna set the kitchen table with plates and cutlery. 'They'll never eat a sausage again!'

'Neither will Nora for that matter,' Edna remarked knowingly. 'That girl is besotted!'

With Julia gone, albeit for a short time, Rosa began to breathe more easily. Guilty about her lack of contact with Roger, and specifically about not having shared her recent experiences with him, she sought advice from Kit, who had just finished her shift and was making her way over to the Phoenix nursery to pick up her son, Billy. Falling into step beside her, Rosa confessed her fears.

'I'm feeling a bit worried about Roger,' Rosa started. 'I just haven't been in the mood to write to him recently, and, if I'm honest, I don't feel quite the same glow of excitement when I think of him these days either.'

Heavily pregnant Kit slowed her pace. 'Love changes,' she said wisely. 'I used to be so much in love with Ian I could barely breathe when I was near him. You mustn't forget you've had a terrible upset recently,' she reminded Rosa. 'What did Roger have to say about all that?'

Rosa blushed and shook her head. 'I haven't told him,' she admitted.

'I think you probably should – he'd want to know,' Kit said firmly.

'I agree, but I'm just too embarrassed to tell him what happened,' Rosa blurted out. 'It was such a pathetic failure.'

Kit raised her dark eyebrows. 'He's bound to ask why you haven't been in touch,' she remarked.

'I could just say I've been working long shifts and I'm exhausted,' Rosa prevaricated.

Kit gave her a baleful look. 'It's really not fair on the lad,' she said quietly.

Rosa blushed. 'I know . . . I know . . .' she sighed guiltily.

Their earnest conversation ceased when they saw the nursery children in the playground; they were holding hands and dancing in a ring, singing, 'Here We Go Round the Mulberry Bush'.

'Look at Billy,' Rosa exclaimed. 'Such a big boy now.'

Kit smiled proudly at her striking son, who had the same silky black hair and deep dark eyes as her. 'He'll soon be big brother to a new baby,' she said excitedly.

'Lucky baby to be born into such a happy family,' Rosa said with a catch in her voice.

That evening Rosa took Kit's sound advice: she forced herself to sit down and write to Roger for the first time in weeks. She talked about the cold weather, her long shifts, overtime and then, as she thought of him on his base way out in the middle of nowhere, her heart constricted. 'Poor chap, facing enemy fire on a regular basis and having a useless girlfriend like me!'

She would make it up to him, she vowed, and signed off with love and kisses – it was the very least she could do.

On her first night at her mother's house in Pendleton, Flora lay in bed beside her two girls; with both fast asleep on either side of her, she felt safe for the first time in months. Though she worried about her husband and what would happen to him, she knew she couldn't put her daughters at risk any more; it was her duty to protect them from harm, and if that meant keeping them apart from their father, then so be it. Murmuring a prayer of thanksgiving, she closed her eyes and drifted into a deep peaceful sleep, which mercifully wasn't marred by a single nightmare.

Downstairs by the crackling fire, Malc and Edna sat smoking in contented silence. It was Malc who broke it by asking, 'Happy?'

'Oh, yes,' Edna said on a long sigh. Close to tears, she added, 'I can't bear to think what the poor kid's been through.'

Malc chuckled. 'She's got a lioness for a mother – now she's here nobody would dare to touch her with you and your trusty rolling pin around.'

'I wouldn't hesitate to use it on anybody who hurt me or mine,' Edna responded passionately.

Malc smiled as he recalled the look of fury on Edna's face when she had flourished the rolling pin at him.

'I don't doubt it, my sweetheart,' he replied. 'Not for a minute!'

24. Home

Julia leant eagerly forwards as the train puffed and wheezed its way into Euston Station. God! She felt like she'd left London a lifetime ago. Almost the first off the train, she virtually ran down the platform – eager to be back in the city that was home.

'Ridiculous, to be so happy,' Julia scolded herself as she manoeuvred a circuitous path around piles of rubble which children (with no better place to play) were picking their way through. 'You've lived here all your life – what's the fuss about? London's even more bomb damaged now than when you left it.'

But it was impossible to wipe the smile off her face. Julia walked through familiar streets and spotted old haunts, pubs and cafés where she'd spent time with friends before she was exiled to the North. Happy to be in the open air, she walked all the way home to Knightsbridge, where the spring sunshine lit on daffodils and crocuses in the parks surrounding the V&A and the Natural History Museum.

When she arrived home, the house appeared to be empty. Dropping her case in the wide hallway, Julia glanced up at the family portraits that hung along the walls.

'Hello,' she called, wondering where everyone was. 'I'm back!'

Savouring the combined smells of beeswax, fresh flowers and something baking in the back kitchen, Julia wandered from room to room, with a contented smile on her face. The dining room, with gleaming china, crystal and silver laid out on the long, highly polished mahogany table. The luxuriously comfortable drawing room, with a thick cream Indian rug set on old parquet tiles that shone with years of polishing, and delicately coloured sofas and chairs banked with pretty silk cushions. Julia's favourite painting in the house hung over the elaborate white marble fireplace: an oil painting of her mother before she 'came out' in society. Staring up at it, Julia realized with a shock how like her mother she now was; they had always shared the deep-gold blonde hair and penetrating green eyes, but she hadn't realized until now that she also had her mother's fine straight nose and full lips.

'It's as if I'm seeing everything for the first time,' Julia thought, as she bent to inhale the fragrant spring flowers placed in a large crystal bowl on the grand piano that only Hugo played.

'Home . . .' she sighed.

Her mind flew back to the home she'd just left: the cowshed with its rusty old wood-burning stove, battered utility furniture, threadbare curtains and rag carpets. The arctic-cold bedrooms and stark kitchen with rickety spindle chairs and scrubbed wooden table; the contrast was so great it made Julia shiver. She thought of Maggie and Nora getting up early every morning to tend their veg and feed their pig just so Maggie would be able to provide a meal of sorts on her wedding day. Julia shook her head – she'd come home for a rest, time away from the place where she'd been so unhappy with a group of women who had actively disliked her. She was here to recharge her batteries before her return North – the last thing she wanted was to think about the Phoenix factory whilst she was on holiday!

In her own large south-facing room that overlooked the gardens surrounding the Natural History Museum, Julia decided to run a deep, hot bath in the bathroom adjacent to her dressing room. Wallowing shortly after in the perfumed bubbles, her eyes strayed to the glass shelves on which stood her favourite (and rather expensive) perfumes, creams and fragrant oils. She couldn't help but recall how she'd dreaded bath nights in the cowshed: taking it in turns to bathe held little attraction, especially when you were last in the line and the water was stone cold. After drying herself on soft white towels warming on the heated towel rail, Julia slipped into her silk dressing gown and sat at her dressing table. Staring into the large mirror, she critically examined herself: her shoulder-length, silky blonde hair had lost its healthy glow and needed a damn good cut and set.

How was she going to fit everything into the few precious days she had at home? Hugo was her priority – she missed him terribly – but more to the point she urgently needed to pick his brains about Rosa's missing brother. If anybody knew about secret underground activities, it was her brother, no matter how much he denied it.

She was longing to catch up with her oldest friends, Rita and Mildred, too, and spend time with her parents, though it was unlikely that her father would be at home, especially now that the third battle of Monte Cassino was under way. Julia knew the days would whizz by and in no time she'd be back in the filling shed handling filthy stinking gunpowder twelve hours a day. Looking at her shredded nails and stained fingers, Julia groaned: it would take more than an expensive manicure to set them to rights.

Finding a recent copy of *Vogue* on her bedside table, Julia lay back against her plump pillows covered in cool silky peach satin and flicked through the magazine, which featured a spring wedding supplement. Julia smiled to herself as she admired one gorgeous gown after another; poor Maggie would weep if she were to see these wonderful and very expensive designs; Nora would just gawp and mutter under her breath, 'They're all too posh for me!'

'There I go again,' Julia thought crossly. 'Thinking about the very women I couldn't get away from fast enough.'

But there was a touch of pathos when she thought of Maggie and Nora. They were so poor and so bloody selfless, one just couldn't help but be impressed by their tough spirit, even if she had to be two hundred miles away to appreciate it.

Tired after her bath, Julia dozed off, and when she awoke it was to the sight of her mother laying a tea tray on the dressing table.

'Welcome home, darling,' she said softly.

'Hello, Mummy,' Julia answered with a happy smile, leaping up to give her a hug. 'It's lovely to be back.'

'We've missed you,' Mrs Thorpe replied, squeezing her daughter hard and breathing in the smell of her.

Julia stepped back to get a better look at her mother in her Red Cross uniform. 'I've been working for the Red Cross too,' she told her.

'I'm surprised you have the time,' her mother said, as she poured Ceylon tea into pale china cups, one of which she handed to her sleepy daughter.

Julia eagerly accepted the tea, which she sipped; then she grimaced. 'Ugh, so weak!' she exclaimed.

'Ceylon's always been your favourite,' her mother reminded her.

Remembering the pint-pot mugs of strong black tea that she drank, especially on the night shift in order to keep herself awake, Julia replied, 'I'm used to a stronger brew these days.'

After they'd finished their tea, Mrs Thorpe left her daughter to make arrangements for the evening. First Julia rang Hugo, who (in the brisk business voice he used in the office) said he'd meet her at the Ritz the following evening; and then she rang Mildred and Rita, whom she arranged to meet for dinner that night. Realizing she'd better get a move on, Julia hurried into her dressing room and rummaged through her vast wardrobe.

'Goodness!' she said out loud. 'I'd forgotten just how many clothes I have.'

In Pendleton she really wore only three sets of

clothes: nightwear, work overalls and day clothes – usually a thick jumper and a tweed skirt. But here she was faced with silk and satin cocktail dresses, pretty crêpe tea dresses, cashmere twin sets, fashionably flared short skirts, even a white fox-fur coat. Savouring the luxury, eventually Julia chose a skimpy sage-green pleated silk dress, high-heeled black suede shoes and new nylons, which she gently pulled on, marvelling at their delicate flimsiness.

'What a treat,' she murmured, as she clasped them to her suspender belt. 'They wouldn't last five minutes in the Phoenix.'

She was careful with her make-up, using rouge to colour her pale cheeks and mascara to emphasize her long lashes. There wasn't much she could do about her hair until she made an appointment at the hairdresser's; cursing the chemicals she worked with, Julia left it long and loose and hoped nobody would notice how dull and lank it looked these days.

When Julia met her old chums at their favourite Italian restaurant in Dean Street, Mildred and Rita were agog to hear her news.

'Quite honestly there's little to tell,' Julia said with a shrug. 'As the saying goes, "It's grim up North!"' she laughed. 'Come on, tell me all about the Ministry of Defence.'

'Well, it's pretty boring typing and answering the phone all day,' Mildred started.

'Though it does have its perks,' Rita teased her friend. 'Mildred's getting married!' she announced.

'You dark horse!' Julia cried. 'Who's the lucky chap?'

Cheeky Rita answered for her blushing friend. 'Horace, one of the bosses, clever ex-RAF pilot with a terrific moustache!'

'Rita's got a chap too,' Mildred giggled like a naughty schoolgirl. 'A handsome GI called Brad!'

'So you're the only single one now,' Rita joked. 'Any chance of finding a chap up North?'

Julia's eyes all but fell out of her head. 'A man?' she cried. 'I work with hundreds of women and live with only women – everywhere I go it's just women, apart from the manager and the supervisors.' She shook her head at the thought of finding a boyfriend in Pendleton. 'It's another world, believe me.'

Over plates of delicious ravioli and a bottle of Chianti, Mildred discussed her wedding plans.

'What kind of wedding dress are you planning to wear?' Julia asked. 'Or will you just wear a smart suit like so many brides do these days?'

'Oh, no! The dress is already made,' Mildred told her.

Rita, who seemed even more excited than the bride about the wedding dress, added, 'White silk and lace with a train the length of Westminster Abbey!' Rita rolled her eyes as she continued, 'Selfless sort that she is, Mildred's already offering her dress to other less fortunate brides-to-be – after she's worn it herself, of course.'

Mildred blushed prettily. 'I really don't care – just so long as I get to wear it first,' she laughed. 'What with rationing getting harder than ever, it seemed the right thing to do, sharing what I'm lucky enough to own amongst friends.'

Julia's eyes flicked over Mildred's tall, muscular body that was not unlike Maggie's slim one.

'Don't think I'd be quite so selfless if it were mine!' Rita joked.

Before Julia could stop herself, she heard herself saying, 'I know this is a bit pushy, but would you consider lending it to a friend of mine?'

'Of course – when's the date?'

'Um, I need to check, but I think it's in early May,' Julia replied.

'Well, that'll be fine, as my wedding is next month, so I can post it on to you if you leave me your address, darling,' Mildred promised.

'You know munitions factories have top-secret addresses which are not for common exchange?' Julia said, as she rolled her eyes dramatically.

'Pigeon-post won't handle it,' Mildred joked. 'Way too heavy.'

'I'll give you the address of my digs, but don't be shocked when I tell you the first line of the address is "The Cowshed"!' Julia laughed.

'God!' cried Rita. 'I've heard that digs can be bad but not that bad.'

'Four of us live there, including the girl who's getting married,' Julia explained. 'I can't tell you what this will mean to her,' she breathed gratefully, feeling a warm glow at the thought of Maggie's face when she saw the dress. 'Maybe,' she thought wistfully, 'they'll all resent me less after this, realize that I'm a good person, and have feelings too.'

As the waiter refilled their glasses with heady red Chianti, Julia could hardly believe the dream scenario she'd just organized for Maggie.

'I must be going soft in the head.'

Her confused thoughts were interrupted by Mildred, who leant across the table to take hold of Julia's hand. 'The wedding's early April – you will come, won't you, Jay?'

'I'd love to,' Julia answered. 'But coming home this weekend has used up all my leave, so it's highly unlikely I'll get more time off,' she said apologetically. 'I'm so sorry – if I'd known I would have saved it up for you, of course.' Seeing Mildred's disappointed reaction, Julia squeezed her hand, noticing a very big, glittering diamond ring for the first time. 'You'll make a ravishing bride, darling. I only hope your fiancé is worthy of a gem of a girl like you.'

After real coffee and Italian brandy, the girls decided to make a run for it.

'We don't want to get caught by the damn siren,' Rita urged. 'I'm so sick of sleeping in the Underground; a night in my own bed would be bliss.'

After giving her address to Mildred and promising to pay the postage for the wedding dress, Julia kissed her friends goodbye, wondering sadly when she would next get a chance to see them. And then she hailed a taxi home, where she immediately snuggled down in her luxuriously comfortable bed. Laying her head on the pillows, she closed her eyes and promptly fell fast asleep for a straight twelve hours.

It was lovely to wake up in her own bed the next morning, with the sun slanting through the pretty curtains. Left to her own devices, Julia would have slept on, but a gentle knock on the door and her mother's voice announcing breakfast made her realize she was starving.

Slipping into her dressing gown, she joined her mother in the dining room, where there were boiled eggs, fresh from the housekeeper's hens, homemade marmalade, warm toast and, best of all, real coffee.

'I bought it on the black market when I knew you were coming home,' her mother admitted guiltily. 'I just couldn't resist it, even though it cost a fortune.'

'This is illegal luxury indeed,' Julia joked as she poured herself a second cup of strong black coffee.

She and her mother swapped notes on their work for the Red Cross, then Julia brought the topic of conversation round to her brother, which was what she really wanted to talk about. 'How is he?' she asked eagerly.

Her mother looked askance. 'You mean how does he compensate for not flying RAF bombers?'

Julia nodded. 'Poor chap – he just adored it.'

'He was lucky – we were lucky – he could have been killed outright.'

'I know, I agree, but I bet he doesn't think that,' Julia retorted. 'Working in the Ministry of Information is never going to be enough for a bomber pilot like Hugo. He'll want to be more involved.'

'He's doing wonderful things,' her mother insisted.

Julia adopted a melodramatic voice as she said, 'What, tracking spies, inventing cyphers, parachuting into France?'

Her mother rolled her eyes at her teasing daughter. 'You and your imagination,' she joked.

Smearing tangy marmalade on her toast, Julia said, 'It must be a lot more thrilling than building bombs.'

Her mother regarded her complicated daughter, who looked wan and pale but had so far voiced no overt complaints about her war work.

'Is it awful, darling?' she asked softly.

'The work's grim but that wouldn't be so bad if everything else wasn't even grimmer,' Julia admitted. 'But the war can't go on forever,' she added with the forced cheerfulness that everybody adopted these days. 'I'll be back in no time – that's what I keep telling myself. What does Daddy say?'

'Not much,' her mother replied with a wry smile.

'Tight-lipped as ever,' Julia retorted knowingly. 'Like father like son!' she added with a laugh. 'Though I am hoping Hugo might be able to furnish me with a little more information tonight. He must know more than we do.'

'Really, is that wise, dear?' Mrs Thorpe said with raised eyebrows.

'Well, the thing is, it's quite specific what I want to ask him. Somebody I share lodgings with is trying to trace her brother, who escaped from a concentration camp. But she's going the wrong way about it, so I feel I should try to help,' Julia told her gravely.

'Let's hope there is a right way. It can't be easy finding someone in those circumstances,' her mother remarked, hoping her daughter wasn't being unrealistic about being able to help.

'It's not like I can ask a host of people for advice on such a delicate matter,' Julia declared. 'Hugo really is the only person I know whom I can ask — he must have some ideas,' she insisted.

'If he's a chip off the old block, he'll reveal nothing,' Mrs Thorpe warned.

The day sped by and before she knew it Julia was on her way to meet Hugo at the Ritz. Wearing a military-style navy-blue hat and a red woollen coat with a swing back and deep pockets and cuffs, Julia felt a rush of excitement. How nice it was to be heading out on a lovely spring evening with the birds singing from lamp-posts and chimney tops, even though their hopeful duets were starkly at odds with the bombed streets and piles of filthy rubble she deftly circumnavigated.

The Ritz exterior was stacked high with sandbags and its revolving doors had been painted a blackout navy-blue. Catchy band music played as waiters in tails scurried back and forth bearing silver trays. As a smiling waiter relieved her of her coat, Julia glanced from right to left and caught sight of Hugo waving at her.

'Jay!' he said, as he stood to embrace his sister. 'You look very nice indeed,' he said, as he admired her short black silk pleated skirt and cream crêpe blouse. 'Very French!'

Julia did a little twirl before she sat down and gratefully accepted the pink gin he'd ordered for her. 'Delicious!' she exclaimed as she took her first sip.

'Mmmmm . . .' She sighed as she studied the menu greedily. '*Consommé frappé*, salmon in white wine sauce followed by ices and coffee, five shillings for three courses, that'll do me!'

Hugo swiftly ordered and they eagerly got started on catching up with each other's news. They talked non-stop all the way through the first and second courses, with Julia as usual asking inquisitive questions that Hugo parried with good humour. It turned out Hugo was able to share with her the fact that he was the officer in charge of the Filter Room, part of the RAF's Fighter Command, and working with mostly female staff and WAAFs at the very nerve centre of the British radar system.

'Gosh!' gasped Julia, who was thrilled to hear all that Hugo's teams were involved in, which included giving warnings for air-raid sirens to be sounded in threatened areas; scrambling fighter squadrons; intercepting incoming hostile planes; and monitoring returning bomber aircraft in difficulty.

'It really is a top-secret job,' she said in awe.

But, as hard as she pushed, Hugo had no intention of sharing any further details with his very persistent little sister.

Julia took a deep drink from her glass of hock, then

shocked her brother by asking a very direct question. 'Hugo, I need to ask you something. How would you trace a Jew who was on the run, trying to find a safe house somewhere in France?'

'Why do you ask?' Hugo asked smoothly as he sipped wine from a crystal goblet.

Julia continued calmly, her voice low. 'A friend of mine, well, she's not really a friend, in fact, she rather hates me; but it's her brother. All she's been able to find out about him is that he escaped from the concentration camp where he was held and she's obviously desperate to find more news of him. I thought you might have some idea of where to start,' she finished, looking up at him hopefully.

Hugo lit up his pipe and nodded for her to continue.

'From what I can gather, she thinks he was initially assisted by underground workers but he dodged them and went solo. Why would he do that?' she asked her brother.

'Fear of compromising them, maybe?'

Deciding it was time to come fully clean, Julia spread her hands on the table and told Hugo the rest: how she'd wilfully foiled Rosa's plan to try to find her brother.

'It may have put you in an awkward position but you did the right thing, sis,' he said when she'd finished. 'What your friend was planning was nothing but sheer madness.'

For the first time in weeks Julia felt some of the guilt

slip away from her. 'I believe I did do the right thing,' she replied. 'But my God have I paid the price for it.'

Hugo looked at her, hearing the pain in her voice. 'So that's why you're still chasing it?' Hugo inquired softly. 'You want to do something to make up for what your friend sees as a betrayal? Even though it wasn't at all!'

Julia cocked her head as she considered his question. 'I suppose so, but it's not just that. It's also because she's so sad and wretched,' she admitted. 'I don't care how she feels about me, but I am sorry I've taken away her hope.'

'So what do you think I can do?' Hugo asked.

'Well, you must have some idea about how someone like that might be traced? Don't tell me you don't have contacts working in the British underground.'

Hugo's face remained impassive. 'Do you have any specific details?' he asked.

Julia shook her head. 'No, nothing, well, apart from this.' She handed Hugo the small black-and-white photograph she'd found in Rosa's bedroom. 'It's a photo of her brother; his name is Gabriel Falco. It looks like they were both held in a concentration camp after they'd been captured by the Nazis in Italy. I know that she got out and he obviously did later. I thought these' – she pointed to the string of letters and numbers – 'might be code names for the undercover workers who helped Rosa escape, though I don't know, it's probably a long shot.'

Hugo stared at the scuffed photo. 'I don't know how you think I can help, sis,' he added, as he caught the waiter's attention.

'Please, Hugo!' she pleaded. 'Can't you just see if any of your colleagues might have ideas, even if you don't?'

As the waiter approached, Hugo appeared determined to change the subject, though she noticed that he kept the photograph she had given him. 'Dessert?' he inquired as if the conversation had never happened.

Instinctively knowing that Hugo would do what he could, she stopped asking questions and rose to her feet.

'No, thanks. Now come on,' she laughed. 'Dance with me!'

25. A Cold Reception

Rosa hadn't expected a letter from Roger to arrive at the Phoenix quite so quickly. She was on afternoon shifts, which meant she'd finish late and then it would be the usual trudge up the lane and bed. She sighed as she rolled one of her strong cheroot cigarettes; it seemed like there was nothing to her life but work, bed, eat and sleep. What had happened to that young girl with long dark hair and wide excited eyes? The other Rosa who'd walked mountains, painted portraits, skied in the Dolomites and lived at peace with her family?

'War happened,' she muttered as she inhaled deeply on her cigarette. 'War and death and loss and separation,' she added bitterly.

Rosa's heart lurched when she saw a letter in her pigeon-hole, nervously opening it to read in a quiet corridor rather than in the noisy canteen, where her friends would be having a last-minute mug of tea and a hasty cigarette before the hooter went.

My Darling,

I was so happy and so relieved to receive your letter – you have NO idea how anxious I've been. I must confess the prolonged

silence from you really troubled me. I even thought you might
have forgotten all about me.

A guilty blush spread across Rosa's cheeks; in truth she hadn't been thinking much about her fiancé in the last few weeks. But she was pleased to hear he was well, though after writing excitedly about his squadron's successful bombing raids, his letter took a quite unexpected turn that sent her pulse racing.

Rosa, dearest, I desperately want to introduce you to my
parents, who were thrilled (and a little surprised) to hear of our
engagement. They are eager to meet their future daughter-in-
law. Is there any way you could get leave to visit them with me
in the near future? I would be so proud to show you off, and I
know that they will love you! Ours is a big old house, full of
dogs, and it's cold so bring your woollies!

After Rosa had finished the letter, she stared at it feeling a little numb. She felt like she'd only just reconnected with Roger – was she ready to meet his family so soon? She supposed if they were marrying it was the natural next step; she just hadn't pictured herself meeting his family just yet. She felt nervous at the idea, but maybe it was a good one – she needed to know all about the man she was going to marry and this seemed like the right place to start. Rosa quickly folded the letter and shoved it into her pocket; she hadn't time to think about Roger's suggestion now, not if she was to start her shift on time.

Rosa's preoccupied mood didn't lighten when she heard later in the canteen that Julia was due back at the Phoenix shortly.

'It will be nice to have her company in the filling shed again,' Kit said cheerfully, as they queued up for shepherd's pie and boiled leeks.

'I can't say the same myself,' Rosa muttered crossly. 'I've enjoyed not having Julia around; the atmosphere in the cowshed is so much better without her.' She gave a loud groan. 'The thought of having to put up with Julia again makes me feel quite sick.'

And at least in part on that basis Rosa made a snap decision: pushing aside her stodgy meal, which she'd barely touched, she decided she'd write to Roger before she went to bed, telling him that she'd be happy to go to Wiltshire with him as soon as they could both arrange leave, and was very much looking forward to meeting his parents.

Julia returned to a frosty reception in the cowshed, which was no more than she expected. Amongst the clothes she unpacked was the wedding issue of *Vogue* that had caught her fancy on her home visit and a photograph of Mildred's lovely wedding gown and veil. Knowing that now was not the right moment to reveal such treasures, Julia slipped them into her chest of drawers along with the extra woollies and thick socks that she'd had the foresight to bring back with her.

'There's tea in the pot and the last of a tin of corned

beef,' Maggie called from the sitting room in a 'take it or leave it' voice.

Seeing Rosa with Maggie and Nora, who were sitting by the wood-burner smoking and drinking tea, Julia confined herself to the cold kitchen, where she made a corned-beef sandwich with two slices of dry white bread, which she hungrily ate with the strong black tea topped up with sterilized milk. Still hungry, but knowing there was nothing else left to eat, Julia slumped into her cold single bed, where she clamped her teeth tightly together to stop herself from shivering. With her feet pressed up against the scalding, heavy stone hot-water bottle, Julia muttered miserably under her bare bedding, 'You're back on the bomb line – damn well deal with it.'

Walking down the cobbled lane to clock on for her shift the following morning, Julia (self-consciously tagging slightly behind Rosa, Maggie and Nora) noticed green shoots sprouting up in Maggie's allotment. She also saw and heard Polly the pig, rounder and fatter than ever, and squealing ecstatically at the sight of her friends. Nora as usual hurried over to chat to the pig and tickle her long pink ears before running to catch up with Maggie.

'How are the wedding plans progressing?' Julia inquired when she and Kit were sitting side by side at their bench in the filling shed.

Kit gave her a long, inquiring look. 'You could ask Maggie yourself,' she said pointedly.

Julia gave a shrug. 'I think we both know that Maggie wouldn't be too keen to chat through her wedding plans with me,' she answered bluntly.

Kit paused to pick up gunpowder from the tray in front of her, and, as she rolled and smoothed the powder with her small, blackened fingertips, she said, 'With not many weeks to go to the big day I'd say it's going less than well.'

Julia looked up, surprised. 'From what I saw on the allotment this morning, Maggie's vegetables are doing well, and that pig of hers is fatter than ever.'

'But the wedding dress hasn't worked out,' Kit said. 'Maggie was borrowing one from the tall, dark-haired girl in the dispatch room, but it got ruined by moths, and poor Maggie's distraught,' Kit said with a sad sigh. 'I feel sorry for the lass; after all her grand talk it looks like she'll be wearing her best Sunday suit on her wedding day.'

Julia's thoughts flew to Mildred's white silk-and-lace dress, which was presently doing the rounds in London. She hadn't planned to say anything just yet, but maybe here was her chance.

'I do know somebody who might lend her a dress,' she said cautiously.

Kit looked up from the file she was filling. 'Really? But would it fit?'

Julia nodded. 'My friend's roughly the same size and height as Maggie, maybe an inch taller, and she's big busted like Maggie too.'

'That's wonderful!' Kit exclaimed. 'Why don't you suggest it, then?'

Julia blushed. 'I don't think Maggie would welcome charity from a "toff" like me,' she answered.

Kit, who'd heard Nora and Maggie calling Julia a 'toff' and a 'snob' more times than she could count, nodded sympathetically. 'I could mention it, if you like?' she suggested.

Julia's green eyes lit up with relief. 'I think that's a very good idea.'

A few days later, as they were setting the kitchen table for their tea, and Rosa was taking a bath, Maggie, who'd been edgy since she got in from work, surprised Julia by asking in a tight, embarrassed voice, 'How was the filling shed today?'

Julia stared at her incredulously; if Maggie had informed her that she'd just circled the moon she couldn't have been more flabbergasted. However, keeping her voice low, Julia managed a civil reply. 'Oh, you know, same as ever.'

Maggie shuffled uncomfortably, then cast a nervous glance at Nora, who pulled a funny face. 'Er . . .' Maggie stammered.

Seeing that Maggie was having difficulty in getting to the point, Nora stepped in. 'She's got something to ask you,' she said bluntly.

Julia knew what was coming but she waited, giving Maggie time to gather her wits, which she did when she finally asked the question all in one breath. 'Kit tells me you know somebody who might lend me her wedding dress? Is it true?'

Continuing to lay the cutlery on the table, Julia

couldn't bring herself to look up, scarred as she was by weeks of rejection and hostility. 'Yes, I do,' was all she managed to say quietly in reply.

Unable to control her curiosity, Maggie, flushed with excitement, pulled out a wooden chair and sat down. 'I can't believe it!' she gasped. 'I never imagined you'd do something like this for me, not after . . .' Her voice trailed away as she avoided saying, 'Not after how rude we've been to you.'

An awkward pause followed in which Julia, undoubtedly pleased that Maggie had initiated the conversation but still lacking the confidence to respond with enthusiasm, nervously rattled the cutlery she was clutching. Maggie, on the other hand, was flushed and fizzing with enthusiasm. 'Have you seen it? Do you know what it's like?' she eagerly asked.

Julia looked up at last. 'I think I might have a photograph somewhere,' she said, as she quickly laid down the last of the cutlery before moving off to her room. Once there, Julia leant against the closed door and panicked. 'Oh, God!' she breathed. 'Have I done the right thing?'

The dress was very grand – would it be too grand for Maggie's modest wedding? Would she upstage everybody by wearing such an expensive gown? Would they turn on her for being 'posh' and knowing 'the right people' and mock her as they had done in the past?

In the kitchen Nora too was having her doubts. Giving Maggie a sharp look, she muttered disapprovingly, 'I hope you know what you're getting yourself into?' Casting a furtive look at Julia's bedroom door to make sure she couldn't be overheard, Nora whispered, 'Are you sure you want to be indebted to Miss High and Mighty Julia on your wedding day?'

She stopped short when she heard approaching footsteps, and Julia returned holding the black-and-white photograph, which she handed hesitantly to Maggie. In the long pause that followed Julia held her breath. Would her generosity backfire and make her life in the cowshed even tougher?

But she needn't have worried. Maggie gazed in rapt wonder at the photograph of Mildred's wedding dress, and when she eventually managed to tear her big, blue eyes away from it she could only gasp, 'Oh, Julia, it's gorgeous! I can't believe you would do this for me.'

Nora dashed to her friend's side to inspect the photograph. 'My God, it's bloody lovely.'

Both girls turned – stunned – to a nervous Julia, who, feeling a little wobbly, quickly pulled out a chair so she could sit down.

'Do you think your friend would really lend it to me?' Maggie asked in a breathless voice.

'She said she would,' Julia replied calmly. 'I could arrange to get it sent up here – as long as you're sure it's what you want?'

Unable to believe her luck, Maggie literally could not speak. Eventually, near to tears, she spluttered, 'All my dreams have come true! How can I ever, ever thank you, Julia?'

The emotional silence that followed was broken by Nora, asking anxiously, 'Do you think it will fit?'

'They're about the same size,' Julia remarked. 'That's what gave me the idea in the first place. But if you need to make some minor adjustments I'm sure Mildred wouldn't mind.'

Before she could even think about what she was doing, Maggie, completely overcome with emotion, threw herself into Julia's arms and wept tears of gratitude on her shoulder. Quite overwhelmed by Maggie's dramatic spontaneity, Julia was lost for words. She hadn't made a mistake – far from it; she'd made a young bride-to-be very happy and seeing her joy filled Julia with sweet relief.

When Rosa walked into the kitchen after having her bath and drying her long, thick hair, which always took a tediously long time, she couldn't believe the scene before her. What on earth was Julia doing clasping a weeping Maggie in her arms?

'What's going on?' she demanded.

Julia instantly dropped hold of radiant Maggie, who told Rosa her good news. 'Julia's borrowed a beautiful wedding dress for me!'

Rosa simply couldn't take it in; in the time she'd been in the bathroom Maggie and Julia had become as thick as thieves. Even Nora was smiling – and all because of a wedding dress! Scheming Julia had wrapped the gullible pair around her little finger; they seemed to have forgotten how she'd been betrayed by the very woman they were now talking to like a friend.

'She's going to get it posted up here,' Maggie gabbled on.

Unable to hide her shock at her friends' radically changed behaviour to the housemate they'd all previously agreed to loathe, Rosa turned away and hurried into her bedroom. Standing against the closed door, she realized with some irony that she and Julia had swapped roles: she was the one who'd slunk away, whilst now Julia was the one who stayed.

26. The Package!

Mildred, the good and generous soul that she was, faithfully kept her promise, and after her own wedding she parcelled up her bridal gown and sent it off to the address Julia had left with her. Once Maggie saw the large cardboard box wrapped in brown paper there was no holding her back.

'It's here, it's arrived!' she babbled to her friends, who'd all just clocked off and were bone weary.

Holding the precious parcel close to her chest like it was gold dust, she relished the moment; then, after asking Julia to unwrap the parcel, she tore off all her clothes apart from her bra and knickers. Trembling with awe, she held her breath as Julia slipped the white silk gown over her head, then gasped in delight as it slithered over her body and landed with a soft sensuous *swish* at her feet.

'Oh, my God!' Maggie exclaimed and promptly burst into floods of tears.

'DON'T CRY!' Nora screamed. 'You'll ruin your dress.'

Terrified of staining the pure silk with her salty tears, Maggie gulped hard to stop herself from weeping.

'I've never seen anything like it in my life,' she murmured as she gazed dreamily at herself in the mirror.

Meanwhile Julia was critically inspecting the dress from all angles. 'The length's good,' she announced. 'And it's a perfect fit around the bust and shoulders,' she added as she checked first the front of the bodice and then the back. 'You might need to watch what you eat a bit in the next few weeks, Maggie,' she said firmly. 'It only just fits you on the hips.'

'Are you saying my bum looks big?' Maggie cried.

'Not at all, it's very shapely – Les will love it,' Julia teased.

Nora, who was rummaging in the cardboard box, gave a loud yell, 'Look at the veil!'

Nora reverently lifted the yards of veiling trimmed with Belgian lace, with a wreath of artificial blossom attached, and carefully arranged it over Maggie's thick glossy hair, then stood back to admire the finished look.

'You look like a princess,' she murmured in wonder. 'It could have been made for you – it's just perfect.' Turning round, she called out to Rosa, who was on the other side of the room building up the fire. 'What do you think, Rosa?'

'It's lovely,' Rosa agreed with a warm smile which didn't extend as far as Julia, who was now urging Maggie to take off the dress and hang it up in her wardrobe so all the creases would drop out.

After she'd hung up her dress, Maggie returned to the sitting room, where Nora was pouring strong tea into pint-pot mugs for everybody.

'It's not fair!' Nora protested. 'Maggie will look like

Princess Elizabeth in her posh white frock and I'll look like her sodding secretary in my Sunday best suit!'

Seeing Nora's stricken face, Julia couldn't help but agree with her point of view; Maggie would indeed look breath-taking but really nobody had thought much about Nora, who was after all going to be chief brides-maid at the ceremony. Hurrying into her bedroom she returned with the *Vogue* magazine she'd been keeping for the right moment.

'Take a look at these,' Julia said, handing Nora the magazine.

Total silence followed as both Maggie and Nora pored over the sumptuous magazine from the front page to the back. Eventually Nora gazed up at Julia and asked in complete innocence, 'Do folks really live in a world like that?'

'It's a bit of a fairy-tale world,' Julia agreed. 'But some of the dresses are very nice.'

'NICE?' Nora cried. 'They're blinking smashing! I love this one,' she said and pointed to a dress with tight-fitting sleeves and a fitted bodice from which flared a full skirt.

'We could copy the pattern,' Maggie said eagerly. 'I've seen Mam draw dress patterns on sheets of newspaper.'

'And what would be the point of that if we've got no material to work with?' Nora asked forlornly.

Determined not to give up, Maggie thrummed her fingers on the arm of the sofa. 'We could unpick the pink bridesmaids' dresses that we wore for Kit's wedding and reuse the material?' Maggie suggested as she grabbed the magazine and scrutinized the design of the dress that Nora liked. 'I'm sure we'd have enough material to make that.'

Nora still wasn't convinced. 'You know I'm no good at sewing,' she reminded her friend.

'Mam's a really good sewer,' Maggie insisted. 'She'd help us.'

'I could help with the hand-stitching,' Rosa piped up.

'And I'd do whatever I can to help,' Julia volunteered.

'So we have a plan!' cried Maggie. 'If we all pull together we can create a stylish new dress for Nora!'

Julia briefly caught Rosa's eye and she knew they were both thinking the same thing: for Nora's sake they would co-operate and work together, and for Maggie's sake they would do it well.

27. The Family Visit

With everybody pitching in to make Nora a new dress, there was an unexpected happiness for Julia in working amicably alongside women she had previously avoided; but for Rosa it was different. She would keep to her work, do her best, not upset the apple cart, but, oh, the strain of being polite to Julia – apparently Maggie and Nora's most favourite person in the world – nearly drove Rosa insane. If she heard Nora say one more time, 'What do you think, Julia, should the train be longer or shorter?' or 'What would you do, Julia, have buttons or press-studs on the sleeves?', Rosa really thought she might completely disgrace herself by saying something very rude and inappropriate.

It seemed to a cynical Rosa that Julia's constant flow of bright ideas was a calculated ploy to pull the two gullible girls more tightly into her manipulative web. She certainly wasn't fooled by Julia's charms – quite the opposite – but for all her resentment Rosa kept tight-lipped. There wasn't much to lighten the load these days. British Bomber Command were raging fury in the skies over Germany, but morale was low, people were tired and hungry, and though nobody ever said it there was always the gnawing worrying thought: 'How long can we *really* carry on like this?'

No, Rosa thought, let Nora and Maggie enjoy themselves whilst they could, just so long as they didn't expect her to join 'The Julia Thorpe Appreciation Society'.

The timing for her to leave for Wiltshire was perfect: even though it was barely two days' leave, Rosa was more than glad to pack her bag. In fact, she was so eager her previous nervousness about meeting Roger's family faded away and she began to count the hours to her departure.

However, the train journey down South reawakened Rosa's bitter resentment towards Julia, bringing back memories of her last disastrous trip when she got no further than London in her bid to find her brother because of Julia's damned interference. Just thinking of her humiliating failure brought tears to Rosa's eyes.

'Come on, lass, give us a smile,' said a cheery sailor who was sitting opposite Rosa. 'Want a fag?'

After she'd gratefully accepted a Senior Service cigarette, which the sailor lit up for her, the young man said, 'It gets you like that sometimes, don't it?'

Embarrassed that he'd noticed how upset she was, Rosa nodded.

'I get emotional every time I think of my girlfriend in Doncaster,' the sailor admitted. 'I worry she might run off with some smart alec who dodged conscription,' he confessed with a rueful smile.

Gazing into his honest open face, Rosa said reassuringly, 'I think you're worrying unnecessarily.'

The sailor smiled. 'Glad you think so,' he retorted gratefully.

The noisy arrival of several soldiers entering their compartment brought their conversation to a halt, and Rosa turned her attention to the changing landscape that was opening up to springtime. As the train travelled deeper into the countryside, newly leafed trees waved their boughs in the sunshine, and all along the railway embankments daffodils flashed bright and yellow. As her destination drew closer, Rosa, now in an empty compartment, took out her powder compact and examined her face in the tiny mirror.

'Gosh! I've aged five years,' she thought as she dabbed powder on the dark bags under her eyes.

Make-up improved her looks, as did combing her long, lustrous dark hair and applying red lipstick to her full pouting lips. Feeling more confident, Rosa reached for her suitcase in the overhead netted rack, then with butterflies swirling in her stomach she made her way along the corridor and disembarked. The minute she stepped on to the platform, Roger was at her side. Wrapping her in his strong arms, he drew Rosa close to his chest, where she inhaled the strong smell of soap and pipe tobacco.

'Darling girl!' he cried in delight, as he hugged her and kissed her over and over again. Tilting her smiling face up to his, he murmured tenderly, 'You look wonderful.'

A rush of relief and happiness engulfed Rosa. 'Yes!' she thought, this was the man she had fallen in love with and agreed to marry; warm, open, laughing, strong and reliable Roger. She'd just had too long away from him — that was all.

'It's good to see you,' she said, surprised at how much she really meant it.

'Come along,' he said, as he relieved her of her suitcase and slipped an arm around her slender waist. 'I'm dying to take you home.'

In Roger's old Morgan, which seemed to judder and rattle more than ever, he prepared Rosa for her first meeting with his parents.

'We're a noisy family,' he said with a grin. 'Everybody's got an opinion – even the dogs!'

'How many dogs have you got?' Rosa asked nervously.

'Three at the last count, but if the bitch has whelped there might be more.'

As they roared along the winding narrow lanes, Rosa marvelled at the wild flowers in the hedgerows: wood anemones, celandine, primroses and tiny daffodils jostled for space, colouring the hedges cream and yellow.

'It's so lovely!' she exclaimed. 'So different from the moors!' she laughed.

'What about your landscape, Rosa?' Roger asked. 'The landscape of home?'

Rosa's thoughts flew back to the old farmhouse in the hills overlooking Padua, which her family had owned for decades. She had an image of Gabriel as a boy, climbing a tree heavy with cherries, which he showered down on his little sister, who spun around down on the ground collecting every ripe red cherry which fell.

After sharing this memory with Roger, she went on

to describe a hillside of ancient olive trees. 'We made our own olive oil from them, and we had vines too, for wine,' she told him proudly.

Roger briefly took his eyes off the narrow lane in order to smile at his fiancée. 'You really are a wonder, darling Rosa – an Italian work of art!'

The spring breeze lifted Rosa's long dark hair and sent it flying around her face, which even after a short time with Roger looked younger and less careworn.

'I hope your parents think so,' she said, as Roger swung off the road and into a drive that wound its way around disused paddocks to a big old grey stone Queen Anne house, where the sun lit up every window, colouring them a vivid blood-orange red.

'Here we are,' cried Roger, yanking on the hand-brake and leaping out of the car, then running round to Rosa's side in order to open the door for her. 'Welcome to Hawksmoor House.'

Catching sight of Rosa's expression as she gazed up at the towering edifice, he said with a chuckle, 'Don't worry, I know it looks like it's falling down, but it's stood for over two hundred years and has another good two hundred to go, so it will see our grandchildren out.'

Rosa smothered a gasp; she'd never imagined bringing up children in England, and certainly not in a vast old house in the middle of nowhere.

'Did you spend all your childhood here?' she asked.

'Yes,' he replied. 'It was a wonderful place to grow up. I roamed the countryside, climbed trees, swam in the rivers and streams, camped out and lit fires. I suppose I was a bit feral,' he chuckled.

'Just you, nobody else?' she asked.

'My sister was around some of the time, but she's much older than me so it wasn't like we grew up together.'

'Weren't you ever lonely?'

'Never! Anyway, I had lots of friends at boarding school so it turned out to be a very good balance.'

Rosa marvelled at her fiancé, who seemed to have the ability to bounce back from any new and potentially strange situation with a bright smile on his face. Her wandering thoughts were interrupted by Roger leading her by the hand up a flight of steps to the solid oak front door; before he could even grip the handle the door was thrown wide open by a tall, lean woman with flowing iron-grey hair and startling blue eyes. Surrounded by barking Labradors whose tails smacked against her legs, the woman firmly shook Rosa's hand.

'You must be Rosa!' she exclaimed. 'I'm Bertha, Bertie to most. Come in.'

'Pleased to meet you,' Rosa said shyly, as she made her way through the licking, barking overexcited dogs.

'Get out of the way, Sherry! Bugger off, Brandy!' Roger cried fondly, as the dogs mobbed him.

A tall man who was the image of Roger except for his shock of thick white hair came striding across the echoing stone-flagged entrance hall.

'Ah, here you are,' he boomed and shook Rosa's hand so hard she winced in pain. 'Cecil Carrington.' Roger's father gave her an appraising look up and down, then nodded as if he approved. 'So you're to be my future daughter-in-law?'

Rosa blushed. 'I hope so,' she answered modestly.

'TEA!' announced Bertie as she led them, dogs and all, into the kitchen, where a long, scrubbed wooden table was laid with a plate of warm scones, clotted cream, homemade jam and a large pot of tea.

'This is wonderful!' Rosa cried at the sight of the fresh food.

'We're fairly self-sufficient here in Hawksmoor,' Bertie told Rosa, as she poured tea into delicate china cups. 'Keep chickens and a cow and grow fruit and veg all year round.'

'Are you a keen gardener?' Cecil asked as he spread his scone with a thin layer of jam and cream.

Feeling like she was failing the first test, Rosa answered truthfully, 'Actually I'm not.'

'Not to worry – I'm sure you'll soon pick it up,' Cecil said with a confidence Rosa certainly didn't feel.

After tea Bertie took Rosa to her room on the second floor, which was spick and span and so cold Rosa immediately began to shiver.

'Don't worry, I've warmed up your bed,' Bertie said, as she threw off the covers to reveal two stone hot-water bottles. 'Now I'll leave you in peace to unpack,' she added and left the room followed by the relentlessly panting dogs.

The minute she was out of sight Rosa threw open her suitcase and took out her warmest woolly jumper, which she pulled on, then hurried to close the windows that stood wide open to the cold East wind.

Feeling better now that she was warmer, Rosa unpacked her few things, then slipped downstairs to find Roger, who insisted that they went for a walk round the estate before supper.

Out in the fresh air Rosa's cheeks turned a soft rosy colour and her dark eyes sparkled with happiness. Now that the ordeal of meeting her future in-laws was over, she began to feel a lot more relaxed.

'They loved you,' Roger announced as they strolled hand in hand through an apple orchard just about to burst into bloom. 'Not that I ever doubted it,' he quickly added.

A walk around the empty paddocks, which Roger optimistically promised would house ponies one day soon for their children to ride, was followed by a close inspection of the rather neglected tennis court, where Rosa had to laughingly admit that she'd never played a game of tennis in her life.

'Don't worry, I'll teach you,' he said with great confidence. 'Come on,' he urged. 'I've something else to show you.'

In the stable block Roger marched past the vacant stalls and entered the tack room. 'Up here,' he called, as he took a flight of low wooden stairs two at a time.

Intrigued, Rosa followed and gasped in delight when she saw that she was in Roger's studio. 'This is wonderful!' she exclaimed, as she examined his easel.

'It used to be the old hayloft,' Roger explained. 'It has the most perfect Northern light.' Taking her in his arms, he whispered, 'Imagine, Rosa: we can paint side by side. I'll set up an easel for you right beside mine and we can swap notes as we work.'

Touched by his excitement and generosity, Rosa stood on her tip-toes so she could reach up and kiss her fiancé's soft mouth fringed by his sandy moustache.

'And how will we make our living, *caro*?' she murmured. 'What did you do before the war? Did you work?'

'I was studying law, hoping to join the family firm as a junior partner,' Roger told her. 'If I'm honest, I love being a pilot far more than being a lawyer.'

'I thought you might say that,' she teased.

Roger led Rosa to a battered old chaise longue littered with sketches, which, with an impatient gesture, he threw to the ground before drawing her down beside him.

'I could stay on in the RAF and we could do a bit of travelling, if you'd like that?'

'Yes, I think I would like that,' Rosa replied. 'But only after I've found Gabriel,' she said firmly.

'Of course,' he whispered, as he softly stroked her long curls. 'That has to be our first priority: finding Gabriel and your parents.'

Moved by her fiancé's tender but hopeful voice, Rosa finally told him about her disastrous attempt to find her brother, concluding with a despondent, 'So, you see, I'm no nearer to knowing where he is or even if he's alive or dead.'

At the sight of her sad, defeated expression, Roger hugged her tightly. 'You brave, reckless girl,' he said.

'There was nothing brave about what I did; in fact, most people accused me of stupidity,' Rosa told him bitterly.

'Darling,' Roger said, as he sat upright and spoke to her earnestly. 'The shift of power is changing: it's Hitler's armies that are on the back foot these days. We've just dropped three thousand tons of bombs on Hamburg, we're gaining the upper hand – and one day soon this blasted war will be over. Imagine, Rosa – peace!'

Frustrated by his reaction, Rosa pushed her point home. 'Yes, but that doesn't address the problem of Gabriel,' she insisted. 'I thought after I'd told you how desperate I've been you might actually have some ideas about helping me to find him,' she snapped.

Roger looked genuinely astonished, both at her words and at her tone of voice. 'Sorry to disappoint you, darling, but I couldn't possibly shine any light on a matter like that.'

'Given your job, I was hoping that you might have a few powerful contacts in the RAF?' she persisted. 'People who could open doors for me?'

'I certainly know a number of powerful men but I really don't think any of them would be of any help in finding Gabriel,' he replied with a regretful smile.

'Oh,' she murmured and blinked hard to hide the tears that were forming in her sad dark eyes.

'Whatever happens, my sweet, we'll face it together,' he promised. 'And don't forget, dearest Rosa, you have a home here now.'

Rosa bit back the cross words that were on the tip of her tongue; how many times did she have to say to Roger that she couldn't begin to settle anywhere if she didn't know where her brother was?

After a hearty supper of Lord Woolton Pie and spring greens accompanied by home-brewed stout, Rosa sat with Roger and his parents in their drawing room, warmed by the crackling fire that blazed in a baroque stone fireplace set with simple square decorations. As Rosa savoured the strong coffee, a mix of chicory and acorn nuts skilfully blended by Mrs Carrington, she felt warm and comfortable, her head drooping on to Roger's shoulder and her eyelids closing.

'Time for bed, young lady,' he said, as he helped Rosa to her feet.

After bidding goodnight to Mr Carrington, Rosa followed Bertie up the back stairs to her bedroom, which was colder than ever, but at least her bed was warm. Snuggled under the heavy blankets and eiderdown with her small feet pressed to the now cooling stoneware hot-water bottles, Rosa jumped in fright when she heard the door squeak open.

'Who's there?' she called.

'Shhh, only me,' Roger called softly in the darkness.

'What're you doing here?' she gasped in surprise.

'Coming to give my beautiful fiancée a goodnight kiss,' Roger chuckled as he lay alongside her on top of the eiderdown.

Feeling the warmth and strength of his body against her back, Rosa wriggled round so she could loop her arms around Roger's neck. 'This is cosy,' she said dreamily as they locked lips.

Rosa was surprised by the passion that blazed through her body, and by how good it felt to be close to Roger again. The touch of his caressing hands, albeit through layers of intrusive sheets and blankets, made her limbs go weak, and being with him felt right in a way she realized she'd been doubting for some time. The thought of abandoning all the fears and anxieties that besieged her daily and giving herself over to a few blissful hours of love-making on a long cold night was deeply appealing.

'*Tesoro*,' she murmured in her mother tongue as she struggled to free herself from the heavy bedding that restricted her every movement.

'Oh, my darling,' Roger groaned as his hands reached inside her nightdress and found her small firm breasts. 'Oh, God, I love you so much,' he sighed as he smothered her neck and shoulders with hot kisses.

A loud cry from downstairs froze them both.

'Roger!' his father's commanding voice boomed out. 'Time to take the dogs out.'

Rosa smothered a disrespectful giggle. 'Damn the dogs!'

But Roger immediately loosened his hold on her. 'Better go – don't want to disappoint the old fella,' he said as he rose to his feet.

The laughter faded from Rosa's voice. 'Don't go, Roger,' she implored. 'Please stay with me.'

Stumbling in the darkness, Roger urgently muttered, 'He's waiting for me, sweetheart.'

'But I need you,' she said close to tears. 'I'm leaving tomorrow – stay and talk to me,' she begged.

'Are you coming?' his father's voice boomed out again, this time even more loudly.

'See you in the morning, dearest,' Roger whispered, as he bolted across the room to open the door.

Bitterly disappointed that he could just leave her, when for the first time in ages she'd really felt close to him, Rosa cried out in frustration and hurt: 'ROGER!'

In an obvious attempt to cover her cry, Roger called loudly, 'COMING!' and, taking the stairs two at a time, he joined his demanding father and the three expectant Labradors in the hallway.

Left alone, Rosa stared miserably into the velvet darkness. She'd meant it when she'd said she really needed Roger to stay with her. It had been unexpectedly good to feel close to him after so long apart, and she'd wanted to share her fears and worries with him before she left. Feeling thoroughly disgruntled, Rosa pulled the covers back over her chilled body.

'Duty first!' she grumbled into her pillow. 'If this is the Carrington way, I'd better learn to live with it!'

28. Encounters

Rosa's next day with the Carringtons was not unlike the previous one: lots of good nourishing food, hearty conversations and blustery walks in the wind and the rain. After her hurt at Roger's abandoning her the previous night, she was in no mood for his passionate attempts to rekindle the moment. She felt let down and made no move to initiate further conversations about her brother, or anything else that was bothering her. She knew she was overreacting, but she couldn't help it. She had needed him last night and he hadn't even realized it.

Feeling not that much happier than when she'd left, Rosa returned to the cowshed to find the dress-making sessions in full swing. Highly motivated Nora and Maggie, helped by Maggie's creative mum, Mrs Yates, had transformed their two pink satin dresses into a single gown with a fitted bodice and long, tight sleeves (just like the one Nora had spotted in *Vogue*). And there was even enough material left over to make a little train, which delighted Nora.

'I can't believe it's really me,' she gasped as she gazed at herself in Maggie's dressing-table mirror.

'You look thinner!' Maggie giggled. 'Maybe it's because you've been giving all your chip butties to Polly,' she teased.

Giddy and happy as she was, Nora's heart sank; time was now seriously running out for her beloved pig. Since Maggie had acquired the dress of her dreams, she ticked off the days to her wedding day on the calendar hanging up on the kitchen wall every morning.

'One day less to go!' she gleefully told Nora, little knowing that her daily countdown was like the sound of a death knell to her beleaguered friend.

On a visit to Wrigg Hall, Nora unexpectedly poured her heart out to Peter, who, after a second skin graft on his face, was making a remarkably fast recovery. Though the stitches were still evident, it was clear that the surgeon, who'd used skin tissue from Peter's thighs to rebuild his face, had done an excellent job. He was now walking better too: daily physiotherapy sessions and regular walks around the hospital grounds had strengthened the muscles in Peter's damaged leg and he was able to forgo the wheelchair in favour of a walking stick.

Seeing Nora weeping uncontrollably moved Peter to tears; he felt so sorry for the sweet, willing girl who spent all her free time helping others. She arrived like a ray of sunshine twice a week without fail: breezing on to the ward, pushing her clattering tea trolley, she brought more than refreshment into their lives. Nora would never know how much she'd personally helped Peter in his own recovery; her regular visits, her patience and compassion had helped to restore not just his body but his mind too. She made him want to talk, to walk, to smile – to live, in fact. To see her with tears running down her cheeks and her wild red hair springing out from underneath her starched cap made Peter's heart ache, and in that moment, quite suddenly, the balance of their relationship shifted. Now he was the strong one helping Nora in her hour of need.

'I might have only one good working eye,' Peter thought to himself. 'But I can see as clear as day that my favourite girl needs help.'

Boldly taking hold of her hot trembling hands, he said softly, 'What is it? What's wrong?'

'It's Polly!' Nora wailed. 'Her days are numbered.'

'But you always knew that, didn't you, pet?' Peter gently pointed out.

'Yes!' Nora cried. 'I tried not to think about it, but now, with Maggie reminding me every single day, I can't *not* think about it. What am I going to do?' she wailed. 'I love Polly so much. I can't bear to think of somebody cutting her throat!'

Peter offered Nora a sip of water from the glass on his bedside table, then he waited patiently for her to regain her composure before he dropped his bombshell.

'You could steal her,' he whispered.

The thought shocked Nora so much she stopped sniffling. 'Steal a *pig*?'

Peter nodded. 'And hide her,' he added.

'B . . . b . . . but . . .' stunned Nora spluttered.

'I'd help you do it,' he said with confidence.

Nora almost laughed. 'Where would we hide a pig? And,' she said as an afterthought, 'and what would Maggie eat on her wedding day?'

Continuing in a calm voice, as if he were talking

about the weather rather than a criminal act, Peter said, 'We'd have to find Maggie an alternative.'

'An alternative pig?' Nora gasped.

Peter gave a solemn nod.

'It'd have to be a well-fed one,' Nora said in all seriousness. 'Otherwise there wouldn't be enough to go round.'

'More to the point you would have to promise not to fall in love with the new pig.'

Nora looked at the young man and started to giggle. 'I don't usually fall in love with pigs!'

'I should hope not!' he joked.

Nora had another troublesome thought. 'It'll cost money to get a replacement.'

'That shouldn't be a problem; I've got money put by,' he confidently assured her.

Nora gazed into Peter's sweet, scarred face with undisguised adoration. 'Would you *really* do that for me?'

Peter squeezed her hands tightly. 'Nora, I would move heaven and earth for you.'

Sitting side by side on the edge of the hospital bed, the two of them could barely take their eyes off each other; the tumultuous passion that flooded through Nora's body made her feel light-headed and breathless. She knew with the certainty that night follows day that she had begun to fall for this brave, damaged and quite wonderful young man since the moment she had first laid eyes on him. And he in return knew that Nora was not only his saviour but the love of his life. Before they could stop themselves they fell into each other's arms.

'I want to look after you,' Peter whispered into her hair, which had tumbled free of her cap and fell in wild curls around her radiant face.

'I want to look after you too,' she murmured.

'Are you sure?' he whispered. 'I'm not a whole man,' he reminded her.

'You're all the man I need,' Nora whispered and for the first time in her life she kissed a man on the lips.

The Bomb Girls, enjoying a welcome break in the Phoenix canteen a few days later, were taken entirely by surprise to see Arthur Leadbetter walking in pushing baby Stevie, now seven months old, in a pram.

'What the 'ell are you doin' 'ere, stranger?' one of the older women called out.

'Just thought I'd pop by to keep you all in line!' Arthur joked in the way they all remembered with affection.

'It'll take more than a man and a babby to keep us lot under control,' another woman teased, as she hurried to give Arthur a quick kiss on the cheek.

Grinning with pleasure, Arthur quickly joined his old friends gathered around the table, drinking tea and having a smoke. After politely shaking Julia by the hand and asking how she was, Arthur wasted no time in handing a gurgling Stevie over to Kit, who'd looked after the little boy when Arthur had been hospitalized after his accident.

'What an unexpected surprise!' delighted Kit said as she cuddled Stevie.

'I had to transport some explosive material to a

factory near Burnley,' Arthur explained. 'I thought whilst I was so close I'd pop in and see my old pals. It's been a long time since Stevie's had a cuddle from any of his "aunties",' he joked.

'How did you get Stevie down here?' Nora inquired.

'I tucked him up in a cardboard box and settled him in the van's passenger seat,' Arthur replied. 'He was as good as gold – slept most of the way down.'

'He's grown so big since we last saw him,' Kit observed.

'I can't keep up with the boy now that he's on solids,' Arthur said with a proud smile. 'He's got the appetite of a horse.'

On hearing this, Nora offered Stevie a chip, which she'd cooled by blowing on it. 'Get that down you,' she giggled.

Stevie waved the chip in the air like a conductor waves his baton, after which he solemnly ate it.

'Here, have a cuddle,' Kit said to Rosa. 'If he jumps on my stomach again I might go into labour,' she chuckled.

Rosa couldn't wait to get her hands on Stevie, whom she'd loved at first sight when she'd seen him some months previously fast asleep in his pram.

'*Ciao, mio carissimo ragazzo*,' she murmured as she held him close and inhaled the sweet baby smell of his soft skin.

Peering over the top of Stevie's head, she caught sight of Arthur watching her cuddling his son.

'How are you, Rosa?' he inquired.

Rosa's heart gave a sudden and rather unexpected

lurch as she gazed at Arthur: tall and lean, with expressive blue eyes, a generous smiling mouth and a mop of thick blond hair, this lovely man was someone whose company she'd really enjoyed. A man who was looking surprisingly handsome today considering the amount of agonizing grief he'd lived through.

When he'd worked in the Phoenix, Arthur could have had any of the attractive young women but that had never been his way. He'd never flirted or pulled rank on anybody, and had eyes only for his beautiful wife, Violet. Rosa realized yet again how much she missed him, and, more to the point, how much she missed little Stevie, who was presently tugging the turban off her head. As her wonderful long dark hair fell in waves to her waist, Stevie grabbed it and wound it around his chubby little fists.

In answer to Arthur's question, Rosa shyly replied, 'I'm well, thank you.'

Feeling a self-conscious blush spread across her cheeks, Rosa was grateful to Stevie for sucking her hair and thereby distracting her.

'*Cattivo!*' she laughed. 'Naughty little boy,' she teased as she gave him a kiss.

When the hooter blew, Julia immediately got to her feet and, after bidding Arthur goodbye, she hurried back to the filling shed. When she'd gone, Arthur gave the girls a knowing look.

'Any friendlier with the newcomer?' he asked with a teasing wink.

Maggie and Nora immediately started talking eagerly about all that Julia had done for them and how much nicer she was these days, whilst Rosa remained distinctly silent.

'Well, I'm glad to hear things have improved,' Arthur answered evenly as he threw Rosa a questioning look.

Kit rose to her feet with an effort. 'Are you staying tonight?' she asked, as she supported her very large tummy, over which she now wore a smock.

'If me and the boy can find somewhere to sleep I'd love to,' Arthur replied.

'You know there's always a bed and a meal for you two at our house,' Kit assured him. 'Billy would love to see his little playmate again.'

Rosa gave an inward sigh as she too rose: if Arthur and Stevie were staying at Kit's, it was more than likely she wouldn't see either of them again this visit. As if reading her thoughts, Kit turned to the girls. 'Why don't you all come round to us tonight?'

With piles of sewing to do, Maggie and Nora declined Kit's kind offer, but Rosa eagerly accepted.

'Yes, please!' she exclaimed before she could stop herself.

'See you later, then,' Arthur said, as he gently popped protesting Stevie back in his pram, then hurried off to the factory office to report to Mr Featherstone.

That evening was one of the happiest that Rosa had spent in a long time. Briefly she forgot her troubles; her anguish and guilt over her missing brother, her recent hurt about Roger's insensitivity, the anger she felt towards Julia, which seemed to be getting worse, and the sense of despair and hopelessness that she carried around in her heart from the moment she woke up to the moment she closed her eyes and fell asleep.

It was simply wonderful being with the babies; cheeky Billy, who treated Stevie like a little brother or alternatively a toy to drag about. Stevie didn't seem to mind; as long as Billy was close he was happy. Rosa could have kissed and cuddled the baby boy who was so like his father all night, but overexcited Stevie had eyes only for Billy and Kit's tabby cat, who he was obsessed with.

After a bath and a story, which Rosa was delighted to read, she sat in the darkened bedroom with Billy in his little bed and Stevie tucked up and sucking his dummy in Billy's old cot. She sang lilting Italian lullabies, the very ones her mother had sung to rock her off to sleep when she was a baby. As she sang sweetly in her mother tongue, tears stung the back of Rosa's eyes.

'Please God, keep my family safe,' she prayed fervently.

Once she was sure the boys were fast asleep, she crept, rather bleary-eyed after sitting in the dark for so long, downstairs, which was thick with a rich savoury smell.

'MEAT?' she asked incredulously.

Ian, who'd arrived home whilst Rosa was upstairs, laughed. 'Rabbit shot on the moors,' he told her. 'Not by me – I'm a rotten shot – but the farmer across the valley keeps us supplied for a ten-bob note.' He waved a bottle of wine in the air. 'He supplies us with this too: damson wine – it's delicious!'

Sitting around the large scrubbed wooden kitchen table, Rosa and Arthur smoked their cigarettes whilst Ian puffed on his pipe. Kit, who'd been a heavy smoker, declined any offers of a cigarette.

'Can't stand the taste of them when I'm pregnant,' she told her friends. 'Probably a good thing.'

Ian helped his wife, who waddled uncomfortably under the weight of her burgeoning belly, to set the table.

'Honest to God I swear Billy was never as big as this one,' Kit groaned, as she gratefully sat down and let Ian serve out a hearty supper of cabbage, mashed potatoes and rabbit casserole, followed by rice pudding and Kit's home-grown plums, which she'd bottled in the autumn. At the end of the evening Arthur offered to drive Rosa home in his van.

'It won't take more than ten minutes,' he said when she protested. 'Anyway, we can't have you walking home in the dark.'

As they bounced over the moors in the draughty van with no headlights to guide their way, Arthur inquired about Rosa's wedding plans; she regaled him with her recent visit to meet her future in-laws in Wiltshire.

'The English middle class,' he said after she'd laughingly told him about the big cold house and the smelly dogs.

'We have no such concept in my country,' Rosa told him. 'Of course we like our children to continue our traditions but to send them away to be educated, to "toughen them up", as Roger's father said, that's not my way.'

'Nor mine,' Arthur exclaimed. 'I want to teach my son the ways of the world myself, guide him through his early life, and maybe one day, if I meet the right woman and fall in love again, give him a little brother or sister to grow up with.'

Rosa was glad of the surrounding darkness that hid her startled expression. She'd never considered the possibility of Arthur's marrying again; even after Violet's death he had always seemed so in love with her that it was impossible to imagine him with another woman.

'So have you set a date?' Arthur asked, oblivious to her reaction.

'No, though Roger would like it to be soon,' she replied cautiously.

'And what would *you* like?' he asked pointedly.

In truth, Rosa dreaded the thought of living in married quarters in a strange barracks far away from the friends she loved; plus, after her recent rather unsatisfactory time with Roger, she knew she didn't feel as romantically inclined as she should.

'*Me?*' she asked with a blush. 'I can't set a date until I know about Gabriel's whereabouts; obviously I'd want him beside me on my wedding day,' she answered; then, before she could stop herself, she blurted out, 'And, if I'm honest, I'm not ready to leave the Phoenix; it's the only home I know these days.'

'Does your fiancé know that?' Arthur inquired softly.

'He knows my feelings about Gabriel,' she said hotly. 'But he hardly pays attention to them.'

'Then you need to be clear about what you want,' Arthur told her firmly before saying with a teasing smile, 'Though leaving the Phoenix would be a sure way of getting away from Julia!'

Rosa looked him squarely in the eye. 'You know, Arthur,' she said sharply, 'I do have a genuine reason for disliking Julia.'

By the time she'd finished recounting why her friendship with Julia had deteriorated on her London trip, Arthur had pulled up outside the cowshed, which was in total darkness.

'Hell fire!' he murmured as he lit up two Pall Mall cigarettes, one for him and one for her. 'Would you really have boarded a ship for France?'

'Absolutely! Without a moment's hesitation,' she said staunchly.

Slipping an arm around her shoulders, Arthur gave her a squeeze. 'You're a brave lass,' he said softly. 'I, for one, am glad you didn't risk it, Rosa. I'm relieved you're here, safe and well. I've had more than enough of losing the people I care about.'

Arthur stubbed out his cigarette, then turned to Rosa. 'Don't go doing anything rash like that again,' he said firmly. 'Everybody's saying this war will soon be over; then you can cross the Channel in safety and find your brother.' Leaning over, Arthur gave Rosa a chaste kiss on her cheek. 'Goodnight,' he said softly. 'Take care of yourself.'

'Goodnight,' she replied, touched by his words as she climbed out of the passenger seat.

'See you on the eighth of May,' Arthur said, as he started up the engine.

'The eighth of May?' she queried.

'Maggie's wedding day, remember?' he teased. 'God bless,' he called as he drove away.

Rosa stood outside the front door until the sound of the van's engine had faded away and Arthur was swallowed up into the darkness of the night.

'God bless you, Arthur Leadbetter,' she whispered, turning to go indoors. 'And keep yourself and little Stevie safe until I see you both again.'

29. The Swap

In order to avoid arousing suspicion, Peter and Nora had to achieve their plan to free Polly and replace her with another pig in a single day. Being hospitalized, Peter wasn't free to come and go as he chose, which meant that Nora was left with all the work of sourcing another pig, finding a hideaway location for Polly and arranging transport for both animals.

'I'm sorry, sweetheart, it's a lot for you to do alone,' Peter said, as they walked around the hospital grounds with Peter leaning on his stick, whilst his free hand encircled his sweetheart's waist.

'It'll be worth it,' Nora said with a grin, though her face then grew serious as she considered all that she had to do. 'Who can I get to drive a truck?'

'I wish I could,' Peter said impatiently.

Seeing the disappointment in his face, Nora stopped him in his tracks. 'Sweetheart, please don't start getting cranky.'

'I'm not cranky, just frustrated,' he admitted, then smiled as he added, 'Don't think for a minute I'm not coming with you, Nora.'

'I'd be a nervous wreck if you weren't there,' she assured him.

As they continued their walk, Nora mused, 'If I could get hold of a truck, I bet Edna could drive it.'

'Is Edna the one who drives up to your factory in her mobile chip shop?' Peter inquired.

Nora smiled. 'She used to come up and cook chips for us Bomb Girls nearly every night; it's less often these days, now that her daughter and grandchildren are living with her.'

'You should definitely ask Edna,' Peter urged. 'If she can handle a mobile chip shop, she'll certainly be able to drive a truck.'

'What're we going to do about Percy?' Nora asked.

'You're going to have to have a quiet word with him,' Peter advised. 'He'll have to be involved at some stage.'

Nora vehemently shook her head. 'No!' she exclaimed. 'What if he goes and blabs to Maggie? That'd really throw a spanner into the works.'

'Better to come clean right from the start,' Peter urged.

'And what if Percy won't help us?'

'We'll do it anyway,' Peter answered staunchly. 'Nobody can stop us buying a pig if we want to – not even Percy!'

Nora leant her head against his shoulder. 'What would I do without you?' she said adoringly.

By this time it was common knowledge on the ward that Peter and Nora were 'walking out' together. Everyone was delighted by the romantic turn of events, though when Sister asked Nora for a quiet word in private Nora suspected she was going to get a ticking off.

'I hope you don't think I'm interfering, dear,' Sister said as she ushered Nora into her office. 'It's just news of your, er, relationship with young Peter Halliday has reached my ears, and I wanted to be sure that you're aware of what you're taking on.'

Nora gazed at her dumbfounded. 'What do you mean?' she blurted out.

'Obviously you're familiar with Peter's disabilities – after all you've been visiting him for some time,' Sister continued.

Nora, who'd keenly observed Peter's recovery with pleasure and relief, answered knowledgeably. 'I know he's lost the sight in his left eye, and part of his face was blown away, but the surgeon's doing a great job rebuilding it, and he was lame but now he's walking, although with a stick, but he's not stuck in a wheelchair any more.'

Sister smiled at Nora's flushed, earnest face and her torrent of words. 'I see you understand the situation perfectly,' she commented. 'But, long term, do you think you can cope with Peter's disabilities?'

Nora felt herself bridle; young and insecure as she was, nothing would make her change her mind when it came to her feelings about Peter.

'If you mean can I care for a half-blind man with a limp who's badly scarred, and who I love with all my heart, the answer's *yes*!'

By this time Nora, incensed, was almost out of her chair.

'There, there,' soothed Sister. 'I have no intention of dissuading you, Nora. I just wanted to be sure you were aware of what you're taking on.'

Hearing her reassuring words, Nora slowly sank back into the chair. 'I thought you were going to tell me to leave the lad alone, and that I wasn't good enough for him,' she muttered, close to tears.

'My dear child, I would never do that!' Sister exclaimed. 'You two have been drawn to each other for some time; it's been sweet to see your affection towards each other grow, and your devotion to Peter has aided his recovery. Since you appeared on the scene, he's come on in leaps and bounds.'

Nora smiled proudly. 'I'd do anything for him, I love him so much,' she whispered.

'We can all see that,' Sister said fondly.

Whilst Nora was in the office, she took advantage of the situation to ask a question that had been on her mind for quite some time.

'When might Peter be discharged?'

'That depends entirely on the plastic surgeon and Peter's physiotherapist,' Sister informed her.

'I know he's got an elderly mother Bradford way – will he go home to her when he's discharged?' she asked anxiously.

'That's for Peter to decide when the time comes for him to leave us,' Sister answered diplomatically.

In the end Nora had no choice but to confess her secret plan to Percy, who went red with indignation.

'You can't do that, yer daft bugger!' he exclaimed.

'I can!' she replied, equally indignant.

'It's thieving!'

'Not if you can find me a replacement,' she insisted. 'I've got money for that.'

'Why bring me into it?' he demanded.

'Because you're the only person I know who could find a pig in this valley.'

Percy didn't argue with that; but he wasn't going to be fobbed off with compliments.

He looked over towards Polly, who was standing on her hind legs so she could see what was going on beyond the confines of her pen. With her head cocked to one side, she actually looked like she was listening in on their conversation.

'And what exactly are you planning on doing with yon pig?' Percy asked.

'I'll find somewhere for her,' Nora answered with a confidence that she didn't actually feel.

'It'll cost you, all this buggering about,' he added irritably.

'I can pay,' she said forcefully.

'When do you want it done?'

'As soon as possible.'

Percy looked her steadily in the eye for several seconds, then said, '*If* I do get thee another pig, you've got to faithfully promise you'll never go near the damn thing. Otherwise you'll be wanting to rescue that one too.'

'Don't worry, I won't,' she promised, knowing he was right and she would indeed have to keep away from the hapless replacement pig before she fell for that one just as hard as she'd fallen for Polly!

'Because I'm telling you straight, lass, I'm not swapping pigs every ten minutes just because you're too soft to see them slaughtered!'

When Nora guiltily confided her plan to Edna, she burst out laughing.

'Yer big soft sod!' she hooted. 'You've got to be kidding me?'

Nora solemnly shook her head. 'It's God's honest truth,' she replied.

'You're serious?' Edna gasped. 'You really think you can swap Polly for another pig?'

'I'll do my damn best,' Nora retorted. 'Will you help me, Edna?' she pleaded. 'I've got to find a truck and a driver . . .' Hoping that Edna would catch on, Nora left the sentence dangling in the air.

Typically Edna replied with her usual generosity. 'Course I'll help you, cock.' Nora sighed with relief.

'Though if Maggie finds out what we're up to, she might never speak to either of us again.'

'Let's hope that never happens,' Nora retorted, as she drew out her packet of Woodbines. 'Now tell me, how are Marilyn and Katherine getting on at their new school?'

Edna beamed. 'Couldn't be better,' she replied happily. 'I have to admit I was worried to start with. Since they moved in with me, the little lasses have barely been parted from their mam for more than a few hours.'

Nora nodded; she'd seen the girls around town,

shopping with their mum, but always holding her hand and never straying far from her side.

'Flora had a private word with the headmistress,' Edna continued. 'She explained to her why they'd moved so suddenly from Penrith; the head was very sympathetic and promised to keep an eye on the girls.'

'Has Flora heard any news about their father?' Nora asked in a low voice.

'Just a few letters that her neighbour redirected down here, from the army, informing Flora that they're looking after him until he's fit for action again.' Edna's face darkened. 'I pray to God he doesn't turn up and drag them poor little chicks back with him,' she said with an emotional catch in her voice.

'I wouldn't worry – it sounds like the man's in no state to whisk the girls away,' Nora quickly assured her friend.

'I hope the army can help to get him better,' Edna said in a guilty afterthought. 'Flora tells me time and again that he wasn't always a bad husband – it's just that not having seen it, I find it very hard to believe.'

After Edna managed to locate a truck, it was then a question of synchronizing the swap on a day that Maggie would definitely not be anywhere near the allotment, and also on a day that Peter would be allowed out of hospital.

'Peter will be joining us,' Nora informed Edna. 'He won't be able to do much but he wants to be there anyway.'

Edna chuckled. 'You two love birds can barely be parted,' she teased.

'Does everybody know we're walking out, then?' Nora asked with a blush.

'Let's just say good news travels fast in these parts,' Edna answered with a wink.

On the appointed day Edna drove Nora up to Wrigg Hall, where she dropped her off, then waited for her and Peter to join her in the truck that Nora had lovingly spread with straw so that her beloved Polly wouldn't have an uncomfortable ride to her secret destination.

Peter's fellow patients grinned when Nora, looking pretty in her best cotton frock and cardigan, arrived to pick Peter up. Surprised not to see her in her volunteer's uniform, the men complimented the blushing girl, whose hair hung long and loose about her smiling happy face.

'You look a picture.'

'Proper bonny.'

As the smiling couple left the ward arm in arm, more good-natured comments followed them: 'Take care of the lad', 'Don't wear him out', 'Bring him back in one piece!'

Peter and Nora, squeezed tightly together in the passenger seat, held hands as Edna, clearly enjoying herself, drove up the steep, cobbled hill that led to the farm. As Peter enjoyed the views of the wild rolling Pennines, Nora gnawed on her nails; her heart was thudding as she thought about what they had to do in the next few hours. What if Maggie, after all her careful planning, showed up out of the blue?

'Cheer up, lovie,' Peter said, as he stroked her knee. 'This is an adventure for me, driving along on a lovely day like today with my girlfriend by my side.' He astonished Nora by suddenly saying, 'One day when I'm fitter I'll teach you to drive, if you like?'

'*Me?*' Nora laughed. 'Give over! I'm too daft to learn how to drive.'

Edna and Peter exchanged a knowing look.

'Now listen here,' Peter said in his firmest voice, 'if you're going to be my lass, I'll hear no more of the "I'm too daft" stuff from you.'

Edna nodded in agreement with Peter's sentiment, whilst Nora looked embarrassed.

'You're one of the cleverest women I've ever met,' he continued.

'I'm not –' she started to protest.

'Hear me out, please. You're clever from the inside, Nora. You understand people, and you have compassion, which is not something you find on a fancy certificate – it's a God-given gift, and you've got it.'

Moved to tears by Peter's earnest words, Edna almost missed the turning to Haworth, but luckily Peter saw it, and after a sharp turn left they followed a narrow farm track, which was rutted with holes.

Edna stayed in the truck whilst Peter exchanged the right amount of pound notes with the farmer, who then led the pig out of his sty.

'Here he is,' he announced. 'I reckon you've got your money's worth.'

'*He?*' Nora gasped. 'It's a boy?'

The farmer nodded. 'And a big one at that.'

In shocked silence Nora gazed at the beast.

'Well, do you want it or not?' barked the farmer.

With a flourish Peter flung open the truck's back doors. 'Aye, of course we want it,' he said loudly.

After a few protesting scuffles the pig was dragged into the truck, and the doors were securely slammed shut.

Peter winked at Edna as he and Nora clambered back into the cab.

'What's up?' she asked.

'Slight change of plan,' Peter replied.

Almost in tears Nora cried, 'It's not a girl! Maggie's sure to notice.'

Edna calmly started the engine and pulled away from the farm. 'Do you really think she'll notice, lovie? I mean, how much time does she spend in the pig sty checking out Polly's whatsits?'

Peter stifled a snort of laughter, whilst Nora considered the question.

'You're right, Maggie does spend most of her time working alongside Percy on the allotment,' she finally conceded.

'So with luck you might get away with it,' Edna said cheerfully.

'And after all,' Peter added, 'a pig's a pig if all you're going to do at the end of the day is eat it!'

*

When Edna drove up to the allotment and saw Percy with a face like thunder holding tightly on to Polly, who had a rope tethered around her neck, she muttered under her breath, 'Aye, aye, here's trouble.'

'Get a soddin' move on,' Percy growled when they pulled up. 'I've been sweating bricks waiting for you two – if Maggie ever finds out what we're up to there'll be hell to pay.'

Nora, after dashing to open the back of the truck and drop the ramp, nervously led out the new pig. But within a few seconds she heard Percy furiously swearing, 'BLOODY HELL FIRE!'

Turning to Nora, he yelled, 'You've gone and bought a fella!'

'I didn't know!' poor Nora protested.

'How do you think you're going to pull the wool over Maggie's eyes with this bugger?' Percy raged. 'Maggie's not daft, yer know.'

'I was hoping she might not notice,' Nora cried apologetically.

Percy pointed at the pig's dangling genitals. 'She'd have to be bloody blind to miss that lot!'

Muttering curses under his breath, Percy led the pig into his new sty, leaving Nora to deal with Polly, who skipped up the ramp and into the truck as if she was going on holiday.

Edna popped her head out of the driver's seat window. 'Let's get out of here before Percy gives us another earful,' she urged.

With Polly grunting contentedly in the back of the

truck, they drove her to her new home on a rather isolated farm a couple of miles from the cowshed.

'It's a bit far out,' Peter observed when they pulled up.

'I thought the further away from Maggie the better,' Nora told him. 'But not so far that I can't visit her,' she added fondly.

'How are you going to get out here to see Polly?' Edna asked.

'I'll cycle out,' Nora replied.

'And what will you say to Maggie when she asks where you've been?'

'I'll think of something,' Nora said, as she led Polly to the sty she'd lovingly prepared for her. 'Here you are, my sweetheart,' she said and removed the rope from around Polly's neck. 'A nice safe place where nobody will ever find you.'

As Polly buried her head in a bucket of pigswill, Peter joined Nora, who was leaning over the gate, watching Polly guzzle.

'We did it,' he chuckled as he hugged Nora.

'I couldn't have done it without you,' she murmured, as she kissed Peter's cheek. 'All the money you've spent – you're wonderful!' she said with grateful tears in her eyes.

Peter gave Nora a deep kiss on her warm pink lips. 'I wouldn't have missed it for the world,' he said, then added with a sparkle in his eye, 'I've not laughed so much in years, my sweetheart!'

30. Hugo

Even though she'd asked Hugo for his help, Julia was nevertheless taken by surprise when a telegram from him turned up in her pigeon-hole at the Phoenix.

Dearest Jay,

Phone me when you have a private moment.

H.

Her heart skipped a beat; she knew instinctively it could only be about Gabriel. Looking down the length of the canteen, Julia could see Rosa, smoking and chatting to Kit and a few other women from the filling shed.

'God!' thought Julia. 'What if it's bad news? She hates me enough already. What will I say to her if Gabriel's been found dead in a ditch?'

The hooter blasting out, recalling the workers, made Julia jump; then, taking a deep breath, she joined Kit in the filling shed, where they resumed the monotonous dirty job of filling shells. Ten minutes in, just as the strains of Vera Lynn's 'We'll Meet Again' were issuing from the factory loudspeaker, Kit suddenly laid down the gunpowder she was smoothing with her fingertips, groaned loudly and got to her feet. Seeing her white, strained face, Julia immediately stood up too.

'What is it, Kit?'

'Terrible back pains,' she replied, as she clutched her lumbar region and groaned again, but this time louder.

'Let's get you out of here,' Julia said firmly, as she took her friend's arm and steered her out of the shed.

In the first-aid room the nurse on duty briefly examined Kit.

'You're big,' she said, running her hands over Kit's bulging stomach. 'How far gone are you?'

'Nearly seven months now.'

'I'm not a doctor but I'd say you're putting too much pressure on your body doing twelve-hour shifts in this place,' the nurse said. 'It's time to put your feet up, lass.'

'I'm not due maternity leave yet,' Kit told her anxiously.

'Your baby doesn't know that,' the nurse replied. 'I suggest you go home right away and make an appointment to see your family doctor, who'll give you a thorough examination. Now,' she asked briskly, 'how will you get home?'

Kit hauled herself up from the narrow examination bed. 'I can get a bus; it's not that far.'

Julia, who'd stayed with Kit, helped her to her feet. 'Shall I pick up Billy from nursery for you?' she inquired.

'Thank you, but I'll get Ian to collect him on his way home,' Kit replied. 'You get yourself back to work, Julia,' she urged. 'I'll be fine.'

Julia returned to the filling shed, where she automatically filled one shell after another, her mind on Kit, but also on how she would manage to secure a private telephone call with Hugo. She knew Malc, the factory supervisor, had a phone in his office, but she didn't feel she knew him well enough to ask him directly if she could use it. But Maggie and Nora were on easy-going terms with Malc, so she decided to ask them to ask on her behalf.

'My brother wants a word with me,' she told them. 'Some sort of family business,' she added with a vague shrug.

Malc didn't mind Julia using his phone so long as he wasn't busy in his office; on hearing this, Julia arranged a time that was convenient for Malc, then phoned her brother in between her breaks.

'Jay, darling, how are you?'

Julia's heart began to pound – what on earth was he going to tell her?

'Fine, what news?' she answered almost curtly.

Dropping his voice, Hugo said, 'There is a chance that Falco may be alive.'

Julia smothered a gasp as she almost dropped the phone she was grasping so tightly.

'If he's using the false name and identity papers he was issued with, then it would seem he's alive and, more to the point, been spotted more than once recently.'

'How do you know this?' Julia gasped.

As Hugo briefly stated the facts, Julia hardly dared to breathe for fear of missing a word he said.

'We know a male who fits Falco's description got himself to underground workers, who vetted him, then hid him in a safe house, where he was given a false name and identity pass. Under his false name he was placed on a train with other rescued Jews, bound for Belgium.'

'Belgium!' Julia cried.

Ignoring her excitement, Hugo concluded, 'We have men on the ground monitoring safe houses across the Belgian coast; if I hear further news, I'll try to let you know.'

'Thank you, Hugo,' she started but he hurriedly interrupted her.

'Sorry, Jay – got to go.'

A sharp click on the other end of the line told her he was gone.

'What now?' she said out loud, as she replaced the handset in its cradle. Now that she had news, should she share it with Rosa, or would it be sensible to wait till she knew more?

After leaving Malc's office, she thoughtfully walked back home but as she got nearer to the cowshed Julia realized she was actually frightened of talking to Rosa, who couldn't even look at her without scowling.

'If I'm going to tell her,' she thought, 'it should be soon, whilst the news is fresh; then at least she won't think I've been keeping secrets from her for weeks.'

The spring days were getting longer and lighter, allowing Maggie and Nora more time on the allotment, tending their now very large vegetables; Julia waved guiltily as she passed them by.

'They could do with another pair of hands,' she thought, but now might be the ideal moment to catch Rosa alone in the cowshed.

Rosa was in fact sitting on the front step, smoking a cheroot, admiring the view of the moors loud with the call of skylarks and curlews. Usually Julia would have deftly sidestepped Rosa and entered the house without speaking a word, but now was not the time to sidestep important issues. Taking a deep breath to steady her trembling limbs, she plucked up the courage to say what she had to say.

'May I have a word with you?'

Rosa looked at her with an astounded expression on her face.

'What about?' she asked rudely.

Julia went for the direct approach. 'Your brother.'

Rosa's face clouded and she covered her mouth as if smothering a cry of fear.

'Should we go inside?' Julia said quickly.

Rosa scrambled to her feet and followed Julia into the sitting room, where they both stood like adversaries facing each other across a wide space.

'I've been putting out feelers, for Gabriel,' Julia started.

'*You?*' cried Rosa.

'And something's come up,' Julia blurted out.

'*What?*' Rosa cried. 'What's come up?' she demanded.

And with that Julia filled in Rosa on all that her brother had told her, trying to be as accurate as possible with the details he'd given her. As she spoke, Rosa's face contracted with an expression that was a mixture of ecstasy and heart-breaking relief; she seemed to fold over with the weight of the news, and Julia had to rush forwards to stop her collapsing on her knees on the hard floor.

'Gabriel,' Rosa sobbed. 'My Gabriel,' she cried, as she wept and shuddered uncontrollably.

At the sound of the relief in her voice, tears streamed down Julia's face too, as she continued to hold Rosa tightly for fear of her falling.

'I can't believe it,' Rosa managed to say, before a look of panic crossed her face. 'But how can we be sure it's true?' she cried.

'Everything I've told you is true, as far as I know,' Julia answered solemnly. 'I trust my source implicitly.'

Guiding Rosa to the old battered leatherette sofa, Julia sat her down by the wood-burner, which she stoked before throwing on more logs.

'I'll make some tea,' she said, but Rosa grabbed her hand.

'No, sit with me, don't go,' she implored, her immense dark eyes wide with tears and wonder. 'Tell me more, please. Stay with me.'

Julia smiled as she sat down beside Rosa, who like a desperate child held her hand and squeezed it hard.

'Why would you do this for me?' she whispered.

'Because . . .' Julia's voice trailed away.

How could she explain her guilt about what she'd done when Rosa was in London? No matter how many times she told herself it was right, and it was *right*, of that Julia had no doubt, Rosa's stricken hopeless face on her return from London had never ceased to haunt Julia.

'I felt I had to try to help after what I did,' was all she said.

Rosa gazed raptly into her face. 'Thank you. And he's alive, *alive*,' she said as if she were in a dream.

Now it was Julia's turn to squeeze her hand. 'Rosa, we must be cautious: Gabriel's still far from safe –'

'But he's got a false identity and false papers!' euphoric Rosa cried. 'And we know he made it on to a train to Belgium – that's enough to give me hope,' she beamed. 'And he's alive!' Rosa repeated rapturously. 'ALIVE!'

Her radiant face, alight with renewed hope, was wreathed in smiles.

'You've given me back my brother,' she said, as she buried her face against Julia's shoulder and wept all over again.

It was at this point that Maggie and Nora walked in with a basket of freshly picked spinach and some sprouts. They both stood gaping in the doorway when they saw Rosa crushed in Julia's arms.

'What's happened? Is she sick?' Nora cried, dropping the basket and dashing forwards to assist Julia.

Rosa lifted her damp face to Nora, and, brushing back her tumbling dark hair, she smiled at them like they'd never seen her smile before.

'Julia's managed to get some news about my brother. It looks as if he's alive!'

For all of Julia's cautioning words, that night in the cowshed was one of happiness, laughter and celebration. Corned-beef fritters were fried in the kitchen, and everybody mucked in, bumping into each other, laughing, as they cooked and set the table together. Julia produced a bottle she'd brought from home on her last visit.

'Brandy,' she said with a grin.

'Where did that come from?' Nora cried.

'Mummy insisted I took it to use for "medicinal purposes"!' Julia laughed as she laced their strong tea with a double measure.

'To Gabriel!' she toasted. 'And to the next stage of his journey. Please God, may he make it back soon — and in one piece!'

Rosa waved her mug in the air as she held Julia's gaze. 'To Gabriel — *and* to friendship!'

Nobody in the room had ever eaten corned-beef fritters accompanied by shots of brandy: the combination was heady and quite wonderful. By bedtime Nora had the hiccups, and Maggie was yawning.

'I must get to sleep,' Maggie said. 'I've got to water the lettuce in the cold frame before I clock on tomorrow morning or Percy will have my guts for garters. And you,' she added as she unsteadily pulled Nora to her feet, 'have got Polly to feed.'

Nora avoided looking Maggie in the eye; she couldn't believe her luck that Maggie still thought the pig in the sty was Polly. Neither could she believe that Percy had kept her secret: though he often shot her a dirty look, so far he'd obviously not let on to Maggie.

Julia, alone with Rosa and feeling a little light-headed, reiterated her words of caution. 'We have to be patient.'

'I know, Julia, but as long as Gabriel's alive surely I'm allowed to feel hope.'

As they said goodnight, Rosa kissed Julia long and hard on both cheeks.

'I still can't believe you did this for me; I thought you despised me,' she admitted.

'Never,' Julia retorted. 'Though I have to admit I was pretty scared of you – you have a hell of a temper, you know.'

'*Mi dispiace, cara*,' Rosa murmured in her mother tongue.

'I know I hurt you badly, but I had no choice,' Julia confessed.

'All these things are in the past,' Rosa said, as she looked into Julia's stunning green eyes. 'You have given me hope, something I thought I had lost forever.'

31. Catching Up

The girls were thrilled to see Kit walking into the canteen one afternoon.

'You were sent home to rest,' Nora teased. 'What're you doing back here?'

'I've come to collect my wages, and to see you all,' Kit announced, as she pulled up a chair and sat down amongst her friends.

'We've missed you, *cara*,' Rosa said, leaning over to give Kit a kiss on the cheek.

'*I've* missed you,' Julia laughed. 'I've nobody to talk to in the filling shed these days.'

'I'll be back,' Kit promised as she rearranged her pretty red duster coat around her even bigger bulging tummy.

Fashion-conscious Maggie eyed the coat with envy. 'Has that nice husband of yours been treating you again?'

Kit smiled fondly. 'He said I needed cheering up, and he was right too – the minute I put on this coat I felt a lot more cheerful – except Billy said I looked like Humpty-Dumpty!' she giggled.

'Oh, to be adored,' Julia teased.

Nora in all innocence said, 'I'm adored these days.'

Her friends couldn't help but smile at her dreamy expression.

'And quite rightly,' Kit said sweetly. 'Peter's a lucky man to have a lovely girl like you looking after him.'

Not to be left out of the picture, Maggie giggled, 'I'm adored too!'

Looking less dreamy, Rosa said in a rather under-stated way, 'I suppose I am.'

Julia grinned as she pointed a finger at herself. 'That leaves me the un-adored odd one out!'

'Never mind,' Rosa said good-naturedly. 'We'll take care of our lonely spinster friend.'

Kit looked incredulously from Rosa to Julia, then back again.

'Did something happen in my absence?' she inquired.

Not wanting to talk about her very private news in the canteen, Rosa just winked. 'Oh, you know, we got fed up with scowling at each other.'

'Well, I'm glad of that,' Kit said with obvious relief. 'Now,' she continued in a more businesslike manner, 'before you all buzz off I've been thinking.'

'She's off,' Maggie cried, as she rolled her blue eyes. 'Kit's been arranging things.'

'That I have,' Kit retorted without a hint of embar-rassment. 'About the cake: I said I'd make one for you, and I will. I'll have eggs from the chickens, if Billy doesn't smash the lot, and we've all been saving our sugar rations.' She waved a hand around the table to include everybody present. 'But it won't be a fruit cake – there's not a raisin to be had in the entire land: the Germans have nabbed the lot!'

Before Maggie could respond, Kit ran on, 'It will be

'iced, white as the virgin that you are,' she said with a cheeky wink. 'And there'll be a darling little bride and groom on a silver pedestal a-top!'

'Oh, thank you,' Maggie cried, as she overenthusiastically squeezed her friend.

'Careful there,' Kit warned. 'One more hug like that and I'll have mi waters breaking in the Phoenix canteen.'

'You'll be pleased to hear my bridesmaid's dress is finished,' Nora told Kit, as Maggie settled back in her chair and lit up a Woodbine. 'Mrs Yates did a grand job fixing it up for me.'

'We seamstresses,' Rosa chipped in. 'Worked our fingers to the bone.'

'How's Billy's page-boy outfit coming along?' Maggie asked excitedly.

'Oh, he looks a treat, though will he never sit still when I'm trying to fit the shirt on him,' Kit laughed. 'You'll have your work cut out walking along behind him, Nora,' she warned. 'I've told Billy to walk slowly and not to step on the bride's veil. God help you, Maggie, if he breaks into a run!'

'He'll look so cute, done up like Little Lord Fauntleroy,' Nora sighed sentimentally.

'Do you know yet when the handsome groom's due home?' Kit asked Maggie, who shook her head.

'He's been granted leave for the wedding, but he doesn't know whether he'll arrive Friday night or in the early hours of Saturday morning.'

'God, that's cutting it fine,' said Kit.

'I know!' Maggie cried. 'And then he has to go back

on the Sunday afternoon. Can you believe it? One night!'

'Better than nothing at all,' Rosa teased.

Having not seen her friends for at least a week, Kit was full of questions. 'How are the arrangements for the wedding breakfast coming along?'

'All organized,' Maggie announced triumphantly. 'Leek and potato soup,' she chanted. 'Roast pork, apple sauce, roast potatoes, sprouts, cabbage and carrots, all the veg from our allotment,' she added proudly. 'Bottled plum tart – and your wedding cake, Kit!' Without pausing for a breath, Maggie quickly added, 'And for tea! Salad, home-grown of course, and meat-paste sandwiches!'

'How we'll be expected to dance the night away at the Black Bull after that I do not know,' Rosa teased.

The hooter going off brought their happy chatter to a close.

'I'd best go and collect my wages,' Kit said, hauling herself up. 'Pop in and see me any time you fancy – the kettle's always on the boil in my house.'

Though Nora cheerily waved Kit off, her heart was heavy, as she told Peter later when she visited him on the ward. These days, as April showers melted into warm spring sunshine, Nora and Peter preferred to spend their time outside, strolling arm in arm around the lovely grounds of Wrigg Hall, admiring the unfolding rhododendrons and bright azaleas.

'Every time they talk about roast pork and apple sauce I thank God Polly's safe, but as soon as that happens I feel guilty about the other one that's not got long to live.' Her brow creased as she continued, 'I over-heard Percy talking to Maggie. He said when the time came he'd take the pig over to Ramsbottom, where his mate has a small slaughterhouse. After he's' – Nora gulped: she just couldn't bring herself to say the words 'slit its throat' – 'after he's done the business, the meat's got to hang for a fortnight in a cool place before eating, so, like I say, the poor beast's not got long for this life.'

'You promised you wouldn't get soft and sentimen-tal when I agreed to buy the new pig,' Peter reminded her.

'And I haven't,' Nora protested. 'I've not looked it in the eye once; I just dump the swill bucket in the pen and walk away. But that doesn't stop me from feeling sorry for it.'

Peter pulled her close and stroked her wild red curls. 'You're a soft lass,' he whispered in her ear.

'Anyway,' Nora continued as they made their way towards the rose gardens, where tender young buds were beginning to peep through the previous year's old growth, 'I've made my mind up – I'm going vegetarian!'

'That won't be difficult, with rationing as it is. I don't think there's more than a shred of meat in anything that we eat – cardboard more like, with a bit of sawdust and tripe!'

'You can scoff, but I'm serious: no meat for me from now on, ever!' she vowed.

Before Nora returned to the hospital to start her vol-untary work, she and Peter discussed the arrangements for Maggie's wedding day.

'Sister's happy for me to go out for the whole day and evening too: she thought it was a good idea in fact,' Peter explained. 'She mentioned I might be going home soon, so I need to start "rehabituating" myself with the outside world.'

Nora tried to smother her gasp of astonishment. 'Going home!'

'I can't stay at Wrigg Hall forever!' Peter laughed.

'No, of course not, not when you're so much better,' she affirmed.

'And getting better all the time, especially since you came into my life,' he teased. 'My little ray of sunshine.'

Nora's heart was beating wildly; whilst she was of course delighted for him, the thought of Peter leaving, of not being able to see him as she did now, virtually every day, brought tears to her eyes. Trying to sound practical she asked, 'Will your mum be able to cope? Nursing you at home? You told me she was getting on.'

'I'll talk to her about it when she next visits and see what she has to say,' Peter replied. 'But I intend to get work, Nora. I don't want to be an invalid all my life!' he exclaimed. 'I can walk now, and see well with my good eye, and I don't frighten people to death with my damaged face any more,' he said cheerfully. 'I want to get back to being a mechanic, working in a garage, fixing cars and trucks – a proper mucky grease monkey, that's me, that's when I'm happiest!'

For all her fear of Peter's moving away, Nora couldn't help but smile at his excitement. After all he'd been through, all he'd suffered, he still had a burning passion for life. Who was she to bar his way if he wanted to move back home and look after his mother and work in the town where he'd grown up? Holding back her tears, she smiled bravely at Peter, who had become the light of her life. Recalling how he was when she'd first seen him, rocking back and forth all day long on his hospital bed, his face covered in bandages, half blind and frightened of every shadow, Nora knew she would never hold him back; he'd come so far and if he wanted to go further, and without her, she would send him on his way with her blessing.

Rosa too was having her own set of anxieties; though she was in regular communication with Roger, she hadn't told him her most recent dramatic news about Gabriel.

'I feel guilty not telling him, but with his RAF connections I thought it might not be a wise move, in case he asked where the information had come from,' she told Julia, as they walked down to the allotment to help Maggie and Nora with the endless task of weeding their precious vegetables.

Julia stopped in her tracks to respond to Rosa. 'You've done the right thing,' she assured her. 'We must never drop Hugo in it, you know.'

'Of course, mum's the word!' Rosa asserted. Linking her arm through Julia's, she chatted on. 'Anyway, Roger's got more than enough on his plate right now: he told me in a letter that Bomber Command suffered its greatest losses recently. Can you believe it? Ninety-five planes failed to return after being heavily attacked by German night-fighters.'

'God help the poor souls,' Julia murmured sadly. 'We nearly lost my brother in a night raid; luckily he was picked up and survived, though it did cost him his left hand . . .'

'How awful!' Rosa gasped.

'That was the end of Hugo's flying days,' Julia added sadly. 'It vexes the life out of him, but he's made the best of it.'

They walked on in companionable silence, which Julia broke by asking a rather unexpected question. 'Have you ever thought of doing something for the war effort other than working in munitions?'

'Actually, I have,' Rosa confessed. 'After I got out of occupied territory, I dreamt of working as an under-cover operator.'

'Really!'

'Well, it was just a dream, but why not? I'm a good linguist, I've had personal experience of being a German prisoner, I detest the Nazis, and I have some first-hand experience of how undercover agents operate,' she pointed out. Giving a philosophical shrug, Rosa added, 'I never got further than dreaming about it – I sometimes regret I didn't actively pursue it – but realistically I don't even know how you would go about getting recruited for something like that. Anyway the Phoenix called and I met you lovely lot!' she joked. 'Now I build bombs to annihilate the Nazis, which I suppose is better than nothing!' She turned to Julia and said with a wicked smile, '*You'd* make an excellent spy.'

'*Me?*'

'Yes, your cool, aloof, English upper-class manner.'

'I'm not upper class!' Julia laughed.

'Oh, you English have such a ridiculous class system,' Rosa mocked. 'Anyway, to me you sound upper class: your voice, your education, your imperious looks! You've only to snap your fingers and people jump.'

Julia grimaced. 'How ghastly!' she exclaimed. 'Do I really come across as a stuck-up toff?'

Rosa couldn't lie, but she spoke with a grin. 'Yes, but it fades once you get to know the real Julia.'

Julia leant across and gave her a pretend swipe. 'Oddly enough, I like it here,' she said, as she lifted her face to the sun and felt it warm her eyelids.

'Me too,' Rosa agreed. 'This place – Kit, Maggie, Nora and now you,' she added shyly, 'are my lifeline.' Her slender shoulders sagged as she confessed with a sad sigh, 'I don't know how I'll survive without you all when I marry Roger and move away.'

Bending to hide her flushed face, Rosa picked up a stone that was lying on the path and threw it over a drystone wall, which she and Julia leant against.

'It's funny,' she continued with a blush, 'I was only talking to Arthur about exactly the same thing when he was up here recently.'

'Arthur,' Julia inquired. 'The man with the little boy?'

'Yes, he used to work here but he and Stevie moved away when his wife died in a factory explosion.'

'Poor chap,' Julia murmured. 'Everybody seems very fond of him.'

'Oh, we all love Arthur,' Rosa said warmly. 'And we miss him too. Anyway, as I said to him, I'm very fond of Roger but his Englishness sometimes overwhelms me,' she admitted. 'And he's in such a rush to get married. I told him I won't do anything until I know more about Gabriel. Ideally I would want him at my wedding.'

'Of course you do, and that's a very sensible idea,' Julia replied smoothly. 'You can't make a big move like that with everything hanging in the air the way it is at the moment. I'm quite sure Roger will understand that. Now come on,' Julia joked as she tugged Rosa away from the wall, 'if we don't show up to help Maggie and Nora with their wretched weeding, we'll never hear the end of it.'

32. Tempers Flare

When the day Nora had been dreading dawned, 24 April, she made sure she was nowhere near either the allotment or the cowshed. She didn't know what time the doomed pig would be loaded and driven away by Percy (who to this day had kept her secret), but she decided to spend the time she wasn't working on the cordite line with Polly.

She found Polly snout down, guzzling contentedly on turnip tops in her spacious new run. When she heard Nora's call, her ears flapped and, with her little curly tail wiggling excitedly, she trotted up to her mistress, who leant over the fence to rub her back.

'Oh, dear, Polly,' Nora sighed. 'It could so easily have been your last day on earth.'

Oblivious to the bullet she'd dodged, Polly stuck her head under the fence and rubbed her head against Nora's legs.

'Silly daft thing!' Nora giggled. 'Now you stay in your run whilst I muck out your sty and put down some nice clean bedding for you to snuggle down on.'

When Nora returned to the cowshed, hot, sweaty and keen to have a bath after mucking out Polly's sty, she walked straight into Maggie, who was blazing with fury.

'You never told me!' she raged. 'All these weeks and you've *never* told me!'

Nora immediately guessed that Maggie must have found out about the swap. But how? Racked with guilt (but not one bit sorry for keeping Polly safe), Nora fought back tears. 'I'm sorry, I shouldn't have deceived you.'

Maggie was striding about the room, wildly waving her hands in the air. 'How can I ever trust you again?' she ranted. 'My chief bridesmaid! My best friend!'

Julia and Rosa, who were keeping themselves well out of the way in the kitchen, grimaced at each other.

'Poor Nora,' Julia whispered.

'Shhh!' Rosa hissed as she listened closely with her ear to the door.

'Why did you do it in the first place?' Maggie demanded.

'Because I just couldn't bear to see Polly go to slaughter,' Nora explained. 'I love her so much,' she gulped.

'Then why not talk to *me* about it?' Maggie cried. 'After all, it was me who bought her in the first place. Don't you think I have a right to know what's happening to my pig?'

Nora crumpled. Everything Maggie said was true: she'd been a rotten friend, a liar, and a thief too.

'I thought if I told you how I felt, you'd say I was being ridiculous –' Nora started.

'You *are* being ridiculous!' Maggie shouted. 'It's a pig we're talking about, not Mickey Mouse!'

'I thought it would be best if I just did a swap on the

298

quiet and told nobody,' Nora blurted out. 'How did you find out – was it Percy?'

'As a matter of fact it wasn't,' Maggie snapped. 'It was the man who slaughtered the pig; he told me it was a male.'

Nora sighed, so it was simply by chance that Maggie had found out.

'I said that my pig was female, and he said the one that Percy had dropped off was definitely male; then I asked Percy and he had to admit the truth. But he didn't want to.'

There was nothing Nora could do but apologize, but at one point in the middle of Maggie's tirade she remembered Peter's words and daringly repeated them. 'They all taste the same in the end, don't they?'

Hearing this and expecting another flare-up, Rosa called loudly from the kitchen, 'Tea's ready.'

Feeling sick to her stomach, Nora said she wasn't hungry and, after a tepid bath, she stayed well out of Maggie's way, which was difficult, because they had always shared their night-time routine: putting in their rollers, having a cigarette, switching out the light, getting into bed and chatting quietly till they both dropped off. But not tonight. In frosty silence Maggie undressed, turned out the light and got into bed; it was the first night in all the time that the girls had known each other that they didn't call out in the darkness, 'Night, night, God bless.'

Nora felt it keenly; turning her face into her pillow, she stifled her sobs, whilst wondering if Maggie would ever speak to her again.

The days that followed were uncomfortable for everybody, and they didn't get any easier when Percy thundered on the cowshed door early one morning.

'The bastard whiteflies have attacked the vegetable patch!' he announced.

Forgetting their quarrel, Maggie and Nora ran down the cobbled lane to the allotment, with Percy panting and cursing behind them. The sight that met their eyes stopped them dead in their tracks: a large section of the patch, which only yesterday was bristling with spinach, broccoli, cabbage and sprouts, had been blitzed by what looked like a cloud of white mould, which clung to the leaves and stems of the vegetables whilst small white-winged insects flitted on the underside of the plants.

'Oh, God!' Maggie cried.

Nora, who'd run to the other end of the allotment to examine the extent of the damage there, called out, 'The carrots are okay.'

By this time Percy had caught up with them and was staring at the pests like they were God's own personal enemy.

'How could this have happened?' devastated Maggie sobbed. 'There was no sign of them here yesterday.'

'They're like a soddin' bad wind; they blow in and they blow out again, leaving ruin in their wake,' Percy growled.

'What're we going to do?' whimpered poor Maggie.

'Well . . .' said Percy as he surveyed the blighted plot. 'This patch here has taken the brunt of it, but that patch over yonder is looking healthy enough.' He nodded in the direction of the healthy carrots. 'We'll have to check where the little buggers are breeding, then sluice every single plant with a solution of soap and water to get rid of 'em.'

'*All* of them?' gasped Nora, surveying the sprawling allotment.

'*All*,' Percy reiterated. 'It'll be back-breaking work, but it's got to be done, and done right away, before they multiply before our very eyes.'

'So it's not as bad as it might be?' Maggie said, grasping at straws.

'If we can get on top of the whitefly, we may only lose this lot,' Percy said, as he pointed at the ruined vegetables before them.

'And the rest might survive?' Maggie asked hopefully.

'Aye . . . if we're lucky,' he replied.

With no time to waste, Percy made up solutions of soap and water in watering cans and galvanized buckets, which the girls lugged along each row, dousing the plants with the liquid, whilst digging up and throwing away all the infested plants. Working in silence, intent on their work, Maggie and Nora fell in beside each other; Nora was surprised when Maggie broke their concentrated silence by asking a very unexpected question. 'Where did you take Polly?'

Playing for time, Nora fiddled with the watering can in her hand. If she told Maggie Polly's whereabouts, would she go to claim her? As if reading Nora's mind, Maggie added, 'It's all right, I'm not about to take her back.' She tried to hide the smile that was playing at the corners of her mouth. 'I don't need to roast two pigs on my wedding day.'

Then suddenly Maggie started to giggle, and in seconds the pair of them were rocking with laughter. Percy, across the way from them, scowled at the hysterical girls. 'What's so bloody funny?' he demanded.

'Oh, just something Maggie said,' Nora, breathless with laughter, tried to explain.

'Well, don't dwell on it too long,' he grumbled. 'You'd best finish this lot before you start your shift 'cos one thing's for sure: I can't do it single-handed.'

With his sharp words ringing in their ears, the girls returned to the job, but a few days later, when the whitefly blight was under control, Maggie walked the few miles with Nora to Polly's new home. Polly was delighted to see Maggie, who she frisked up to, grunting a greeting.

'You look comfortable, missis,' Maggie joked, as she scratched Polly's ears. 'In your smart new place far away from wicked Maggie and the butcher's knife.'

Blushing Nora apologized again. 'I'm sorry I lied to you, Maggie, it was wrong, I know.'

Big-hearted Maggie threw an arm around Nora's slumped shoulders. 'It's all in the past, kiddo; now all we've got to worry about is Percy and the wrath of the returning whitefly!'

Unfortunately Maggie spoke too soon. Just as they were recovering from the shock of the whitefly attack, Kit, who always treated the cowshed like her second home, walked in looking as white as a ghost.

'Billy's got chicken pox!' she announced.

Rosa, Julia and Nora, who were in the kitchen making a pot of tea before they headed off to the Phoenix to clock on for their afternoon shift, stared at her in dismay.

'He's covered in spots,' Kit added mournfully. 'There's no way he's going to be better in time for the wedding.'

Nora slumped into the nearest chair. 'Maggie's going to go nuts!' she whispered.

'Who's taking my name in vain?' Maggie called cheerily as she breezed into the kitchen, then stopped in her tracks when she saw her friends all nervously staring at her.

'I've got bad news,' Kit started.

Assuming the worst, Maggie clutched the side of the kitchen table.

'Not Les? Please not Les . . .'

Before her legs buckled beneath her, Kit grabbed Maggie's arm and sat her down on one of the wooden chairs. 'No, thank God, not Les. It's Billy. I'm not sure he can be your page boy . . .'

After hearing Kit's news, Maggie was disappointed indeed, but, because she'd been expecting something a thousand times worse, she didn't go to pieces; instead she took a more practical approach.

'He might be better in time?' she said hopefully.

'He might but I don't want to infect the entire congregation,' Kit answered with a smile. 'I'm on my way to the Phoenix nursery right now to ask Matron's advice.'

As she made a move towards the door, she called over her shoulder, 'I'll report back as soon as I can.'

On the way to work Maggie's resolve weakened. 'It's a shame,' she said sadly. 'I thought Billy would look so cute dressed up as a page.'

'And such a waste of the sweet little outfit Ian bought for him,' Nora commiserated. 'The wedding photographs won't look anything like as nice with only me next to you,' she added glumly.

Before spirits sank lower, Rosa quickly said, 'Kit might come back to us with good news.'

Later, when the hooter went for tea-time, the girls rushed to their favourite table, where Kit was waiting for them.

'What did she say?' cried Maggie, as she sat down next to Kit and lit up a Woodbine.

'Once the spots are dry and Billy's showing no sign of a cough or a cold, he won't be contagious.'

'So he could be all right?' Maggie replied.

Kit was busy counting the days off on her fingers. 'I think he could be all clear by your wedding day.'

'That's good news,' Maggie said with relief. 'We wouldn't want the guests breaking out in spots a week after my wedding!' she giggled.

With the big day fast approaching, Julia suggested to Maggie that she might try out a new hair-style in advance of her wedding day.

'I think you'd really suit that Lauren Bacall look,' she said, as she showed Maggie a picture of the beautiful film star with her long hair looped in golden waves around her face. 'Your hair's long enough to take it – shall we give it a try?'

Intrigued and excited, Maggie immediately agreed. 'Yes, that style would look lovely with my long veil.'

'I've done it before,' Julia reassured her. 'On a friend of mine: we used setting lotion and heated rollers, and it looked stunning.'

Taken with the idea, Maggie agreed that they'd have a trial run at the end of the week of afternoon shifts, which gave Julia time to purchase the setting lotion and borrow some heated rollers and a portable hairdryer from a woman she worked with in the filling shed. On the appointed night Maggie washed her mass of thick auburn hair. After running the setting lotion through Maggie's hair, Julia rolled long strands around the heavy rollers, then carefully arranged the hairdryer that was attached to a bag over Maggie's head.

'Now all we've got to do is set the timer and wait,' Julia said with a confident smile.

Maggie smoked several Woodbines as she sat on an upright chair, talking loudly over the noise of the dryer.

'It's beginning to feel warm,' she told Julia, who checked the time on her wristwatch.

'Just another ten minutes,' Julia replied.

'Are you sure? It feels very hot under here,' Maggie fretted.

'Quite sure,' Julia asserted, checking the timer. 'I know what I'm doing.'

When the timer finally shrilled out, Rosa and Nora

gathered around excitedly as Julia carefully removed the hairdryer bag from Maggie's head. But, as she pulled the bag away, her confidence abandoned her – for there was no mistaking the smell of singed hair.

She stood, frozen, hardly daring to look at Maggie, or her hair. There was a horrible pause before anyone spoke.

'Oh, Christ!' wailed Maggie, as she clutched her hands to her head. 'What on earth's happened?'

Terrified of what she would find, a white-faced Julia tore out the rollers with trembling, clumsy fingers. Exchanging horrified looks with Nora and Rosa, who could see as well as Julia that the hair on Maggie's crown was badly burnt in several places, Julia made things even worse by running cold water over the area, which made the singed smell stronger.

'What have you done to me?' Maggie yelled as she leapt from the chair and ran to the mirror hanging on the wall.

Though the rest of her golden-auburn hair fell in silky waves around her face, there were chunks of hair on top of her head that were standing on end. The sight of the burnt bits scattered on the floor sent Maggie into weeping hysterics.

'Oh, no!' she wailed. 'No . . . no . . .'

Beside herself with remorse and panic, Julia gabbled, 'I'm so sorry – I have no idea what's gone wrong. It worked perfectly when I did it before, truly it did.'

'Well, it's not worked now,' Nora said bluntly.

Though all three friends offered reassuring words, Maggie was beyond any kind of comfort.

'My wedding's doomed,' she sobbed. 'First the pig, then the flies and Billy's chicken pox – and now this – I'll be bald on my wedding day!' Putting her head in her hands, she wept uncontrollably. 'Les will never want to marry me looking like this!'

When she was a little calmer, it was Rosa who came to the rescue, managing to soften the brittle burnt hair with some setting lotion, and then carefully looping it into little pin curls which she assured Maggie would give her a softer look in the morning. Still weeping, Maggie prayed that Rosa's words would come true, but the next day, when the pins were removed, her damaged hair sprang up like a chicken's coxcomb. Utterly devastated, Maggie returned to her bed, where she lay wide-eyed, staring up at the ceiling.

'We've got to do something,' Nora hissed to Rosa and Julia, who were in a huddle in the sitting room.

'I've done more than enough,' Julia said miserably. 'I can't believe I find her the dream wedding gown, then burn her hair just before her wedding day.'

'This damned wedding has worn her out,' Nora said crossly.

'It's turned into a nightmare for the poor girl,' Rosa agreed sympathetically.

'I can't think of anything to say that will help,' a defeated Julia admitted.

Nora, suddenly wide-eyed, exclaimed, 'Wait – I know exactly who can talk to her.'

'*Who?*' Rosa and Julia asked in unison.

'Her sister, Emily.'

Rosa and Julia looked blank. 'How's that going to help?' Julia asked.

'Maggie hero-worships her big sister; she used to work here at the Phoenix,' Nora explained. 'But then she got married and moved to Bolton. She's the best person in the world to talk Maggie down. I've seen her do it many a time; she always talks sense.'

'How do we get hold of her?' Rosa inquired.

'She regularly visits her mum,' Nora said, as she snatched up her coat. 'I'll go and ask Mrs Yates if Emily's due for a visit soon.'

Nora returned an hour later with a smile on her face.

'Mrs Yates said their Emily will be popping over this week; she said she'd send her up here to have a word with Maggie.'

'We can only hope and pray,' Julia said with a heavy sigh.

They didn't have long to wait. A few days later a grinning Emily knocked on the cowshed door. 'Hiya,' she said. 'Where's our kid?'

Julia and Rosa gaped in amazement at Maggie's older sister, who had the same colouring as Maggie and (if it were possible) even bigger blue eyes.

'In the bedroom,' Nora whispered. 'Trying to do something with her burnt hair,' she added, rolling her eyes.

'It's my fault,' guilty Julia blurted out. 'I should never have suggested waving it.'

Recognizing her Southern accent, Emily said, 'Are you the one who found the lovely frock for Maggie?'

Julia nodded. 'Yes, one good deed followed by a bad one,' she groaned miserably.

'Leave her to me,' Emily said briskly, as she walked towards the bedroom door.

The girls in the sitting room sat tensely, waiting to hear a shout or a sob or something being thrown at the wall, but all was strangely quiet. Inside the room, Emily sat on the bed beside her sister, who cried in her arms. Taking advantage of her position, Emily was able to peer down at Maggie's singed crown.

'I'm not going to lie to you,' she said. 'It's a bloody mess.'

'I know,' Maggie wept. 'Les will hate it.'

Emily held her at arm's length. 'Les won't see it,' she announced.

'What?' Maggie spluttered. 'You're not suggesting I wear a wig?'

'Don't be so daft!' Emily laughed. 'Come on now, get me the wreath and veil.'

Maggie rose and went to the wardrobe, where the veil hung, yards and yards of it trimmed with delicate lace.

'Right, now stand up straight with your arms by your side,' Emily instructed.

Like a child being told what to do, Maggie got into position.

'Head up,' Emily commanded.

Concentrating hard, Emily arranged the wreath of artificial blossom on the crown of Maggie's bent head, then gently pulled the veil around it.

'When you walk down the aisle, the veil will be over your face, like this,' she said and smoothed down the veil. 'After you've taken your vows, the veil will be thrown back and all that the congregation will see is your beautiful smiling face and your long, shining hair topped with a pretty wreath that completely hides all the burnt bits.'

Maggie gazed into the mirror and slowly smiled. 'That works if you move the wreath back a bit,' she agreed. 'But what about at the pub, when I'm dancing? I can't keep the veil on, can I?'

'No, but you can keep the headdress on,' Emily explained as she released the wreath from the clips that held it to the veil and popped it back on Maggie's head. 'It looks charming, don't you think?'

Maggie stared at her reflection and nodded. 'It does look nice,' she said in surprise. Then she thought of something else; blushing she whispered, 'What about later, when I'm in bed with Les?'

At which point Emily burst out laughing. 'Sweetheart, believe me, when you two get between the sheets it's not your hair that Les will be looking at!'

The sound of the sisters' loud raucous laughter brought a smile to the faces of the girls waiting tensely in the sitting room. Nora gave a cheeky grin as she gave Churchill's famous victory sign.

'Looks like Emily's cracked it!' she whispered.

Before Emily left, she eyed Nora, Rosa and Julia, who were all smiles now that Maggie was happy.

'Promise me none of you will do anything daft

before the eighth of May?' she said firmly. 'No mad diets, hair colouring, dodgy skin creams or tantrums,' she said, emphasizing the last word as she winked at her kid sister. 'See you on your wedding day, sweetheart. Stay calm,' she added, and, blowing a kiss, she walked back down the hill to her mum's house in town.

Maggie sank on to the old leatherette sofa, where she lit up a Woodbine.

'Stay calm,' she laughed, as she remembered the government poster that was pinned up on the canteen wall: STAY CALM AND CARRY ON.

33. Visitors

Gladys had written to say that she and Reggie would be arriving on the seventh of May for the wedding and staying at Yew Tree Farm with Kit and Ian.

> *I'm so excited, Mags – I wouldn't miss your wedding for the world! First we'll be going to Leeds – it's time I introduced Reggie to my parents – but we'll be with you on the eve of your wedding, in the cowshed, just like old times, so get the kettle on, sweetheart. Can't wait to see you.*
>
> *Lots of love,*
> *Glad*
> *xxx*

Maggie grinned as she folded the letter. 'Good job you've started on that Italian soup, Rosa. We'll have a lot of mouths to feed.'

Her friend grinned back as she sliced potatoes and carrots into chunks before throwing them into the bubbling mixture on the stove.

'*Zuppa di fagioli, cara*,' Rosa corrected Maggie, who raised her eyebrows and rolled her eyes.

'*Zuppa di fagioli!*' she mimicked Rosa in a perfect Italian accent. 'It smells good whatever it's called,' she added, coming closer to sniff the soup. Rosa had soaked dried beans overnight, picked fresh thyme from the moors and used all the vegetables that Nora and Maggie could spare from their allotment. 'Will there be enough there for everybody who's coming for supper tonight?' she asked anxiously, as she peered into the depths of the big pot Rosa had borrowed from the Phoenix canteen.

'I could do with more vegetables,' Rosa admitted before quickly adding, 'But I don't want to take any that you've set aside for the wedding breakfast.'

'We'll be picking salad and veg from the allotment later,' Maggie told her. 'There's bound to be some stuff left over.'

'I hope there'll be enough,' Rosa fretted. 'There'll be quite a crowd later on.'

Rosa's thoughts strayed to Roger, who'd been granted twenty-four hours' leave to attend the wedding and would be arriving later that day.

'He's probably on his way,' she thought nervously. 'Driving up the A1 in his old Morgan, battered by the wind and the rain.'

Blissfully unaware of Rosa's anxious thoughts, excited Maggie babbled on about the domestic arrangements. 'Kit's promised to bring a batch of her freshly baked bread to go with the soup, and I'm going to collect a big apple pie from Mum's – there should be plenty, especially if Ian turns up with some damson wine,' she laughed.

Happiness zipped through the cowshed as the girls

busied themselves with their tasks. Nora insisted on doing all the prepping for the wedding breakfast.

'Peter's getting the bus over from Wrigg Hall to help me,' she told Maggie with a ring of pride in her voice. 'I've already told the landlord of the Black Bull that we can lend a hand preparing the roast if he's short staffed.'

At the mention of 'the roast' both girls exchanged a secretive smile.

'I'm glad we're not eating Polly!' Maggie confessed with a cheeky wink before she hurried off to pick up the apple pie her mum had prepared.

After the Lauren Bacall burnt-hair disaster, Julia hadn't volunteered her services again, so when Maggie asked her to iron her wedding gown, Julia was a complete bag of nerves.

'I don't know why Maggie even asked me,' she confessed to Rosa in a frantic whisper. 'After what I did to her hair imagine what I could do to her dress?'

'She thinks because the dress came from your friend in London, you'll know best what to do,' Rosa assured her.

'I thought I knew best when I waved her hair,' Julia answered drily.

'Keep the iron on a cool heat and don't take your eyes off it for a second,' Rosa advised.

With everybody busily dashing back and forth, Rosa stayed in the kitchen stirring the *zuppa*. As the steam from it clouded her vision she let a terrible, heinous thought enter her head. 'I'd be so much happier if Roger wasn't coming to this wedding!'

Before she could let the vicious thought take root, Rosa laid down the wooden spoon and lit up a cheroot, which she inhaled deeply as she gazed out of the kitchen window at the rolling moors that changed in colour, the wild, blustery sky turning constantly from blue to grey and back again.

'What is wrong with me?' she raged at herself. 'Why can't I behave normally and look forward to seeing my fiancé like any other woman would?'

Even though the girls could have accommodated Roger at the cowshed, what with Maggie away on her honeymoon night, Rosa had booked him into the Black Bull. It wasn't just about giving him some privacy, which is what she planned to say to him when he arrived; the truth was her passion had cooled considerably after the visit to his parents. She also vividly recalled Arthur's advice after she'd poured out her troubles to him in private on his last visit.

'And what would *you* like?' he'd asked.

She recalled her own words too. 'I can't set a date until I know about Gabriel's whereabouts; obviously I'd want him beside me on my wedding day.' Her face flushed, not as a consequence of the steaming soup but because she knew in a few hours' time Arthur would be with them and darling baby Stevie too. How could her reactions be so different? It should be Roger whom she was excited to see, not Arthur. Her fiancé was kind, considerate, and he adored her – so he was a bit of a traditionalist, but she'd known that when she agreed to marry him. But the truth that was dawning on her right now was that she really did wish Roger was driving South, away from her, not North towards her.

In the sitting room Julia, who was breaking out into a nervous sweat, spat on the iron to check it wasn't too hot before holding her breath as she slid it over the glistening satin that was so white it momentarily blinded her. Gaining confidence Julia ironed out the creases in the long train and the full-waisted skirt, before turning her attention to Nora's pretty pink dress. As she was carefully pressing the fitted sleeves, Nora came and stood beside her.

'Isn't it lovely?' she sighed.

'It's gorgeous,' Julia agreed. 'Mrs Yates did a wonderful job.'

'I just can't wait for Peter to see me wearing it,' Nora admitted. 'He's never seen me dressed up in something as posh as that,' she said with a modest blush.

'He'll love you in it,' Julia assured her, as she swept the dress off the ironing board and carried it into the girls' bedroom, where she carefully hung it on the back of the door beside the freshly ironed bridal gown. 'Now,' she said as she turned to Nora with an excited smile, 'what's next?'

'It would be great if you could help with the veg,' Nora suggested.

'Rightio, lead the way,' laughed Julia.

As Julia marched down the cobbled lane to the allotment with Nora chattering at her side, she realized how very happy she was; a month ago she would have willingly packed her bags and walked away from the cowshed and everybody in it. Now she was giddy with excitement about the forthcoming wedding; she'd even been nominated official wedding photographer. She was the only person with a camera (bought by her generous father whilst she was at boarding school); but she loved sharing what she had with her friends. She loved their company, their humour, their individuality but, most of all, now that she'd got to know the different ways of each of the girls, she just loved *them*. The thought that after months of waiting and planning, weeping and fretting, Maggie's big day was about to happen filled Julia with joy; she couldn't wait to see her walking down the aisle arm in arm with Les.

After returning with an enormous apple pie, Maggie finished packing her trousseau into a small brown suitcase: it consisted of her only pair of nylons, a new nightie, which she'd saved coupons to buy, a light cotton frock and a warm cardigan, all neatly folded and ready for her brief honeymoon in a smart hotel in Grange-over-Sands. Every time Maggie thought about the moment she would be alone with her husband, her legs went weak and her pulse raced; what would it be like making love to Les for the first time after all these frustrating months of waiting?

'Only one precious night,' she thought. 'Better make the most of every precious minute, kiddo!'

*

Rosa and Maggie were so preoccupied with their own thoughts that they never heard Gladys and Reggie drive up in the car he'd borrowed for their long journey North.

'Anybody home?' Gladys called, as she stepped into the sitting room.

On hearing her voice, Maggie came bolting out of her bedroom and threw herself headlong into Gladys's open arms.

'Sister of the Groom!' she said with a happy laugh. 'I'm so glad to see you!' Gazing into Gladys's lovely face, she was vividly reminded of Les: brother and sister had the same sparkling smile and dark-blue eyes and the same rich dark-brunette hair. 'Rosa! Rosa!' she called. 'They're here.'

When Rosa came hurrying out of the kitchen to greet them, Reggie was astonished at the change in her demeanour.

'Good to see you again,' he said as he shook Rosa warmly by the hand.

'And you too, Reggie,' she said with genuine pleasure.

'How were your mum and dad?' Maggie asked eagerly about her future in-laws.

'Very excited about the wedding,' Gladys replied. 'They'll be driving over tomorrow first thing in the morning.'

'And Les . . .' Maggie asked with a quaver in her voice. 'Does anybody know when he's arriving?'

'He's already here,' the voice Maggie loved most in the world sounded softly behind her.

'LES!'

Maggie spun round and there, framed in the doorway, was her beloved fiancé. 'Oh, Les!' she cried, and, running into his arms, she burst into floods of tears.

'I wanted to surprise you, sweetheart, not make you cry,' he said, as he kissed away her tears.

'How did you get here in such good time?' Maggie sobbed.

'I drove up with Glad and Reg,' Les said, then added with a cheeky wink, 'I hid in the back of the car so you wouldn't see me.'

Leaving the rapturous lovers locked together, Gladys, Reggie and Rosa made a strong pot of tea, which they carried into the sitting room just as Julia and Nora returned from the allotment, hot and streaked with mud. Dragging themselves away from each other, Maggie and Les joined the happy group round the wood-burner, where Maggie simply couldn't take her eyes off Les. If she had, she might have seen a gold band glinting on Gladys's wedding finger, but it was Rosa who spotted it first.

'Is that what I think it is?' she gasped.

Gladys gaily waved her left hand in the air. 'We got married a week ago!' she cried.

'You got married?' Maggie gasped. 'Without telling anybody?' she added incredulously.

'We knew we wanted to get married,' Reggie explained with a proud smile. 'But with our shifts and the long hours we keep, we never seemed to have a moment to arrange it.'

'We were walking past the local register office after work one day,' Gladys giggled. 'Actually we were on our way to Lyons Café, and I said to Reggie, come on, let's go and see how long the waiting list is.'

'Can you believe it?' Reggie laughed. 'They'd had a cancellation and said they could marry us right there and then.'

'We had no ring, so we used my engagement ring, and no witnesses either, so one of the secretaries stood in,' Gladys told her friends, who were hanging on her every word.

'Ten minutes later we were standing outside, man and wife,' Reg said, completing the story with a triumphant smile. 'Best thing I ever did,' he added, as he put his arm around his radiantly happy wife.

Maggie, who'd been meticulously planning her wedding for months, couldn't believe that anything could be so simple.

'What did your parents say?' she asked Gladys.

'They only met Reg yesterday when we drove up from London. Obviously they were shocked, and I think Dad was a bit disappointed not to give me away,' she admitted. 'But Les turning up took their mind off everything else and knowing that tomorrow is his wedding day made up for us not having one.'

Still incredulous, Maggie continued, 'You really didn't mind not having a white dress and bridesmaids and a big do with all your friends and family?'

It was perfectly clear from the joy on both their faces that Reggie and Gladys didn't mind at all.

*

After drinking their tea and smoking several cigarettes the newlyweds drove over to Yew Tree Farm, where they were staying, whilst Maggie and Les, arm in arm, walked out on to the moors with eyes only for each other. Nora packed her bicycle basket with the veg and salad she'd picked with Julia, then set off down the hill to the Black Bull, where she'd arranged to meet Peter.

Left alone, Rosa went into the kitchen to check on the soup, but her heart skipped a beat as she heard the unmistakable sound of Roger's old Morgan sports car clanking and popping as it made its way along the cobbled lane.

'Oh, no,' she muttered. 'He's here already.'

Trembling, Rosa took a deep breath, then walked to the door to greet her fiancé. She was struck by how different this reunion was from the one she'd witnessed only an hour ago, when Maggie had laid eyes on her beloved for the first time in months. Unlike utterly rapturous Maggie, Rosa felt tight and edgy, and she had to take another deep breath to steady her jangling nerves.

'Darling!' Roger cried, as he vaulted over the driver's door and rushed towards her. 'It's so good to see you.'

Swinging her round in the air, he pressed his lips to her rich dark hair that fell in waves to her waist, then reluctantly set her back down on the ground, where, dizzy and disorientated, Rosa swayed for a few seconds.

'Roger,' she said rather breathlessly, fighting down the feeling of panic that was threatening to overwhelm her, 'how was your journey?' she managed.

'Excellent!' he boomed as he followed her into the cowshed. 'For two hundred miles I thought only of your face, your voice, your smile waiting for me here.'

'You must be hungry,' Rosa prevaricated. 'Sit down by the fire whilst I make you some tea.'

'It's lovely to be back in the old place,' Roger said, as he flung himself full length on the old sofa, which groaned under his weight. 'I've missed you so much, darling,' he called out to her as he reached for his pipe and matches.

'I've missed you too,' she replied from the kitchen, where she wasted as much time as she could, fiddling about with teaspoons and a milk jug and searching for cups and saucers, things they never used normally but that she felt, after having tea at Hawksmoor House, might be necessary for Roger.

'Here we are,' she announced brightly, as she laid the tea tray down close to the sofa from where Roger reached out a hand. 'Sweetheart, bugger the tea, kiss me,' he begged.

Feeling deeply uncomfortable, Rosa allowed him to pull her close and gave him a quick chaste kiss.

'No, no, no,' he chided, as he kissed her deeply, pushing open her mouth and flicking his tongue against her clenched teeth.

At that exact moment, when Rosa was wriggling awkwardly, the door was flung wide open and a little squeaky voice called out, 'Rosee! Rosee!'

'Who in God's name's that?' growled Roger, as Rosa sprang gratefully away from her fiancé and turned towards little Stevie, sitting upright in his pram with his arms flung wide open in greeting.

'*Caro!*' she cried as she rushed to the little boy and gave him the kind of welcome that Roger would have died to receive.

'Rosee!' little Stevie chanted, as she lifted him from the pram and kissed him on both rosy-red cheeks.

'Do I get one too?' Arthur chuckled as he followed behind.

'Of course,' Rosa cried, her cheeks scarlet as she clutched Stevie, who sat comfortably on her hip, playing with her long black hair, and stood on her tiptoes to give Arthur a kiss too.

It was only as she pulled away that Arthur spotted Roger on the sofa.

'I'm sorry,' Arthur immediately apologized. 'We've come barging in and interrupted you.'

Roger gallantly approached to shake Arthur's hand and tweak Stevie's cheek, at which the boy loudly protested.

'Have some tea, Arthur,' Rosa said. 'Come and sit down.'

'No, no, we'll leave you to it,' Arthur said diplomatically. 'We're just on our way over to Kit's, but Stevie wasn't passing your door without saying hello to you,' he said jovially.

For all his polite smiles, Rosa knew Arthur well enough to see he was embarrassed and keen to get away.

'We'll see you later,' he added as he scooped Stevie from Rosa's arms.

Furious that he was being denied more kisses and cuddles, Stevie kicked up an almighty fuss, but Arthur firmly plonked him back in the pram and left the cowshed with the boy's angry cries ringing in their ears.

'I can see you've got a fan there,' Roger chuckled.

Disappointed that they'd gone, Rosa said rather feebly, 'I used to babysit Stevie when he lived on the Phoenix site.'

Anxious that Roger was going to start kissing her all over again, Rosa started to edge away, then jumped in surprise when yet again the cowshed door was flung wide open and Nora walked in announcing loudly, 'Just got to pick up the pigswill bucket!'

When she saw tall, imposing Roger in his dapper RAF uniform, Nora blushed. 'Oh, sorry,' she stammered. 'Didn't know we'd got company.'

'Not at all,' urbane Roger replied. 'How are you, Nora?'

'Fine, fine,' flustered Nora replied. 'Got to dash – Polly's waiting for her tea!'

When she'd sped away on her bicycle with the bucket of pigswill swinging from one of the handlebars, Roger slumped back on to the sofa, where he gave a loud groan. 'God almighty! It's like damn Piccadilly Circus in here!'

Rosa smothered a smile. 'I'm afraid it's only going to get worse,' she said apologetically. 'Several friends are staying here overnight and everybody's arriving at six for supper.'

Roger's face fell. 'Am I to get no time with you at all?' he said desperately.

Keen to get him out of the house before somebody else came bursting through the door, Rosa took his arm. 'Why don't we drive down to the Black Bull and drop off your things?' she suggested.

'If it means we can have five minutes together, I'm all for that,' said Roger, as he gripped her hand and pulled her to him. 'I just can't wait to get you on your own, sweetheart.'

'Oh, Lord,' thought Rosa as yet again she wriggled uncomfortably in Roger's grip.

All the happy comings and goings of the afternoon, the joyous reunions and declarations of joy, had done nothing but highlight Rosa's discontent. There was no doubt in her mind about whose company she really wanted and unfortunately it wasn't her fiancé's; it was the man who'd just walked away pushing his little boy in a pram. The crushing truth of her situation bore down on Rosa; she had to stop lying to herself and, in fairness to Roger, she had to tell him the truth.

34. Home Truths

Rosa spent the best part of two hours trying to extricate herself from Roger, who was very keen to spend time with his fiancée after so many weeks apart. But, as she tried to leave, his beseeching expression made Rosa feel racked with guilt, so, perching ready for flight on the edge of the bed, she let him pour out his heart to her.

'These last few weeks have been as tough as hell,' Roger started. 'Our workload has increased tenfold,' he added, lowering his voice. 'Strategic bombing in Europe has been taken over by President Eisenhower; we're preparing for the Allied invasion, darling – it could be very soon.'

Rosa gasped as she held a hand to her mouth. She knew of the advances in Europe but an Allied invasion, a massive joint force of British and American troops moving on the Germans, made her heart sing. Could it be that, with this imminent attack, peace might come and she would finally be reunited with her family?

'That's wonderful news,' she cried.

'We've lost so many men,' Roger said sadly.

On top of her guilt about the conversation Rosa knew she must have with Roger, she now felt genuinely sorry for him.

'Please,' she begged as she lay down on the bed beside him, 'don't speak like that.'

'Why not? It's the bloody truth.' Near to tears, he gave a long, heart-felt groan as he buried his face in her thick, dark hair.

'Shhh,' she soothed, as she kissed and caressed him, until he fell into an exhausted sleep. When his breathing was steady, Rosa crept from the room and headed downstairs, where she immediately bumped into Nora and Peter.

'What are you two doing here?' she asked in surprise.

Peter, now unaided by a walking stick, was paying great attention to laying cutlery on the long dining table that ran the length of the large, upstairs reception room. Squinting through his good eye, Peter, clearly taking great pleasure in his work, placed every knife, spoon and fork with accuracy and precision.

'We offered to help the landlord if he was short staffed and he jumped at it,' Peter told Rosa with a proud smile.

'Edna was hoping to be here,' Nora added. 'But what with the chip shop's opening hours and the little girls she's minding, she's not got a spare minute, so Peter and I said we'd take over.'

She glanced adoringly at Peter, who looked back at her with just as much adoration.

'Why am I surrounded by people who are madly in love?' Rosa thought in frustration.

Shaking selfish thoughts from her head, she smiled

at the happy couple: Peter out and about, at ease with the world because of Nora's love and devotion; and Nora, who'd never thought she'd be in love, utterly besotted by her brave boyfriend. Feeling choked with emotion, Rosa couldn't stop herself from giving them both a quick kiss.

'Don't be late for tea,' she said, as she hurriedly buttoned up her coat and headed for the pub door. 'Everybody will be there, and they all want to meet Peter.'

'And I want to meet them,' said Peter eagerly.

By the time Rosa had run up the steep hill and along the cobbled path that led to the cowshed, she was panting for breath; and when she saw the cowshed door wide open and heard music and singing, she rushed forward to see what was going on.

'I'll be loving you always,' Maggie and Les sang in perfect harmony. 'With a love that's true, always . . .'

Kit, who was standing on the doorstep breathing in the cool air, winked at Rosa.

'Will you look at the two love-birds,' she said fondly. 'God love 'em.'

Seeing Rosa's eyes stray to her burgeoning belly, she tapped it gently. 'I know what you're thinking: look at the size of it!'

Rosa was no expert on pregnancy, but Kit's tummy really was enormous.

'Poor you,' she commiserated. 'Hopefully it'll soon be over.'

'Don't kid yourself – I've weeks to go,' Kit chuckled.

'Go on,' she urged, 'get yourself in there – little Stevie's been all over the place looking for you.'

With a knowing smile, Kit watched Rosa dash off to find Stevie. 'And somebody else has been looking out for you too,' she added under her breath.

Inside the cowshed, clutching her Brownie camera which fortunately had a flash, Julia, looking elegant and stylish in slim-line tweed trousers and a bright-green sweater tucked into her waistband, circled the room, snapping photographs of Gladys and Reg having a secret kiss, the radiant bride and groom who couldn't stop hugging each other, and Kit's husband, Ian, with Billy, who was still spotty but, much to everybody's relief, completely recovered from chicken pox. Looking up, Julia saw Rosa standing in the doorway with the sun setting behind her.

'You look a picture!' Julia cried. 'Don't move an inch!' she said and she took the shot.

Momentarily motionless, Rosa heard a voice whispering softly behind her, 'Penny for them.'

Trembling, she turned to see tall, handsome, blue-eyed Arthur smiling down at her.

'Oh, Arthur,' she sighed and, unable to stop herself, she instinctively leant her face against his chest, where, feeling the solid strength of him, she relaxed for the first time all day.

Laying a hand on her glorious dark hair, Arthur didn't move; for a few seconds they both stayed perfectly still, hardly daring to breathe, and in that moment

Julia caught them in the photograph they would treasure for the rest of their lives.

'Rosee!'

Reluctantly releasing Arthur from her embrace, Rosa bent down to scoop up little Stevie. '*Carissimo*,' she murmured, as she kissed him gently, and with their arms encircled they stayed close, the three of them entwined, until Stevie wriggled impatiently and Rosa set him down, but Stevie held tightly on to her hand.

'No! No!' he squawked crossly.

Seeing his sad little face, Rosa gently pulled him back into her embrace. 'Don't worry, *carissimo*, you can stay with me as long as you like,' she assured him.

The meagre supper the girls had been worrying about was much improved by everybody's generous contributions. Les had somehow got his hands on a crate of stout and a bottle of whisky (nobody asked any awkward questions); Kit had brought some fine Lancashire cheese, which the neighbouring farmer's wife had given to her; Arthur had arrived with a box of chocolates that sent the two little boys into a frenzy of excitement; and Edna, whom the girls hadn't seen much of lately, dropped by with two dozen potato fritters.

'Heat 'em up in the oven,' Edna instructed before she rushed off home in her little blue van to open her chip shop. 'Believe me, they'll be gorgeous!'

Roger arrived in time for supper, bringing Peter and Nora along with him. Before the meal began, Les rose to his feet and, holding up his glass of whisky, he gazed into Maggie's big sky-blue eyes.

'To my darling girl,' he said. 'Here's to the rest of our lives together.'

As the guests clapped and drank their whisky, Roger, squeezed up tight beside Rosa, covered her hand with his.

'It'll soon be our turn, my sweet,' he murmured.

Rosa turned to him, discomfort nagging at her. 'You haven't forgotten what I said about Gabriel, have you?' she asked carefully.

Seeing him looking blank, she added impatiently, 'About waiting until I find my brother before we set the wedding date.'

'Yes, of course,' he blustered. 'But surely you must understand that we can't wait forever, sweetheart – life goes on.'

Feeling hurt, Rosa abruptly stood up and straightened her dishevelled clothes. 'Life may go on for you, Roger, but without knowing what's happened to Gabriel, I don't think I'd make a very happy bride.'

'Don't take the hump,' Roger begged as he grasped her hand.

Rosa, who rarely drank, took a deep pull of her whisky. How was she going to get through the night? Glad of an excuse not to stare any longer into Roger's yearning eyes, Rosa busied herself circulating plates of piping hot *zuppa*, then took the two little boys, who didn't seem at all interested in eating anything but chocolate, out on to the moors, where they sat in the heather and watched the sun go down. Seeing Stevie yawning widely and rubbing his eyes, Rosa held him to her breast and rocked him gently; after a long, over-excited day the little boy soon dropped off in her arms.

Billy, who'd recently turned three, stroked Stevie's silky blond hair.

'Stevie has no mummy,' he lisped.

Rosa stared at Kit's son, who had his mother's intense dark eyes. 'That's right, Billy, his mummy died, but he has a daddy who loves him very much.'

'You be his mammy,' Billy said with a bright smile.

Rosa's heart skipped a beat; Billy in all innocence had articulated what she'd always wanted to be: Stevie's mummy. And, if she was not mistaken, Arthur's wife too.

As the party indoors got merrier and louder, Kit came to join Rosa and the boys. 'I'd better get this one home,' she said, as she tousled Billy's raven-black hair. 'Other-wise there's going to be one very tired, and spotty, page boy!' she chuckled.

One by one the visitors left. Les, who had to be vir-tually wrenched away from his fiancée, called out as he went, 'Don't keep me waiting at the altar, darling!'

Blowing kisses, he staggered into Reggie and Gladys's car, where he was joined by Arthur and his sleeping son.

'See you in the morning, Rosa,' Arthur called, as he and Stevie settled in the car beside Les.

Rosa stood waving and smiling in the twilight, until the car had disappeared over the hill; then, tilting her chin, she walked back into the cowshed to do the very thing she'd been dreading all day long.

She found Roger sitting disconsolately by the wood-burner, puffing on his pipe. Hearing Nora, Peter and Julia washing up amidst much laughter in the kitchen, Rosa closed the kitchen door before sitting down beside him, where she lit up one of her cheroots. There was a long awkward pause as they both smoked, then Roger turned to her. 'It's all right, Rosa, I know.'

Tears rushed into her eyes; racked with guilt, she simply didn't know what to say.

'It's never been quite the same for you as it has for me,' Roger continued slowly. 'You've blown hot and cold most of the time.' He gave a heavy sigh. 'In retrospect I shouldn't have rushed you; taking you to meet the family wasn't such a clever move.'

'They were very nice to me,' she quickly interjected, taking his hand. 'I liked them.'

'But they're a lot to take on, especially when you haven't got a family of your own at the moment,' he admitted with a guilty smile.

'Roger, I can't tell you how sorry I am,' Rosa murmured, feeling utterly wretched, as she fiddled with the engagement ring on her finger. 'I do love you, you're a good, good man, but –'

'You don't love me enough,' he said, finishing the sentence for her.

Knowing this wasn't the time for lies or feeble prevarications, Rosa bowed her head in shame.

'I thought I did when I agreed to marry you,' she confessed, struggling to find the words to express her emotions. 'But perhaps we did rush into things; perhaps I just didn't know you well enough?'

Roger stood up and tapped his pipe on the woodburner. 'I'm surplus to requirements here,' he said with a resigned sigh.

Trembling Rosa stood too, and, twisting the antique ring off her finger, she handed it back to Roger. It seemed like a cruel act, but she knew she was doing the right thing – for both of them in the long run.

'I hope one day soon you'll find someone a lot worthier than me to wear your grandmother's ring.'

Roger stared at the twinkling dark stone before taking it from Rosa and dropping it into his pocket. When she saw him picking up his RAF flying jacket, Rosa began to panic. 'What will you do now? Where will you go at this time of night?'

Roger gave a weary shrug. 'Pick up my things from the pub and drive back to Norfolk,' he replied.

'But it's going dark,' she protested. 'And it's such a long drive.'

Looking her square in the eye, Roger gave a wry smile. 'I don't think I'll be sleeping much tonight wherever I am, and apart from everything else I don't want to be a spectre at the feast at Maggie's wedding.'

Forcing herself not to cry, Rosa followed him to the door. *Why* had she not done this earlier?

On the doorstep, with the sound of owls hooting as

they hunted on the dark moors, Roger stroked her long, dark curls for the last time.

'I've loved knowing you, beautiful Rosa,' he said. 'I hope you find your brother when this war is over.'

And with that he turned his back and walked away. For the second time in less than an hour, Rosa stood and watched a car disappear into the night, but this was one she knew she would never see again.

Feeling not one bit proud of herself, Rosa walked back into the cowshed, where, determined not to say or do anything that would darken Maggie's happiness, she forced a bright smile to her face as she helped her friend prepare for her wedding day.

35. The Big Day . . . at Last!

Maggie's wedding couldn't have gone more smoothly.

'Glory be to God!' exclaimed Kit, as she succinctly summed up the day. 'After all the tempers and tantrums, the tears and the grief, it was *perfect*.'

And it was. Maggie looked like the princess of her dreams, and her sister, Emily, was right: the last thing that anybody noticed, least of all Les, was the patch of burnt hair on the top of her head. As Maggie, on her proud father's arm, entered the church to the strains of 'Here Comes the Bride', there was a collective gasp from the congregation. In all five years of the gruelling war that they'd lived through, none present had ever seen a bride more radiant or a dress more beautiful.

As Maggie progressed slowly down the aisle, the satin fabric of her bridal gown seemed to shimmer as it caught the light spilling through the stained-glass windows. The veil over her face hardly hid her rapturous smile as she approached Les waiting for her at the altar, and behind her little Billy walked steadily, just as his daddy had instructed. Still spotty, the little boy in his charming page-boy suit, with his wild black hair slicked down, completely stole the show. Mrs Yates said it all when she exclaimed, 'For the love of God! Will you look at the little lad!'

Billy assiduously avoided stepping on the veil that puffed out and filled half the aisle, but he didn't avoid grinning at everybody he passed and neither did he avoid waving gaily at his mum and dad. Nora, bringing up the rear (trembling from head to foot), looked unrecognizable in the elegant pink gown that hugged her voluptuous figure. But it wasn't just the gown that enhanced Nora: it was the glow that emanated from her, the look of a woman in love.

Rosa had decided, as she tossed and turned all night long, that she wasn't going to say anything to anybody about what had passed between her and Roger the previous night. She had no intention of darkening Maggie's big day with her own unhappiness. In fact, she needn't have worried: with all the hullabaloo of the wedding preparations, nobody even mentioned Roger. It wasn't until after the service that Julia, smart in a wine-coloured suit that accentuated her tall, slender frame, suddenly called out, 'Rosa, Roger, can I have a photo please?'

Blushing Rosa hurried over to Julia. 'He's gone,' she whispered behind her hand.

Julia looked blank. 'Gone where?'

Rosa's eyebrows shot up. 'Please, Julia, please don't say another word – I'll explain later.'

Julia nodded and, smiling brightly, continued to photograph the guests, who were showering the bride and groom with confetti as they left the church and walked the short distance to the Black Bull, with the wedding party following close behind them.

As soon as she was inside the pub, Rosa slipped into the ladies', where she washed her face in an attempt to cool her flaming cheeks.

'You've got to get through this without making a fuss,' she firmly told herself, as she brushed her hair and examined her pale reflection in the mirror.

In the upstairs room, guests were sitting down at their marked places. Rosa found hers and Roger's too; glancing round to make sure nobody was watching, she snatched up the card with Roger's name on it and shoved it into her handbag; then, feeling very self-conscious, she quickly sat down next to the vacant chair. Considering she hadn't wanted to draw attention to herself, the gapingly empty chair beside her seemed to shout, '*Where's Rosa's fiancé?*'

Looking down at the bowl of hot soup that the smiling waitress placed before her, Rosa thought she was going to completely disgrace herself by bursting into tears. She jumped when she heard the sound of what should have been Roger's chair scraping on the ground, and, to her amazement, astonishment and pure delight, Arthur sat down beside her.

'Arthur,' she gasped in sheer relief.

Never one to beat about the bush, Arthur said in a low voice, 'I see Roger's not here.'

When his deep-blue eyes locked with her dark brooding ones, Rosa felt her stomach swirl.

'He's left, Arthur,' she murmured. 'He left last night.'

Arthur quickly looked down, so it was impossible to read his face, but Rosa continued anyway. 'I didn't need to tell him I wasn't ready to marry him – he guessed.' She added, 'That's why he left.'

'Tough on the poor chap,' Arthur mumbled, still staring at the table.

'I should have had the guts to speak out sooner,' she said in a guilty rush.

When Arthur finally did look up, he smiled as he patted Rosa's hand. 'It must have been tough for you too,' he said.

As his intense gaze bore into her, Rosa felt as if all her bones were melting. When she finally dragged her eyes from him, she was aware of several people looking at her curiously, though the only person who spoke was a grinning Edna, who said in a loud whisper, 'Bugger me!'

After that everything was a blur for Rosa. The food so lovingly prepared barely passed her lips; the speeches seemed far away, like a distant echo; faces came and went as if she was in a dream; the only thing that seemed real was Arthur, right by her side.

Luckily Stevie slept throughout most of the meal, but when Edna saw the little boy stirring in his pram she hurried over, popped a soft bread crust dipped in a bit of milk into his hand and beckoned to her two little granddaughters.

'Sweethearts,' she said quietly, 'will you push Stevie round the room in his pram, and let him play with Billy if he gets restless? His daddy's busy at the moment.'

Marilyn and Katherine could not have been keener. They very self-importantly looked after the little boy, entertaining him with songs and games and little nibbles of wedding cake.

After the tables were cleared and stacked against the wall, a local band tuned up and the bride and groom took to the floor; to the achingly romantic strains of Vera Lynn's 'Yours Till the Stars Lose Their Glory', Maggie and Les waltzed around the polished floor, gazing deep into each other's eyes. As the song faded away and a new one started, Arthur rose to his feet and held out a hand to Rosa. 'May I?'

Rosa took his hand, then put her other hand on his broad shoulder. After encircling her tiny waist, Arthur expertly led his partner into another waltz, holding her close to his chest, so close Rosa could hear his heart beating.

'You're so much taller than me,' she cried, tipping back her head so that she could smile up at him.

'And you,' he murmured tenderly, 'are just perfect!'

Rosa could have danced till dawn, but all too soon newly married Les and Maggie were leaving for their honeymoon. Stunning, stylish Maggie, wearing a military-style navy-blue swing coat over her going-away suit, waved to her guests, before she tossed her posy of spring flowers into the air. As it fell to earth, Nora held out her hands and caught it.

'You'll be the next!' Kit cried, as everybody laughed at Nora's blushing, excited face.

Across the room Peter smiled; he had something special to say to his girlfriend, but not now, he thought; to make it right he'd need another person present – well, to be correct, he chuckled to himself, he'd need a rather special pig!

The next day was a whirl of goodbyes; so many people were leaving, and, with the bride and groom already gone, a sense of anti-climax was beginning to descend on those in the cowshed, who were all recovering from a very late night. Though Rosa knew Arthur was leaving soon, she couldn't take the smile off her face, and when he appeared, tall and handsome, his blue eyes roving the room for her, she threw caution to the wind and ran straight to him.

'I missed you,' she cried.

'I missed you too!' he replied, then laughed at himself. 'And it's only been ten hours!'

Still laughing, he couldn't take his eyes off her before Stevie claimed her attention, and all three went for a walk, Rosa pushing the pram and chatting in Italian to Stevie, who babbled back, whilst Arthur smiled in delight at their excitement in each other.

Julia was aware, like all of the girls, of the shift that seemed to be taking place within Arthur and Rosa's relationship, and she smiled as she watched them go. Her smile widened when she spotted Peter walking up the cobbled lane towards the cowshed. Surrounded by romance on all sides, Julia laughed to herself. 'Oh-o! Here comes another besotted one!' she chuckled.

Nora was surprised to see Peter so early in the day. 'How did you get here?' she inquired.

'I got a lift in one of the ambulances,' Peter replied

with a smile. 'I thought I'd help you with Polly this morning.'

Delighted Nora gave him a kiss. 'What a treat,' she said, and went in search of the pigswill bucket.

It was a perfect May morning: robins, blackbirds and thrushes were singing their hearts out, whilst skylarks rose high into the arching blue sky. And in the shade rolling banks of bluebells blazed against the dark bark of oak trees.

'They're so blue they make me blink!' Peter laughed, as he strode along, swinging the pigswill bucket with one hand whilst holding on to Nora's hand with the other. He stopped as he looked in wonder from the flowers to Nora's face. 'You've got bluebell eyes!' he exclaimed.

Nora couldn't believe she was capable of such happiness. The sight in Peter's only eye was strong and clear these days; he now walked without a stick and barely limped, except when he was overtired. Physically he went from strength to strength, which Nora thanked God for every day.

'But now,' she thought, 'he'll soon go away.'

Determined not to spoil the beauty of the day, Nora pushed her dark thoughts to the back of her head.

'Live for the moment,' she remembered her late mother's advice. 'Make the most of God's given gifts.'

Polly met them with grunts of excitement; as soon as Peter lowered the bucket into her run, she buried her head in it, and the contented slurps and burps that Polly made as she gobbled her breakfast made Nora giggle.

'When you hear her you really understand the expression "greedy pig",' she laughed.

Grabbing the spade, Nora was all set to muck out Polly's sty, but Peter stopped her. Laying a hand on her arm, he led her to an improvised bench made from an old wooden crate.

'Let's sit down for a minute,' he said, as he drew her down beside him.

Nora smiled up at the sun bathing her face in a warm glow. 'Hah, this is nice,' she sighed as she closed her eyes.

When she opened them there was a bunch of blue-bells tied with a pretty blue ribbon in her lap.

'How lovely!' she cried, picking them up and inhaling their woody sweetness. Feeling something attached to the ribbon, she looked at Peter. 'What is it?' she asked.

'That's for you to find out,' he said with a mysterious smile.

Nora loosened the ribbon and gasped in surprise. 'It's a ring!' she cried.

'A sapphire,' he added proudly.

Speechless, Nora gazed at the beautiful, clear-blue stone surrounded by tiny sparkling diamonds. Completely overcome, she whispered, 'It's too good for me, Peter.'

Seeing her start to cry, Peter took the ring and slipped it on to her wedding finger. 'My sweetheart, *nothing* in the world is too good for you,' he whispered;

then, raising her hand to his lips, he said, 'My Nora, please will you marry me?'

Nora gazed into Peter's scarred but beautiful face. She was so full of love she wanted to sing out loud, 'Yes, yes, yes! Oh, yes, my love, I will marry you!'

Some hours later, as the newly engaged couple walked back to the cowshed, Nora poured out all her former anxieties. 'I thought you'd go back to your mam's in Bradford; I thought I might never see you again,' she exclaimed, as she flashed her new ring this way and that, so that it could catch the light from the slanting sun.

Peter stopped in his tracks. 'You really thought I'd up sticks and leave you, after all you've done for me?' he asked in amazement.

Nora dumbly nodded her head.

He pulled her close and kissed her wild, unruly curls. 'I love you, you're my girl, I want to spend the rest of my life with you, make a home for you and our children,' he added softly.

Nora blushed to the roots of her red hair. 'Oh, Peter . . .' she said on a sob.

'I told you before,' he said as they continued walking along hand in hand, 'I'm not short of money: when Dad died before the war, he left me and Mam with a tidy sum. I intend opening up a business here in Pendleton, a little garage and repair shop,' he said with a determined ring in his voice. 'I'll get Mam to move over here so I can keep an eye on her, and we'll have our own home, my sweetheart, right here in the town where you grew up,' he announced.

Giddy with excitement, Nora flung her arms around Peter's neck and kissed him long and hard. 'I love you so much,' she whispered as she gazed into his face. 'And I promise I'll love you always.'

36. All Change

In the week that followed Maggie's wedding and Arthur's departure, things slowly got back to normal, or as normal as possible, given Nora's surprise engagement and poor Maggie's emotional outbursts.

'It was so wonderful,' she said over and over again.

'The wedding or the honeymoon?' Rosa teased.

'Everything!' Maggie exclaimed. 'But, oh, that night at Grange-over-Sands,' she said with a dreamy, romantic smile. 'The hotel was gorgeous and the view was unbelievable –'

Nora, flushed with love, was keen to hear about what happened inside the bedroom rather than outside. 'Who cares about the sodding view!' she scoffed. 'What was it like?' she asked in a low voice. 'You know, in bed . . .'

Cheeky Maggie gave her friend a saucy wink. 'Let's just say it was well worth waiting for; I could have stayed there for weeks,' she groaned, as she reached for her packet of Woodbines. 'But before we knew it we were back on the train and heading home.' She slumped glumly in her chair. 'Saying goodbye to Les was awful – we were both in tears. It's just not fair!' she fumed. 'I don't even know when I'll see my husband again.'

Luckily Julia had just picked up the first set of wedding prints, which she handed to Maggie.

'These should cheer you up,' she said with a smile.

Maggie stared rapturously at the black-and-white photographs that captured her perfect day, exclaiming in delight at the different images.

'Look at Billy waving at his mum and dad, cheeky little monkey,' she chuckled. 'And Nora!' she gasped. 'I knew you looked bonny when you set off for the church but there you are, walking down the aisle like a princess – no wonder Peter proposed to you the next day!'

'I felt like a princess,' Nora said wistfully. 'It was the happiest day of my life.'

'Mine too,' Rosa murmured dreamily.

She was disturbed from her romantic reverie by Julia asking Nora a question. 'Does Peter know when he might be discharged from Wrigg Hall?'

Nora grinned as she replied with a bit of a swagger. 'You mean my *fiancé*?' she teased.

'Get away with you!' mocked Julia.

'We haven't got a definite date,' Nora continued on a more serious note. 'But it'll be soon,' she said confidently.

'Then will he go back home?' Julia questioned.

'*No!*' Nora exclaimed. 'He's staying right here, with me,' she giggled. 'He'll lodge with mi dad, poor bugger. Once Dad gets going, Peter will never hear the end of Accrington Stanley Football Club.'

'Has Peter told his mum the news?' Rosa inquired.

'We're going over to Bradford to tell her together,' Nora replied. 'We're hoping she'll move over this way when we get wed – it's not that far from Bradford.'

With a nervous smile Maggie turned the conversation

from Nora to Rosa. 'I still can't get over you and Roger,' she cried.

'Believe me, neither can I!' Rosa replied in all honesty.

'I only heard when I got back from our honeymoon,' Maggie said, as she shook her head in disbelief. 'Do you think you'll ever hear from him again?'

A shadow fell across Rosa's face. 'I shouldn't think so – it's not as if I treated him well, is it?'

Seeing guilty tears well in Rosa's brooding dark eyes, Julia said gaily, 'Well, it looks like yet again you and I are the only Bomb Girls who aren't spoken for,' she joked.

'Somebody will come swinging by one day soon and steal your hearts away,' Maggie assured her.

Julia gave a good-natured shrug. 'Honestly, Mags, I really couldn't care less. With all the talk of mobilizing troops in Europe, and Bomber Command dominating enemy skies, this blasted war might very soon be over and I intend to take up where I left off and go to Oxford,' she declared with an excited smile.

Nora, who hated being more than five minutes from those she loved most, looked tragic. 'I thought you liked it up here?' she said in a hurt voice.

'I do like it, darling, but a girl has to get an education if she's to compete with men when the war's over,' Julia said robustly. 'No, seriously, time at Oxford will help me kickstart my writing career.'

Poor Nora looked even glummer. 'How can you even think of writing all day long – just penning a letter gives me a headache,' she sighed. 'I bet you'll never speak to me once you leave here and start mixing with all them posh clever girls down South,' she concluded on the verge of tears.

Laughing, Julia threw her arms around Nora. 'I'd be proud to call you my dear friend wherever I am, in fact,' she added with a mysterious wink, 'I might even put you in my novel.'

Rosa smiled as she listened to Julia gently teasing Nora. Who would ever have imagined that 'the snobby bitch from down South', as they used to unkindly call Julia, would turn out to be such a gem of a friend? Rosa knew, even though their relationship had begun so badly, that she would always trust Julia, as she had done in the days after Roger's sudden departure, when she had turned to Julia for sound advice and reassurance.

The factory hooter recalled the girls back to their workbenches, all with different preoccupations: Maggie was desperate to finish her love letter to her husband, now back on active service; Nora was thinking about Peter's discharge date from hospital; Julia had recently had the first stirrings of an idea for a novel about women and their war work, which was beginning to take shape in her mind; whilst Rosa could not stop her thoughts from returning to Arthur and Stevie.

A few days later Julia found a telegram in her pigeon-hole, and, tearing it open, she eagerly read Hugo's cryptic message.

Would you two like lunch on my day off next week?

There was no doubting the significance of the message: it was clear that Hugo wanted to meet up with her and Rosa as soon as possible. But how would they get to London? Quickly folding the letter, Julia went in search of Rosa, whom she needed to talk to urgently and in private too.

Julia found her opportunity when they were walking home from work later that evening.

'I had a telegram from Hugo today.'

Rosa stopped dead in her tracks and gripped her arm. 'Gabriel!' she gasped.

'He didn't say,' Julia replied. 'But he wants to see us soon.'

'In London?'

Julia nodded. 'It'll be a very short visit,' she quickly added. 'But first we have to get permission to take time off.'

'It's only a day – surely we're owed that?'

'With our recent instructions to push out more bombs, we might be turned down,' Julia commented.

'I'll ask Malc if he can swing it for us with Mr Featherstone,' Rosa said, as she quickened her step, then stopped again as she turned to her friend. 'Your brother *must* have found something out,' she insisted, hope burning bright in her eyes. 'Otherwise why would he ask to see *both* of us?'

Worried that Rosa was running ahead of herself, Julia quickly cautioned her, 'Let's see what Hugo has to say first and, more to the point, if we can actually get time off to go to see him.'

Rosa asked Malc to approach the factory manager on their behalf, and he agreed to grant them twenty-four hours' leave. 'But you'd better be back on the line bang on time the next day,' Malc warned. 'Bomber Command waits for no man – or woman either for that matter.'

Once permission was granted Julia hurriedly sent Hugo a reply.

We'd love lunch, what day best suits you?

Jay x

Hugo's reply came winging back almost immediately.

Table booked, usual place, 1 pm Monday. H

'God!' Julia thought. 'Hugo's definitely not hanging about.'

To be on the safe side, Julia suggested they travelled down to London on Sunday evening, after they'd finished their shift.

'We can't risk travelling on Monday,' she told Rosa. 'If the train should be delayed, we'll miss Hugo altogether.'

Vividly recalling how excited Rosa had been when they'd previously heard from Hugo, Julia repeated her warning: 'You know, Rosa, it's vital that you keep our meeting a secret.'

'I know you think I'll blab to Arthur,' Rosa said with a knowing smile. 'But I won't – I'll keep my mouth shut, promise.'

Nora and Maggie were nonplussed by their friends' plans.

'You're going all that way just for a day?' gasped Nora.

'I promised ages ago I'd go to see Mummy on her birthday,' Julia lied.

'And Rosa's going with you?' Maggie asked.

'I'm meeting up with an Italian friend from university,' Rosa also lied. 'I've only just found out she's in London.'

Exchanging guilty looks, Julia and Rosa felt bad about deceiving their best friends, but needs must; the last thing they could afford to do was to tell them the truth.

After finishing their long shift, the girls managed to get on a packed train just after six at London Road Station in Manchester. Too tired to talk, they fell asleep with their heads pressed together, Julia's golden blonde hair contrasting with Rosa's long, dark, winding tresses. When the train, packed with exhausted servicemen, shunted slowly into Euston Station, yawning Julia gave Rosa a nudge. 'We're here,' she said gently.

Unable to cope with the Underground so late at night, Julia hailed a cab on Euston Road, and once they were settled in the back seat the cabbie – keen for company – reiterated the news they'd heard, of the German surrender in the Crimea. The driver nattered on, gleefully predicting the outcome. 'We've got the Hun on the run for sure,' he chuckled. 'What with our lads south of Rome and the Soviets now on the offensive, bloody Jerry won't be crowing much longer!'

Relieved to get out of the taxi, Julia quickly paid the driver, then, after unlocking the front door to her darkened house, led sleepy Rosa to the guest room before going in search of her mother.

When Rosa woke up the next morning, for a single wonderful minute she thought she was back home in Italy. The crisp, ironed linen sheets on her comfortable bed smelt of lavender, just like hers used to; the big room full of morning light was warm and pretty, with pictures on the wall and fresh flowers in vases; and when she sniffed she could smell coffee – real coffee. Jumping out of bed, Rosa rushed into the bathroom, where she started to run a bath, and as she waited for it to fill up she looked at her steamy reflection in the mirror – would today be the day she had dreamt about for almost three years?

'Please, God,' she prayed as she closed her eyes, 'let me hear my beloved brother is alive and well.'

37. The Usual Place

Julia's family always jokingly referred to the Ritz Hotel as the 'usual place', so Julia was in no doubt where she and Rosa would be meeting Hugo for lunch. She thought it wise not to mention this to her mother, who, though delighted to see her daughter and to meet Rosa, was clearly disappointed that their visit was so brief.

'What a shame,' Mrs Thorpe sighed, as she poured the girls a second cup of rich, dark coffee. 'I thought we'd have more than a few hours together.'

'I'm so sorry, Mummy,' Julia apologized.

Rosa quickly added, 'If we're not back on the bomb line first thing in the morning, we'll be in big trouble!'

'We're doing more overtime than ever these days,' Julia said with a grimace. 'Bomber Command are going through bombs like nobody's business.'

'I'm surprised you could be spared from the workplace,' Mrs Thorpe remarked.

'Believe me, Mummy, it wasn't easy!' laughed Julia.

Before the girls left, Mrs Thorpe handed Julia a shopping basket packed with goodies from her own pantry.

'I have to confess,' she told Rosa with a guilty smile, 'that my housekeeper procures coffee for me from the black market – at an extortionate price, I might add.'

She rolled her eyes in mock shame. 'I know it's wicked and not at all patriotic, but it really is my only sin!'

'I think we can live with your wicked sins,' Rosa said with a conspiratorial smile.

'Come back soon, darling,' Mrs Thorpe urged, as she kissed her daughter. 'You too, Rosa. Goodbye!'

Julia and Rosa took the bus to the West End, passing shattered shops, blasted factories and tenement blocks caved in on their own foundations.

'I sometimes wonder if London will ever recover from this onslaught,' Julia said, as she gazed sadly out of the grimy bus window. 'How much more can Londoners take?'

'God knows what I will find when I eventually return home,' Rosa murmured. 'I don't really care about anything, if I'm honest,' she blurted out. 'Buildings, museums, works of art – I just want my family safely back.'

Julia gave Rosa's hand a comforting squeeze. 'Have you ever talked to Arthur about your brother?' she asked curiously.

Rosa quickly answered, 'Oh, yes! Arthur knows everything.' She grinned as she added, 'He even knows about me running away to London.'

Julia tentatively asked a question that had been on her mind since Maggie's wedding. 'I hope you don't mind my poking my nose in, Rosa,' she started to say, 'but it's perfectly obvious to me, and to others too,' she said with a cheeky wink, 'that you've taken a shine to Arthur Leadbetter.'

Rosa blushed. 'Is it that obvious?' she asked shyly.

'Oh, yes!' Julia teased.

'But it's hopeless!' Rosa exclaimed.

'Why?' Julia cried.

'He was *so* in love with Violet. And she was my dear friend.'

Rosa gave a heavy sigh as she recalled the terrible tragedy of Violet's death in the explosion at the Phoenix, which had also left Arthur badly injured and hospitalized for several weeks.

'I think if it hadn't been for Stevie,' Rosa told Julia, 'Arthur would have lost the will to live, but he had to keep on going for his son.' Rosa turned to Julia with tears in her eyes. 'It was love at first sight for me with Stevie; I adored him, and still do,' she admitted. 'But I don't know when my feelings for Arthur started to change. I've always been fond of him, and we all felt so sorry for him and missed him when he went to work in Dundee, but it really was no more than that.'

'What changed things?'

'I think it's just been a gradual thing,' Rosa replied. 'When I started to dither about setting a wedding date with Roger, Arthur was supportive, which made me feel a bit less guilty. And then I just gradually started to realize I was much happier in Arthur's company than Roger's. And that feeling has grown and grown over time.' She smiled as she recalled Arthur's words of advice, 'He told me, *You should take your time and not be rushed*. Which, to be honest, was very comforting.'

Julia laughed softly. 'Well, that advice certainly paid off!'

A waiter in tails led them to the table where Hugo was waiting for them with cocktails.

'Thought we might need these,' he joked, as he kissed his sister and shook Rosa by the hand.

Rosa was so nervous she could have downed all three cocktails, but determined to keep her head clear she took only a sip from her glass.

'How are you, darling?' Julia said, as she sat close to her brother and smiled at him adoringly.

As Hugo grinned and chatted with his younger sister, Rosa was struck by how similar they were: both tall and lean, the same penetrating, intelligent green eyes and straight nose, though Hugo's hair was brown rather than silky blonde like Julia's. They had the same manner too: confident, at ease with the world; it was only when Hugo ordered lunch that Rosa noticed the stub which was all that remained of his left hand.

'You're from northern Italy?' Hugo asked as he turned his attention to his guest.

Rosa nodded. 'Padua, though I've not been back since the outbreak of war.'

Suddenly impatient of small talk, Rosa leant forward in her chair and said in a low, urgent voice, 'I can't tell you how grateful I am to you, Hugo – you and Julia have given me hope that my brother might still be alive,' she finished with an emotional gulp.

Hugo glanced nervously around. 'We still don't know that for sure, I'm afraid.'

'But you have news?' Rosa insisted.

With his good hand, Hugo raised his cocktail glass,

which he drank from before carefully placing it back on the table. 'One of our field agents who works the Belgian coast got a message out to us last week.'

The waiter arrived bearing three bowls of soup on a silver tray.

'Madam,' he said, placing a bowl before Rosa, who spread a white linen napkin across her lap and took a warm roll from the breadbasket. 'Thank you,' she said; then, with her heart beating double time, she waited for him to finish serving so she could hear what Hugo had to say.

'Every month a submarine surfaces close to the Belgian coast. For obvious reasons the location changes all the time; its purpose is to pick up prisoners of war,' Hugo explained. 'Under cover of darkness, those chosen to meet up with the vessel wait for the sub's signal, then row or swim to it.'

Rosa held her breath. She could almost hear the lap of the freezing cold water as the sub surfaced offshore; then, at the appointed time, a few flashes to the desperate men, women and children awaiting rescue in the shadows. What if the Germans were lying in wait too? What if they'd tortured the field agent and knew about the clandestine operation? They could pick off the escapees as they ran to the boats, leaving them to float out, dead or dying, on the tide.

Seeing Rosa tensely gripping her soup spoon, Hugo quickly added, 'It's unquestionably risky – there's danger at every turn – but every month escapees make it to Southampton.'

Rosa laid a hand over her mouth to smother her cry. 'Are you telling me Gabriel is one of them?'

Hugo answered honestly, 'We won't know till the sub's safely home and the passengers have disembarked – and I don't know the names of those on board either,' he quickly added; then, feeling sorry for Rosa, who was desperately fighting back tears, he said, 'What I can tell you is *if* your brother is still using the identity papers he was issued with, then he would have had a fair chance of being selected to board the vessel.'

Wanting to say something positive, Julia smiled brightly as she added in an upbeat voice, 'Surely those with false identities stand a better chance of getting on the sub than those without?'

She looked inquiringly at her brother, who nodded back at her. Julia knew what his demeanour meant: that was as much good news as he could give them; from here, they would just have to wait and see.

Visibly trembling, Rosa reached for her cocktail glass, which she drained in one. 'Thank you, Hugo,' she managed to say in a quaky voice.

Julia gently patted her arm. 'Darling, the search is getting closer,' she said reassuringly.

'I thought it was important that I spoke to you personally about this matter,' Hugo added. 'It's not the sort of information I can put in a letter or speak of over the phone.'

'Of course,' Rosa replied hastily. 'I quite understand.'

After picking at her lunch, Rosa begged to be excused.

'I'm sure you two have a lot of catching up to do,' she said sweetly. 'And, to be honest, I'd like to be alone for a while,' she admitted.

Bidding Hugo farewell and kissing him lightly on both cheeks, Rosa left the restaurant with every man's eyes following her slim, shapely form.

'God! She's a bit of a stunner,' Hugo said, as he stared admiringly at Rosa's long dark hair swinging around her slender shoulders.

'She's lovely,' Julia replied with a fond smile.

'I thought you told me that she hated you,' Hugo recalled as he tucked into his jam roly-poly.

'Oh, she certainly did,' Julia retorted as she savoured her ice-cream. 'But, after coming to an understanding, we realized we liked each other enormously.'

Over coffee (not as good as her mother's black-market coffee, Julia thought wryly), she asked Hugo what Gabriel's chances of survival really were.

'As I told Rosa, if he's on that sub I'd say excellent,' he answered. 'The pick-up is the most dangerous time; if he made it to the sub and didn't get shot or drowned in the process, the chances are he'll be docking in Southampton very soon – but, for God's sake, don't get Rosa's hopes up too much – she's nervous enough as it is.'

After finishing his meal, Hugo sat back and lit up a cigarette. 'Things are speeding up fast, Jay,' he said, and, lowering his voice to a whisper, added, 'There's talk of an imminent invasion on the French coast. If we keep gaining ground, young Rosa might even be able to return home sooner than she thinks. And let's hope it's alongside that brother of hers.'

The journey back North was long and arduous, but Julia and Rosa dragged themselves out of their beds the next morning and clocked in on time at the Phoenix, albeit with dark circles under their eyes and both of them yawning non-stop.

'Shut yer gob, there's a bus coming!' Malc joked when he saw Julia smother another yawn.

Julia burst out laughing. 'I've never heard that expression before,' she told Malc, who was full of Northern witticisms.

'That's 'cos you're from down South and you speak different from us heathens up here,' Malc pointed out.

'I think I might be picking up a bit of a Northern accent,' Julia confessed.

'Keep working on it, cock: it takes a life-time of practice,' Malc joked as he wandered off to the dispatch room.

As the Bomb Girls' shifts got under way, they heard over the clanking of the conveyor belts the eight o'clock news bulletin, which had the entire factory riveted:

'Supreme Allied Headquarters have issued an urgent warning to inhabitants of the enemy-occupied countries living near the coast. The warning said that a new phase in the Allied Air Offensive had begun. Shortly before this warning the Germans reported that Le

Havre, Calais and Dunkirk were being heavily bombarded and that German naval units were engaged with Allied Landing craft. A new phase of the Allied Air Offensive has begun.'

Women in every part of the factory stared at one another in disbelief; Maggie on the cordite line whooped for joy. 'At last, we're breaking through the German defences!'

'We can't be!' Nora gasped incredulously. 'Jerry always knocks us back.'

'Not this time!' Rosa laughed excitedly. 'Allied Headquarters wouldn't issue a news bulletin like that if we were losing!'

As Joe Loss and his orchestra followed the dramatic early-morning news bulletin, the workers automatically carried on assembling bombs, but every one of them sent up a prayer for those brave boys on the beaches.

The atmosphere throughout the entire factory was electric as the clock ticked towards noon. When the pips for the news sounded out, hardly a soul moved, and they were right not to: the news was what every woman, and man too, had waited five long years to hear:

'*D-Day has come!*'

A roar of sheer joy went echoing round the factory.

'Shhh! Shhh! Shhh!' workers keen to hear the rest of the news hissed at their neighbours.

'Allied troops were landed under strong naval and air cover on the coast of Normandy early this morning. The Prime Minister has told the Commons that the commanding officers have reported everything going to plan so far, with beach landings still going on at midday and mass airborne landings successfully made behind enemy lines.'

When the hooter went for their next break, there was a rush to get to the canteen, where the Bomb Girls chain-smoked and drank tea, as they talked incredulously of the news reports.

'We're behind enemy lines!' Maggie gasped. 'Did you ever think it would happen – we're fighting on enemy territory?'

Her eyes clouded with fear as she thought of her new husband. 'Where are you, my love?' she wondered. 'Stay safe, Les: come home to me, please don't die,' she prayed earnestly to herself.

Julia broke through her anguished thoughts as she jumped to her feet and yelled across the canteen with fierce conviction, 'Today begins the liberation of Europe from Nazi occupation!'

A cheer went up as the women around the room agreed with her.

'We'll soon be free!'

'Our boys will come home!'

'The war will be over.'

'We've waited long enough for it.'

Rosa, sitting quietly smoking a cheroot, thought of those who would never come home, and of the mothers, daughters and wives whose lives would never be the same again, even when peace was declared. Their sacrifices would bring this bloody war to its final conclusion, and then they would pick up the pieces and live half a life without the one they'd lost. God! How she hated these wars that men created; all around her were women, hundreds of passionate women with one burning desire: peace.

In the middle of all the heated discussions Kit literally came waddling across the canteen floor towards her friends.

'What're you doing here?' Maggie gasped in amazement.

'I got fed up with being cooped up at home, so I thought, seeing as it's such a glorious day, I'd come and pick up Billy and catch up with mi mates whilst I was at it,' Kit said, easing herself, groaning, into an uncomfortable upright metal chair.

'Have you heard the news?' Julia eagerly asked.

Kit grinned. 'Have I heard the news? D-Day has come! The whole nation must be sitting by their wireless sets.'

Nora, who had thoughtfully picked up a mug of hot strong tea for Kit, gazed in awe at her friend's enormous pregnant belly.

'Oh, my God!' she exclaimed. 'Are you sure you should be out? You look like you're going to drop it any minute.'

Kit smiled. 'Don't worry, Nora, the baby's not due till the end of the month.'

'Heavens!' Nora thought to herself. 'The poor girl will explode before then.'

The girls chatted excitedly about the joyous news, but nothing stopped the bomb-making machinery rattling, so when the hooter recalled them to work they stubbed out their cigarettes and said a hasty goodbye to Kit.

'Don't you worry about me,' she said, as she waved them off. 'I'll finish my tea, then stroll over to the nursery to pick up Billy.'

Half an hour later Malc came dashing into the cordite shed, where the first girls he spotted and beckoned to were Nora and Rosa.

'Over here!' he called.

'What's up?' Nora asked, as he led them to his office.

'It's Kit: she's in my office with her little lad.'

They found Kit sitting in Malc's chair with Billy balanced precariously on her knee.

'Glory be to God!' she exclaimed when she saw her friends. 'I couldn't make it to the bus stop, so I had to come back here. I think I might have to get Ian to come and fetch us.'

Seeing little Billy looking uncharacteristically subdued, Nora said with a warm smile, 'Would you like to come and help me feed Polly? I could take you on the back of my bike,' she said, as she threw Malc an inquiring look.

'Aye, go on, then,' Malc agreed indulgently. 'But one of you lasses must stay with Kit until her husband's picked her up.'

'Don't worry, I'll stay,' Rosa volunteered.

Billy glanced up at his mother, who smiled reassuringly.

'Good boy,' she said. 'Run along with Nora – she'll take care of you.'

As Nora led the little boy away, Malc offered Kit his office phone. 'You'd best call that fella of yours right away,' he said, before he left his office and returned to work.

Kit was told that Ian wasn't in his office, so she left a message with his secretary, asking her husband to pick her up at the cowshed as she was too tired to make it home.

'Do you mind me waiting for Ian at the cowshed?' she asked Rosa. 'It's more comfortable than sitting here troubling Malc.'

'Of course not,' Rosa said, as she helped Kit to struggle to her feet.

Leaning against her friend, Kit started to breathe heavily as they made their way up the steep cobbled lane.

'It's not far now,' Rosa said cheerfully. 'We'll have a nice cup of tea when we get there –'

But she never finished the sentence, because, with a gush, Kit's waters broke and amniotic fluid flowed down her legs and landed in a puddle at her feet.

'Jesus, Mary and Joseph!' Kit cried out in alarm; then, full of fear, she turned to her friend and said, 'This shouldn't be happening, Rosa – it's too early!'

38. D-Day Landings

Somehow Rosa got Kit up the cobbled lane and into the cowshed, where she led her into her own room.

'Lie down and rest,' Rosa said gently, settling Kit on her bed, before opening the window as wide as it would go; and, as she did so, she heard happy skylarks singing their glorious rhapsody as they soared higher and higher in the hot June sky.

'Stay with me,' Kit begged. 'Don't leave me.'

'*Carissima*, dearest,' Rosa murmured, smoothing Kit's long, dark hair off her hot face. 'I promise I'm going nowhere.'

Kit reached out to take her friend's warm hand. 'I was on my own most of the time when I was in labour with Billy – my sister took fright and ran a mile – but she did fetch an owd biddy to cut the cord and clean me up.' She sighed as she recalled her beloved son's birth. 'It was tough.'

'This will be easier,' Rosa said with a confidence she certainly didn't feel.

Kit interrupted her with a loud groan: 'Oh-oh, the contractions are starting!'

As the contraction grew in strength, Kit's distended stomach looked as tight as a football, but she breathed through the pain and loosened her grip on Rosa as the pain faded.

'Oh, thank God for that,' Kit gasped as her body relaxed.

Wondering what to do for the best, Rosa quickly said, 'Can I get you anything, sweetheart?'

'Some water, please,' Kit murmured, as she sank back on the pillows and closed her eyes.

Whilst Rosa was running the tap in the kitchen, she saw Nora and Billy walking towards the cowshed. Rushing to the front door, Rosa dashed outside.

'Kit's in labour,' she whispered behind her hand in order to avoid alarming Billy.

Nora's blue eyes all but rolled out of her head. 'Jesus!' she squeaked.

'Take Billy away.' Rosa frantically added, 'He can't stay here.'

Putting on a big, bright smile, Nora turned to Billy and said, 'Let's go to the allotment and pick some carrots.'

'Want Mammy!' Billy started to wail.

'Don't cry,' Nora pleaded, and then had a change of mind. 'Forget about the silly carrots; let's go to Edna's chip shop instead.'

'CHIPS! CHIPS!' yelled Billy as he skipped away.

'Wait for me, sweetheart,' Nora called and set off running after the little boy.

When Rosa returned to her bedroom, she found Kit half sitting up as she panted her way through another contraction.

'They're coming faster and getting stronger,' she said when the pain eased and she was able to gratefully sip from the glass of water that Rosa held to her lips.

'God!' she fretted, pushing her damp hair off her face. 'Where is Ian? Do you think he got my message?'

Rosa was asking herself the same question. What if Ian was out of the office all day and hadn't even got the message?

'Christ,' she whispered under her breath; then, holding back a wave of suffocating panic, she quickly asked Kit, '*Cara*, who is your midwife?'

'Nurse Hodson,' Kit replied.

'Where does she live?'

'In Pendleton, near Edna's shop,' Kit told her.

Rosa's mind was racing. Dammit, Nora had just left; she could easily have taken a message to Edna for the midwife.

'Maybe I could catch up with her?' Rosa frantically thought. 'She can't have gone far, not with Billy.'

Turning to Kit, she said gently, '*Cara*, I have to go outside for just a few minutes?'

Kit's big dark eyes grew wide in alarm. 'You said you wouldn't leave me,' she wailed.

Torn between her desperation to catch up with Nora and her guilt about abandoning her friend in labour, Rosa dithered at the end of the bed. Her heart leapt when she heard Nora shout from the sitting room, 'I'm just picking up Billy's coat.'

'Nora!' Rosa gasped, and she all but bolted out of the bedroom. 'Nora – stop!' she cried as she grabbed her friend's arm.

Looking scared, Nora asked, 'What's the matter? You're as white as a sheet.'

Rosa dropped her voice to an urgent whisper: 'Can you tell Edna to fetch Nurse Hodson up here right away?'

Turning ashen, Nora nodded, then ran out of the house, just as poor Kit was gripped by another contraction.

'Rosa! Rosa!' she called.

Taking a deep breath to steady her nerves, Rosa returned to Kit, who was howling in pain, first holding up one finger, then another, and another, and another. 'They're coming every four minutes,' she panted.

After gently mopping Kit's brow with a flannel she'd dipped in the bowl of cold water, Rosa murmured soothingly as she removed Kit's clothes, leaving only a slip over her sweating body.

'Lie back, sweetheart, I need to make you cool.'

'Arghh!' Kit grunted, as she eased herself down the narrow bed. 'Have you sent for the midwife?'

Keeping her voice steady, Rosa answered, 'She's on her way; she'll be here very soon.'

Kit looked Rosa steadily in the eye. 'If I start bearing down, there'll be no stopping the baby,' she warned. 'You might have to deliver it yourself.'

A panicked Rosa blurted out, 'Tell me what to do!'

'I'll need clean sheets underneath me,' Kit told her. 'And plenty of hot water, towels too – and sharp scissors, sterilized,' she quickly added.

Feeling sick, Rosa hurried into the kitchen, where she gripped the edge of the table to stop herself from shaking; then, after she'd put the kettle on to boil, she went in search of clean sheets and towels.

*

Nora had never run so fast in her life; with Billy skipping along beside her, she virtually tore down the steep hill that led into town.

'Faster, faster,' little Billy laughed in excitement, thinking it was a game.

By the time she reached the chip shop, Nora was gasping for breath.

'EDNA! EDNA!' she cried.

Seeing Nora's flushed sweating face, Edna immediately laid down the whisk she was using to beat a large bowl of frothy batter. 'What is it, lovie?'

Nora dropped her voice to pass on Rosa's message: 'Kit's in labour, in the cowshed – Rosa said you're to fetch the midwife right away.'

Not one to waste time on words, Edna simply said, 'Stay here and watch the shop whilst I run round to Nurse Hodson's house.'

Nora hardly had time to catch her breath before Edna returned with the midwife in tow.

'Can you stay on here whilst I drive the midwife up to the cowshed?' Edna quickly asked Nora.

'Yes, yes, just go,' Nora urged.

Billy cried hungrily, 'Chips, chips!'

'Later, sweetheart,' Edna promised. 'Keep an eye on the little lasses,' Edna added. 'They're in the back room; they'll entertain Billy whilst I'm gone.'

Back at the cowshed, Kit was desperate to push. 'It's coming, Rosa, the baby's coming,' she moaned, as she fell back on the bed, heaving and shuddering with exhaustion.

At her wits' end, flustered Rosa nearly wept with relief when she heard Edna calling out from the sitting room, 'The midwife's here.'

'Thank God!' Rosa gasped, making her way for the calm, buxom lady in a clean uniform with a nurse's bag and a reassuring professional smile.

'How are you, dear?' Nurse Hodson asked, as she stepped forward to expertly assess her patient. 'I need hot water – right away,' she quickly told Edna.

Leaving Edna to do as instructed, Rosa went outside for a smoke. Through the open window she could hear the midwife talking firmly to Kit, who was groaning in pain. 'Good girl, it won't be long now. I can see the baby's head – one more push should do it.'

'Poor kid,' Edna murmured, as she joined Rosa and lit up a Woodbine.

'Thank God you got here just in time,' Rosa said. 'I hadn't a clue what I was doing.'

'You did a grand job –' Edna started to say, but she stopped as they both heard the sound of a baby wailing.

'She's had it!' Rosa exclaimed and burst into tears of pure relief. 'Kit's given birth!' she said, as she tossed away her cigarette.

Creeping into the bedroom, Rosa and Edna saw the midwife wrapping a clean towel around a small, wet, pink baby.

'A girl,' she announced as she laid the newborn in Kit's arms. 'A beautiful baby girl.'

As weeping Kit clutched her daughter, Rosa and Edna wept too.

'Well done, sweetheart,' Edna whispered.

The sweet relief on Kit's face suddenly disappeared when Nurse Hodson, who was expertly cleaning up her patient, suddenly gasped.

'What is it?' Kit asked. 'Is something wrong?'

Looking up, the midwife said in a brisk voice, 'Mrs McIvor, you'd better brace yourself: if I'm not mistaken there's another baby on the way.'

'*Another?*' Kit gasped in disbelief.

'Yes,' Nurse Hodson answered tersely as she removed the baby from Kit's arms and handed her to an astonished Rosa.

'Outside, ladies, now,' she barked.

Standing in the sitting room, Rosa gazed in rapt wonder at the tiny creature she was holding; the little girl's hazy blue eyes blinked at the bright light but then she started to stare at the world she'd just been born into.

'Look at her,' Rosa whispered in complete awe. 'She's perfect.'

Edna smiled fondly at the baby, but her thoughts were with Kit, who, from her cries and grunts, was now in the process of bearing down for the second time.

After what seemed like an eternity but was in fact only fifteen minutes, the midwife assured Kit that all was going well.

'Keep going, Mrs McIvor! One more push and I think you'll have your baby.'

As exhausted Kit gave one last heroic push, Nurse Hodson with infinite care delivered the second, much smaller baby, who lay mewling between Kit's outspread legs.

When Edna and Rosa (still holding the firstborn) heard the plaintive wail of the second baby they slipped back into the bedroom, where the midwife announced with a triumphant smile, 'Another girl – two strong, healthy, lovely babies!'

After the midwife had tidied up her tired but utterly ecstatic patient, Kit lay in a freshly made bed with a baby asleep in each arm – and that's how Ian found her an hour later.

Sweating with anxiety and breathless with running, he rushed into the cowshed with his heart in his mouth. 'I've just got the message!' he gasped. 'Where is she?' he asked Rosa, who was on her own after Edna had left to drive the midwife home.

Pressing a finger to her lips, Rosa led Ian to the bedroom, where his wife and daughters lay peacefully sleeping. Completely stunned, Ian gazed from his wife to the babies and back again. 'TWO!' he gasped.

'Twin girls,' Rosa said softly.

'Girls,' Ian murmured, as he tenderly touched each warm pink cheek. 'My little girls,' he sobbed and tears rolled unchecked down his face.

Closing the door softly behind her, Rosa left the happy family to themselves.

Back at the Phoenix, Maggie and Julia had been on tenterhooks all day. Malc had told them that Rosa had taken Kit up to the cowshed to wait for Ian to come and pick her up.

'He'll be on his way as we speak,' he said with supreme confidence.

But, as the hours passed and neither Rosa nor Nora returned to work, Julia and Maggie became increasingly agitated. Because they worked in different parts of the factory, they could only talk to each other on their last break.

'What's keeping them?' Maggie fretted.

'Maybe Ian's been delayed,' Julia suggested.

'Delayed ALL day?' Maggie cried incredulously.

When the hooter announced the end of their shift, they tore up the lane to the cowshed, where to their astonishment they saw Kit being carefully lowered into Ian's car. Seeing Maggie and Julia standing open-mouthed and staring at them, Billy waved excitedly.

'Mammy's had twinnies!' he cried.

Clutching a baby in each arm, Rosa quickly explained: 'Kit gave birth a few hours ago – in the cowshed!'

After Rosa, Billy and the twins were safely in the back seat, Ian drove away, leaving Nora, who'd only recently returned with Billy, to tell her astounded friends about her and Rosa's dramatic D-Day experience.

'Honest to God, I don't know what was harder: keeping Billy entertained all day or being up here all on your own with Kit in labour.'

Julia shook her head in disbelief. 'And all the time we were listening to the news bulletins about the advance on the French coast, we had no idea of the drama going on right here in the cowshed!'

Later, when Ian dropped Rosa back home, he handed

her a bottle of brandy, which he told her he'd been keeping for a special occasion.

'Wet the babies' heads,' he said with tears in his eyes. 'I'll never be able to thank you enough for helping Kit and my daughters,' he added with a proud smile.

As the sky darkened and the twittering birds on the moors grew quiet, the tired girls lit the wood-burner, then sat around it drinking brandy and smoking cigarettes.

'What an auspicious day to be born,' Julia sighed, as she savoured the heat of the spirit slipping down her throat. 'The sixth of June 1944: the day we finally routed the Germans!'

'Obviously we missed all the news bulletins,' Rosa said with an ironic smile. 'But tell us,' she urged. 'Tell us the news.'

'There were bulletins throughout the day,' Maggie said. 'A cheer went up when Churchill announced that troops had been dropped behind enemy lines.'

With her green eyes burning bright with excitement, Julia exclaimed, 'Four thousand ships, along with several thousand smaller crafts, crossed the English Channel! Imagine what a sight that must have been.'

'It's happening,' Rosa said with a sob in her voice. 'Dear God, it's finally happening.'

Julia suddenly jumped up and switched on the wireless set. 'We mustn't miss the nine o'clock news,' she cried.

It took a while for the old set to warm up; after a series of annoying crackles and beeps, they finally heard the newsreader's report:

'All still goes well on the coast of Normandy. Fighting is going on in the town of Caen, while the Allied navies bomb the German coast defences in support of our troops. Our great air-borne landings, the biggest in history, have been carried out with very little loss.'

'Thank God for that!' Maggie gasped with tears in her eyes.

When the news ended, Julia raised her glass. 'To all our brave boys on the French beaches,' she cried.

Nora, who was in floods of tears, sobbed, 'God bless and keep them safe.'

'And God bless our little D-Day twins!' Rosa said with a fond smile.

Raising their mugs, they chinked them together as they said in earnest unison: 'PEACE!'

Epilogue

Spirits were high on the Phoenix bomb line in the week that followed the D-Day landings.

'That's shut up Herr Bloody Hitler,' one of the women crowed in the canteen.

But a week later Hitler lashed back with his first V-1 bomb attack on London: the Buzz Bomb which hit Bethnal Green, killing six civilians and injuring many more.

'Jerry's not going to go down without taking a lot of innocent buggers with him,' Malc growled angrily when they heard the grim news on 13 June.

Spirits sank, then soared again when, a few weeks later, news came through of US troops liberating Cherbourg; and shortly after that British and Canadian troops captured Caen.

'It's like being on a roller-coaster,' Julia exclaimed. 'You don't think you can go any higher, then suddenly you're ricocheting back down again.'

Though horrifying stories and film footage of Hitler's death camps had been in circulation for some time, more news of further atrocities were flooding into the public domain. The horrifying images were unbearable for anybody to look at for long, but for Rosa they were pure torture.

'Oh, God!' she sobbed in front of her friends, who could only comfort her with tender words of loving reassurance. 'When will this hell be over – when will I know if my family are alive or dead?'

'You must stay strong,' Julia urged.

'You've been strong for so long,' Maggie reminded her weeping friend. 'Don't give up now, lovie – not now when we're winning. Be strong for just a bit longer,' she implored.

Hardly a day went by when Rosa didn't take Julia to one side to ask, 'Any news?' Or 'Why is it taking so long? The sub was due back in Southampton round about the time we saw Hugo in London.'

'Hugo said the sub would surface only if there were no more missions scheduled,' Julia reminded her. 'Who knows where it went after picking up POWs on the Belgian coast?'

Rosa's edginess, combined with her highly emotional state, were in the forefront of Julia's mind when she finally did receive a telegram from Hugo. It was written in the same cryptic form as before:

Mother's birthday present should arrive shortly,
she apologizes for the delay, she's not been well
since she got back home.

Regards
H

Julia's heart skipped several beats. It didn't take a genius to decode the message: Gabriel was in England but

379

hadn't been able to make contact for some reason or another; illness perhaps, or maybe an injury. Julia's thoughts were in turmoil; should she tell Rosa now and risk the chance of her bolting off in a wild attempt to find her brother? Julia sighed. For the second time in her life she felt guilty about playing God with Rosa: who was she to decide when was the right time to tell the poor anguished girl that her brother was alive?

Julia's decision was further complicated by the fact that Kit and Ian had asked both Rosa and Arthur to be present at the baptism of their D-Day twins – aptly named Joy and Hope. Arthur and Stevie were due to arrive in a few days for the christening, and Rosa (when she wasn't working) was busy helping Kit. Seeing Rosa so happy and excited was what finally swung Julia's decision to delay; best to get the christening over with, then break the news.

When Arthur arrived on a short leave with his son, Rosa thought her heart would burst with happiness. The sight of Arthur's tall, lean body made her pulse race; his face, though scarred from so many accidents, was still strikingly handsome and his blond hair (now shot with silver) fell in a charming boyish sweep over his stunning blue eyes. There was no doubting now how she felt about this man. But dare she hope her feelings could ever be returned?

Laughing, Arthur greeted Rosa with a huge hug. Without a doubt she could have stayed in his embrace for a very long time, but a little hand reaching up to Rosa instantly made her drop her hold on Arthur.

'Stevie!' she gasped, as the little boy grasped her skirt and hauled himself upright. 'You can stand!' she cried in delight, sweeping him into her arms and covering his cherubic rosy cheeks with warm kisses. 'Nearly one year old, and you can stand, big man!' she exclaimed joyfully.

'He's been pulling himself up for a week now,' Arthur told her proudly. 'He'll be walking soon, running circles around us.'

Arthur led her and his son into Kit's beautiful summer garden, fragrant with roses, lilies, delphiniums and phlox.

'Let's sit down and have a little time in private,' he murmured, as he led her to a low drystone wall where they sat with Stevie pressed warmly between them. Rosa was more than happy to be alone with Arthur, though she was quite sure he would hear her heart hammering in her chest.

'How was your journey?' she asked shyly.

'Not bad,' he said, as he took a packet of Pall Malls from his pocket.

When she noticed how much his hand trembled as he lit up two cigarettes and handed one to her, Rosa's heart contracted with love for him. 'Poor lamb,' she thought tenderly. 'He seems a total nervous wreck too!'

Fortunately, innocent, guileless Stevie reached up to lace his chubby little arms around Rosa's neck. 'Squeeze Rosee!' he chuckled.

'Squeeze Stevee!' she joked and stood up, dancing him round in a circle. With the baby on her hip, she laughed as she held out her hand to Arthur. 'Come on, let's go and look for butterflies!'

After the christening in Pendleton Church, everybody made their way to Yew Tree Farm, where Kit and Ian had laid on a splendid spread. Malc, Ian and Arthur offered lifts in their cars, but the biggest surprise was Peter driving up in his new Ford, which he'd had specially adapted for him to drive. Nora was beside him looking like the Queen on her way to the races!

'Can you believe it?' she cried, jumping out of the car so others could hop in. 'Peter's driving and' – she paused as she turned to her beaming fiancé – 'you tell them, lovie,' she urged.

'I'll be discharged next week and lodging with Nora's dad till we find a nice place of our own,' Peter added with a little manly swagger.

'Make sure you live near Polly,' Maggie teased. 'Otherwise you'll never see Nora! You know she prefers pigs to folks,' she joked.

When the guests, including the babies and the toddlers too, were packed into all the available cars, the convoy set off over the moors, which were awash in pale-golden sunshine and loud with the song of skylarks.

As Arthur gazed at Rosa in the passenger seat, cradling his sleeping son in her arms, he was struck by how perfect they looked together. After the death of his wife, he'd never expected to trust another woman with his only child, but right from the beginning, even when he was a baby, Stevie had chosen Rosa to love. Arthur had always admired Rosa – she was a strong, clever, talented woman – but he was now more than aware that every time he saw her his feelings for her were growing stronger and stronger, to such an extent that he'd recently taken to dreaming about her! He'd been pleased for her when she told him she was engaged, but he had to confess he'd been even more pleased when he heard she had called it off. But did he dare to hope that a beautiful woman like Rosa would want a middle-aged, heart-broken widower?

The christening tea was a treat: the fruits of Kit and Ian's garden and vegetable plot graced the table that happy Sunday afternoon. Apart from the usual sandwiches spread thinly with meat paste, there were a couple of fruit pies and jellies made from Kit's blackcurrants and redcurrants; bottled gooseberries had been made into a fruit crumble; and there were just enough eggs from Kit's hens to make a few custard tarts too. Their neighbouring farmer had generously donated a round of his own soft, creamy Lancashire cheese and two bottles of heady damson wine.

The little girls slept sweetly throughout the meal, side by side in the big Silver Cross pram that had a fringed canopy over the hood to keep the warm sun off their faces. Though it was early days, Joy was beginning to show signs of having Kit's dark hair, whilst Hope had her father's tawny brown colouring. Arthur and Rosa had cooed over the little girls throughout the service, and now smiled at them as they lay sleeping peacefully; without saying a word to each other, both were thinking the same thought: when would they have children of their own to love?

Arthur had to leave after tea in order to drive back to Dundee in the car he'd borrowed. After packing his and Stevie's luggage into the boot of the car, he bade a fond farewell to the twins and their doting parents.

'Come back soon,' Kit begged. 'We miss you so much.'

'Not as much as I miss you,' Arthur said, as he kissed her goodbye. 'I had to go as far north as Dundee to realize all the riches I'd left behind here.'

'And we all know which richness in particular you're talking about,' Ian teased as he watched Arthur's eyes turn to Rosa, who was sitting in the car with Stevie bouncing on her lap.

Deciding to throw caution to the wind, Arthur opened up his heart to Kit and Ian, and with tears in his eyes he blurted out, 'After Violet I thought I would never love again. But you two know I do, don't you?'

'We could see it coming,' Ian said with a knowing smile. 'And I can't say that we're sorry.'

Kit, who'd known Violet well, also smiled at Arthur. 'I'm sure Violet is looking down from heaven and blessing you,' she said, fighting back tears. 'She would want it no other way.'

Waving goodbye to all the guests, Arthur drove Rosa to the cowshed, where he planned to say his goodbye to her in private, but, as they bounced down the cobbled road and neared the cowshed, all the colour drained from Rosa's face. A noise like a painful groan burst from her lips when she saw a man sitting on the cowshed doorstep; hearing the car approaching, he stood up and, squinting in the sunshine, he covered his eyes to see who was coming.

'STOP!' Rosa screamed to Arthur. 'STOP THE CAR!'

Rosa hardly waited for Arthur to slam on the brakes before she thrust Stevie into his arms, then leapt from the car and ran like a thing possessed towards the man, who was now running towards her. When they met they virtually fell on each other – crying and weeping, they clung on tightly as if they would never let each other go. Arthur got out of the car and, after lifting Stevie on to his shoulders, he walked slowly towards the pair, whose sobbing he could hear from a distance. When Rosa raised her tear-stained face to Arthur, he knew who the man was.

'Arthur,' she said with a catch in her throat. 'Meet my beloved brother, Gabriel.'

Arthur smiled in amazement; he could have been staring into Rosa's face. Though much taller than his sister, Gabriel had the same stunning dark eyes and thick, jet-black hair. His face was marked with pain, though, and quite unlike Rosa's delicate heart-shaped face; and he was so thin that the jacket he wore hung off his body. This man has suffered, Arthur thought with immense compassion. Taking hold of Gabriel's right hand, he gripped it in his own and held it firmly there as he spoke.

'She's waited a long time for this moment, Gabriel,' then adding with a catch in his voice, 'It's an honour and a privilege to finally meet you.'

Shortly after, Arthur left brother and sister alone.

'I have to get back, Rosa,' he said, as he kissed her goodbye. 'And you have much to discuss with your brother.'

Though ecstatic to have Gabriel close by, Rosa's sweet face dropped. 'Oh!' she gasped involuntarily.

Though Arthur was desperate to pour his heart out to Rosa, he knew, like the wise and considerate man that he was, that this was not the right time for her: there were other, more important issues for her to address right now.

'But please,' he hastily added, 'can we come and visit you again soon?'

'Yes!' Rosa exclaimed breathlessly. '*Very, very soon!*'

As Arthur settled his son in the car, Stevie started to cry. 'Want Rosee,' he bawled.

'Want Rosee too!' Arthur joked, as he gave a final wave, then drove away.

Arthur was right: there was so much to talk about! Brother and sister talked well into the night, and early the next morning Julia found them curled up beside each other on the old battered sofa, Rosa's head resting on Gabriel's shoulder, with his arm clasped around his sister as if he would never let her go.

Though she was utterly exhausted, emotionally and physically, Rosa had no choice but to go to work.

'Promise me you'll be right here when I get back,' she begged Gabriel, who laughed as he replied, 'Don't worry, I won't go running back to Europe!' He then bent to kiss her tenderly on both cheeks. 'I'll be right here waiting for you when you come home.'

In the Phoenix changing room, Julia came clean with Rosa. 'I have to confess,' she started with a guilty blush, 'I did get a telegram a few days ago. I was hanging on, hoping to get more information before I told you,' she blurted out, before continuing rather shame-facedly, 'Hugo informed me that Gabriel had been ill on arrival; he didn't say where Gabriel was, or how he was, and I thought you'd go haring off, like you did before, and leave Arthur . . . and the christening . . .' Julia's voice faded away. 'Oh, Rosa, I'm so sorry,' she gulped, on the verge of tears.

'Don't be sad,' Rosa said, as she gave Julia a big hug. 'You were right, Julia — I would have run off, God knows where, but that would have been my instinct, as it was Gabriel's to come to find me. And, in doing so, he's met all the people I love best in the world.'

Over their tea-breaks throughout that day, Rosa told her friends about Gabriel's long and terrifying journey to England; she was careful not to mention Hugo's involvement in her brother's rescue, or how much Julia had acted as an intermediary.

'What will Gabriel do now?' Julia inquired.

'Get fit, put some weight on — he's nothing but a bag of bones,' Rosa fretted. 'We're both desperate to find our family, but that will have to wait until the war is over.' Rosa stubbed out her cheroot as she added bleakly, 'With all that is going on right now in Europe, I pray to God they're still alive.'

Later that week Arthur phoned Malc's office and asked to speak to Rosa. 'How's your brother?' he immediately asked.

'Getting stronger, and he's got work at the Phoenix, packing bombs in the dispatch room. Oh, Arthur! Isn't it wonderful?' she exclaimed. And then, before she could think about what she was saying, the words spilt out of her mouth. 'All the men I love most in the world are finally in one country!'

There was a long pause that nearly made her heart stop. 'Well . . .' Arthur said, the smile in his voice unmistakable. 'If that's the case, now that Gabriel is here, do you think you might have room in your life for an older man who worships you, and a little boy who dreams of you every night?'

Rosa could hardly breathe as she stammered out her shaky reply. 'Arthur, you have no idea how empty my life would be without you and Stevie.'

'Sweetest Rosa,' Arthur said with a catch in his voice. 'I never thought I'd ever feel happiness like this again.'

On hearing his heartfelt words, Rosa's previous life flashed before her: the agony of war, the pain of separation, the loss of her family, her life as a Bomb Girl, her wonderful friends, and now the promise of a future with Arthur and Stevie. With her heart overflowing with love and gratitude, Rosa whispered incredulously into the phone: '*Il mio amore*, I can't believe this is happening! I hardly dared even imagine that you might feel the same as me.'

A silence hung in the air as they both waited uncertainly for the other to speak.

'I was going to wait until I saw you next to ask this, but I can't wait, my dearest. May Stevie and I dream of building a new future with you, Rosa?' Arthur asked hesitantly.

Rosa's knees went so weak she had to clutch on to Malc's desk to stop herself from falling over. 'Oh, yes, yes!' she cried, giddy with happiness. 'With Violet's blessings, you, Stevie and I have a whole new world before us.'

Now it was Arthur's turn to sound incredulous. 'A new world!' he gasped with a sob in his voice, quickly adding, 'And, as for Violet, I know in my heart that we will have her blessing.' Then, as if he couldn't hold back a moment longer, he exclaimed, 'Oh, when can I see you, darling Rosa? When can I hold you in my arms and tell you just how much I care for you?'

'Just as soon as you want!' she replied with a joyous laugh. 'I'm all yours, and Stevie's too,' she added with a giggle.

After they'd made a plan to meet up in the very near future, Rosa put down the phone and, smiling widely, she walked back on to the cordite line, where her friends needed no explanation: the look on their friend's radiant face was the look of a woman who had finally found love.

None of them could have wished for anything more for their dear Rosa, who had waited long for this moment. If any woman deserved peace, happiness and a safe haven, it was Rosa Falco. As the clattering conveyor belts rolled relentlessly on, Rosa's friends diligently returned to their war work, each saying the same prayer: God bless Rosa as she enters into a new era of her life, now with Arthur by her side. Julia, the so-called clever snob who became a friend and a mentor to all the Bomb Girls, prayed for all her wonderful friends: Maggie with her Les; Gladys with Reggie; and sweet Nora, the radiant bride-to-be. They all deserved nothing but happiness and blessings in their future lives, in a world where they could live in peace when the war was finally over.

Acknowledgements

I'd like to thank all my readers who have enjoyed my 'Bomb Girl' books. I love corresponding with you on Facebook. You have no idea how much I value your comments, especially on days when I sit staring at my blank computer screen; it's then I recall your remarks with pleasure and they urge me on – so please don't stop!

I particularly want to thank the Royal National Institute for the Blind (RNIB) Talk and Support Group. A few months ago Faye, Peggy, Diane, Anne, Urma, Marise and I logged in over the phone to talk about *The Bomb Girls*. They asked lots of insightful questions and supplied me with some fascinating personal history, too, as some of them were children during the Second World War. The stipulated hour just flew by and when our time was up we were all reluctant to stop, so I suggested the group read (in large print) or listen to the audiobook of *The Bomb Girls' Secrets*, which we'll discuss in our next session. Really looking forward to it!

Also by
Daisy Styles...

Out Now

Also by
Daisy Styles ...

Out Now

Also by
Daisy Styles...

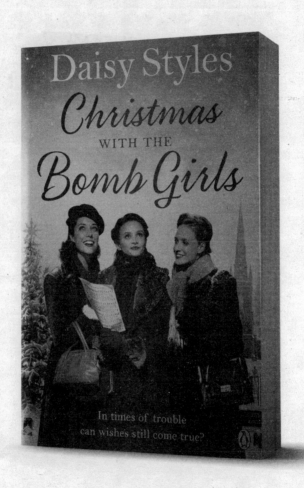

Out Now